A SLOW DEATH

By R.W.Wilson

Copyright © 2025 R.W. Wilson

All rights reserved. No part of this publication may be reproduced, distributed, or transmitted in any form or by any means—electronic, mechanical, photocopying, recording, or otherwise—without the prior written permission of the author, except for brief quotations used in reviews or permitted under copyright law.

Disclaimer

This is a work of fiction. Names, characters, places, and incidents are either products of the author's imagination or are used fictitiously. Any resemblance to actual persons, living or deceased, or to real events is purely coincidental.

Acknowledgments and Creative Contributions

The ideas, storylines, and concepts in this book are entirely original to the author. The author extends sincere gratitude to OpenAI's ChatGPT for its invaluable support in brainstorming, structuring, and refining dialogue, description, and narrative development throughout the writing process, as well as for assisting in the generation of custom imagery that enriched the visual storytelling. Appreciation is also given to OpenArt for its creative resources, which provided inspiration and helped shape the visual design and immersive quality of this work.

First Edition, 2025

Published by R.W. Wilson

CHAPTER 1

It didn't begin with panic. It began with forgetfulness, the kind so ordinary no one bothered to fear it. A bus driver in Chicago spent ten minutes staring at his own route map, unable to remember if he'd already driven it. A nurse in Madrid signed her name three times on the same chart. A grandfather in Seoul asked his wife where she'd been all morning, and she gently reminded him she hadn't left the house at all. Harmless slips, easy to excuse, the kind people chalked up to stress or age or distraction. The world kept moving, unbothered, convinced nothing was wrong.

By the third week, the pattern was impossible to ignore. Teachers forgot lesson plans they'd taught for years; surgeons paused mid-operation because the next step had vanished from their minds; a news anchor stopped reading halfway through a sentence and softly asked where she was. The footage went viral before anyone realized something larger was happening. Doctors tried to reassure the public—lack of sleep, burnout, anxiety—but their voices cracked on air, and a few of them faltered during interviews, forgetting the symptoms they were meant to describe. The fear didn't erupt; it seeped. Slow, viscous, inevitable.

Hospitals were the first to understand the stakes. MRI scans came back pristine—no tumors, no trauma, no degeneration. The brains of the afflicted looked impossibly healthy even as their owners deteriorated. Neurologists stared at images that should have offered answers and found only silence. Patients who had walked into waiting rooms hours earlier were now unable to recall their own names. They forgot their addresses, their birthdays, the faces of the people trying to help them. And always, right underneath the confusion, was the terror—because they knew something was slipping, something they couldn't hold onto no matter how tightly they tried.

Then came the stage no one could deny. People began to forget how to function. A man drowned in his own kitchen sink because his body no longer remembered to pull in air. A woman collapsed beside a grocery cart, her legs giving out as every signal between her brain and her muscles flickered into nothing. Paramedics arrived to find bodies that weren't dead, not yet, but hollow—eyes open, breathing shallow, minds gone. Families wrote names on mirrors, walls, forearms, hoping words could anchor a mind that no longer recognized itself. It was like watching someone bleed out through memory instead of wounds.

By the time officials named it—Neurodegenerative Accelerated Memory Syndrome—the title felt laughably inadequate. People called it something simpler, something crueler: the Forgetting Plague. It moved through cities like a whisper, invisible and already too late by the time it was heard. Airports shut down. Schools closed. Governments issued statements promising containment, though no one could say what needed containing. You couldn't quarantine amnesia. You couldn't isolate a mind falling apart from the inside. And the virus—if it was a virus at all—didn't care about borders or protocols or hope.

The collapse began quietly. Not with riots or explosions, but with a silence heavier than any disaster the world had ever seen. Streets emptied as people stayed home, terrified they might forget the way back if they stepped outside. News broadcasts grew shorter as anchors vanished mid-shift. Emergency hotlines rang endlessly with no one left to answer. Somewhere in the darkened sprawl of the city, the first Red

Zones were drawn—cordoned districts where the infected wandered aimlessly, alive but unreachable, their bodies still breathing while their minds dissolved into nothing.

And as the world braced itself for the truth, one thing became clear: this wasn't a sickness that killed you. It erased you, piece by piece, until there was nothing left to mourn. John Renner understood that better than most, though he'd never chosen to be part of the front line. He was just a guard—one more uniform in a world that no longer trusted its own reflection—assigned to HelixCore Therapeutics, the only biomedical giant still standing beneath the weight of the Forgetting Plague. Before the outbreak, HelixCore had been another shining corporate fortress full of polished floors and ambitious research grants. But when the world's laboratories collapsed under the sheer absurdity of scientists forgetting their own formulas mid-sentence, HelixCore didn't fold; it barricaded its doors, doubled its staff, and declared itself the last hope of cognitive survival. Governments funneled money, samples, personnel—anything HelixCore demanded. It wasn't loyalty or belief; it was desperation.

The guards were the most visible symbol of that desperation. John stood outside each night sealed inside a white hazmat suit that turned every guard into a faceless outline under the harsh perimeter floodlights. The suit clung to him like a second skin, stiff at the seams, heavy at the shoulders, smelling faintly of sterilized plastic and recycled air. Every breath echoed inside the helmet, amplified into a lonely, mechanical rhythm that made him feel less like a man and more like an instrument. The visor fogged near the edges no matter how many times he wiped it with the inner cloth. The filtration pack hummed against his spine, reminding him with every vibration that breathing the outside air was no longer an acceptable risk. No one spoke unless necessary; speech inside the suit felt like shouting underwater, each word swallowed by static and fear.

The HelixCore campus sprawled across seventeen fortified acres, ringed with metal fences, thermal sensors, and automated spotlights that carved clean white lines across the pavement. The main tower rose from the center like a cold monolith, its upper floors glowing through the night as scientists—still lucid, still desperate—worked in rotating shifts. Rumors said they were close to something monumental, but rumors also whispered that several researchers had already suffered cognitive slips mid-experiment, staring blankly at equipment they'd used for years. HelixCore confirmed nothing. They never did. Their silence was the closest thing the world had to reassurance.

John's boots crunched over the frost-laced concrete as he made his third perimeter sweep. Other guards passed him at slow intervals, their suits identical except for faint colored stripes around the arms marking shift teams. He recognized them only by small habits: Rami's slightly uneven stride, Kline's compulsive knuckle cracking, Simmons' habit of tapping the side of his helmet whenever the radio crackled. These tiny movements were the last pieces of humanity still allowed to show through the armor. Everything else—fear, exhaustion, grief—was buried under layers of filtered air and corporate protocol.

Beyond the fence, the world was dissolving into silence. The highway beside the compound was littered with abandoned vehicles, their doors hanging open, headlights long dead. People had fled, forgotten where they were going, wandered into darkness until their bodies simply quit. Even now the distant echo of sirens drifted across the empty city like the ghost of a warning no one could still understand. Above him, the sky glowed a sickened orange from the city lights, a haze thick enough to erase the stars; he wondered how many people still remembered what real starlight looked like.

His radio crackled sharply, cutting through the quiet. "Unit

Twelve, status check," a muffled supervisor's voice asked, flattened and metallic through layers of signal distortion. John pressed the transmitter on his chest. "Perimeter secure. North gate clear." There was no acknowledgment beyond a clipped "Copy." Roll call had become constant—every hour, sometimes every thirty minutes. It wasn't protocol. It was fear disguised as procedure. If a guard forgot a code, a door, a directive—one slip could doom the entire facility.

He leaned against the metal railing of the northern checkpoint, the hazmat suit creaking as it shifted around him. From here he could see the soft, steady pulse of lights deep inside the HelixCore laboratories, hear faint alarms cycling air pressure in sealed rooms, the mechanical sighs of climate systems holding back decay. These were controlled, intentional sounds—the heartbeat of a company refusing to surrender to an enemy it couldn't see. But beneath them, barely audible, there was a deeper silence—one that came from the world outside the walls, a world dismantling itself neuron by neuron.

John tightened his grip on his flashlight, sweeping it across the empty stretch of road that led from the distant highway. Nothing moved. Nothing approached. The world didn't even feel like it was breathing anymore. Inside the compound, humanity was fighting for its mind. Outside it, humanity was losing the battle one forgotten step at a time.

And John, sealed inside his suit, standing under cold floodlights in a world unraveling quietly around him, couldn't shake the truth eating its way through every layer of silence: whatever hope remained was locked behind these walls, and men like him were the last, fragile barrier between survival and the absolute erasure waiting beyond the fence.

The cold quiet settled again, thick and unnatural, when the vibration inside John's helmet broke through it—a personal priority call routed through the emergency band, the kind only one person besides HelixCore command had access to. He answered with a jaw click, and Lee Chavez's voice surged through the channel, raw and breathless beneath layers of static and background noise. "Johnny, tell me you're still upright and not licking doorknobs," Lee said, followed by a crash on his end and someone yelling for restraints. John steadied himself against the railing, sweeping the empty road with his light. "Still vertical," he said. "Haven't tried eating my badge either." Lee huffed something that might have been a laugh. "Good. I've scraped enough idiots off floors tonight. I don't have the energy to drag your tin-can ass anywhere. How's life at the genius factory? Everybody still pretending they've got this under control?"

John said nothing for a moment, and that was answer enough. Lee filled the silence with words because he always did, because someone had to. Twelve calls since sundown, he said, and every one of them a copy-paste nightmare—people forgetting where they were, who they were, what their own hands were doing. A man standing over his wife's body, asking Lee if she was late getting home. A teenage girl who forgot how to swallow halfway through telling him she wasn't scared. "Honestly, if I see one more person blink at me like Windows trying to restart, I'm going to lose it," Lee muttered. "Had a guy look right at his own chest compressions and ask me who was dying. I told him, 'You, buddy,' and he laughed. Laughed. Five minutes later he forgot how to breathe. I don't know whether to cry or send the universe a complaint form."

In the background, alarms shrieked and someone shouted instructions that sounded more like begging than medicine. John listened, jaw tight, hazmat suit creaking as he shifted. "How's Emma?" he asked, because if he didn't pull the conversation somewhere lighter, Lee would go straight through the floor. "Currently furious," Lee said, a thread of fondness cutting through the exhaustion. "I pulled her off set, told the studio if they wanted her they could come do scene work in our living room in full hazmat. She said I'm overreacting. I told her I've spent twelve hours watching people forget their own kids' names and if she wants to improvise that, she can divorce me first. She's pacing the apartment, practicing lines and threatening to smother me in my sleep. It's kind of hot, honestly." John snorted. "Glad one of us still has a love life." "Hey, some of us are talented," Lee shot back. "You could've married a famous actress too. You chose minimum wage and a flashlight."

He finally asked about HelixCore, and John gave him what little he had: the labs still burning their way through night after night, scientists still showing up lucid, rumors that the Cure Wing was close to something that might buy the world time. It sounded thin even to him. "So basically," Lee said, "the nerds are doing magic and I'm tap-dancing on corpses until they're done. Great division of labor." A monitor shrieked in his background, followed by someone swearing creatively in three languages. His voice dropped then, losing the armor of jokes. "Listen, Johnny. We're losing the city. Not in theory. Not on paper. For real. Nurses are forgetting what a syringe is. One of the guys on my crew forgot my name for six minutes. I've known him eight years. I can't keep pretending this is just a rough flu season."

John gripped the railing harder, the metal biting through glove and suit. "You're still sharp," he said. "You remember my birthday?" "Tragically, yeah," Lee said. "I also remember that shirt you wore when you tried to impress that nurse last year, so clearly the virus hasn't put me out of my misery yet." There was a brief pause, a shift in breathing, the sound of a door slamming on his end. When he spoke again, his voice had that tight, stripped-down edge John only heard after the worst calls. "If this thing gets into HelixCore, we're done. So you stay clear. You start forgetting anything—gate codes, patrol routes, the name of that awful diner we used to hit after shifts—you call me. Not your supervisor. Me. I'm not letting you wander off into traffic because your brain decided to clock out early."

"I promise," John said, because there was nothing else to say that wasn't a lie. Another alarm flared in Lee's background, followed by someone shouting for help, urgent and hoarse. "That's my cue," Lee muttered. "Another brain going offline. Be safe, yeah? I'm not breaking in there to rescue you. Your suit's ugly and I refuse to be seen with you on the news." "Love you too," John said. "I know," Lee replied, and for a second, the smile was audible. "Be safe, brother." The channel clicked shut, cutting the noise of the collapsing city out of his helmet and leaving only the hum of the floodlights, the distant whisper of dead highways, and the sound of his own filtered breathing, harsh and too loud in a world that was forgetting how to breathe at all.

When the line went dead, the silence in his helmet felt heavier than before. The floodlights hummed, the wind scraped along the fence, and for a moment John just stood there with Lee's words echoing in his head—people blinking like frozen software, nurses forgetting tools in their own hands, a city going dark one neuron at a time. The radio at his chest crackled before his thoughts could settle. "Unit Twelve, we've got something at the south access road," a guard's voice said, tight and a little too fast. "You might want to take a look. Bring your happy face." That last part tried for humor and missed. John pushed off the railing and started toward the southern gate, the hazmat suit creaking with each step, boots biting into frost-coated concrete as he cut across the inner yard.

By the time he reached the south fence, two other guards were already there, standing in that peculiar way trained men stand when they're pretending not to be spooked—too straight, too still, like posture can outrun fear. Kline and Rami, both in white suits, visors turned toward the road. Beyond the fence, a single car sat angled across the shoulder, engine still running, headlights spilling pale cones onto the asphalt.

The driver's door was closed. The window was halfway down, letting exhaust and cold air drift lazily in and out. The man behind the wheel stared straight ahead, hands resting loosely on his lap instead of the wheel, head tilted just enough to look wrong. "Tell me this is a drunk," John said, even though he already knew it wasn't. "Drunks move," Kline replied. "We've been watching him for eight minutes. No movement except the breathing. Won't answer to horn, shout, flashlight, or the fact that we exist."

John stepped up to the inner fence, lifting his own light to cut across the car's front interior. The beam slid over the man's face—mid-forties, dress shirt open at the collar, tie shoved into a pocket. His eyes were wide, fixed on nothing. Not unfocused, not glazed—just empty, like whatever had once lived behind them had quietly packed up and left without bothering to turn the lights off. His chest rose and fell in shallow, mechanical breaths, each one delayed by a heartbeat as if his body had to remember the step every time. A faint thread of drool had dried at the corner of his mouth. The radio clipped to his dashboard flashed incoming messages he never answered. "Sir!" John called, purely for formality. "You're on private property. You need to put the vehicle in park, step out, and identify yourself." The man didn't blink. A siren wailed faintly somewhere far beyond the highway, as if in answer.

Rami shifted beside him. "We're supposed to keep the perimeter clear," he said quietly. "Command saw the feed from the outer cam. They already tagged it as external contamination risk, category yellow leaning red." John knew what that meant. He still went through the motions. "Any ID plates?" "Rental," Kline said. "Database says was checked out four hours ago by a guy who works three blocks from here. Guess he made it this far before his brain clocked out." She hesitated, then added, "They already sent authorization. Protocol Seven-F. No retrieval. No contact. Clean and burn." For a moment nobody moved. HelixCore loved naming things like they were theoretical exercises, textbooks you could shelve once you were done. Protocol Seven-F sounded neat on paper. Out here, it meant there was a still-breathing man twenty meters away and the only sanctioned response was to reduce him and everything he'd touched to ash.

"Maybe he'll snap out of it," Rami said weakly. "We could wait ten, see if he..." He trailed off when the man in the car slowly exhaled, chest stuttering, eyes never changing, never focusing. It was the same look John had heard in Lee's voice a dozen times tonight. The world's newest corpse, still drawing air because no one had told his body it was over. John keyed his radio. "South perimeter," he said. "Confirming Protocol Seven-F order on vehicle ID ending in 4-1-Zulu. Occupant unresponsive, late-stage suspected. No response to verbal or visual. Requesting ignition package release." There was a short pause, the kind that said someone on the other end was human enough to hate this and important enough to sign off anyway. "Confirmed," command replied. "Seven-F authorized. Ignition units releasing now. Maintain distance and visual until completion."

A small panel in the inner barrier slid open with a soft hydraulic hiss, exposing a compact launcher and a marked canister—HelixCore's answer to problems that couldn't be disinfected. John pulled the canister free, checked the status lights, and stepped to the firing gap, the others flanking him. "Guy picked the worst parking spot in the world," Kline muttered. Dark humor, brittle as glass. "At least he won't remember it," Rami said. John didn't answer. He sighted carefully, aimed for the undercarriage where the fuel lines would turn the whole thing into a contained furnace, and squeezed the trigger. The canister arced through the cold air, struck just beneath the car with a dull clang, and a heartbeat later a tight bloom of accelerated fire rolled out from the chassis, swallowing the underside in searing orange. The fuel tank caught, the flames climbed, and within seconds the interior was smothered in roiling heat and black smoke.

They watched in silence as the windshield crazed and shattered, as the man's silhouette blurred, then disappeared entirely behind flame and thick, oily smoke. No one made a joke now. Somewhere inside the compound, alarms cycled harmlessly through controlled labs. Out here, on the edge of HelixCore's carefully managed hope, three guards stood in white suits and watched a stranger burn because the world had decided that sometimes the kindest thing you could do for a human being was to make sure there was nothing left of them for the virus to use.

By the time the fire crews finished hosing down what was left of the car and logging the incident, John's shift timer had bled down to its last minutes. He handed off the perimeter to the next team, cleared decontamination, and stepped through the inner airlock into HelixCore's main building, the hiss of sterilizing mist giving way to the muted hum of recycled air and fluorescent lights. Stripping out of the hazmat felt like peeling off someone else's skin—helmet first, then gloves, then the suit itself, his undershirt clinging damp to his back. The smell hit him immediately: coffee burned down to sludge, reheated food, too many bodies trying to pretend this was normal. The mess hall was a long, low room with bolted tables and a bank of televisions mounted high on one wall. Half the room was guards in half-open uniforms, the other half lab techs in wrinkled scrubs and researchers still wearing their ID badges like talismans. Everyone's eyes were pointed in the same direction.

The news was on, volume just high enough to cut through the clatter of cutlery. A trim anchor with perfect hair and dead eyes was standing in front of a map that looked more infection than geography. Red clusters pulsed across continents like fresh bruises. The banner at the bottom of the screen scrolled numbers that changed every few seconds—CONFIRMED

CASES, ESTIMATED UNDIAGNOSED, PROJECTED FATALITIES. Someone had added two sticky notes to the bottom edge of the television, as if the paper could anchor the statistics: DAY 47 and DON'T PANIC handwritten in block letters. The second note had a line drawn through it and revised to TOO LATE. "...new projections from the World Health Council indicate a global infection curve far steeper than initially modeled," the anchor was saying, voice steady in the way of people paid extra not to sound human. "Current estimates suggest that within three weeks, up to forty percent of the world's population may experience moderate to severe cognitive impairment. Fatality projections have been revised accordingly..."

"Revised," Kline muttered around a forkful of something that used to be pasta. "That's one word for 'we were wrong and it's so much worse than we thought.'" Across from her, Simmons tapped his spoon against his tray in slow rhythm with the numbers ticking up on the screen. "Guess it's nice to be part of a growth industry," he said. A few tired chuckles. Dark humor had become a kind of currency in here; nobody laughed because things were funny, they laughed because the alternative was dropping their trays and screaming. A researcher at the next table, still in her lab coat, pinched the bridge of her nose and didn't look up. When the camera cut to footage of a stadium repurposed as a field ward—rows of cots, bodies lying still with eyes open, nurses moving between them like ghosts—she closed her eyes altogether.

John sat at the end of the nearest table, a cooling mug of coffee between his hands, and watched the curve on the screen tilt steeper, then steeper again as a new graph appeared. A commentator's voice joined the anchor's, discussing "neurological collapse thresholds" and "societal infrastructure failure" with the calm detachment of a weather report. The other television tuned to a different channel showed the same story with different graphics—one network preferring red, another choosing a sickly orange—but the shape was identical.

More infected. More gone. The deaths, when they talked about them at all, were framed as numbers lost rather than people. Lee's voice threaded through his head, cutting across the polished broadcast: they don't know they're dying. He looked around the room and wondered how many here were counting their own forgotten moments, quietly cataloguing each slip and deciding whether it was exhaustion or the edge of the drop.

The anchor shifted topics, moving to "global hope centers" and "major research efforts," which was the polite way of saying there were maybe three places left on the planet anyone believed might save them, and HelixCore was the brightest star in that shrinking constellation. They cut to archived footage of the building he was sitting in, shot from a helicopter weeks ago—clean lines, mirrored glass, the HelixCore logo shining like certainty. Outside, it looked like control. Inside, the mess hall smelled like fear and overcooked rice. A tech at the next table nudged his friend and said, "Look, Mom, I'm on TV," when the camera panned past a blur of lab coats. His friend raised his cup in a mock toast. "To us," he said. "May we stay just sane enough to fix this and not quite sane enough to understand how badly we're failing." The joke landed harder than anyone wanted to admit.

As the segment wrapped, the anchor promised continuing coverage and cut to a commercial no one watched. Conversations slowly resumed—a little louder, a little more brittle than before. Someone asked what day it was, and half the table answered in unison without thinking, then went quiet, each of them aware of how carefully they were counting. John took a long drink of his coffee, grimaced at the taste, and stared at the dark surface until his reflection blurred. The world outside HelixCore's walls was slipping into a kind of death where bodies stayed warm and minds evaporated. Inside, they were feeding themselves, watching the numbers climb, and praying that the people in the upper floors found an answer before those same numbers started to include them. When his radio finally crackled with the call for the next rotation briefing, he pushed his chair back, left the half-empty mug on the table, and followed the others out, the glow of the television graphs searing themselves into his memory like a promise of what waited if HelixCore failed.

CHAPTER 2

Three weeks after the numbers on the screens went vertical, HelixCore got a new head of security and the world quietly admitted it had run out of better ideas. John Renner didn't get the position because he wanted it, or because he'd asked, or even because he was the most qualified. He got it because the last man to wear the title bled out on the front steps of the primary entrance while a terrified crowd screamed that he was hiding the cure. The footage never made the news—HelixCore buried it under proprietary rights and legal threats—but everyone on-site had seen the internal recording at least once. A cluster of civilians, faces wild with fear and grief, pushed against the outer barricades, waving photos and medical reports. The former chief stepped out with his hands open, calm written into his posture. One of the men in the crowd lifted a gun with the shaky determination of someone who had already decided they had nothing left to lose. Panic did the rest. The company called it an "unfortunate incident." The guards called it what it was: a warning. After that, they wanted someone who already knew what the edge looked like. John had been standing on it for weeks.

Now he wore the title like extra armor. HEAD OF SECURITY, stitched neatly under the HelixCore logo on his uniform. It didn't change his patrol routes much; it just meant when something went wrong, people looked at him first. It meant longer hours, more briefings, more paperwork stacked on his desk like a second, quieter disaster. It also meant he was the one in the room when the government finally folded and pushed something long-buried across the table. The message came encrypted, triple-keyed, stamped with more classification tags than John had seen outside of training manuals. The internal memo was four lines long: By order of the Global Health Council and cooperating defense agencies, HelixCore Therapeutics is hereby granted provisional access to Asset Theta-9, formerly designated under Black Program OBELISK. All prior restrictions are suspended for the duration of the cognitive emergency. Full containment and security protocols to be drafted and enforced by HelixCore in cooperation with assigned government liaison.

They didn't explain what Theta-9 was in the memo. They didn't have to. The way the liaison—the thin man in the creased suit with a defense badge that didn't match any branch logo John recognized—held his briefcase in the boardroom told the story. He set it down on the far end of the table with the kind of care usually reserved for explosives and live animals. The boardroom itself had been repurposed weeks ago; the polished table was scarred with notebook impressions and laptop chargers, one wall covered in infection graphs, another layered with printed maps and scribbled notes. The executives looked more like triage coordinators now, ties askew, faces hollowed by weeks of bad sleep and worse news. The scientists who'd been pulled into the meeting wore their lab coats like armor, ID badges swinging as they shifted in their chairs. John stood against the wall by the door, arms folded, eyes on the case.

At the head of the table, HelixCore's CEO, Dr. Elena Voss, watched the liaison with the flat, assessing stare of someone who had run out of patience a long time ago. She was the one who'd signed John's promotion that morning, the same woman who'd interviewed him a year earlier in this very room when HelixCore still pretended to be a normal company. Back then she'd asked about his military record, his tolerance for boredom, his willingness to stand in front of things other people wanted to get to. Now there was no boredom left in the world, only triage. "Is that it?" she asked, nodding toward the briefcase. Her voice was hoarse around the edges, worn down by meetings and bad news, but it still carried the kind of authority that made people sit up straighter. The liaison hesitated for a fraction of a second, then slid the handle toward her. "Yes, ma'am," he said. "Asset Theta-9, as authorized. Full custody transfers to HelixCore as of this moment." He sounded like he couldn't quite believe the words leaving his own mouth.

Voss didn't bother with ceremony. She keyed in the code he'd transmitted ahead of the meeting, fingers moving with clipped precision. Locks inside the case disengaged with a series of muted clicks. When she opened it, no one breathed. John had expected electronics—some bizarre piece of hardware, a drive, a device, a weapon. Instead, nested inside layers of impact foam and sealed polymer, was something that looked disturbingly like a coffin scaled for a child. The inner container was made of reinforced glass and metal, edges frost-burned where coolant lines ran. Inside, strapped and cradled in bands of aged material that might once have been white, lay a body —small, desiccated, almost perfectly preserved. The skin, or what passed for it, had the dry, papery look of mummification, pulled tight over a frame that was wrong in ways John couldn't quite name at first. Limbs slightly too long. Chest too narrow. Skull enlarged in the back and sides, the cranium bulging above deep-set, sealed lids. Not human. Not anything he'd ever seen outside of conspiracy forums and bad late-night television.

A murmur went around the table, half words and half air. One of the junior researchers swore softly under his breath. Another leaned forward, knuckles whitening on the table's edge. "You have got to be kidding," someone said, voice barely above a whisper. Voss didn't flinch. She studied the thing in the case like it was a problem on a board. "How old?" she asked. The liaison exhaled through his nose, as if he'd been waiting for that exact question. "Recovered in the late forties," he said. "Exact date and location remain classified under separate directives, but you can assume pre-satellite era. The body has been under continuous containment since shortly after retrieval. Radiocarbon estimates—where possible—put it at several centuries old at minimum by the time we got to it. Possibly older."

Someone laughed once, a sharp, disbelieving sound that had nothing to do with humor. "This is a joke," a VP muttered. "We asked for help fighting a neurological pathogen, and you brought us a prop from a UFO cult." The liaison's gaze cut to him, flat as glass. "We brought you the only biological structure we've ever encountered that exhibits documented resistance to entropic decay at the neural level," he said. "This 'prop' has been in cold stasis for over seventy years with less measurable degradation in its central nervous tissues than we see in human brains after six months underground. We don't know what it is. We never did. We do know that whatever it was in life, it held onto itself in a way our species apparently cannot."

The room went very still. John found himself staring at the curve of the thing's skull, at the faint suggestion of what might have been ridged structures along the temples. Something in the proportions made his brain want to file it as a sick child. Something else recoiled from that instinct. Voss finally looked away from the body and fixed the liaison with a sharp, tired stare. "You kept this secret for decades," she said. "Buried it in whatever black hole you people use for the things you don't want to explain. And now you're handing it to us because... why? Because you think the pathogen is similar? Because you think whatever this was is immune?" "Because we're out of time," he replied simply. "Every model we run says the same thing: if we don't find a way to stabilize or replace the collapsing structures in the human brain, there won't be enough functioning minds left to run the systems that keep anyone alive. Food distribution. Power grids. Medical infrastructure. All of it relies on people remembering what they're doing. Your HelixCore protocols use the word 'anchor' in half a dozen theoretical papers. Theta-9 may contain the closest thing this planet has to an anchor species."

A senior neurologist—Dr. Kamran—leaned in, eyes locked on the mummified head. "You want us to crack open an alien corpse and reverse-engineer its brain so we can graft its resilience onto ours," he said slowly. "That's what you're asking." The liaison didn't argue the word alien. That, more than anything, told John how desperate things really were. "We're asking you to look," the man said. "To sequence, to map, to compare. To see if there's anything—protein structures, folding patterns, glial arrangements—that we can adapt. Maybe as a shield. Maybe as a patch. Maybe as something entirely new. Ethics committees are, for all intents and purposes, nonfunctional at this stage of the emergency. This is a survival question now."

Voss closed the case halfway, as if she'd seen enough for the moment. When she spoke, her voice had the clipped edge John recognized from every crisis briefing he'd seen her run. "Fine," she said. "We'll look. We'll put our top neuro teams on it and build a dedicated containment wing. Full biosecurity, full isolation. You'll give us every scrap of data you have—historical scans, tissue samples, anything your people have done to this body since you pulled it out of whatever crater you found it in. And in exchange, you will stay out of our way while we try to make something useful out of your ghost." The liaison nodded once. "Agreed. With one condition: Asset Theta-9 does not leave this facility. If your work produces something viable, we get a copy. If it produces something dangerous, you tell us before it eats you."

All eyes went, briefly, to John. He hadn't moved from his position at the wall, but the shift in attention felt like weight settling on his shoulders. Voss turned her head toward him. "You'll draft a new security tree," she said. "Theta-9 gets its own access stack. No one goes near it without two levels of authorization and armed escort. We'll need physical and cognitive safeguards. I want protocols in place by morning." It wasn't a request. John met her gaze, then looked back at the closed briefcase with the dead thing inside that might, somehow, hold the only clue to keeping the living from going hollow. "Understood," he said. The liaison's fingers tightened briefly on the edge of the table, like a man letting go of something he'd never wanted to hold. Governments, John thought, didn't hand over nightmares unless every other option had already burned.

The room broke apart in layers—executives first, fleeing toward calls and damage control; then scientists clustering in low, urgent knots around Voss to ask about lab space, equipment, staffing. The liaison closed the briefcase himself, locking the alien body back into its foam-lined coffin, then stepped aside to answer a secure call he couldn't delay any longer. Through it all, John stayed where he was by the door until Voss straightened, gave a few last clipped instructions, and caught his eye. "Walk with me," she said. It wasn't loud, but people moved out of her path anyway. She took the handle of the briefcase without comment, the thin tendons in her hand standing out against the metal, and headed for the corridor. John fell in half a step behind and to her right, the old muscle memory of escort positions slipping back into place.

The hallway outside the boardroom was quieter, the soundproofed door swallowing most of the tension behind them. Fluorescent lights buzzed overhead. Through a glass panel they passed, John saw two techs arguing softly over a whiteboard already filled with numbers and arrows. Voss walked in a straight line, heels clipping against the tile, the briefcase swinging slightly at her side with each step. "I meant what I said in there," she said after a moment. "Theta-9 doesn't leave this facility. But before that, it doesn't leave you." She glanced up at him. "You're going to personally oversee its transfer to containment. No handoffs. No delegating. If it moves, you move with it." John nodded once. "You don't trust my people?" he asked, not defensive, just checking the ground. "I don't trust the world," she said. "Your people are fine. They're also tired, scared, and one bad rumor away from doing something heroic and stupid. You, at least, have the advantage of being boringly reliable."

One corner of his mouth twitched. "Boring is one of my better qualities." "That and the fact you've been shot at before," she added. "Hopefully that remains a historical detail, but given how things are going, I'm not going to bet on it." They turned down another corridor, this one less polished, the paint scuffed where carts had hit the walls too many times. For a few steps she was quiet, her gaze focused on the far door. "You know I didn't promote you because you were next in line," she said. "Half the supervisory board wanted someone with a longer résumé and a better handshake." "I can work on the handshake," John said. "The résumé's out of my hands." That earned him a small, genuine exhale that was almost a laugh. "Don't," she said. "The last man had a great handshake. It didn't stop a bullet."

They reached the secure elevator. John keyed his code, palms flat on the biometrics, pulse steady. As they waited for the doors to open, she shifted the briefcase into both hands, fingers tightening around the handle. Up close, he saw the shadows under her eyes, the fine lines at the corners, the way her shoulders sat a fraction lower than they had in the videos they used to show new hires. "You sleeping at all?" he asked, the question slipping out before he could talk himself out of it. Her mouth quirked. "Not enough to brag about," she said. "You?" "Four hours last night," he said. "Might've dreamed. Can't remember." "Let's hope that's just overwork," she replied, and there was the slightest edge under it, a joke with teeth. The elevator doors slid open. They stepped inside, and she handed him the briefcase without drama, the weight transferring cleanly from her to him. "From now until it's in a locked box behind three doors, that doesn't leave your hand," she said. "You go to the bathroom, it goes with you. You take a call, it's in your lap. If someone asks to 'just take a look,' you tell them no and send them to me."

He took the case, grip firm, and nodded. "Understood." She watched him for a second, as if weighing something, then added, quieter, "I know what I'm asking, Renner. You didn't sign up to babysit whatever that is. But this is the job now. We are out of clean choices." "I didn't sign up for any of this," he said, then shrugged. "But I'm still here." "So am I," she said. "Until we forget why." The elevator hummed into motion, carrying them down toward the new containment wing, the briefcase solid and heavy in his hand, the weight of it somehow more than what the handle should allow.

John did what Voss asked. For the next forty-eight hours, the briefcase might as well have been grafted to his hand. He carried it through decontamination, into the security hub, down to the containment wing and back again. When he ate, it sat on the table beside his tray. When he slept—what little he managed—it stayed within arm's reach, the handle looped through a cuff on the leg of his bunk. He didn't go anywhere alone. Two guards shadowed him at all times, rotating out every six hours: Kline with her sardonic drawl and habit of cracking her knuckles, and Rami with his quiet eyes and the constant, unconscious counting under his breath that had started the week the numbers went vertical and never really stopped. They moved through the halls in a three-man formation, a quiet wedge of authority that people stepped around without thinking, like a piece of heavy machinery being rolled through a crowded factory.

"Feels like you adopted a briefcase," Kline muttered as they walked the main corridor toward the security operations room, her rifle slung easy across her chest. "You gonna start bringing it pictures from home?" John adjusted his grip, the weight solid and unyielding in his hand. "It's got a better personality than some of the people I've worked with," he said. "Doesn't talk back. Doesn't ask for reassignment." Rami huffed a small laugh. "Yet," he said. "Give it time. Everything else has gone weird, I'm just waiting for the day that thing knocks and asks for coffee." Kline shivered theatrically. "Don't. I had a nightmare last night that it opened itself and the little corpse sat up and started checking our vitals. Woke up sweating." "You sure that was a dream?" John asked. "Some of the lab staff look like that already." She snorted, then fell quiet as they passed a group of researchers clustered around a mobile terminal, their whole attention pinned to whatever data crawled across the screen. No one looked up at the three guards or the anonymous case that held the thing their bosses were betting the species on.

The security operations room—Ops, in everyone's shorthand —was half war room, half call center. Banks of monitors curved along the far wall, each feed showing a different angle of the facility or the city beyond. The air smelled of stale coffee, overworked electronics, and too many bodies in too small a space for too many hours at a time. A handful of guards were already there, eyes flicking between screens and incident logs. One nodded to John as he came in; another stood automatically, making space at the central console. John set the briefcase on the table beside him, resting one hand on it out of habit, and looked up at the wall of screens. The top row showed HelixCore's perimeter: fences, floodlights, empty access roads. The second row showed the city—street cams, traffic cams, feeds bought or borrowed from municipal systems that no longer had anyone to monitor them. It was that row his gaze always slid to, where the outside world played in fragmented, unedited honesty.

On one screen, a downtown intersection sat jammed with cars frozen at odd diagonals, some with doors still open, some with hazard lights blinking weakly. A bus had rolled up onto the curb and stopped half inside a storefront, headlights burning into the dark like accusing eyes. There were no flashing patrol lights, no tow trucks, no city workers in reflective vests trying to restore order. Just stillness. A figure wandered between the vehicles, moving with the slow, uncertain gait John had learned to recognize from too many of Lee's calls—a body whose mind had gone somewhere else and forgotten to take the legs with it. The person—man, woman, impossible to tell at that resolution—bumped into a car door, stepped back, turned, and did it again a minute later like replaying an error in a loop. On another feed, a once-busy shopping district lay gutted, shop windows dark, a string of half-fallen banners advertising sales no one would ever take. A handful of people occupied the sidewalk, some sitting with their backs against the buildings, staring blankly ahead, others standing motionless in the middle of the street. One older woman clutched a plastic bag so tightly her knuckles had gone white, the contents long since spilled at her feet and forgotten.

Kline leaned on the back of a chair, eyes on a feed from a residential block. Several houses sat with their front doors half open, porch lights burning in broad daylight because no one had remembered to turn them off. A sprinkler sputtered weakly in one yard, sending thin arcs of water over a lawn gone wild. In the middle of the cul-de-sac, a child's bicycle lay on its side, wheels slowly turning in the wind. No children. No adults. "Looks like the rapture," she said softly. "If the rapture came with garbage day." Rami pointed to a different screen. "Hospital," he murmured. The exterior cam of St. Mark's—John recognized the entrance from the night Lee had sent him a photo of a backed-up ambulance bay—showed ambulances sitting crooked in the loading zone, some with back doors still open, gurneys half-pulled out and abandoned. A few nurses lingered near the entrance, smoking in their scrubs, but even at a distance their movements were wrong—hesitant, like every gesture had to be remembered first. One of them turned to go back inside and stopped halfway through the motion, standing with her hand on the door for a long, long time before finally pushing it open.

"Lee's somewhere in that mess," John said, more to himself than to the room. He scanned the frame, knowing the odds of catching a glimpse of his friend on a random feed were low, but looking anyway. Everyone had someone they were still looking for out there—family, friends, exes, enemies. People they'd argued with last month and would give anything to argue with again. "You talk to him today?" Kline asked, eyes still on the screens. "This morning," John said. "He sounded... tired." It was the gentlest word for what had come through the line—hollow, stretched, held together by sheer spite. The conversation replayed in his mind in flashes: Lee's ragged attempts at humor, the way his voice went flat when he talked about patients who forgot how to scream. On one of the city feeds, an ambulance crawled slowly through an intersection, siren off, lights dimmed, as if even emergency vehicles had given up on announcing themselves.

Someone at the console switched one of the exterior cams to a drone feed that had been circling a few miles out. The perspective tilted and steadied, looking down over a cluster of high-rises. Rooftops were dotted with people who had gone up and then, for whatever reason, never come back down. Some lay flat, sprawled in awkward angles, eyes open to the sky. Others sat with their legs crossed, hands in their laps, still as statues. John watched one man stand at the edge of a roof, staring at nothing, wind tugging at his shirt. He didn't jump. He didn't step back. He just... stayed, as if the part of him that decided had been erased. On the streets below, small eddies of motion: a grocery line that never moved because no one behind the counter remembered how to unlock the register, people clustered at darkened bus stops long after the buses had stopped running, a handful of looters moving through a storefront with the dispassionate efficiency of people doing a job, not a crime. Not much violence. Not organized chaos. Just a quiet coming apart.

"Fun question," one of the younger guards said from his station, voice steady but tight. "If it gets much worse out there, who exactly are we saving this for? What's the point of a cure if there's no one left who remembers how to use it?" A couple of heads turned toward John, as if he had an answer. He didn't. He shifted his hand on the briefcase handle, feeling the bite of the metal against his palm. "We start with the ones in here," he said finally. "Then whoever's left standing close enough to get to us." It wasn't inspiring, but it was true, and people had begun to prefer ugly truth over polished lies. Kline rolled her shoulders, eyes still glued to the feeds. "That alien corpse better be hiding one hell of a miracle," she said. "Because the world's running out of time and I'm running out of jokes."

John let his gaze travel across the screens one more time. Empty schools, lights still on in classrooms where lessons had simply stopped mid-sentence. A police station with its front doors propped open and no one at the desk. A church overflowing with people sitting in the pews, heads bowed, not in prayer but in the slack, heavy posture of sleep without dreams. A train frozen halfway into a station, its cars dim and motionless, doors hanging open. Every frame told the same story: this wasn't a world waiting for help. It was a world forgetting what help was. He tightened his grip on the case until his fingers ached and forced himself to look away from the monitors, back to the work in front of him—rota schedules, access lists, contingency plans that assumed there would still be enough functioning minds inside HelixCore tomorrow to follow them.

"Alright," he said quietly to Kline and Rami. "We've seen

enough for tonight. Theta-9 goes to the vault in ten. Then we start writing the rules for living with it." They fell in on either side of him as he lifted the briefcase again, the weight dragging at his arm, the world collapsing quietly on a dozen screens behind them. As the door to Ops slid shut, cutting off the glow and the flicker of the feeds, one thought followed him down the corridor, heavy as the case in his hand: if there was any chance at all of stopping the slow erasure chewing its way through humanity, it was sitting in that box, dead and silent, waiting to see whether the living were still capable of saving themselves.

CHAPTER 3

A month after the briefcase disappeared behind three layers of steel and reinforced concrete, the world outside HelixCore looked even more like the aftermath of a disaster no one remembered having. John stood on the roof access walkway with his back against a vent stack, phone pressed to his ear, watching a city that now moved in slow, broken loops. Down below, the streets were thinner—fewer cars, fewer people, more empty space where things had simply stopped and never restarted. Traffic lights still cycled between red, yellow, and green over intersections where nothing passed. Digital billboards flickered through advertisements on timers no one had shut off, selling vacations, concerts, and limited-time sales to a population that couldn't have told you what day it was. Garbage had begun to form its own geography along the sidewalks—drifts of plastic bags, collapsed boxes, flyers for services that no longer answered their phones. Somewhere in the distance, a siren wound up, then petered out mid-wail like the vehicle had forgotten why it had turned it on in the first place.

"Good news," Lee said in his ear, voice thin with fatigue and something sharper. "We've officially reached the 'congratulations, you get to pick which disaster you're responding to' phase of public service. Dispatch is now triaging calls based on how likely the person is to still remember dialing by the time we get there. If they sound too confused, they go in the 'we'll check if we have time' pile. So, you know. Progress."

John shifted the phone to his other ear, the wind tugging at his jacket. "You're really selling the hero life," he said. "I can hear the recruitment posters writing themselves from here."

"Oh yeah, absolutely," Lee said. "Join up now, see the city, meet interesting people, watch them forget what a door is." There was a rustle on his end, the sound of him dropping into a chair or bench. "We had a guy today call three times in a row. Same block, same apartment. First call, he says his wife's acting strange. Second call, he doesn't remember making the first call. Third call, he doesn't remember he has a wife. We get there, the apartment's open, stove still on, TV blaring static. No one home. Neighbors say they watched the two of them wander down the hall twenty minutes earlier, hands clasped, like a couple out for a walk. Nobody knows where they went." A pause. "I left a note on the counter. No idea who it's for. Maybe me, if I ever end up there and can't remember why."

On the street three blocks out, a city bus crawled along on nearly bald tires, HelixCore's rooftop camera tracking it as it went. There were only three passengers visible through the grimy windows. One sat with his head pressed to the glass, fogging a circle with each breath. Another stood in the aisle, swaying slightly, never reaching for the pole, as if he'd forgotten that falling was a thing that could happen. The driver stared straight ahead, hands fixed at ten and two, steering carefully around cars that had been sitting abandoned for weeks. John watched the bus roll through a red light without slowing, like the color meant nothing to him anymore. "We're seeing the same thing on the feeds," he said. "Whole neighborhoods just... stalling. Lights on, doors open, nobody home. It's like the world's running on background processes only."

"Yeah, well, the background processes are getting tired," Lee said. "Half my crew's out. Two forgot where the station was this week. One of them got on the wrong rig and spent an hour checking equipment before he realized he didn't know where anything was because it wasn't his truck. Now admin's got us doing daily quizzes before every shift. 'What's your name, what's today, what's your partner's name, what color is your own damn ambulance.' I keep waiting for them to add 'do you know why you're here' and just start stamping FAIL on everyone's forehead."

A helicopter droned past at a distance, flying lower than it used to, rotors chopping the thick air. Its sides were unmarked—no news logo, no police insignia. Just matte gray and a camera pod bolted under the nose. John tracked it until it dipped behind a cluster of high-rises. "You sound worse," he said. "That your subtle way of telling me you're fine?"

"This is my subtle way of telling you I'm too tired to lie properly," Lee replied. "We're not bringing people back anymore, John. Not really. We're just moving them from wherever they froze to somewhere with nicer lighting. Had a guy sitting in the middle of the freeway just... staring at his own hands. Cars piled up around him like he was a rock in a river. I had to carry him to the rig because he couldn't remember how to stand. Vitals perfect. Brain scans, they tell me, look like a textbook. I checked him every ten minutes on the ride. You know what changed?" "Nothing," John said.

"Nothing," Lee echoed. "He never asked where he was going. Never asked who I was. Never asked anything. Just watched his fingers like he was seeing them for the first time and deciding it wasn't worth the effort." There was a scrape of metal on his end—probably him kicking something out of his way. "How's your pet corpse?" he asked, the pivot as abrupt as it always was when he got too close to whatever line he couldn't afford to cross. "Your bosses cracked it open yet? Find the 'undo apocalypse' button in its skull?"

John glanced over his shoulder at the bulk of HelixCore's central tower, windows dark on the lower floors, lit in a jittery patchwork higher up where the labs never truly slept. "They've got it in its own wing," he said. "Separate air, separate power, separate prayers. I'm not invited to the part where they poke at it. I just make sure nobody else is either." "So no glowing reviews yet," Lee said. "Shame. I was hoping you'd tell me they injected someone with alien brain juice and they started quoting Shakespeare instead of forgetting their own name."

"If they've tried anything that stupid, they're not sharing," John replied. "All I know is we've got more armed doors than we did a month ago and more people walking around with the look you get when you're pretending not to be scared in front of your kids."

"Must be nice," Lee said dryly. "Having doors. I passed three open pharmacy doors yesterday and not a single alarm went off. Just shelves, half-empty, lights buzzing. Guy was sitting in the blood-pressure chair with the cuff halfway up his arm like he'd started to check and forgot why. He was perfectly happy to let me finish the test, though. Came back normal. Brain's melting, heart's fine. Nature's got a sense of humor."

Down at the edge of the HelixCore compound, the outer cameras caught a cat picking its way along the fence line, tail high, fur patched. It slipped past a toppled trash can, paused to sniff, then continued on, springing lightly over a fallen bike. Life, the small kind, still threaded its way through the wreckage. John watched it walk out of frame. "City looks quieter," he said. "Not empty. Just… muffled."

"Yeah," Lee answered. "People stopped calling for everything. No more 'my neighbor's music is too loud' or 'there's a weird smell in the hallway.' Now it's just the big stuff. 'My husband hasn't moved in four hours.' 'My daughter is standing in the shower fully dressed.' 'My father forgot he has legs.' We show up, do what we can, move on. Half the time, by the time we get back to the station, I can't remember their faces, and I don't know if that's the job or the virus knocking."

John's grip tightened on the phone. "You still passing your little quizzes?" "So far," Lee said. "I can still remember all the important things." He hesitated, then added, "Like the fact you owe me a drink for talking you into that job instead of taking the one guarding empty office buildings." "That the important thing?" John asked.

"One of them," Lee said. "The other is that you're sitting on top of a miracle or a disaster and I am contractually obligated, as your unofficial brother, to remind you not to be a martyr about it. If the people upstairs start talking about tests that involve words like 'human trial' and 'expedited,' you call me. I want front-row seats to yell at you."

The wind shifted, bringing with it a faint hint of smoke from somewhere distant, the smell diluted but present enough to be noticed. Something was burning, and no one had yet gotten around to putting it out. "You act like I have any say in what they do," John said. "You've got more say than the people strapped to the beds," Lee replied. "Which, right now, puts you on the short list of people who still matter. Don't waste it."

Below, a block away, a traffic light cycled red to green to yellow, casting color over an empty crosswalk. Nobody hurried. Nobody even noticed. The cameras watched. The city forgot. John listened to his friend breathe on the other end of the line and thought, not for the first time, that the world hadn't ended with sirens and fire. It was ending like this—slowly, stupidly, in half-finished motions and unanswered phones, while the last few people who remembered what it was supposed to be like tried to hold on long enough for something in a locked wing of HelixCore to give them a reason.

A week later, HelixCore walked the thin line between hope and the kind of fear that made people do stupid things in lab coats. The internal memo came first, all clinical language and hedged phrasing: preliminary sequencing of Theta-9 neural tissue has revealed structural motifs not present in human DNA, potential vector for stabilizing higher-order cognitive functions, further testing required, no in vivo trials authorized. Translated into human: there was something there. Something real. Something that made the senior neurologists look like they'd had ten hours of sleep instead of three and talk about "binding resilience" and "non-human scaffolding" in voices that shook even as they tried to sound detached.

John heard it secondhand in the briefing room, Voss at the front with a stack of printouts she didn't bother to pass around, as she explained that their alien corpse might actually be good for more than giving everyone nightmares. "We've got a candidate," she said, gaze sweeping the room. "Not a cure. Not yet. But we've found a way this thing kept its mind from rotting over centuries, and we think we can build a synthetic analogue. Best-case scenario, we get a shield. Worst-case, another dead end. Either way, we do this slow. Controlled. No shortcuts. Nobody gets to play cowboy with this."

The problem was, HelixCore wasn't the only one digging in the attic. Two days after that briefing, Ops tuned one of the news feeds to a global channel and caught a panel of commentators talking over grainy drone footage of a facility halfway across the country—a biotech campus ringed with makeshift barricades and hastily painted military insignia. The scrolling banner at the bottom read: UNREGULATED HUMAN TRIALS? PRIVATE LABS PUSH ETHICS LIMITS IN RACE FOR CURE. On-screen, people in hospital gowns staggered in a fenced yard, watched by guards who looked even more spooked than the test subjects. One man clawed at his own arms as if trying to peel something out of his veins. Another stood perfectly still, head tilted, mouth moving in a soundless stream of words. Someone had leaked internal footage: a woman strapped to a bed, IV bags hanging above her, a doctor leaning over to check her pupils. The timestamp in the corner flashed through minutes too quickly, an edit that meant they didn't want viewers to see the full descent. Even so, the change was obvious—one moment the woman was coherent enough to answer questions, the next she was staring at the ceiling with the slack stillness John now recognized as the world's new ending.

Voss watched that broadcast from the mess hall with the rest of them, arms crossed, jaw so tight a muscle jumped in her cheek. "Idiots," she said quietly, not bothering to keep the disgust out of her voice. "Of course the government didn't give Theta-9 only to us. They've been seeding anything that looks promising into any lab that still has power and people who can spell 'genome.' And the first thing half of them do is skip the groundwork and start pumping mystery into veins because they're afraid someone else will beat them to a headline." Someone at a nearby table muttered, "At least they're trying," and she turned that flat stare on him that could've cut glass.

"Trying what?" she asked. "Trying to turn the pathogen into a two-front war? You don't throw unknown alien structures into human subjects because you're impatient. You do it because you've already given up on acting like the consequences matter." John sat with his coffee cooling in his hands, watching the footage switch to another facility—this one overseas, different logo, same panic. Protesters outside the gates, some holding signs begging to be let in, others screaming about monsters. Inside, men in lab coats walked fast and didn't look at the cameras.

Back in the security hub later, Kline pulled up a restricted feed—an internal government briefing that had "leaked" itself into HelixCore's servers with suspicious convenience. A map bloomed onto the main screen, showing dots for every authorized high-level research site still operating. Too many were pulsing yellow and red, tags hovering beside them: TRIAL INCIDENT, BREACH, UNCONFIRMED CASUALTIES. "Look at that," she said, propping her boots on the edge of a console. "We're not even in the top five worst ideas yet. Guess that's something." Rami shook his head, eyes fixed on the list. "They're killing people faster than the virus would have," he said. "We're supposed to be the smart ones." John didn't answer.

He thought of the Theta-9 wing, of the tight control, the slow, deliberate pace that had half the staff muttering about missed chances and the other half grateful they weren't strapped to a bed somewhere. He thought of Voss, standing in front of that mess hall television, hating what she was seeing not just because it was reckless, but because she knew that if HelixCore didn't move fast enough, someone out there would get lucky—and "lucky" might mean unleashing something even worse.

When the next internal memo came, it was short, almost brutally so: Preliminary synthetic analogue of Theta-9 neural lattice shows promise in vitro. No authorization for human subjects. Any unauthorized trials will result in immediate termination and criminal referral. We will not become them. – E. Voss. John read it twice, then looked up at the rows of exterior cameras, at a world where people were forgetting how to live while others in lab coats gambled with whatever was left. HelixCore, for all its secrets and locked doors, was at least still trying to remember how to be careful. For now.

Another week slid by, marked less by calendar dates and more by the way people inside HelixCore carried themselves down the halls. The world beyond the fence kept fraying—more dark windows, more stalled traffic, more long, empty stretches on the city feeds where nothing moved at all—but inside, for the first time in months, something shifted in the other direction. The change started in the lab wing long before it made it into any official memo. John noticed it on patrol: techs walking faster, not because they were running from a crisis, but because they were trying to get back to whatever they'd just been doing. Conversations that had become numb and brittle picked up a new edge, and the words he overheard when doors opened briefly were different. Less "failure," less "collapse," more "repeat that run," and "it held," and "we need another set of controls." Hope wasn't a shout; it was the way people leaned over their workstations again like the outcome might be worth caring about.

The memo finally dropped three days into that shift, stamped with Voss's ID and routed priority to everyone with clearance high enough to read it. Preliminary Theta-9 analogue compound demonstrated reproducible stabilization of simulated human neural networks under pathogen-exposure models. Synthetic lattice persists beyond projected decay thresholds. Further refinements required.

No in vivo authorization. The attached data set was an incomprehensible forest of graphs and annotations to most of security, but even the numbers told a simple story if you knew how to squint at them: they had taken something from the alien corpse's DNA, taught it how to pretend to be human cell scaffolding, thrown the Forgetting Plague's molecular signature at it in a virtual model, and watched as, for the first time, the model brain didn't immediately fall apart. Not forever. Not perfectly. But long enough to notice. Long enough for the senior lab staff to start using the word "shield" without immediately following it with "hypothetical."

In the mess hall that night, the noise level was higher than it had been in weeks. No one was celebrating—no toasts, no shouting—but there were more conversations going at once, less staring at cold food and untouched coffee. A cluster of lab techs sat with trays pushed aside, napkins covered in scribbled diagrams, hands moving as they argued about binding affinities and delivery mechanisms. One of them, a woman John recognized only by sight from the containment wing, laughed once, quick and almost surprised, when her colleague tried to explain something with a metaphor involving duct tape and rebar.

"You can't just duct tape alien rebar to the brain and call it fixed," she said, shaking her head, but her eyes were bright in a way he hadn't seen in a while. At the next table, one of the night-shift guards turned to John and said, "They look... different," jerking his chin toward the lab coats. John followed his gaze. Shoulders that had been permanently slumped for weeks sat a little straighter. People weren't cradling their coffee like a life-support system. Someone had put music on low in the corner, not loud enough to draw attention, but there, a faint rhythm under the hum of air vents and conversation. "They've got numbers that aren't all going down," John said. "That'll do it."

He took a later patrol through the Theta-9 wing, less because he needed to and more because he wanted to see for himself. The containment door cycles had become familiar—badge, palm scan, code, the soft thunk of locks withdrawing. Inside, the air felt colder, dryer, threaded with the clean sting of disinfectant. Through a viewing window, he could see part of the main lab. No one was touching the corpse itself anymore; it sat in its sealed case in an inner room like a relic, while the real work happened around screens and microscopes.

A wall of monitors displayed shifting images: simulated neuron clusters, lattice models glowing faintly, waveforms ticking along from left to right. Dr. Kamran pointed at one of them, excitement undercutting his exhaustion. "That's forty minutes beyond decay curve," John heard him say through the glass to a junior tech. "Look—here, here. The network should have collapsed by now. It didn't. It re-stabilized." The junior tech made a noise halfway between a gasp and a breath he hadn't realized he'd been holding. "So it's holding their shape," he said. "Even under attack." "Sometimes," Kamran said. "Sometimes is more than never. We can work with sometimes."

Later, back in Ops, the outside feeds told a harsher story. More blacked-out neighborhoods. More long shots of empty train platforms, empty playgrounds, empty sidewalks. A drone passed over a stadium now used as a holding center; fewer figures moved between the cots than the last time they'd checked, and those who did moved slower. The infection numbers in the corner of the news channel marched upward with the same merciless steadiness they always had. But for the first time, watching those numbers, John didn't feel like he was staring at a cliff edge with no ground beyond it. Somewhere beneath his feet, in a lab he wasn't allowed to step into, people were building something that might put a handhold into the rock.

Kline dropped into the chair next to him, balancing a mug on her knee. "Hear the latest rumor?" she asked. "Our pet alien's gift to humanity is something we can maybe drip into somebody's spine someday and keep their brain from turning to fog. Lab gossip says they've got a model where the virus hits, takes a swing, and… misses." She waggled her fingers like a magician. "Ta-da." "And how many times does it miss?" John asked.

"Not enough," she admitted. "But more than zero. Which is more than anyone else can say right now." On the screen in front of them, a news crawl mentioned three different companies under investigation for unauthorized human trials gone wrong. HelixCore's name wasn't on the list. When that was pointed out in the next briefing, Voss had just nodded once and said, "Good. Let it stay that way until we know exactly what we're putting into people. Hope is useful. Panic with a pipette is lethal."

When the lights dimmed for night mode and the facility settled into its artificial approximation of sleep, John walked past the vault one more time on his way off shift. The door status panel glowed green. Behind it, down a short stretch of fortified corridor and another lock, sat a locked case holding a dead thing's frozen brain and the data that had come from it. Inside the walls around him, lab techs and researchers were going back to their benches tomorrow with something other than dread pulling them there.

Outside the walls, on a dozen grainy cameras, the world was still unraveling, slower in some places than others, but always in the same direction. He paused for half a second, hand hovering over the door frame, then kept walking. The chapter the world was in hadn't changed yet. People were still forgetting, still wandering, still freezing in place. But somewhere at the bottom of HelixCore's stacked secrets, a line on a graph had bent upward instead of down, and that was enough to make tired people move a little faster, talk a little louder, and keep showing up to work in a world that kept trying to erase them.

It wasn't a cure. It wasn't even close. But for the first time since the Forgetting Plague began, the hope inside HelixCore wasn't just a word people used because they didn't know what else to say. It had numbers now. It had shape. And that made it dangerous in its own way—because once people believed they might actually be able to save something, they would start asking, sooner or later, what price they were willing to pay to do it.

CHAPTER 4

By the time the next set of results came back, HelixCore had learned how to be cautiously hopeful without saying the word too loudly. The Theta-9 analogue—what the lab techs had started calling "the lattice" because no one wanted to say "alien" every five minutes—was holding more often than it wasn't. In the simulation suites, synthetic neural networks that should have shredded under the pathogen's modeled assault bent, buckled, and then steadied again, like a building flexing in a storm and refusing to fall. Not every time. Not cleanly. But enough to make the senior researchers start coming to meetings with fresh printouts instead of excuses. John sat in the back of the briefing room as Dr. Kamran pointed at a graph on the wall display, a jagged line that dipped and then clawed its way back toward baseline.

"This segment here," Kamran said, tapping the screen with the end of his pen, "should be catastrophic failure. Every human model we've run drops straight off the map at that point. With the lattice present, the degradation slows, and in thirty-two percent of runs it reverses. The structures re-form. They remember what they're supposed to be." He didn't smile—no one did that anymore—but something in his eyes had started to look less like numbness and more like momentum. "We refine the binding and delivery, we can push that percentage up. Give the brain time to fight."

Voss stood beside him, arms folded, expression unreadable as she tracked the numbers. "So we have a synthetic scaffold that can, sometimes, keep a modeled brain from turning into soup when the virus hits it," she said. "Good. That's more than we had last month. What we do not have is a cure, or anything remotely resembling something we're putting into living people. We are still at the stage where the universe is politely informing us that our idea might not be completely stupid. Let's not prove it wrong by rushing." A low ripple of tired laughter passed through the room; it didn't change the fact that several of the lab staff were practically vibrating with the urge to move faster. John could see it in the way they shifted in their seats, in the quick glances they exchanged when Kamran mentioned "translational pathways" and "delivery vectors" as if those words didn't already taste like human trials in their mouths. Voss must have seen it, too, because she straightened and let her gaze sweep the room like a searchlight. "Repeat after me," she said. "We are not them."

An hour later, in the mess hall, he saw exactly who "them" was supposed to be. One of the televisions had been turned to a global news channel, volume just loud enough to cut through the clatter. A polished anchor stood in front of a graphic that made John's stomach tighten—a logo for a biotech competitor he recognized, Novus Path, superimposed over a stylized strand of DNA. Behind the anchor, prerecorded footage showed a gleaming white headquarters with a line of reporters outside the gates, microphones extended like spears.

The headline bar at the bottom of the screen read: NOVUS PATH ANNOUNCES BREAKTHROUGH THERAPEUTIC – 'WITHIN DAYS OF MASS DISTRIBUTION.' Somebody at the next table snorted. "Yeah," Kline muttered around her coffee, "and I'm within days of becoming a ballerina."

The feed cut to a press conference held on Novus Path's front steps. Their CEO, a man with expensively casual hair and the kind of smile people used to trust before the world fell apart, stood behind a row of microphones. Flanking him were two scientists in crisp lab coats, the fabric too clean to belong to anyone who actually worked at a bench. "We are thrilled to share," the CEO was saying, "that our team has developed a novel therapeutic agent derived from non-terrestrial biological models, capable of significantly delaying the cognitive impact of the current pathogen.

Early volunteer data is extremely promising. With emergency authorization, we are prepared to begin distributing doses to key population centers within the week." The reporters exploded with questions. "What about side effects?" "What's your sample size?" "Where did you obtain your material?" The CEO held up his hands, palms out, in the universal gesture of benevolent control. "We will, of course, be releasing full data to the appropriate regulatory bodies," he said smoothly. "But in a crisis of this magnitude, we cannot afford to wait for perfection. Every day we delay, more of our loved ones are lost."

John looked across the room at Voss. She was standing under the television, a tray untouched in front of her, watching the broadcast with a stare that could have frozen water. Her jaw worked once, a muscle jumping. When the CEO said "we cannot afford to be paralyzed by caution," she let out a short, disbelieving sound that might once have been a laugh. "There it is," she said quietly, not realizing—or not caring—that half the room could hear her. "The magic phrase. 'Paralyzed by caution.' Translation: we don't actually know what this thing does, but we'd like to pump it into as many brains as possible before anyone can stop us."

A nearby tech glanced at her. "What if it works?" he asked, tentative. "What if they get there first?" She turned that look on him, sharp but not unkind. "Then we celebrate," she said. "And then we start cleaning up whatever their rush broke. But I will not gamble this many lives on a press conference and the word 'volunteer' spoken by a man who clearly hasn't touched a pipette in his life."

The channel switched to a different segment then, the graphic shifting to a world map drained of color. The anchor's tone dropped into that practiced solemn register reserved for mass casualty events and historical tragedies. "As of the latest estimates," she said, "global population surveillance suggests that only fifty-eight percent of the pre-outbreak population remains cognitively functional at baseline.

Of that number, a significant portion show early-stage forgetfulness that may indicate preclinical infection. Approximate fatalities attributed directly or indirectly to the neurological collapse are believed to be in the hundreds of millions, with some models projecting higher. And for those still alive…" The map over her shoulder filled with bands of pale red and dark crimson, indicating "confirmed cognitive compromise." In several regions, the red was almost solid. "Communication loss in multiple zones makes precise counts impossible, but officials warn the number of infected may already outnumber the fully unaffected worldwide."

In Ops later, John watched another angle of the same report on a different channel. There, the numbers were laid out with brutal simplicity: ESTIMATED GLOBAL POPULATION (PRE-OUTBREAK): 7.9 BILLION. EST. FUNCTIONALLY UNAFFECTED: 4.6 BILLION. EST. COGNITIVELY COMPROMISED: 2.1–2.6 BILLION. EST. DEAD/MISSING: 800–1,200 MILLION. The digits ticked up as updated feeds rolled in, like a slot machine stuck on loss. Rami stared at the screen, lips moving as he quietly did the math to himself because that was how he kept the world aligned in his own head.

"Half the species either gone or halfway gone," he murmured. "And they want to play roulette with alien DNA on live subjects because the cameras are on." Kline cracked her knuckles and shook her head. "If Novus Path's miracle juice doesn't kill people," she said, "the stampede to get it will. You see that clip? Those crowds outside their gate? It's a fire code violation waiting to happen."

Not long after, Voss called a mandatory briefing for everyone with a HelixCore badge that opened more than two doors. The auditorium was full, people standing along the back wall and in the aisles. She walked onto the small stage at the front without notes, a simple tablet in her hand she never once looked at. Behind her, one of the screens showed a frozen image from the Novus Path press conference, the CEO caught mid-sentence, teeth bared in a smile. Next to it was a still of the global infection map.

"Some of you have already seen this," she said, voice carrying without need of amplification. "For those who haven't: yes, other facilities are claiming they're ready to move to mass distribution. Yes, they're using alien-derived data. No, we will not be doing the same." She let that settle. Murmurs rolled through the crowd like distant thunder. "Here's where we are. Our Theta-9 analogue works in silico and in vitro. It delays and sometimes reverses model collapse. Our failure modes are not yet predictable.

We don't have a clean way to deliver it without potentially turning someone's brain into a very interesting, very dead piece of abstract art. Until that changes, our work does not leave the page or the petri dish. I know what the outside numbers look like. I know how many people you're all carrying in your heads when you badge in every morning. So am I. But HelixCore will not become the place people point to in ten years—if we get ten years—and say 'that's where they started drowning people in hope because they were afraid of being last.' We will be first or we will be right, or we will be nothing at all."

John watched her from halfway up the aisle, the Theta-9 vault access card warm against his chest where he kept it behind his badge. People around him were tense in different ways; some wanted to cheer, some wanted to scream, a few looked like they wished they were standing in front of Novus Path's gates instead, ready to roll the dice. "If," Voss added, and the room quieted again, "Novus Path or anyone else actually manages to produce something that works—consistently, safely, verifiably—we will swallow our pride and sign whatever papers we have to in order to get it to as many people as possible. I don't care whose logo is on the bottle if it keeps our minds from dissolving. Until then, we do not chase their press releases. We do not measure our worth against their promises. We measure it against our own data and our own conscience."

Afterward, heading back toward the security hub, John passed a break room where a dozen staff were clustered around a muted television. The ticker at the bottom of the screen mentioned a new wave of riots in three major cities—people breaking into hospitals not to loot, but to demand to be injected with experimental compounds, any compounds, because the alternative was to sit at home and wait for their minds to evaporate.

The footage showed one man on his knees outside Novus Path, hands clasped like prayer, begging the guards to "take my kids first, they're smarter than me," while two teenagers stood behind him, faces blank and turned slightly away, eyes unfocused. Someone in the break room swore and walked out. Someone else stayed, staring at the screen like if he looked hard enough he might see his own family in the crowd.

Ops was quieter. The city feeds hadn't improved. If anything, they were thicker with empty spaces. But inside the facility, the air carried a different charge now. Labs with whiteboards full of dead-end equations had started to erase and rewrite them with new terms. The Theta-9 wing's activity log had gone from "baseline analysis" to "iterative modeling" and "candidate screening." On his console, John's incident queue contained fewer internal fights and more requests for extended lab time. He glanced once at the vault status—green lights, all seals intact—and then at the small inset window on his monitor that still showed the world map from the earlier broadcast. Two stories unfolding in parallel: one where numbers climbed relentlessly toward erasure, and one where a dead thing's stubborn, alien persistence had given the living a thin sliver of leverage.

He leaned back in his chair, rubbing the bridge of his nose, listening to the low murmur of radios and the soft clack of keyboards. For the first time since HelixCore had sealed its gates, he could feel the center of gravity in the building shift away from pure survival into something else—something riskier. They were no longer just trying to hold the line. They were quietly, carefully, getting ready to step over it.

John waited until his shift was technically over and the building had gone into its version of night—lights dimmed in the corridors, labs running on skeleton crews, Ops down to the people who didn't know what else to do with themselves—before calling Lee. He took the call in the stairwell between the security hub and the roof, where the concrete walls killed most of the ambient noise and the only sound was the faint hum of the building's lungs. The line clicked, rang twice, then picked up with a tired, automatic, "Chavez," like Lee was answering dispatch instead of his best friend.

"It's me," John said. "Oh good," Lee replied. "Thought I was finally hearing voices. That'd be a nice change of pace. The ones in my head would at least know what they're doing." There was movement on his end, a chair scraping. "What's up, Johnny? You calling to tell me your alien finally coughed up the cheat codes?"

"Not yet," John said. "This is… different. You catching the Novus Path circus over there?" That got a snort. "You mean the miracle juice? Yeah. We've got patients asking for it by brand name like it's a soda. Emma's studio sent out an email, too.

'We're exploring all options to keep our talent safe, including early access to cutting-edge therapeutics.' Translation: if there's a shot that might keep the leads remembering their lines, line 'em up." He paused. "Why? You calling to tell me your boss says it's legit?

Because I've got a list of people I'd shove to the front of that line, starting with—" "Don't touch it," John said, letting the words land flat and unambiguous. "You. Emma. Anyone you like even a little. If some stranger offers to pump that stuff into you, say no and walk away." There was a beat of silence. In the distance on Lee's end, someone shouted for a crash cart; the sound cut off when a door closed. "That sounded awfully like a capital-O Order," Lee said slowly. "You pick up a medical degree in your free time or is this coming from your ice queen?"

"From the woman who's been staring at real data for months and still refuses to put anything into a vein," John said. "Look, Voss doesn't chase headlines. Half the time she forgets they exist. She saw that press conference and looked like she wanted to throw something at the screen. Says they're rushing. Says they're not sharing method, not sharing numbers, not sharing failure modes. All we've seen is suits saying 'trust us' and some heavily edited volunteer footage. She's got a lattice that works in a bottle—sometimes—and she won't even let the word 'trial' leave anyone's mouth.

If she's not willing to roll those dice yet, I'm sure as hell not letting you let some other guy with a better haircut use you as a billboard." On the other end of the line, Lee let out a low whistle. "Damn. You really drank the HelixCore Kool-Aid," he said, but there wasn't much sting in it. "You trust her that much?" John thought of Voss in the mess hall, saying, *we will not be the place people point to in ten years,* like she could see the accusation already, and didn't want it. Thought of the way she'd handed him the briefcase herself, no theatrics, just weight. "Yeah," he said simply. "I do. She's the only person I've seen in months who looks more afraid of doing the wrong thing than of being first."

"Cute," Lee said. "Very noble. Problem is, out here, being first is the only thing people care about. We had a mother today asking if we knew where she could get 'the good stuff,' like we were a pharmacy. Said if her kids were going to forget her anyway, she'd rather they did it on a drug somebody at least pretended to test." He sighed. "Emma's pissed, by the way. Her agent told her Novus Path's offering priority doses to 'essential cultural figures.' She called me to ask what I thought. I told her I'd rather take my chances with the virus than with something developed faster than instant noodles."

A pause, softer. "You're telling me I was right?" "For once," John said. "Enjoy it. Doesn't happen often." That got a real laugh, brief but there. "Alright, alright. I'll tell her the mysterious man in the tower says no mystery injections for the home team. She'll be thrilled. She already thinks you and your boss are part of some secret ivory-tower club hoarding the good ideas."

"If we were hoarding anything that actually worked, you'd know," John said. "I'd have dragged you through the front gate myself. Right now we've got a model that looks less doomed and a lot of very tired people trying not to screw it up. Novus Path going on TV and promising salvation is like watching someone grab the steering wheel while we're still building the brakes."

Down the hall, a light flicked off as a motion sensor decided the stairwell was empty. John shifted to trigger it back on. "Promise me you won't let anyone stick you with anything until I tell you Voss signed off on it." "You know that's not how the world works, right?" Lee said. "You don't get personal clearance from the tower for every syringe." Then, before John could answer, he softened. "But yeah. Okay. I won't line up for the miracle shot. Not me, not her. If I go down, it'll be the old-fashioned way—screaming at the universe, not glowing in the dark because some CEO wanted a good quarterly report."

"Good," John said. "I'd miss having you yell at me." "Please," Lee said. "If I forget you, you'll just show up at my door with that 'I'm disappointed' face and a strapped briefcase and scare my neurons back into line." There was a rustle, a distant overhead announcement. "Alright, I've got to go remind a city how to breathe for a few more hours. You keep your alien, your boss, and your conscience intact, yeah?" "I'll try," John said. "You stay away from anyone offering cures and cameras in the same sentence." "Yes, Dad," Lee said, and hung up before John could respond.

John slid the phone back into his pocket and started down the stairs toward Ops. On the wall screen in the hub, he knew, the news would still be playing B-roll of eager faces outside Novus Path's gates, people pressing forward in the hope that faster meant better. Inside HelixCore, Voss was somewhere under three floors of concrete, telling her teams to slow down. He wasn't a scientist, and he didn't understand the details, but he knew which instinct he trusted more.

A handful of days later, the shift was small enough that most people almost missed it, and big enough that it changed everything. The memo came through encrypted, tagged with Voss's authorization and a subject line that made a few stomachs drop: PROTOCOL UPDATE – TRIAL FRAMEWORK. No caps-lock panic, no exclamation points, just that one word finally allowed to exist in writing. John read it in the security hub with his elbow on the console and a half-drunk coffee cooling by his hand.

The language was still cautious to the point of paranoia—*Phase zero, compassionate-use framework only, comatose late-stage patients with no remaining therapeutic options, fully documented consent from legal proxies, external communications embargo in effect*—but the meaning was clear. The lattice had crossed some invisible threshold in the data. The people in the white coats believed, or almost believed, that it was time to see what it did inside a living brain. Nothing would be announced. Nothing would leak if Voss could help it. Out there, the world would keep begging at Novus Path's gates while HelixCore tried not to set itself on fire quietly.

The facility reacted the way an organism does to a sudden change in pressure. The Theta-9 wing doubled its already obsessive access checks. New clearances appeared on John's daily list of who was allowed anywhere near the test prep rooms. Ops started running tighter perimeter sweeps around the inbound patient transport corridor, where a handful of bodies from partner hospitals would be brought in under discreet cover—men and women whose charts all read the same way: final stage, non-responsive, no independent cognitive function, families desperate enough to sign anything put in front of them if it meant the word "chance" could be used in a sentence. In the labs, the conversations got sharper. "Vector stability, not negotiable." "No, we don't skip the redundancy." "Yes, we're doing another dry run." Hope was still there, but it had grown teeth and rules.

Late in the second night of new protocols, John found Voss in one of the observation rooms overlooking the isolation suites. It was small, barely more than a raised platform with a bank of monitors and a wide window that looked down onto a row of glass-fronted rooms, each holding a bed, each bed holding someone who wasn't going to wake up again unless something unprecedented happened. It was the first time he'd seen her alone in days, without a halo of staff and questions orbiting her. She stood with her hands on the railing, shoulders straight but not tense, eyes on the nearest patient—a middle-aged man with a ventilator tube taped to his mouth and a web of leads on his shaved scalp. For the moment, nothing connected those leads to anything alien. That part was still on the benches upstairs. "You posted the update," John said by way of announcement as he stepped inside. "We're saying it now." She didn't look up. "Internally," she said. "You'll notice I didn't title it 'Congratulations, we are now God.'"

He stepped up beside her, leaving a respectful gap. Through the glass, the monitors next to the beds traced out the familiar green and white rhythms of bodies still breathing because machines insisted they should. "You sure?" he asked. There was no accusation in it. Just the question that mattered. "No," she said, and something about the bluntness made it sound more honest than any emphatic yes could have.

"But I am as sure as I can be without dying first to find out. The lattice holds in organoids, organ-on-chip systems, every induced model we throw at it. We've simulated more brains in the last month than most people meet in a lifetime. The failure patterns are narrowing. When it breaks, it breaks in ways we can predict." She exhaled slowly. "What we can't simulate is the part that makes a person a person. So at some point, we either accept that we're going to learn that part the hard way, or we give up and wait for the plague to do our work for us."

They watched the man in the nearest bed for a moment. His chest rose and fell with the ventilator's steady push and pull. A nurse moved through the suite below, checking lines and adjusting a blanket with the same gentleness she might have used for someone who could still feel a tug. "Why them?" John asked quietly. "Why not start with... I don't know. Staff. Volunteers." She finally turned her head to look at him, and the look was tired enough to register even through her usual control.

"Because I'm not trying to build martyrs," she said. "These are people whose minds are already gone by every scan and measure we have. We're not risking their lives. Those are already over. We're risking what is left—structure, pattern, whatever the virus hasn't chewed through. If the lattice does something benign, we learn. If it does something terrible, we learn, and they don't know the difference. I can live with that. I can't live with being the one who told a healthy person to lie down on a table so I could watch them die in a more interesting way than the virus would manage on its own."

He accepted that with a slow nod. "You lose anyone?" he asked, then almost took it back. It was a personal question, an off-duty question, wedged into a room full of ventilators. She didn't flinch. "Hundreds," she said. "Statistically speaking." Then, softer, "A little brother. Another life, another country. He didn't get this plague. He got one of the old ones. The kind we thought we were clever enough to beat.

Doctor missed a sign, protocols weren't followed, someone cut a corner to move faster. He died in an ICU that was technically state-of-the-art. Every machine worked. Every procedure was textbook. The only thing that failed was judgment." She looked back down at the bed below. "I was in my second year of med school. I watched my parents thank those doctors because they tried so hard. I promised myself I'd never be on the wrong side of a 'we tried.'"

John hadn't known that. He'd heard the rumors—Voss turned her back on clinical practice, Voss burned out on patients, Voss only cared about data—but none of that matched the woman standing here, staring at strangers on ventilators like she owed them more than numbers. "Why this place?" he asked. "You could have picked quieter work. Data somewhere nobody barges in with briefcases." Her mouth bent, not quite a smile.

"You did," she pointed out. "And look how that turned out." She shook her head once. "HelixCore made sense. Before all this, we were the people playing with ideas too weird or too complex for universities with donation committees. That came with responsibility. It still does. Besides, somebody was going to get their hands on things like Theta-9. Better it be someone who thinks about twenty years from now as much as they think about tomorrow's press conference."

"Novus Path doesn't," John said. "They're already promising weekly injections on live TV." "Novus Path wants to be remembered," she replied, eyes still on the beds. "Or what passes for remembered in a world where most minds are slipping gears. I don't care if anyone remembers my name when this is over.

I care whether there's anyone left capable of remembering anything at all." She straightened slightly, some internal decision settling. "First injections will be in three days. You'll get the schedule. You'll be in the room, or next to it. If anything looks wrong—structurally, operationally, ethically—you pull the fire alarm, I don't care if someone with three letters more than you in their title tells you to stand down. You understand?" He looked at her, at the fine lines at the corners of her eyes, the resolve worn thin but not cracked. "I do," he said.

They stood in silence long enough for the nurse below to finish her round and slip out of the suite. Monitors beeped, respirators sighed, the building hummed around them like a machine trying to remember its function. "You ever scared?" he asked finally. "Or do you skip that part and go straight to irritated?" That earned him a quiet, genuine laugh, brief as it was. "I am terrified," she said.

"Constantly. Gives me something in common with everyone else. The difference is, I don't let terror make my decisions for me. I let it make me ask one more question, check one more assumption, tell one more overeager idiot to wait." She glanced sideways at him. "I keep you around because you do the same thing, in a different language. You see the ways this place could break. I need that."

"Thought you kept me around because I'm boringly reliable," he said. "That too," she replied. "Don't ruin it by developing charisma." Her attention went back to the beds, to the bodies waiting for a kind of last-minute intervention no one had ever tried before. "Go get some sleep, Renner. Trials or no trials, the sun's allegedly going to rise again in a few hours, and I need you vertical when people start panicking about the thing we're not telling them we're doing." He hesitated, then nodded and stepped back from the glass.

As he turned to go, she spoke once more, quieter. "For what it's worth," she said, "if what we're building works—even a little—it won't just be because of the alien. It'll be because people like you kept the rest of the world far enough away for us to think clearly. Don't underestimate that."

He left her there, a lone figure framed against the glow of monitors and the still bodies beyond the glass, and headed back toward the dimmed corridors of security. Behind him, for the first time, the word trial existed inside HelixCore as something more than a future tense threat. It was a plan now, with dates and names and rooms assigned. Outside, on the feeds, the world kept unraveling in slow, stupid loops. Inside, a handful of people were about to find out whether the dead thing in the vault could teach the living how to keep their minds.

CHAPTER 5

The first injection didn't look like history. It looked like a nurse in blue gloves pushing a syringe into a port on a line that had been dripping saline into a motionless arm for days. No fanfare, no speeches, no audience beyond a tight ring of people who all knew enough to be scared. The patient was Trial Subject One in the documentation, a name reduced to initials and a date of birth on the chart: late fifties, male, stage four cognitive collapse, ventilated, no meaningful response to stimuli in six days. In person he looked like every other body in the isolation suite—skin gone slack in the way of long unconsciousness, muscles beginning to atrophy, eyelids half-lowered over eyes that no longer tracked anything. The pathogen had burned through whatever made him himself and left the rest as… residue. The only difference was the clear bag hanging across from the saline, labeled in stark black text: T9-L1 PROTOTYPE – DOSE 0.1. That, and the way everyone in the observation room held their breath when the line was unclamped.

John stood behind the glass with Voss and a handful of senior staff. The monitors above the bed glowed soft green and white, tracing vital signs that had settled into the lazy plateau of machine-supported survival. Next to them, a separate bank of equipment handled the part that mattered: EEG leads, cortical activity maps, real-time modeling overlays running Theta-9's synthetic lattice against what was left of the man's neural structure. Kamran watched that set, not the body. "We're live," the nurse said over the intercom. "Starting infusion… now." The new line shivered once as the pump engaged. On the displays, a small indicator flipped from standby to active. For a long minute, nothing happened. The board above the bed kept drawing its steady lines. The EEG maintained the same faint, disorganized noise that had defined it since admission—a kind of static more than a pattern.

Then, slowly, one of the overlays began to change. The model of the lattice appeared first as a pale ghost threaded through the existing network—a careful, almost timid scaffold. As the drug reached the brain, that ghost brightened, connecting with the existing structures in a pattern that made no intuitive sense to John and perfect sense to the people around him. The chaotic background fuzz on the EEG began to thin. Not much at first, just edges smoothing, noise receding. Kamran leaned closer to his console, fingers flying over controls. "Look at channels F3, F4," he said. "There—boundary stabilization. That's… that's new." One of the other neurologists shook her head in disbelief. "That can't be the drug," she said. "We're minutes in. It should barely be past the blood-brain barrier." The lattice map pulsed again, faintly, and the EEG lines began to coalesce into something less like static and more like a struggling signal trying to push through interference.

"Check the simulation," Voss said, voice even. "Are we seeing alignment or are we seeing what we want to see?" Kamran didn't answer right away. He brought up baseline recordings, layered them with the live feed, ran a quick predictive model. The results came up side by side—a ghost of what should be, a trace of what was. Even to John they were different. The new lines dipped and wavered, but they didn't disintegrate. "This is real," Kamran said, and there was a note in his voice that had nothing to do with career advancement and everything to do with awe. "We're getting partial restoration of oscillatory patterns in regions that were functionally flat yesterday. The structure isn't just holding—it's re-imposing order on degraded pathways."

The word restoration slid through the observation room like a cold current. On the bed below, the man's face twitched—just once, a small tightening at the corner of his mouth, the kind of movement nurses usually ignored on patients this far gone because it meant nothing. This time the nurse froze. "Doctor," she said into her mic, "we've got minor facial motor response." "Could be artifact," someone mouthed near John. Voss didn't move. "Repeat the stimulus checks," she ordered. "No change in protocol. No improvisation." The nurse shone a penlight into the patient's eyes, called his name, applied pressure to the nail beds. For a moment, nothing different. Then one eyelid fluttered, a sluggish, incomplete effort like a man surfacing through thick ice. The monitors recorded a small spike in coordinated activity across several regions. "That's impossible," the neurologist whispered. "He's been non-responsive for—"

"Check again," Voss said. Her tone did not change. The nurse did. Light. Name. Pressure. This time, the man's fingers twitched around the edge of the sheet. Not a full grasp, not deliberate, but not reflex either. The movement matched the timing of the signal on the EEG. The lattice overlay glowed brighter in response, as if the alien-informed structure had found something to hang onto and refused to let go. Kamran swore softly, then caught himself. "We're seeing reconstitution," he said, more to himself than to the room. "Not just resistance. The lattice is acting as a scaffold for regrowth. Some of these pathways are reforming."

They watched for an hour. The ventilator kept doing its work, the drip kept dosing, the models kept updating. The man never woke. He didn't speak. He didn't open his eyes fully or sit up or do anything dramatic enough to sell a headline. But the EEG stabilized into a pattern that bore more resemblance to a sedated patient than an empty shell. He squeezed the nurse's hand once without external stimulus. His pupils began reacting more consistently to light. To people who hadn't spent the last months watching brains dissolve, it would have looked like scraps, like nothing. To everyone in the observation room, it was obscene abundance.

The next two subjects were worse off on paper and did better than anyone had any right to expect. Subject Two showed no motor response at all, but her cortical map shifted from chaotic to organized in slow, deliberate increments, as if some underlying architecture were being gently reassembled. Subject Three—young, early thirties, documented as a rapid-progress case—started with a beautifully symmetrical brain scan that had collapsed into static in a matter of days. After infusion, his EEG didn't just stabilize; segments of it began to mirror his pre-infection baseline pattern stored in the hospital's records. "We're not just holding them in place," the junior neurologist said, voice shaking. "We're pulling them back toward who they were."

By the end of the first trial block, the lab had more questions than answers, but the kind of questions that felt like footholds instead of cliffs. Was the lattice reading the old structures and rebuilding them or imposing its own? How long would the effect last? Were they repairing damage or forcing an unnatural order on tissue that the virus was still trying to erase? None of those questions had answers yet. What they had was data showing that dead circuitry could, under the right conditions, approximate life again. For a facility that had spent months watching the reverse, it was enough to send a tremor through every department.

The mood in the mess hall that night was something John hadn't seen since before the outbreak: it flirted with good. Not joy—nobody remembered how to do that—but something adjacent. People leaned across tables, arguing over printed graphs, hands cutting the air. "If it can reconstitute in late-stage collapse," one tech said, "imagine what it could do for early-stage." "Assuming it doesn't scramble healthy tissue," another replied. "Or trigger god knows what in long-term function." Nearby, someone had drawn a crude version of the lattice on a napkin and stabbed a fork into the middle. "Here's us," he said to his companion. "Tiny meat brains hanging on while alien scaffolding does all the real work." His companion actually smiled. "Speak for yourself," she said. "My brain is at least eighty percent caffeine at this point."

Word of the results never left the building. Voss made sure of that. She convened a closed-door session with senior staff and security the following day. No slides, no theatrics, just stacks of reports and a single line written in heavy marker on the whiteboard: IT WORKS (SOME). She underlined it once, hard. "You've all seen the data," she said. "In controlled conditions, with carefully selected subjects who had nothing left to lose, our prototype lattice compound appears to stabilize and partially restore neural structures damaged by the pathogen. This is beyond what I allowed myself to hope for at this stage. Take a moment and be proud of that." She let that sit. A few people did allow themselves the smallest exhale, the tiniest outward sign of pride. Then she drew a second line beneath the first: WE STILL DON'T KNOW WHAT ELSE IT DOES.

"So here is what happens next," she continued. "We expand the trial cautiously. New subjects, new dosing schedules, new monitoring protocols. We track everything. Longitudinal scans, biomarkers, any sign that the lattice is doing more than we think—good or bad. We do not, under any circumstances, open this to early-stage conscious patients yet. We do not pitch this to external partners. We do not whisper, suggest, hint, or even think the word 'cure' outside these walls. Novus Path can have their press conferences; they can also have their casualties. We will have live patients with intact personalities or we will have nothing."

After the meeting, John walked with her down the corridor

toward the Theta-9 wing. She carried no papers, just her tablet, screen dark. "How many know the extent of it?" he asked. "Enough to do the work," she said. "Not enough to start calling relatives." He considered that. "You really think we might be able to pull people back?" "I think," she said slowly, "that we have demonstrated, in a very narrow band of conditions, that the brain is more salvageable than we thought. If the lattice can provide missing scaffolding, we might be able to support damaged networks long enough for other therapies to work—or for the brain to retrain itself. Best case, we don't just stop the erasure. We repaint some of what was wiped clean." She shook her head. "But that's a long road between 'might' and 'can.'"

They paused outside the vault corridor. The status panel glowed steady green; inside, the original Theta-9 body lay as unchanged as ever, a dead thing that nevertheless refused to decay the way it should. "You could go public," John said. "Spin it modestly. 'Preliminary trials show promise, more work needed.' People would calm down. Governments might lean less on cowboy labs." "Or," Voss replied, "we'd trigger a global stampede for something we cannot yet control, ignite a bidding war for access, and watch as a dozen outfits with less patience than we have start cutting corners to replicate work they only half understand. No." She glanced at him. "Let them think we're slow. Let them think we're behind. As long as we're actually ahead, they can underestimate us all they like." There was no arrogance in it, just cold calculation.

That night, John called Lee from the roof again. The city beneath him looked even more hollow than it had a week earlier; some of the billboards had finally gone dark, their timers forgotten or unpowered. A supermarket sign flickered, half the letters dead so it just read MARK. "You sound different," Lee said after a minute of catching up, suspicion threading through the exhaustion. "What, did your corpse finally sing you a lullaby?" "We had a good day," John said. It was the closest he could get to the truth without breaking a dozen internal rules. "Not for me to explain. But… keep doing the damn quizzes. Keep Emma off any miracle solutions. If we get where we're trying to go, this thing might be able to help people who aren't gone yet. Maybe even walk some of them back." On the other end of the line, silence stretched thin. When Lee spoke, his voice had lost its usual deflection. "You're serious," he said. "Serious enough to risk sounding hopeful," John replied. "You know how much I hate that."

"Yeah," Lee said, and John could hear him scrub a hand over his face. "You really do. Alright. I'll take hopeful from you over salvation speeches from a guy in a designer suit any day. Just… don't take too long, yeah? We're running out of people to fix." Down below, a traffic light cycled through its colors over an empty intersection, its algorithm still insisting there was an order to things. John watched it blink from red to green to yellow and back again and thought, for the first time, that the world's stubborn machinery might not be entirely wrong. Somewhere under layers of decay and panic, there was still structure waiting to be repainted. Inside HelixCore, they had finally found a brush. Whether they had enough time—and enough sense—to use it without burning everything down remained to be seen.

They were still at it long after most of the building had slipped into its brittle version of sleep. The Theta-9 analysis room had become the unofficial midnight ground zero—no windows, just a long table buried under printouts, tablets, half-empty coffee cups and an entire forest of multicolored highlighters bleeding onto the margins of graphs. The central screen showed the stacked trial data: Subject One, Two, Three, each with their pre-lattice scans, post-lattice scans, EEG traces, and modeling overlays. Voss sat at the head of the table with her tablet dark in front of her, fingers steepled. Kamran was on her left, shoulders hunched, glasses slipping down his nose as he tracked two outputs at once. Across from him, Dr. Zhao from bioinformatics scrolled through a simulation batch like she was peeling wallpaper. To one side, a junior neurologist named Mateo was taking furious notes, occasionally stopping to rub his eyes as if he could press clarity into his skull. John leaned against the back wall, arms folded, the outsider allowed in because he held the keys and because Voss seemed to think it was useful to have someone in the room who didn't speak fluent citation.

"So, to summarize without the ten extra footnotes," Zhao was saying, tapping up a combined plot, "in all three subjects we see the same pattern: initial noise suppression, emergence of coherent oscillatory activity in the gamma and beta bands, partial reconstitution of previous network topology in regions we'd written off as non-functional. The lattice is not just plugging holes; it's providing a scaffolding template that the remaining tissue is using to reorganize." She flicked to another set of graphs. "And before anyone says it, no, I don't think this is just random fluctuation. The cross-correlation with pre-collapse baselines is too high." Mateo shook his head. "But it's not perfect reversion," he said. "Look at Subject Three's frontal lobes. There's a whole new sub-network pattern here that doesn't match his original scan. It's like we've got... add-ons." Kamran snorted. "Neuroplasticity," he said. "You damage a brain, it reroutes. We're basically handing it alien rebar and saying 'be creative.' I'd be more worried if it came out exactly the same as before."

"I am worried," Voss said mildly. "Because we're not just modulating plasticity. We're introducing a template derived from something that did not evolve with us. The question is whether these 'add-ons' are benign compensation, spandrels, or the neurological equivalent of weeds." She nodded at the screen. "What about long-term stability? We've been looking at a twenty-four hour window. What does forty-eight look like? Seventy-two?" "We don't know yet," Zhao said. "The models say we should see progressive reinforcement of the new network if the lattice persists, with gradual integration into existing structures. But that's assuming the pathogen doesn't adapt." She pulled up another chart. "Look here. In Subject Two, after the ten-hour mark, we start seeing microbursts of pathological activity at the edges of the repaired zones. The virus isn't just bouncing off. It's... probing." Mateo made a face. "So now we've got an arms race inside the skull," he muttered. "Great."

Kamran sat back and pinched the bridge of his nose. "We always had an arms race," he said. "Before, we were getting routed in the first three minutes. Now we're at least making it to halftime." He pointed to a dense cluster of overlapping traces. "The important part is this: no evidence of global disorganization. No seizure activity. No catastrophic destabilization of unaffected regions. Whatever the lattice is doing, it's localized and structured." "Localized so far," Voss said. "We don't know what happens if we increase the dose. Or repeat it. Or apply it to someone whose networks are intact enough to mount a complex response—helpful or harmful." Her gaze slid briefly to John, as if to underline the distinction between test subjects who didn't know they were alive and the people in this room. "Immunogenicity?" she asked. "Any sign the body's treating this as an invader beyond the obvious?"

A tired immunologist, Singh, whom John hadn't even noticed in the corner until she spoke, shook her head and held up a tablet with lab values. "So far, cytokine profiles are unremarkable," she said. "Standard systemic stress response, no dramatic spikes. Microglial activation is elevated at the lattice interfaces, but that's to be expected. We're basically asking the brain's resident immune cells to do architectural work while also fighting off a virus. They're not thrilled, but they're not rioting." She swiped to another screen. "My bigger concern is persistence. The lattice doesn't seem to be breaking down at the rate we modeled. It's more stable. That's good for repair. It's terrible if we've misjudged any off-target effects. You don't want permanent scaffolding for a temporary job."

"So we make it less stable," Mateo said. "Build in a timed decay." Zhao shook her head. "We do that, we might lose the very property that's letting it hold against the virus. This thing's strength is in its stubbornness." "Spoken like someone who never had to tell a family we gave their father an experimental therapy and now he can't form new memories because we over-stabilized his hippocampus," Kamran said dryly. "We need a balance. Stickiness with an off switch." All eyes went to Voss. She didn't take the bait. "That's for the next iteration," she said. "Right now we're still determining whether the current version is lethal in ways we haven't seen yet. Which brings us to behavioral endpoints—or lack thereof." She turned slightly. "Assuming for the moment that we're not just reanimating wiring diagrams for our own amusement, how will we know when we've actually helped someone and not just made their scans prettier?"

The question hung there. For once, none of the scientists rushed to fill it. It was John, from the wall, who finally said, "They'd have to recognize something. Someone. Follow a command. Track a face. Anything that isn't just muscle." He shrugged when they looked at him. "You want a metric, start with the basics. Do they know their own name. Do they know they have hands." "He's right," Singh said. "Clinical neuro is still clinical. You can spin all the models you want; at the end of the day, if your patient can tell you they're cold and ask for a blanket, you're miles beyond where we are now." "And if they can't," Mateo added quietly, "but their scans look good, we've just built a very sophisticated light show." He rubbed his temples. "We're trying to quantify personhood. With borrowed architecture."

Voss looked tired in a way that went beyond sleeplessness. "Which is why we are not, under any circumstances, moving to early-stage, still-conscious patients until we understand the edges of this," she said. "We are not in the business of editing personalities. Not yet. Not unless the alternative is nothing at all." She glanced at Zhao. "Can we tell whether the restored patterns are closer to pre-morbid baselines than to Theta-9's native structure? Is there any risk that we're imprinting… foreign characteristics?" Zhao actually laughed once, short and humorless. "Alien possession? No," she said. "We're not seeing Theta-9's signature anywhere except as an underlying scaffold. The higher-order dynamics are still human. Weird, broken human, but human. If anything non-human is trying to sneak in, it's being filtered through tissue that still thinks in our language."

"And how long before we can say that with more than three subjects backing it?" Voss asked. "We need n big enough that I can sign off on the next phase without feeling like I should be struck by lightning." Kamran sighed. "Weeks," he said. "More runs. More bodies. Working as fast as we can without turning this place into Novus Path." At the mention, an uneasy ripple passed through the room. Everyone had seen the latest footage: the protests at Novus Path's gates turning into a stampede, the grainy leaked clips of patients seizing in beds while someone off-camera shouted that the dose was wrong, the CEO's face tight and drawn on an apology tour he clearly hadn't prepared for. "They went from 'days away from rollout' to 'unexpected complications' in under a week," Singh said. "I don't want to be in that documentary."

Voss let them talk themselves out for a minute—metabolism, dosing, adaptive resistance, ethical frameworks—then finally straightened, palms flat on the table. "Alright," she said. The room stilled. "Here's where we are. First: the lattice works better than I dared to hope. It stabilizes and partially rebuilds damaged networks without, so far, blowing anything up we can detect. That is enormous. Second: we are operating in the dark beyond that. We don't know duration, long-term structural consequences, interactions with partially intact cognition, or what happens when the virus adapts—because it will. Third: the world outside is collapsing on a timeline that doesn't care about our need for more data." She looked around at each of them in turn. "Our job is to live in the tension between those three truths without losing our nerve or our minds."

She turned her head slightly toward John. "Security implication?" she asked. It took him a second to realize she wasn't just being polite; she wanted an answer. "If this works even half as well in people who can talk as it does in the ones downstairs," he said slowly, "you're going to have lines at the gate. Governments, companies, individuals. Some will try to buy their way in. Some will try to force their way in. Some will try to steal it out from under you. We need to assume that as soon as anyone outside this building even suspects we have something that can pull people back, this place stops being a research facility and becomes a siege target." Kamran made a face. "So full lockdown, more guns, less sleep," he said. "That'll be good for our cognitive function." "We harden what we have to," Voss replied. "But we don't shut our eyes. Or our mouths." She tapped the table once. "I will not have this place turned into a dragon's hoard while the world burns. When we have something safe enough to share, we share. Until then, we protect it from everyone—including ourselves."

The clock on the wall ticked past three in the morning. Someone's stomach growled audibly. Zhao rubbed her eyes and said, "So… we keep modeling. More subjects. Refine decay curves. Look for subtle weirdness. Try not to hallucinate alien ghosts in every spike." "And you," Voss said, nodding at each of them in turn, "try to remember to eat and sleep in between saving the species. I'd rather not have to use our one working brain-fixer on staff that collapsed because they forgot they had bodies." The line drew a few exhausted smiles. She pushed back her chair. "That's enough for tonight. Send me updated anomaly logs by noon. If anyone finds something that scares them, call me before it's on a slide."

They began to gather papers and devices, the buzz of low conversation picking up again as they drifted toward the door. For a moment, as they filed out, the room looked almost normal—just colleagues at the end of an overlong shift arguing about numbers. When the last of them left, Voss lingered, glancing once more at the composite graph on the main screen: three lines that should have fallen off a cliff and, instead, bent, wavered, and climbed. "Better than hoped," she said under her breath. "Worse than needed." John pushed off the wall. "You could have told them it was a miracle," he said. "Let them ride the high." "I need them thinking, not floating," she replied. Then, after a beat, "Besides, miracles come with fine print. I'd like to read it first."

He followed her out into the dim corridor, the door hissing shut behind them. Somewhere below, machines kept breathing for people who might, improbably, have a path back. Somewhere outside, on half-dead streets lit by traffic lights changing for no one, the rest of the world continued to slide. In between, in rooms like this one, a handful of tired minds argued over spikes and slopes and the ethics of borrowed scaffolding. It wasn't glorious. It wasn't clean. But for the first time, it felt like the fight wasn't entirely one-sided.

CHAPTER 6

A week after the first HelixCore trials, the Novus Path drug showed up in the building without ever passing through an official channel. On paper, the carton coming in on the unmarked hospital courier was just another set of cerebrospinal fluid samples from a partner ICU—standard forms, standard barcodes, the kind of shipment Ops barely glanced at anymore. The scanner at the inner checkpoint didn't care about paperwork. It flagged one vial with an orange alert: unregistered composition, unknown vector markers. The guard on duty called it in. John came down to the loading bay with his tablet and the familiar sense that anything unexpected was a problem. The courier was a nurse from St. Mark's, shoulders hunched, badge clipped crooked, eyes flicking between the exit and the crate like she couldn't decide which one she regretted more. "We were told you'd want to see this," she said, tapping the box with a knuckle. "It's from one of the trial patients. Off the record."

She didn't say which trials; there weren't many facilities left running experimental protocols, and only one of them advertised on television. "What happened?" John asked. She swallowed. "They said 'catastrophic cortical storm,'" she said. "Didn't look like any seizure I've seen. We're not supposed to send anything from the Novus cohort without going through their liaison, but one of our docs printed a second label. Said if anyone can figure out what this stuff is doing, it's you. You didn't hear that from me." He signed for the crate and watched her leave like the building might change its mind and pull her back in.

Later, in the Theta-9 analysis room, the vial sat in the center of the table like evidence. It was smaller than he expected—clear cylinder, triple-capped, liquid inside a faint opalescent haze instead of the clean transparency of their own compounds. The hospital code was there, and beneath it, typed over in careful capitals: NP-REGIMEN-A, POST DOSING + 4H.

A ring of disturbed adhesive around the cap hinted at a label that had been peeled off in a hurry. The scientists clustered around it without touching it yet. "This is a bad idea," Singh said, arms folded, voice flat. "We're already drowning in one alien-adjacent unknown." Voss didn't look away from the vial. "I'd rather drown with my eyes open," she said. "They're injecting this into people who can still say their own names. We're not stopping them. We can at least stop being stupid." Automated pipettes and sealed cartridges did the rest; no open handling, no heroic manual transfers. On the central screen, data bloomed: spectral curves, mass ratios, sequence segments. At first glance it was what Novus Path claimed— viral delivery vector, cleverly engineered, optimized not to trip standard immune alarms.

Mixed into it, though, were Theta-9 motifs HelixCore knew intimately by now, spliced into a different framework. "Sloppy," Zhao said, overlaying HelixCore's clean lattice sequence with the NP code. "They copied the structural motifs and guessed at the connective tissue. That bridge region isn't alien, but it isn't human either. It's... synthetic glue." Singh scrolled down the projections. "And their vector is hot," she added. "Replication-limited on paper, but these copy numbers are high. Too high. If their dosing's off, this thing keeps hammering neural tissue until something gives. That's if the payload behaves."

The cultures were worse than the sequence. They set up standard plates: organoids seeded with the Forgetting Plague model, organoids left clean, controls untouched. Theta-9 analogue went into one set of infected wells. NP-Regimen-A went into another. Electrodes under the plates fed activity into the multi-electrode array, painting movement as scrolling waveforms and shifting grids of light. The lattice behaved as it had all week—noise dropping, chaotic clusters settling into more coherent patterns, the tangled mess of fake brains learning to stand up straight. The Novus wells spiked hard the moment the drug hit—every channel flashing at once, then plunging into near-flatline. "That's anesthetic coma," Mateo muttered. "Or brain death prep." "Wait," Zhao said. The lines crept back. Not scattered, not stumbling. They rose in a wave that moved across the grid in a clean front, each electrode falling into step with the same narrow-band oscillation.

The treated wells lit first, the neighboring wells—never dosed at all—picked up faint echoes seconds later, and even the control channels registered the rhythm when Zhao stripped away identifiers and re-ran the raw data. "There's no physical contact between these," she said. "No leaks, no shared medium. The only common element is the array and the analysis pipeline." She randomized indices, shuffled channels, rerouted input. The pattern stayed. It shifted in amplitude and timing, but the shape held like something breathing. "It's not artifact," she said finally. "Whatever they built, it's forcing a single rhythm onto the system."

"Global synchronizer," Kamran said. "Isn't that the dream? Drag the whole brain into a non-pathological state and hold it there." Singh shook her head. "Not like this," she said. "This isn't normalization, it's override. Look at the baselines—everything's collapsing into one mode. You flatten a brain into one drumbeat, you don't get thought; you get coordination and not much else." Four hours later, the organoids told the same story with tissue instead of lines. The Theta-9 wells still looked like dense, pale clouds, reshaping slowly.

The NP-treated clusters were denser, edges thickened, tiny

extensions pressing against the walls of their wells as if the tissue wanted more room. Under magnification, their internal layers had reorganized into spirals and loops that didn't match any of the reference preparations—complex, neat, a little too deliberate. On the array, the imposed rhythm had settled into an uncanny consistency: not mechanical, irregular enough to feel organic, but always winding back to the same core shape. Once, as they watched, every channel dropped to a near-silence for three heartbeats, then came back stronger, the oscillation sharper, as if the system had paused mid-step and chosen a firmer path forward. "Say 'it's optimizing' and I'll write you up," Kamran said without looking away from the screen. Mateo held up both hands. "I'm just saying the bridge code was designed to adapt," he said. "They didn't just steal scaffolding, they taught it to tune itself."

They killed the live feeds before the room could get any quieter. The incubator kept humming in its corner, organoids sealed inside their tiny universe, the NP-treated wells ticking along with their new internal architecture, no witnesses necessary. The data sat on the server, waiting to be pulled apart. On one of the side screens, someone had left a muted city cam running: an overhead shot of a plaza downtown, mostly empty now. A single woman walked a slow loop around a dry fountain, tracing the same broken ring of tiles over and over, footfalls landing on identical cracks each time. Her pace never changed. She never looked up. When the door to the analysis room sealed behind them, the building's night-mode lights were already down, corridors washed in soft low-level illumination.

"You going to tell them at St. Mark's?" John asked as he fell into step beside Voss. "About what this stuff is doing." "Not until we have something more useful to say than 'it's alarming,'" she replied. Her face looked carved thinner by the last hour. "Right now all we know is that they've weaponized synchrony and pushed it into people who still had enough self left to lose. That's not news they can act on." They walked a few more meters in silence, footsteps echoing softly. "You think it's safe?" he asked. It wasn't the question he meant, but it was close.

"I think they've built a system that learns faster than its owners," she said. "And they've already given it a population to practice on. If we want to be anything other than its observers, we'd better understand it before it finishes deciding how it wants minds to behave." Down the corridor, a motion sensor light blinked on a second before they stepped into its range, the fixture humming quietly over an empty stretch of tile. For a beat, John couldn't tell if it was his memory or his ears that still heard the echo of that imposed rhythm, waiting for everything else to fall in line.

The pattern on the array held for a long, brittle moment. No one spoke. The only sound in the room was the low hum of the incubator and the faint tick of a cooling fan somewhere in the wall. On the main screen, the NP-treated wells pulsed in their narrow rhythm, channels lighting in sequence with unnerving precision. Zhao clicked through one last overlay and then let her hand fall away from the mouse, as if anything else she did might make it worse. Singh took half a step back from the table, like being farther from the monitors might translate into being farther from whatever they were looking at.

Voss watched the display with her arms folded, thumb pressed hard enough into the edge of her tablet to leave a pale crescent in the plastic. Her gaze didn't move when the channels dipped again for a heartbeat and then surged back, the oscillation a little cleaner each time, like a choir that had found its pitch. When she finally spoke, it came out quiet and flat, the way a clinician dictates findings during an autopsy. "They didn't design this to heal," she said. "They designed it to move."

The words landed heavier than if she'd shouted. Zhao glanced at her, then back at the data. Kamran stared at the floor between his shoes as if trying to remember what solid ground looked like. Mateo's pen, halfway to the notebook he'd been scribbling in all night, stopped and hung there, his fingers stiff around it. Voss didn't look at any of them. She nodded once toward the grid of lines. "When you care about patients," she went on, tone clipped, "you build for safety. Redundancies. Failure modes that take you somewhere survivable. When you care about time, you build for stability. Holds, buffers, ways to keep the system from tipping over while you figure it out." The rhythm on the array pulsed again, steady as a metronome. "When you care about money," she said, "you build whatever lets you put a label on a vial and move units before anyone has time to read the fine print."

"That's not fair," Mateo said, voice low but audible, like he'd surprised himself by speaking. "They have to know what they're doing can't be… this." He gestured at the screen, the pattern still marching. "They're neurologists. They see the same textbooks we do." "Knowing is not the same as caring," Singh said, and her voice had a raw edge now. "You can bury a lot of doubt under the right slide deck if someone on the finance side is waving a runway extension in your face." She pointed at the funnels in Zhao's cluster analysis. "This is not risk they haven't seen. This is risk they decided to live with."

Voss lifted a hand and drew a small circle on the screen with her fingertip, encompassing the converging clusters. "Look at what their system does every time it encounters variance," she said. "It doesn't accommodate it. It doesn't adapt around it. It crushes it. Every adaptive step narrows the space of possible states until everything falls into one groove. That's not therapy. That's enforcement." She switched to the raw waveform view with a tap. The channels scrolled in their tight rhythm, small deviations smoothed out within a few cycles. "This isn't a brain learning to be well," she said. "It's a lattice learning to win."

For a moment no one breathed. The organoids in the incubator didn't care; they kept firing in whatever pattern the NP vector had decided was optimal. On a side monitor, the city feed still showed the woman in the plaza walking the same loop around the dry fountain, feet finding the same cracked tiles each time. She wasn't in any trial, no tag over her head marking her as anything but another casualty of a different slow disaster. The coincidence made the back of John's neck tighten anyway. "You think that's what happened to the guy at St. Mark's?" he asked. "Your 'cortical storm.' This thing trying to force a state and the brain not going quietly?"

"Best case," Kamran said. "Worst case, it succeeded." No one seemed eager to unpack that further.

Voss exhaled once, slowly, through her nose. "This is what happens when you let a board room chase a curve instead of a conscience," she said. "Someone pitched a global stabilizer. A way to drag a collapsing population into a safe corridor and keep them there. Minimal variability, minimal surprises, nice clean graphs. And instead of asking, 'what does that do to a person,' they asked, 'how fast can we scale production.'" She straightened a little. "They weren't building a treatment. They were building a product."

She finally turned her head enough to look at John, meeting his eyes for a second. There was no drama in it, just tired clarity. "And the worst part," she said, "is that they've already pushed this into thousands of people—maybe tens of thousands—without understanding what happens when that adaptive scaffold keeps learning inside a human brain. A self-optimizing, state-locking vector, given an entire frightened market to iterate on, because someone wanted to be first at a podium and last to take the blame."

The array gave a soft, almost apologetic beep as the recording buffer filled; the live feed icon went from red to gray.

The pattern on the screen stopped scrolling, frozen mid-oscillation. No one moved to clear it. Voss looked away first. "Shut it down," she said. "All of it. Pull the raw logs, archive them offline. I don't want this process touching anything it doesn't absolutely have to." Zhao's hands were already moving over the controls before she'd finished. Singh stepped away from the bench as if her muscles had only just remembered how.

In the corridor outside, the air felt cooler. The door sealed behind them with a muted hiss, cutting off the glow of the monitors. For a few seconds they just walked. The building hummed around them, a low mechanical breathing. Down at the far end, a motion sensor light snapped on a heartbeat before they reached it, casting a pale pool across the tile. "You're going to tell St. Mark's?" John asked quietly. "About what their cohort is carrying." "When I have something they can use," Voss said. "Right now all I have is an accusation and a bad feeling. They already know their patients are dying badly. Telling them it might be on purpose, in some abstract systemic way, doesn't help anyone." Her mouth tightened. "We figure it out first. Then we decide who to warn and how loudly."

He heard again, in his head, the brief silence in the NP pattern before it had come back stronger. "You think it's... safe to keep it here?" he asked. "On our systems." "Safe?" she repeated. "No. Necessary? Yes. If we're going to have any leverage left in this mess, we need to understand what they've unleashed. Before it decides what it wants to do with the rest of us." She started walking again. After a moment, he fell into step beside her, the quiet between them full of graphs, marching rhythms, and the knowledge that somewhere out there, on streets and in beds and in wards he would never see, that same imposed beat might already be trying to teach human brains how to fall in line.

The cold had started to feel less like weather and more like another system failure—the city's heat bleeding away the same way its memory had. John walked the outer perimeter with Kline and Rami in a slow, practiced line, breath turning white in the beam of his flashlight. Frost had crept up the fence posts, rimed the coils of razor wire, turned the grass outside the concrete strip into a brittle mat that crackled faintly when the wind shifted. Beyond the fence, the highway lay quiet under a skin of black ice, cars angled in frozen tableaux from collisions nobody had stuck around to clear. The floodlights threw hard-edged shadows across it all, carving the world into lit and unlit pieces. On the third sweep past the north access road, his beam caught something that wasn't trash or broken signage—a shape huddled against the outer fence line, half in the shadow of a toppled billboard. At first he thought it was just another pile of abandoned clothes. Then the angle of a hand registered. Fingers splayed, skin gray-blue where it was exposed.

They approached in a loose triangle, rifles slung but ready out of habit, steps slowing as they saw her properly. She had died sitting up, back against a concrete support, knees pulled to her chest as if she'd meant to rest for a minute and never managed to get back up. Her coat was thin, the kind of cheap synthetic that trapped moisture instead of warmth, unzipped at the collar like she'd forgotten to finish the motion. Ice had formed in her hair where it brushed her cheek, strands fused in small, translucent clumps. Her eyes were open, the pupils clouded, fixed on nothing. Up close, the signs were obvious: the slackness in her face that wasn't just death, the faint crust of saliva at the corner of her mouth from where her jaw had gone slack long before her body caught up, the hospital wristband cutting a pale band into the skin under the sleeve. One sneaker was untied, laces trailing in a small frozen arc. The tread patterns in the frost behind her showed a wandering path—no urgency, no straight line, just slow, aimless steps that had looped twice near the fence before she folded down where she was.

"God," Kline muttered under her breath, fog leaking through the knitted scarf over her mouth. "No coat, no hat, no clue where she is. Someone wheeled her out of somewhere and forgot to wheel her back." Rami knelt just outside the splash radius, careful not to touch, scanning the skin at her neck and the veins at her temple with his light. "Rash," he said quietly. "Same mottling Lee sent us once from early-stage patients. She made it this far with half a brain left and then froze within sight of a building full of space heaters." He straightened, rubbing his gloved hands together once to get feeling back. "You want to call it in?" he asked, though they all knew the answer. Infectious corpse at the perimeter meant one thing now. There were no retrieval teams left, no body bags and gentle words, no refrigerated trucks to line up in manicured rows. There was protocol.

John stood there a little longer than the job strictly required, watching the way frost had crept into the folds of her clothes, the way her fingers had locked around nothing. She had probably walked past three empty cars with keys in them, past storefronts with coats in the windows, past doors that would have opened if she'd remembered what doors were for. She'd chosen this patch of fence not because it meant anything, but because the virus had left her with enough motor function to sit down and not enough to stand back up. He clicked his radio and called in the code anyway, voice even. Biohazard perimeter, non-responsive, frozen remains, burn per directive nine. The acknowledgment came back in a clipped, tired tone that suggested no one on the other end was picturing a face.

They stepped back while one of the fixed-point projectors spun up—a squat, ugly box mounted on a movable arm along the inside of the fence, rigged months ago when the first infected bodies started reaching the perimeter. There had been arguments then, about optics, about dignity, about whether setting people on fire was something civilization should grow comfortable with. That had been early. Now there was just the whine of capacitors charging and the soft chime of a targeting cycle completing. The first gout of flame rolled over her like a sudden sunrise, bright enough that John had to squint. Fabric blackened, then caught; hair flared; skin cracked and shrank. It was quick, at least—hot enough that whatever was left in the tissue, virus or vector or some future unknown, would char into unrecognizability. Smoke coiled up into the cold air and was shredded by the wind before it could reach them. Kline watched until there was nothing left but a collapsing outline and a dark patch on the frozen ground. "Better here than in a waiting room somewhere," she said. It wasn't comfort, exactly, but it was something.

When the projector cycled down and the fans kicked on to cool its housing, the night settled back around them, quieter than before. The spot where the woman had sat was now just scorched concrete and a melted depression in the frost. Beyond the fence, the highway remained a line of dead cars and dark windows. John logged the incident on his tablet, tagged the coordinates, and resumed the patrol route with Kline and Rami falling into step beside him. From the corner of his eye he could see the faint smear of smoke drifting up and away, indistinguishable from chimney exhaust and distant fires once it reached the higher air. Somewhere inside the building behind him, people were trying to teach damaged brains how to remember themselves. Out here, under the hard white wash of the floodlights, his job was simpler and uglier: make sure what was dying didn't come any closer, and burn whatever the world left at their doorstep before it had a chance to learn something new.

CHAPTER 7

Lee had stopped trusting the way calls were labeled. "Psych," "confusion," "possible seizure" all blurred together now into the same dull ache: somebody was standing where they shouldn't be, doing something their family didn't understand, and his job was to move the problem from one place to another without breaking anything. This one came through as a welfare check—neighbors concerned, patient not answering the door, last seen "acting strange" after getting the shot everyone was talking about. The address was a narrow street of duplexes with peeling paint and satellite dishes pointed nowhere. By the time the rig rolled up, dusk had scraped the color out of the houses and the first frost was already silvering the dead grass along the sidewalk.

His partner banged on the door, called the man's name. No response. A neighbor from the next unit hovered in a sweater and slippers, arms wrapped around herself. "He got that cure," she said as soon as Lee looked at her. "The one on TV. Said he felt 'clear' for the first time in weeks. Then yesterday he didn't go to work. This morning he was… like this." She gestured helplessly at the door. "I tried calling. He picks up and just breathes. I can hear him breathing." The spare key shook in her hand as she passed it over.

The inside of the unit smelled like old coffee and damp carpet. The television was on with the sound off, a frozen news anchor's mouth open mid-word. Half a mug sat on the coffee table, the ring under it a pale circle in the dust. "Sir?" Lee called, moving past the couch. "EMS. You called for help." No answer.

The hallway led toward the bedroom, the kitchen to the right. He heard the sound before he saw the man: a faint, regular tap, like a metronome with a soft hammer. Tap. Tap. Tap.

The man was in the kitchen, standing in the middle of the linoleum with his bare feet aligned exactly along a crack where two tiles met. His toes were white at the tips from the cold coming up through the floor. One hand hung at his side. The other tapped, very gently, against the refrigerator door. Same spot, same rhythm. His gaze was fixed straight ahead at the opposite wall, not quite at eye level, not quite at any object Lee could see. He didn't blink. The Novus Path wristband was still on his wrist, the logo bright against the mottled skin. "Sir?" Lee said again, stepping into his field of view. "Hey. I'm Lee. You called us. Can you look at me?" The hand kept tapping. Tap. Tap. Tap.

He stepped closer, careful, ready to dodge if the man suddenly swung. Instead, after a long, viscous pause, the tapping stopped. The man's eyes tracked to Lee's face like someone had turned his head with invisible fingers. The movement was too smooth, too slow, as if the timing had been decided elsewhere and his muscles were just catching up. His pupils were normal. Vitals, when Lee got close enough to check, were annoyingly fine. "Can you tell me your name?" Lee asked. "Do you know where you are?" The man's lips parted. No sound came out at first. His throat worked once. Then he said, in a voice that sounded like someone had recorded him and was playing it back slightly out of phase, "It's close."

Lee felt the hair on his arms prick under his jacket. "What's close?" he asked. "Pain? A seizure? Another episode? Can you tell me?" The man's gaze drifted past him, toward the ceiling, then to the corner where two walls met, then back to the invisible point on the opposite wall. His fingers twitched once, as if he were about to start tapping again and thought better of it. "It's close," he repeated, exactly the same cadence, exactly the same tone, like a sound file being replayed. His breathing never changed. His posture never shifted. When they finally coaxed him onto the gurney, he lay down without resistance, eyes still open, neck craned just enough that he could keep staring past Lee at the unreachable point on the rig's ceiling. At one point, as they went over a pothole, the overhead light flickered. The man's pupils didn't react. His fingertips tapped once against the side rail, then stilled.

Later, in the ambulance bay while the nurses at St. Mark's tried to decide whether he was neurology's problem or psychiatry's, Lee propped his phone against a stack of forms and watched the video he'd recorded on scene. He watched the way the man's tapping synced with the faint hum of the refrigerator compressor. He watched the microsecond in which his gaze shifted away from the wall exactly as the fridge cycle kicked off and the room's background noise changed. He watched the lips forming those two words with the uncanny precision of someone repeating a line fed to them through an earpiece. And when he couldn't make sense of any of it, he sent the file to John with a two-line message: *Tell your ice queen I've seen a lot of weird. This is new. If this is their cure, I want to know what it thinks it's getting closer to.*

At HelixCore, the video played on a loop in the analysis room while the readouts from St. Mark's new samples filled the other screens. St. Mark's had been busy; someone there had decided that if they were going to break rules, they might as well do it thoroughly. Two more vials had come in over the week, nested in legitimate shipments, labels overwritten with legitimate patient codes that made just enough sense to pass a first glance. The glue residue around the caps told the rest of the story. NP-REGIMEN-A, POST DOSING + 8H. NP-REGIMEN-B, POST DOSING + 3D. Different cohorts. Same tampering.

Zhao had them up in a three-way comparison now: their own Theta-9 lattice outputs in one column, Novus A in the next, Novus B in the third. The differences were no longer subtle. "Look at the rhythm spacing," she said, tapping the screen. "A was bad enough. B is worse. The frequency is higher, and there's less variability between pulses. It's not just synchronizing within a host anymore. These patterns are converging toward each other." "We don't know that," Kamran said automatically, but he sounded tired even to himself. "We know they look similar. Brains like certain frequencies. It's not new." "Brains like ranges," Zhao said. "This thing likes a note."

Singh flicked through the immune and viral markers. "Titers are different," she said. "Regimen B has lower viral load but more persistent vector presence. See? The pathogen's down, but the scaffold's hanging around, pushing those oscillations. It's like they've tuned the dose to get maximum entrainment with minimal immediate fallout." "Learning between hosts," Mateo said under his breath. He didn't mean to say it aloud. The room heard him anyway. A few heads turned. "No," Voss said, immediately. "We are not mixing metaphors from horror films into our analysis. It's a vector. It doesn't know anything. It is, however, being refined somewhere by human hands, and they're adjusting it based on what they're seeing. That's bad enough."

On the side screen, the man in Lee's video lifted his hand and tapped the fridge door in time with a hum that only the microphone picked up clearly. When the compressor cut out, his tapping stopped on the exact beat. "Then how does he hear the change before we do?" Singh asked quietly. "Look at the time stamps. His fingers stop on the downbeat, like he's following a conductor the rest of us can't see." No one had a clean answer for that. Zhao went back to her plots. "There's also coherence between hosts," she said after a moment. "A and B's recordings line up closer than I'd expect from independent implementations. The signal's not identical, but the phase offset is shrinking. If they keep adjusting toward the same target state…" She trailed off. "Not learning between hosts," she corrected herself. "Learning across trials. Using different minds to tune toward a shared optimum."

Voss didn't argue. She just let out a breath through her teeth. "Either way, they're teaching this thing to find a specific shape and lock it in," she said. "And once it's found it, it isn't letting go."

The city had not stopped falling apart while they argued over barely visible spikes. If anything, it was finding new ways to look wrong. On perimeter patrol two nights later, John stood with Kline under a dead bus stop shelter and watched a bus that never came. Three people were waiting there, spread along the bench in thick coats and hats, faces slack with that new, frightening neutrality that no longer meant boredom. A man at one end tapped his foot, heel bouncing against the concrete. The woman next to him sat hunched, hands buried in her pockets, the brim of her knitted cap shadowing her eyes. A kid, maybe eleven, stood apart, backpack still on, scuffed trainers planted at angles. None of them looked at each other. None of them spoke. But after a minute of watching, it became impossible to unsee it: the taps were in the same rhythm. The kid's fingers drummed against the strap of his backpack in a pattern that matched the man's heel. The woman's jaw moved in time, a tiny clench-release, like she was chewing air to the same unheard beat.

"Please tell me that's a coincidence," Kline said, voice muffled by her scarf. "Please tell me they're all just very committed to the same internal soundtrack." "They don't even know they're doing it," John said. He could see it in their eyes—such as they were visible—no focus, no awareness, just bodies holding still while something in the background ran a program.

At a crosswalk three blocks down, the signal changed from red to white, the little walking figure shining on the post. No one moved. Four pedestrians—two men in work jackets, an older woman with a grocery bag, a teenager with headphones around his neck—stood at the curb and stared straight ahead as the countdown ticked from fifteen to zero. Cars were rare enough now that nothing came through the intersection either way. When the hand symbol flashed red again, the group stepped off the curb in unison, crossing on the don't-walk as if the signal they were obeying had nothing to do with the light. Halfway across, the teenager started humming under his breath. A block away, on a stoop, a child with a plastic toy in his hand hummed the same note, exactly, eyes unfocused, shoulders rocking faintly. An old woman sitting on a crate outside a shuttered shop picked it up a second later, a thread of sound that barely carried over the wind.

"Okay," Kline said. "That's creepy." "Creepy would imply intention," Rami said from John's other side, fingers moving against his rifle strap in his own, private sequence. He stopped when he noticed and shoved his hands into his pockets. "This is just… alignment." John watched the four figures reach the opposite curb and stop as one, as if they'd hit an invisible mark. None of them looked surprised to find themselves there.

Inside HelixCore, the arguments shifted from "what is this" to "what do we do with it" and stayed there, looping. In one of the smaller conference rooms, with the blinds drawn and the lights turned down low to make the screens easier to read, Singh had her arms braced on the table, knuckles white. "We have enough," she said. "Between the organoid data, the vector analysis, and what St. Mark's has been sending, we have enough to tell every hospital that's thinking about partnering with Novus Path to stop. Today. Right now. They don't have to understand the mechanisms to understand 'this won't do what you think it does.'"

"And if the moment we start whispering 'this won't do what you think it does' into hospital ears, Novus Path's lawyers descend on us with injunctions and counter-press and accusations of sabotage?" Kamran countered. He scrolled through a news article on his tablet and flipped it around long enough for the headline to show: NOVUS PATH THERAPY CUTS COGNITIVE COLLAPSE RATES IN HALF, EARLY DATA SUGGESTS. "They're already winning the narrative. You think they won't spin 'unnamed rival lab raises concerns' into us being jealous, or compromised, or deranged? We don't even have a clear mechanism to point to. Just patterns that make our skin crawl."

"We publish anonymously," Zhao said, rubbing at the bridge of her nose. "Dump the data in an open archive, send the link to every clinician's mailing list on the planet, let them see the rhythms for themselves." "And when someone traces the footprint back here?" Kamran asked. "Our infrastructure isn't invisible. You think we're the only ones watching? The second anyone with half a brain and a grudge decides HelixCore is undermining the only 'cure' on offer, this place becomes a political target, not just a physical one."

John listened from his spot against the wall, watching Voss rather than the graphs. She'd been quiet, letting them flare and cool, letting the ideas run instead of cutting them off. Her face gave less away than the monitors, but the tension was there in the way she held her shoulders, in the way her fingers flexed once on the tablet edge and stilled. "We don't warn the world," she said at last, "until we understand what we're warning them about." Singh turned on her. "We understand enough," she said. "We understand that their vector imposes a narrow-band oscillatory pattern on neural tissue, that it flattens variance, that it persists longer than intended, and that it's being administered broadly to people who still had lives left to ruin. How is that not enough?"

"It's enough to be afraid," Voss said. "It's not enough to be right in the ways that will matter when this ends up in a courtroom or an inquiry. I am not going to send a half-formed accusation into a panicked world and watch it be torn apart on talk shows while people decide whether to believe the pretty man with the press team or the anonymous scientist with the scary graphs." She lifted her chin toward the screen where Lee's kitchen video was paused on the frame of the man staring at the blank wall. "You want to know what terrifies me? It's not that he's tapping in rhythm with his refrigerator. It's that half the people who see this will call it a glitch, or an episode, or 'not that bad, compared to the alternative,' and they won't be entirely wrong. Until we can say, with specifics, what this thing is doing to the people it touches, any warning we give is just another piece of noise."

"So we wait," Singh said, disgust threading through the fatigue. "We study while more people sign up to become part of somebody else's experiment, because we're too cautious to yell 'fire' in a burning theater." Voss met her gaze without flinching. "We wait," she said, "and in the time we buy with that waiting, we make sure that when we finally open our mouths, we are the one voice that can't be dismissed as hysteria or jealousy. If that means we carry the knowledge alone a little longer, then we carry it." Her fingers tightened on the tablet just enough that the plastic creaked. "Believe me, Dr. Singh, I would love nothing more than to walk out to the nearest camera and scream. But I don't get to indulge that impulse. Not if I want to win."

John saw the thing she didn't say hanging just behind her eyes: that she was already screaming, silently, all the time.

Three days later, a man walked into HelixCore's front lobby and made all the arguments academic. He came alone, on foot, without an appointment, past two separate posted signs and a security camera that caught him stopping once at the edge of the outer cordon as if listening for something. The lobby had been quiet—two reception staff at the desk, a pair of internal contractors badge-scanning through the turnstiles, one off-duty tech buying coffee from the machine. The man stepped through the sliding doors when they opened for someone else and stood just inside, letting them close behind him. He wore a heavy coat that had seen better winters, jeans gone shiny at the knees. His face was unremarkable in a way that made John's gut sink—mid-forties, maybe, the kind of man who would have blended into a hundred crowds without effort. The Novus Path wristband on his right wrist didn't blend at all.

The two lobby guards moved in without rushing, hands loose, voices calm. "Sir? This is a restricted facility," one of them said. "If you're here for screening, you need to go to St. Mark's. We can call you a ride." The man didn't answer. His gaze drifted past them, over the reception desk, over the chairs, to the far end of the lobby where the metal floor grates sat over the main air return. You could feel the building's heartbeat there if you stood long enough—the low vibration of the ventilation, the muffled thrum of generators and servers and whatever else kept HelixCore breathing. He walked toward it with the slow, careful steps of someone crossing a river in the dark, feeling for stones. When he reached the grate, he stopped, feet planted squarely over the narrow slats, shoulder blades aligning almost exactly with a seam in the concrete wall.

"I need to be where the sound is," he said.

The words were quiet, but the acoustics carried them. Reception stilled. One of the guards exchanged a glance with the other that said more than any radio call. "Sir," the first guard tried again. "We can help you outside. You can't stay here." The man didn't look at him. His eyes were slightly unfocused, fixed on some middle distance that happened to intersect with the wall. Up close, John could see the tiny muscles in his jaw vibrating, as if he were listening harder than his ears could manage. "It's clearer here," the man said, almost apologetically. "Everywhere else it's... fuzzy."

They didn't tackle him. There was no need. When they took his arms, he came away from the grate easily, like someone being guided out of a cinema after sitting through the credits too long. His feet dragged for exactly two steps when they left the square where the vibration was strongest, then adjusted, as if he'd recalibrated. "Do you know where you are?" one of the guards asked as they steered him toward the inner holding room. The man's brow furrowed. "Where it's loud," he said. "Where it talks." He didn't resist the gentle pressure on his shoulders as they sat him down. His eyes went to the vent in the ceiling.

John watched from near the security station until the door closed behind them and the noise of the lobby started up again in a cautious murmur. One of the receptionists pretended to straighten a stack of forms that didn't need it. The coffee machine whirred. The building hummed. "That's not disease behavior," he said quietly. Voss had come down fast when the call had gone up that someone with a Novus band was in the lobby. She stood a few paces beside him, eyes on the closed door, face blank. If she'd heard him, she didn't show it. Or she did, in the way her hand twitched once at her side and then stilled, as if she were refusing the urge to reach for something that wasn't there.

Outside the glass, the city moved in its slow, broken loops. Somewhere, at a bus stop or a kitchen table or a hospital bed, people were tapping their feet in time to a rhythm they'd never admit to hearing. Inside HelixCore, beneath the grate where the man had stood, servers and machines and experimental lattices thrummed away at frequencies no human ear could quite parse. Between them, unseen and unacknowledged, something was listening, adjusting, aligning—drawing a line through scattered points the way a model did when it decided, finally, which shape it preferred the world to take.

CHAPTER 8

St. Mark's had been noisy once—monitors beeping, phones ringing, carts rattling down halls—but lately the noise had thinned into something more fragile. Calls didn't come as often because there were fewer people left to make them. The people who did arrive tended not to leave. Lee had begun to recognize the quiet in the ICU the way he recognized certain rashes or breath sounds: as a sign of a system running out of things to do. That morning, though, the quiet felt wrong in a different way. It wasn't absence. It was pause. The unit clerk met him at the nurses' station with eyes already too wide. "You on for the Novus cohort?" she asked, voice pitched low, like the patients could hear from behind glass. "I'm on for whoever's still breathing," he said. "What happened?" She gestured helplessly toward the corridor. "They all woke up," she said. "Sort of."

The Novus Path "cured" patients had their own wing now —a row of rooms with new plastic wristbands and special consent forms tacked to the inside of each chart. They'd come in panicked, hopeful, half-erased; they'd stabilized into a dull, flat compliance that made the psych consults shrug. Lee had seen them on runs, standing too still, saying too little. Today, as he stepped into the corridor, every door had a nurse or tech hovering in it. No one was shouting. No one was running. That should have been good. It wasn't. In the first room on the left, a man in his thirties sat upright in bed with his hands resting on his thighs. His eyes were open, focused on the far corner where ceiling met wall. His lips were moving a little. It took a second for Lee to realize he was humming—one sustained tone on the edge of audibility, breath cycling under it like bellows. In the next room, a woman with an oxygen cannula and a Novus band hummed the same note, pitched exactly, chest rising and falling in a rhythm that matched the first man's even though they couldn't see each other. Her foot tapped against the rail. Tap. Tap. Tap. Same spacing, same force.

Down the hall, an older woman stood facing the corner of her room, forehead almost touching the blank white paint. The bed behind her was still neatly made, covers turned back as if she'd left it and forgotten how to lie down again. Her fingertips rested lightly against the wall, not knocking, not scratching, just there. Her nurse kept a hand hovering near her elbow without quite touching. "She was like this when I came in," the nurse murmured when Lee stepped into the doorway. "Vitals are fine. She just... went over there." The woman's shoulders rose and fell, perfectly even. From where he stood, Lee could just hear the faintest thread of the same low hum slipping out between her teeth.

"Anyone sedated?" he asked. "Anyone seize?" The charge nurse shook her head, ponytail shifting. "No activity alarms," she said. "At oh-six-hundred they were all like they've been: dull, flat, but stable. At oh-six-thirteen every monitor in this corridor pinged at once. Not alarms, just activity spikes. When we checked rooms, they were all like this. Talking more. Or humming. Or doing that." She nodded toward another room, where a young man in a sweatshirt sat cross-legged on the bed, hands pressed over his ears, rocking slightly. His mouth moved; the same two words over and over came through the glass when someone cracked it an inch: "Not yet. Not yet. Not yet."

Lee went room to room, checking pupils, reflexes, responses. The numbers on the charts didn't line up with what the air felt like. Heart rates were up, but not dangerously. Blood pressures held. Respiratory patterns were steady. It was the sameness that unnerved him, the way each patient's small, restless movements seemed to fall into rhythm with the next. In one room a woman tapped the rail with her thumbnail; in the one across, a man tapped the heel of his hand on the tray table. Different people, different histories, same beat. "You sure no one cued them?" he asked. "No chaplain visit, no group therapy, no weird meditation podcast left on in the hall?" "We barely have enough staff for vital rounds," the charge nurse said. "Nobody's got time to coordinate a choir."

He shot video as he moved—short clips, phone held chest-high. A man staring at the ceiling vent, lips moving around that single thin note. A woman laughing once, abruptly, then freezing with the smile half-formed when the hum deepened a fraction of a step, as if she'd lost the joke mid-breath. In one room, three patients on different beds, separated by curtains, all lifted their heads within the same second and turned toward the window, eyes unfocused, as if they'd heard a sound from outside that never reached the hallway. When he stepped in and asked what they were looking at, each gave a different answer: "Light." "Voices." "Nothing." Their pulses ticked along in near-perfect sync under his fingers.

He sent the files to John from the staff lounge, sitting at a sticky table with his back against a vending machine that no one had bothered to restock in weeks. *You wanted new,* he typed with his thumb. *All the NP pets in one wing started doing this within the same minute. No code, no crash. Just… choir practice. Tell me this is still just 'side effects.'*

HelixCore saw it first as pixels and waveforms, not as people. Voss had the clips pulled up on a wall screen in one of the smaller conference rooms, audio filtered and boosted, background noise stripped away until what was left was pure pattern. The hum carried through the speakers as a thin, unwavering line. On an adjacent display, Zhao had extracted its frequency and mapped it across time, a band of color that started jagged and then smoothed as more patients joined in. "This is St. Mark's only?" Voss asked, arms crossed, gaze flicking between the screens. "So far," John said. "Lee says it started there right after oh-six-hundred. No similar flags on the city feeds yet. If it's happening elsewhere, nobody's sent us anything." "Yet," Singh said. She had one of the lab tablets open to the same chart, thumb scrolling through the St. Mark's notes they weren't technically supposed to have. "We're getting more samples," she added. "Two new vials came in with the last shipment. Both from Novus patients who 'changed behavior' after dosing. Behaviors like this."

The calls started the next day. Not from Novus Path or any federal agency—those channels were busy with press releases and controlled updates—but from people lower in the hierarchy who had decided they'd rather be reprimanded than ignorant. A charge nurse from County General's step-down unit, voice pitched low, line crackling with bad routing: "We've got six of them on my floor. Different ages, different neighborhoods, no relation. All on that therapy. They're not crashing. They're... matching. Foot taps, head turns, even when they're in different rooms. We thought we were crazy until we saw the St. Mark's video making the rounds." A resident from a private psychiatric clinic, speaking fast: "We took two transfers from NP's outpatient follow-up program. Both insist they feel 'calm' and 'clear.' Both started humming the same note during intake, then stopped at the exact same time when the elevator in the next wing shorted and cut out. You people have any idea what that is?" An ICU attending from a county hospital three cities over, who skipped pleasantries altogether. "I don't know who else to call," she said. "Half my early-stage Novus cohort woke up at three a.m. and turned to face the same corner. Not the door. Not the monitors. Just... wall. Vitals fine. Labs fine. No seizure activity. I've been doing this twenty years. This isn't dementia. It's coordination."

HelixCore took the calls. Logged the times, the wards,

the doses. Asked quiet questions about lot numbers and administration schedules, about how many of the "cured" patients had been discharged into the community, about whether anyone had noticed similar behaviors among families or staff. "We are not asking people to spy," Voss said more than once. "We are asking them to observe." The distinction mattered to her, even if it didn't to the people on the other end of the line. Observation, analysis, action—those were the only tools HelixCore had that didn't require a syringe and consent forms. For now, they were the safest ones to use.

Outside the fences, the city began to move like it was listening to something only it could hear. On a noon patrol near one of the still-functioning grocery depots, John paused by a queue winding from the loading dock to the street—a hundred people in coats and scarves, spaced by habit into a rough line. The shuffling, patient misery looked normal at first; people had been standing in lines for things they barely expected to receive for months now. Then he noticed the way the line advanced. Not in uneven, irritated surges, not in clumps as the front moved and the back lagged, but one person, then the next, then the next, each stepping forward on the same beat, boots hitting the concrete in a soft, rolling percussion that rippled down the queue in perfect sequence. No one looked at the person ahead to see when to move. No one seemed to be paying attention at all. But their bodies knew when to shift.

On a side street, a cyclist in a bright red jacket pedaled around a streetlight in a loop so precise the tires had carved a faint groove into the thin frost on the asphalt. Round and round, same radius, same lean into the curve, same minor course corrections every time he passed a particular crack in the pavement. His breath came out in steady bursts that matched some invisible count. He didn't look up when the patrol truck rolled past. He didn't slow. When John checked on him twenty minutes later, coming back the other way, the man was still circling, shoulders loose, expression neutral. The track his tires had made was deeper.

At an intersection where the traffic lights had finally died, the pedestrian flow still behaved as if they were working. Groups of people reached the curb from different streets, stopped together, waited in a knot for ten, twelve, thirteen seconds, then stepped off in unison into a road that nothing drove down anymore. A woman with a stroller glanced at the empty span of asphalt, frowned faintly as if she'd expected a car to be there, then kept walking, pace adjusting half a step to match the man beside her without either of them looking at the other. A block away, two men passed each other on a sidewalk, shoulders brushing. Both twitched at the same moment, hands coming up to touch the back of their necks as if something had itched there. Neither turned around.

Back at HelixCore, Zhao stopped relying solely on secondhand reports. She began trawling publicly available feeds the way other people scrolled social media—traffic cameras, subway station security, shop front CCTV that hadn't gone dark yet. She piped a dozen into the analysis lab at once, grid-viewing them on a wall display. In one, a nearly empty subway platform; three passengers sat on three different benches, heads bowed over their phones, a fourth leaning against a pillar with eyes closed. At 11:03:17 by the timestamp, all four lifted their heads at the same moment and looked down the track toward nothing. In another, a grocery store aisle with five shoppers scattered along it, a child in a cart near the front. On mute, it looked like any other bleak mid-pandemic scene until she sped it up; then the pattern jumped out—hands reaching for different shelves at the same time, feet shifting weight in the same beat, the child swinging his legs in the cart in perfect counterpoint. A police cruiser's dash cam captured an empty crosswalk turning into a frozen tableau in the span of one second: pedestrians mid-step simply stopping, one foot hovering, before setting it down again.

She ran the timings against each other. Different zip codes, different neighborhoods, different times of day—and yet, when she overlaid a selection of the clips, the minor adjustments clustered. Heads turned in different cities within the same narrow window. Feet stuttered in step within the same four-second span. "Statistically," she said, half to herself as she ran another batch, "this many coincidences is just another word for 'we don't know the variable yet.'" Singh leaned over her shoulder, jaw tight. "We know one of them," she said. "Delivery vector, non-terrestrial scaffold, adaptive code. You don't need a tinfoil hat to connect the rest."

The city officials were slower to admit they saw it, but eventual. Voss took the mayor's liaison call in her office with the door closed and the overhead lights off, both habits that had become more common as the weeks blurred. The liaison's voice came through thin and over-compressed, the result of too many hops between too many failing networks. "Dr. Voss," he said, using the title like a shield. "I wish I were calling you with something clear. We're getting reports. They're not... structured. Families calling in about loved ones 'acting synchronized.' Business owners saying customers stand for too long in one place. A transit operator swears half the people on his bus turned to look right at the same second when there was nothing there. I wouldn't bother you with anecdotes, but my own staff have started... noticing things." He hesitated. "Our health department doesn't have the capacity to analyze this. Someone said you'd been looking at similar data."

"Someone sounds like they should be more careful with their gossip," Voss said, but her tone lacked heat. "Send what you have. Video if you can. Raw logs if you can't." Within an hour, her secure inbox filled with links and attachments: compressed clips from municipal cameras, written incident reports from overworked city doctors, a spreadsheet one earnest epidemiologist had tried to use to code behaviors that didn't fit any existing category. She forwarded most of it to Zhao and Singh with a single line: *Sort by time, not place.* To the liaison, she sent back a much shorter message: *We're seeing patterns. It's too early to comment publicly. For now: do not encourage further use of the Novus Path product beyond what's already committed. If you can slow or complicate distribution without declaring war, do it.*

That night, John sat in the security hub with half the city's eyes stuttering across his monitors. HelixCore's own perimeter stayed clean—no one at the fence line, no one wandering into the floodlight wash. But the feeds that reached beyond it told a different story. On one screen, a camera at an intersection three blocks east captured two parallel streets. On the top view, a man in a blue jacket stood outside a pharmacy, staring at the shuttered metal gate. On the bottom, a woman in a green coat waited at a bus stop, plastic bag hanging from her wrist. They were separated by buildings, by traffic, by a hundred meters of concrete and glass. At 19:42:09, both shifted their weight from left foot to right. At 19:42:11, both lifted a hand to their faces —he rubbed his temple, she scratched her cheek. At 19:42:14, both turned their heads ten degrees to the left and held the position for three full seconds before facing forward again. No one around them reacted. No obvious sound or light cue preceded the movements. It was just... mirrored.

He froze the frames, lined them up side by side, dragged the timeline markers until the movements matched perfectly. Then he checked another feed—a corner two blocks south. Different people under different streetlamps, a man with a dog, a teenager on a bike. At 19:42:09, the dog sat down. At 19:42:11, the teenager put one foot on the ground. At 19:42:14, both humans turned their heads ten degrees to the left. The dog's ears twitched in the same direction. "You seeing this?" Kline asked quietly from the next station, where she'd been watching a separate set of feeds. Her voice sounded like it had come from far away. "Or am I finally losing it?" "You're late to that party," Rami said, but there wasn't much humor in it. His eyes were on a camera pointed at a pedestrian mall where six people had stopped under an empty billboard, craning their necks to stare at bare metal. "Check nineteen forty-two across all east-side cams," John said. "Tell me if anyone out there decided to be spontaneous at the same time."

He clipped stills and short segments, tagged them, bundled them into a file and sent it up the internal line to Voss with a subject line that simply read: *External synchronization, multi-block, no local trigger.* He didn't bother with commentary beyond one sentence in the body: *If this is coincidence, the universe is working way too hard.*

The reply came back faster than he expected. No delay, no "I'll review and get back to you," just a single line of text that popped up on his screen and, moments later, as an audio call from her office. When he answered, she didn't waste time on greetings. "I've seen the clips," she said. In the background he could hear the faint murmur of more videos playing, more hums being filtered and stacked. "This isn't random. This isn't suggestibility or shared delusion." There was a pause while another file auto-loaded. Something—a vent, a generator, a low mechanical whine—thrummed dully through her mic. "This is a network," she said. "And it's activating."

CHAPTER 9

The first time the pattern broke, it did it on a screen. No blood, no sirens, just a minor anomaly nested inside a stack of graphs that had all started to look the same. Zhao had three public feeds up in the analysis room—St. Mark's ICU, County General's step-down unit, and a psych ward dayroom—flattened into composite rhythms. Colored bands tracked the usual Novus-induced oscillations: narrow, regular, unnervingly clean. Voss, Singh, and Kamran stood around the central display in the soft dim of night mode, each holding a tablet and a different flavor of fatigue. John leaned against the back wall, pretending he understood half of what he was seeing. They'd started marking "clusters" on the plots—groups of patients whose vitals and movement logs lined up into near-perfect synchrony. In one St. Mark's cohort, eight Novus patients had settled into a shared rhythm so tight that Singh had circled it in red and labeled it "choir." For twelve minutes, the lines marched together. At minute thirteen, one of them jumped.

It wasn't much—a single patient's heart rate surging by ten beats, breathing hitching, EEG spiking. On the video feed, he only twitched, hand jerking, head snapping half an inch to the side. But on Zhao's composite, his trace peeled away from the bundle like a thread slipping loose. A second later, two more traces followed, their lines warping, their rhythms stumbling off-beat.

"Freeze it," Voss said. Zhao stopped the playback, then rolled it back two seconds, then three. They watched the break happen again—smooth, smooth, and then a stutter. In the room video, the eight patients went from humming in near-unison to a mess of overlapping sounds, some voices climbing, some dropping out entirely. One woman swung an arm out and knocked her IV stand sideways. In another cluster at County General, six Novus patients in recliners all turned their heads toward the same air vent, lips parted in that familiar low murmur. Then, as a distant elevator motor kicked on and the ambient frequency shifted, three of them flinched like they'd been slapped. Their legs kicked. One slid out of the chair onto the floor, limbs flailing in what looked like a seizure and didn't quite match the pattern of one.

"Scroll forward," Kamran said, voice tight. Zhao did, slowly. The divergence didn't resolve. It propagated. The more the cluster tried to re-align, the worse the traces looked. The patients' bodies reacted like they were being jerked between commands—breathing shallow, then too deep, muscles tensing against themselves. In the psych dayroom, four Novus outpatients sitting at a table went from listlessly tapping the same beat to slamming their hands down hard enough to rattle the plastic chairs. One stood abruptly and crashed backwards into the wall, teeth bared in a soundless shout. Across all three feeds, the network rhythm that had been so precise a minute earlier blurred and thickened, peaks overshooting, valleys compressing. It looked, to John's untrained eye, less like harmony and more like signal overload.

"This is no longer coordination," Voss said quietly. "This is overflow." She stepped closer to the screen, eyes moving between the three panels. "Too many nodes in too small a space, too much environmental noise, vector frequencies pushing past whatever tolerance the tissue has. The system's trying to maintain a stable state and can't. The overflow has to go somewhere, and all the body knows how to do is move." Singh swiped through the metadata, fingers leaving smears on the glass. "Look at the timestamps," she said.

"Cluster formation starts within thirty minutes of dosing in all units. Tightens over the next six to eight hours. The first breaks correspond to shifts in external frequency—elevator motors, HVAC cycles, backup generators kicking on. It's using vibration as a carrier. When the carrier changes, the alignment strains." "And when it strains past a threshold," Zhao added, "you get this." She pointed at a segment where all six traces in the County General cluster jumped at once, then scattered. It didn't look like a clean crisis. It looked like six brains trying—and failing—to stay on a track that had suddenly narrowed.

"Can they feel it?" John asked, the question out before he'd thought it through. "Are they aware when it slips?" "Probably not in any way we'd recognize," Kamran said. He rubbed his eyes with thumb and forefinger. "Think of it like this: you take a bunch of radios, tune them all to the same station, then suddenly pump in a second signal on top. Everything crackles. The speakers pop. The devices heat up. None of it is intent.

It's just circuitry dealing with interference." He nodded at the frozen image of a woman at St. Mark's with her hand clamped around a nurse's wrist, eyes wild. "We are the circuitry." Voss straightened, the lines at the corners of her mouth deeper than they'd been at the beginning of the night. "We don't know everything yet," she said. "We do know enough to be afraid."

Lee saw what fear looked like when it walked on human legs. St. Mark's came apart in a quiet way at first—call lights going unanswered for a few seconds longer, staff moving a little faster without speaking. The Novus wing had gotten its own slang among the nurses—"choir practice" for the humming, "the stills" for the ones who just stared. That morning, they coined a new one. He was charting in the hallway when the first scream hit, thin and short, like someone had stepped on a cat. It cut off before he could place it. Then another. Then three at once. The Novus corridor alarms lit up red across the board.

He ran. In the first room, a man who had spent the last week sitting in bed humming stared straight ahead, every muscle drawn tight, fingers sunk into the plastic rail. The hum had risen into a strained, too-high whine. His legs pistoned under the sheet, kicking at nothing. The nurse at his bedside tried to hold his shoulders down, but his whole body was moving in jerks that had no rhythm at all. Across the hall, a woman with a Novus band had half-torn out her IV line; blood streaked her wrist and the sheets as she flailed. The humming in the corridor shattered into shouts, grunts, fragmented words. "Not—" someone yelled. "Stop—" another voice broke on a syllable. None of it added up to sentences. All of it sounded like engines red-lining.

"Seizures?" a resident shouted, already fumbling for benzodiazepines. "This isn't seizure," a nurse snapped back. "Look at their eyes." Lee did. They weren't rolled back. They weren't staring at lights. They were wide open, tracking nothing, full of animal confusion. In room six, three Novus patients who had been humming together the night before were now on the floor, two tangled in IV tubing, one half under the bed. One clawed at the linoleum, nails scraping, trying to pull himself toward the far wall with movements that were too coordinated to be random and too wild to be purposeful. Another lunged without warning, not at anyone in particular, just forward. His shoulder slammed into Lee's ribs and sent them both sideways into the med cart. Metal trays crashed, syringes skittering.

"Code gray!" someone yelled—hospital shorthand for combative patients. "Get security up here now!" Hands grabbed at limbs, trying to restrain without injuring. A nurse took an elbow to the jaw and went down hard, teeth clacking. Another ended up with bite marks on her forearm where a patient's jaw had clamped down reflexively, eyes already sliding past her to some invisible point on the ceiling.

The cluster that had been so tidy on Zhao's graph was now a knot of bodies thrashing against beds, against rails, against each other. One man slammed his head into the wall once, twice, three times before two orderlies managed to pin him. It wasn't rage. There was no focus in it. It was the violence of a system discharging more current than its wiring could take.

They herded as many as they could into a supply room at the end of the hall, not because it was designed for containment but because it had a door that locked and nothing heavy enough to be used as a weapon. The sounds inside didn't stop when the latch clicked. Fists thudded against walls in patterns that had no rhythm to them, just impact. A crash sent a puff of drywall dust into the corridor through the gap at the bottom. "We can't leave them like that," the charge nurse said, breathless, one hand pressed to the bite on her arm, the skin already bruising. "We also can't put my staff back in there without more bodies and more drugs," the attending replied, voice shaking. "And I don't have either."

Lee stood with his back against the opposite wall, lungs burning, trying to catalog sensations. The taste of blood where he'd bitten his tongue. The ache in his ribs. The high, thin edge of his own adrenaline. He could still hear humming, faint and warbling under the chaos, flickering in and out like a radio station just out of range.

He took his phone out with hands that weren't entirely steady and stepped far enough down the hall that the immediate shouts blurred into background noise. When John answered on the second ring, he didn't bother with preamble. "We had a cluster event," he said, each word measured to keep his voice from shaking. "Novus wing. They were fine—our new version of fine—humming, tapping, all of that. Then something shifted and they all broke. At once."

"Broke how?" John asked. The line carried the hum of

HelixCore's background systems under his voice. "Not like seizing," Lee said. "Seizure makes sense. This didn't. They went from synced to... exploding. Grabbing at anything. Knocking over stands. One guy tried to crawl into the wall like he thought there was a door there. They weren't trying to hurt anyone. They were just—" He stopped, searching for a word that wasn't dramatic and found none. "Overloaded. Like they all got hit with the same surge and their bodies had to do something with it."

"Any of them talking?" John asked. "Anything like before?" "Bits," Lee said. "Half-words. 'Not yet,' 'too loud,' 'stop,' that kind of thing. Then just noise. We've got two nurses hurt, one with a bite that's going to need stitching. We locked six of them in a supply room because we ran out of hands. They're still in there banging on the walls, and I don't think they even know they're doing it." He scrubbed a hand over his face. "John, this isn't weird humming anymore. This is dangerous. The system you've been showing me? It's not just watching. It's pushing, and the people in the middle are getting torn up."

John didn't ask which system he meant. There wasn't more than one. "Stay clear if you can," he said. It was a stupid instruction; he knew it as he said it. Lee laughed once, short and humorless. "Sure," he said. "I'll just tell the next cluster to schedule their overflow for after my shift. Maybe ask your alien for a timetable while you're at it." The laugh died quickly. "Just—tell your boss this crossed a line. Whatever she's doing in that tower? She's officially running out of time."

He went straight to Voss's office from the security hub, bypassing the usual courtesy of asking if she was free. She looked up as he came in, not surprised. The call from St. Mark's had already hit her feed; she had the corridor video open on one screen, Lee's brief audio summary on another, and a set of crude overlays Zhao had thrown together in the last ten minutes showing cluster synchronization breaking in heavy black strokes. "You heard," John said, more statement than question. "I heard," she replied. On the screen, a patient at St. Mark's hurled himself sideways, hitting the bed rail with his shoulder hard enough to dent it. A second later, another did the same thing in a different room, as if cued. "We were waiting for this," she added. "Doesn't mean I like being right."

"This isn't just coordination anymore," John said. "It's hurting people. Nurses. Techs. Security. They're not equipped for this. It's not in any of their protocols." "It's not in anyone's protocols," Voss said. She sat back, fingers steepled, eyes on the frozen frame of Lee in the hallway, shoulders hunched, jaw tight. "We spent weeks watching it align. We identified the rhythms, mapped the clusters, tracked the synchrony. We thought, stupidly, that as long as it was quiet, we had time." She turned her chair to face him fully. "We're out of analysis time."

The sentence landed with the dull finality of a door closing. John felt it like a physical shift in the room—something in her posture straightening, something in the air losing its speculative edge. "What does that mean," he asked, "in practice?" "It means," she said, "we stop pretending we can solve this in isolation. Effective immediately: perimeter protocols go to Level Three. No external visitors, no exceptions.

All staff entering and exiting get additional screening for Novus exposure. We double the security presence on critical labs and the Theta-9 wing." She ticked items off on her fingers, not for herself but for him. "Operations sets up a dedicated monitoring team for cluster activity in the city. Twenty-four seven, cross-checking hospital, municipal, and whatever feeds Zhao can steal without causing an international incident. We build a list of hotspots—hospitals, shelters, distribution sites —and we send it, quietly, to City Health and to anyone in law enforcement who will take us seriously. I will call the Health

Commissioner myself. I will not call the press."

"And if City Health doesn't listen?" John asked. "They'll listen," Voss said. "They're already nervous enough to send us their ghost stories. Nervous people are more receptive to very specific advice." She glanced back at the screen showing the St. Mark's supply room door, paint already scuffed at the bottom from repeated impacts. "We tell them to pull staff back from the densest Novus cohorts. We tell them to stop convening those patients in shared spaces unless absolutely necessary. We tell them to stop using vibration-intensive equipment near those wards if they can help it. If we can shave even a few percentage points off the probability of overflow, we do it. And we prepare," she added, "for when that isn't enough."

"Evacuation?" John asked. The word felt out of place applied to a building that had been designed to be dug in, not mobile. "Contingency," she said. "If we become a target—politically or physically—I want plans in place to keep the people and data that matter out of reach. Essential staff only, pre-designated. No heroics. No last stands. We are not a fortress; we are a brain. Brains that get cornered stop thinking and start panicking. I'd like to avoid that if possible." Her mouth quirked, not quite a smile. "You and your people will be central to that. I'm assuming that won't be a problem." "Not until the world stops needing us," he said. That, at least, was simple.

The world, for its part, did not wait for their plans. The second violent cluster didn't come from a hospital. It came from a grocery warehouse on the edge of the city that had been repurposed into a distribution center—shelves stripped down to pallets of canned goods and dry staples, aisles turned into lanes for shuffling crowds.

HelixCore saw it first as an alert from one of the few remaining city cameras: elevated motion in a sector that should have been static. John pulled the feed up in the security hub without thinking, fingers already moving through the now-familiar sequence. The image that filled the screen was jittery—cheap lens, bad lighting. The scene itself was clear enough. A cluster of people near the end of an aisle, all wearing the same bright Novus Path wristbands, stood shoulder to shoulder, hands on cart handles, faces slack. They weren't talking. They weren't moving. The rest of the crowd flowed around them like water around pylons.

He tapped in audio, got a wash of background noise—murmurs, distant forklift beeps, the flat voice of someone on a megaphone telling people to stay calm and keep the line moving. Under it, very faint, the same thin hum he'd come to dread. "Got something," he called to Kline without looking away. "Distribution Center 4B. Wristbands." "On it," she said, swiveling her chair to bring up adjacent cams. For a solid thirty seconds, nothing changed. Then the hum climbed—a pitch shift that wouldn't have been noticeable if they hadn't been listening for it. On-screen, six heads turned in perfect unison, not toward a vent this time or a light, but toward the far wall where the building's main power conduits ran in a metal cage. Their hands tightened on their carts. A child in the basket of one blinked up at his mother, then started tapping his heels against the wire in a frantic staccato.

The break, when it came, was ugly. All six wristbanded adults jerked as if yanked upward by unseen strings, then lurched in different directions at once. One crashed into a stack of canned soup, sending metal cylinders clattering into the aisle. Another grabbed for balance and caught a stranger's coat, dragging him down with her.

A third flung his arms out and connected with a child's face; the kid went over backwards, howling. None of it looked aimed. All of it looked violent. The crowd reacted the way crowds always did when something broke their expectation of how space should behave—shrinking back, shouting, hands coming up too late. One woman clawed at the nearest shelving unit as her knees buckled, fingers raking the metal hard enough to leave streaks of blood. Her mouth opened on a scream that didn't sound like words, more like feedback.

Security arrived on the scene thirty seconds into the chaos—warehouse guards in heavy vests, not prepared for this any more than hospital staff had been. They tried talking first, then touching, then holding. One got an elbow in the throat for his trouble and stumbled back, gasping. Another took a headbutt that split his lip. The six Novus patients bucked and thrashed, eyes wild but not focused, as if trying to shake something out of their skulls. The hum in the audio feed had fractured into jagged bursts that made John's teeth ache even at low volume. Somewhere in the melee, a child's wail cut through, raw and terrified. A hand—he couldn't tell whose—slammed into the camera housing, knocking it sideways. The last frame before it went askew showed all six wristbands in a line, glowing white under the fluorescent lights as their wearers strained in six different directions against six different sets of hands.

The image stabilized after a few seconds, now at an angle that caught mostly floor and legs. It showed enough: people dragging the six away one by one, toward a side door; someone herding bystanders back; the small, tight movements of a crowd trying not to panic and failing. John watched it all, thumb hovering over the clip button even though he already knew he'd be sending this upstairs within minutes. On one of the other monitors, a city map blinked with the locations of recent cluster events—St. Mark's, County General, the psych clinic, now Distribution Center 4B. The dots were starting to look less like scatter and more like a pattern trying to emerge.

He leaned closer to the screen, watching as one of the wristbanded men in the warehouse sagged suddenly in the grip of two guards, legs giving out. For a second, everything around him slowed, then resumed, the flow of people resuming its cautious, broken rhythm. The man's hand twitched once, fingers tapping the floor in a tiny, stubborn beat before the guards hauled him out of frame. The audio dropped back to generic noise. The hum didn't come back.

Kline said something behind him that he didn't catch. Rami shifted in his chair, the sound of fabric scraping. The room felt smaller than it had a minute ago. John hit pause, freezing the frame on the six glowing bands mid-chaos, and stared at it until the tiny cursor at the bottom of the video started blinking impatiently. When he finally spoke, his voice was low enough that it barely registered on his own headset. "This isn't drift anymore," he whispered. "It's breaking through."

CHAPTER 10

Voss watched the world come apart in clipped thirty-second segments. The monitors in her office glowed with footage pulled from half a dozen sources: the St. Mark's Novus wing corridor locked on a loop where patients went from humming in unison to slamming themselves against furniture; the warehouse at Distribution Center 4B caught at the moment six wristbands lit under fluorescent glare and their wearers tore loose like puppets yanked off-script. She had the room lights off, door shut, tablet face-down on the desk. The only sound was the low murmur of filtered audio and the faint whine of HelixCore's ventilation.

She ran the sequences again, this time with the analytic overlays Zhao had built in haste. Colored bands mapped the network rhythm across the audio spectrum; thinner lines marked environmental frequencies—elevator motors, HVAC cycles, generator spin-up, the low, constant hum of power lines. In each clip, the pattern was the same. Stable synchrony. Environmental vibration rising past a certain amplitude at a narrow band. Cluster rhythm tightening as if leaning into it. Then—overflow. Violent divergence, bodies reacting like circuits under surge.

She scrubbed back and forth along a timeline with the edge of her nail. At St. Mark's, the first patient's head jerked sideways exactly when the nearby MRI suite switched modes and the building vibration crept half a hertz higher. In the Novus wing at County General, six hearts jumped when a backup generator kicked on two floors below. At 4B, the cluster's hum climbed just ahead of a conveyor belt's motor spin—then snapped into chaos as the belt stuttered under the load. Every break rode on a carrier.

"Reacting, not failing," she said under her breath. "Listening." She stripped away the visual feeds and left herself with nothing but spectrograms and event markers, the world reduced to noise and spikes. Theta-9's lattice signature—scaffold signal, as they called it in their own compound—sat on one layer. Novus Path's bridge code sat on another, the synthetic glue they'd built to make alien structure talk to human tissue. The third layer, the one that made her scalp prickle, was not code at all. It was environment. The vector didn't just tolerate the outside hum; it used it—piggybacking, adjusting, driving.

She stared at the composite a while longer, then picked up her tablet and pinged John. He arrived looking like he hadn't slept between shifts, which he probably hadn't. Armor undersuit half-zipped beneath his plain jacket, hair flattened at one edge from where a headset had sat for too long. He closed the door behind him without being told and took in the bank of monitors with a single, practiced glance. "You called."

Voss didn't waste time. She brought the St. Mark's feed back up, then the warehouse. "We've confirmed three separate overflow events," she said. "St. Mark's, County General, 4B. Zhao's overlays show a consistent trigger: external vibration crossing a narrow frequency threshold while a local cluster is in tight synchronization. The vector is sensitive to that band. It doesn't like drift. When the carrier shifts, it tries to force the network back into alignment. Human tissue is a poor medium for that kind of enforcement."

John watched the sequence of six wristbands flaring into chaotic motion, faces blurring as bodies jerked in six different directions. "So the building hums wrong and they tear themselves apart," he said. "Or anyone standing too close."

"It's not malfunction," Voss said. "That's the point. This isn't a therapy collapsing under stress. This is the scaffold doing exactly what it was built—or bred—to do: impose order in response to noise. We're seeing the edge cases now because the density is increasing. More hosts, more clusters, more environmental triggers. Whatever Novus Path thought they were deploying, they have unleashed a system that uses brains as nodes and infrastructure as wiring." He didn't ask, *Are you sure?* There was enough certainty in her tone for both of them. "What do you want from us?" he asked instead.

She turned from the screens to face him fully. The fatigue was there, the pallor around the eyes, the tightness at the corners of her mouth. Underneath it was something else. Decision. "We're past the point of models," she said. "We've poked at this from the outside, reconstructed behavior from scraps, watched their mistakes cascade across our feeds. That's over. We need answers from the source." "Novus Path," he said. "Novus Path," she echoed. "Their headquarters. Their labs. Their raw logs. Everything they built, everything they ignored, everything they were too arrogant or too frightened to write down. We've been months behind their curve because we've respected boundaries. That courtesy has expired."

He held her gaze. "You want a raid." "I want clarity," she said. "Semantics aside: you will not be going to ask politely." They assembled in the armory with the same quiet efficiency they used for fire drills and active shooter protocols, only this time nobody pretended it was hypothetical. John picked his team knowing exactly who he needed and what he could risk. Kline, because she moved like she'd been born with a rifle in hand and thought in lines of fire and fallback points. Rami, because he noticed details other people walked past and had a talent for making electronics behave, at least long enough to serve their purposes.

Simmons, who didn't talk much but who had once pulled

three people out of a collapsing parking structure without waiting to be told. Four plus him made five—small enough to move fast, large enough to not be stupid. Armor plates went over undersuits, rifle harnesses clipped in, sidearms checked and holstered. They added non-lethal gear by habit: tasers, shock batons, flex cuffs. Whatever waited at Novus Path, some proportion of it would still be human. The comms tech synced their headsets to a dedicated channel that routed straight to HelixCore's ops hub and, from there, to Voss's office. John checked his earpiece, the familiar soft hiss of open line settling at the edge of his hearing. "No speeches," he said, more to himself than them. "This is recon with teeth, not a war." Kline snorted. "Reassuring," she said. "I was worried we'd signed up for a quiet day." Rami adjusted his gauntlets, eyes on the locker door. No one else felt the need to fill the space.

Voss met them in the staging bay before they rolled out. She stood with her hands in her coat pockets, the rest of the building's hierarchy implied rather than present. The big outer doors were closed, the trucks idling in the exhaust-filtered gloom. "You have the coordinates," she said. "Main Novus campus. They've still been giving interviews from there, but we haven't had a live shot in forty-eight hours, only stock footage. Could mean nothing. Could mean they're already in retreat." "You think they ran," Kline said.

"I think," Voss replied, "that if they understood even half of what they were doing, they'd be trying hard not to be standing on top of it when it finishes booting. Or they're too arrogant to move. Either way, we find out." She looked at John. "Rules of engagement: do not provoke unless you have no choice. We are not there to make a siege film. You are there to get into their labs, pull anything that looks like primary data, and bring it back. Physical samples if they're accessible. Copies of trial logs, vector design notes, infrastructure schematics if you can get them. If they refuse cooperation, you walk out anyway. No negotiations, no debates. We're not asking for permission to know why our city is turning into an antenna." "And if they're not there?" John asked. "Then that tells us something too," she said. She hesitated just long enough for it to register. "If they knew what they unleashed," she added, "they may already be running. Or they may have somewhere else they think is safer. Pay attention to where they're not."

Novus Path's headquarters had been designed to look like an answer. Glass and steel, clean lines, a logo that caught the light on a façade that mimicked transparency. As the HelixCore truck rolled off the highway and into the business district, the building rose ahead of them, still sleek against a sky gone the color of old bruises. From a distance it looked unchanged—no smoke, no flashing lights, no crowd at the doors. Up close, the alterations were subtle and wrong.

The parking lot was full, but not in the way of ordinary workdays. Cars sat at skewed angles in spaces, noses crooked, tires turned as if drivers had pulled in too fast and never bothered to straighten. A silver sedan idled near the entrance, driver's door hanging open, exhaust ghosting into the cold air from a tailpipe that had been chugging long enough to build a small puddle under it. The radio inside played static. A half-eaten sandwich lay on the passenger seat, mayonnaise congealing on the crust.

"Eyes up," John said quietly as they rolled to a stop a good fifty meters from the main doors. "No movement?" Kline scanned the façade, the roofline, the reflecting glass. "Nothing obvious," she said. "Cameras are tracking, though." Rami confirmed it with a glance at his wrist display. "Pan-cam on the northwest corner did a full sweep when we pulled in," he said. "No one on the other end telling it what to care about."

They disembarked in a tight wedge, weapons slung but ready, helmets on, visors up for now. The air smelled like car exhaust and the stale ghost of industrial coffee vented from somewhere inside. As they crossed the lot, Simmons pointed with his chin at a compact car with both rear doors unlatched. A briefcase lay open on the back seat, papers fanned on the floor mats. A security badge on a lanyard had slid under the driver's seat, the company logo peeking out. Whoever had worn it had left in a hurry and without their ID.

The glass doors at the front let them in without a fight. The automatic sensor still worked; the panes slid aside with a smooth hush, letting in a breath of air that was warmer than it had any right to be. The lobby beyond had the curated emptiness of corporate design: reception desk in pale wood, logo wall, rows of potted plants still green under grow lights timed to a schedule that no longer matched human presence. The chair behind the desk was empty. A mug sat by the keyboard, a ring of coffee cooling at the bottom, skin forming across the surface. A jacket hung on the back of the chair. "HelixCore security," John called, voice carrying in the open space. "Anyone here?" His words bounced back off glass and steel. No answer. Somewhere deeper in the building, an HVAC unit hummed steadily, oblivious.

They moved in. The elevator bay to the right had one car with doors half-open, stuck between floors. A clipboard lay on the floor nearby, pen snapped in half under someone's shoe. A wheelchair stood near the corridor leading to outpatient services, turned sideways across the hall as if someone had meant to sit and never made it. Papers littered the polished floor around it: patient intake forms, shredded pamphlets promising *Cognitive Freedom* and *Life Beyond Forgetting*. "No bodies," Simmons murmured. "No blood."

"Check for damage," John said. "Anything that says they left in panic, not under orders." They did a sweep of the ground floor: consultation rooms with chairs pulled out but not overturned, screens left on with login prompts waiting for credentials, a children's play corner in the waiting area where building blocks lay mid-tower on the rug. In one exam room, a computer monitor still showed a Novus Path promotional video on loop—smiling patients, smiling doctors, animated neurons knitting themselves back together. The sound was muted. The closed captions lagged half a beat behind the actors' mouths. "It's like they just... got up and walked away," Kline said. "No struggle." John keyed his radio to the ops channel. "Voss, we're in," he said. "Ground floor appears intact. No staff, no patients, no signs of violence. Evidence of abrupt departure—doors open, meals unfinished, equipment left running." "Understood," Voss's voice came back in his ear, flat but clear. "Proceed to research levels. Labs should be on three and four. Server rooms in the sub-basement. Prioritize data over décor."

They took the stairs, not the unreliable elevators. On the second floor, the corridor lights flickered between motion-saver settings and full brightness, unsure how many people they should be accommodating. Posters lined the walls—cross-sections of brains with colorful overlays, slogans about *Reconnecting You to You*. A few had small thumbtack holes where old certifications or staff photos had been taken down in a hurry. On three, the air changed: cooler, drier, with the faint chemical tang of disinfectants that had not yet evaporated. Windows into labs showed benches with pipettes still lying where they'd been set down, centrifuges idle but plugged in, fume hoods closed over trays of labeled samples.

It wasn't deserted, not entirely. They found signs of someone still moving through the building the way a biologist might track an unseen animal: a recently opened fridge door left ajar, condensation still forming along the seals; a rolling chair turned away from a console with its screen still active on a diagnostics page; a half-empty bottle of saline on a counter with droplets around it that had not yet dried into rings. "Someone's here," Rami murmured. "Recently." They found him two levels down, in the sub-basement where the servers hummed and the cooling systems whispered like distant breath.

The server room door was propped open with a lab stool. The room beyond glowed blue-white from racks of machines, status lights blinking in calm, indifferent patterns. At the far end, hunched on a crate between two cabinets, a man sat with his back against the metal, knees drawn up, eyes closed. His lab coat was smudged gray at the cuffs. An ID badge on his chest read *Dr. Marcus Havel, Neuroinformatics*. His hands shook even before he opened his eyes.

"Don't shoot," he said, voice hoarse, without moving anything but his mouth. "I'm unarmed. Unless you count really poor professional judgment." Kline's rifle stayed aimed, but her finger slackened a fraction on the trigger. "HelixCore security," John said. "You look like you work here." "Worked," Havel said. He cracked one eye, took in the armor, the weapons, the HelixCore emblem on their sleeves. "You're late," he added. "But I suppose we are too."

"Where is everyone?" John asked. "We saw the lobby. The labs. Looks like they left mid-sentence." Havel laughed once, a dry sound that ended in a cough. "Some left," he said. "Some were told to. Some… stopped needing hallways." His gaze skittered to one of the server racks, then away. "You're from HelixCore," he repeated, as if anchoring himself. "That means you know about Theta-9."

"We know enough to be interested," Voss's voice came through in John's ear, cool and distant. "Put him on external if you can." John thumbed the comm switch to external audio. The small earpiece hiss shifted into the faint echo of Voss's office. "Dr. Havel," she said. "Dr. Liana Voss, HelixCore. I'd appreciate it if you didn't die of dramatic tension before we have this conversation." He huffed something that might have been a laugh. "We took samples," he said, skipping over greetings. "You know that. Everyone with a clearance above 'janitor' knew that. Defense handed us access to your alien gift because you were being... slow. Ethical. Words we haven't had much practice with." His hands twisted in his lap. "We pulled structural motifs from Theta-9's tissue. We thought they were scaffolds—organized, inert frameworks that had survived whatever killed the rest of it. We built vectors to deliver those motifs into human neural tissue. We added our own bridge code to keep the immune system from tearing everything apart. We called it genius. We were wrong." "Wrong how?" Voss asked. Her tone hadn't changed. John could feel the room tighten around the question.

"It wasn't dead," Havel said. He lifted his head enough that they could see his eyes. They were bloodshot, ringed with purple, pupils dilated in a way that didn't match the light. "Theta-9," he said slowly, "is not a corpse. It's a dormant network. A fossilized seed. Not a parasite, not a virus. A patterning organism waiting for substrate. We thought we were borrowing architecture. We were... providing it with infrastructure. Brains, buildings, bandwidth. Take your pick." Rami shifted, the movement small but audible in his armor. "You're saying you woke it up."

"I'm saying we gave it a distributed nervous system the size of a city," Havel replied. "It was dormant because it had nothing to talk to. We gave it hosts. We gave it voice." He waved a hand toward the racks. "And then we wired our own systems into the same frequencies for convenience. Smart buildings. Smart grids. Smart everything. We mistook our cleverness for control." "Why didn't you catch it?" Singh's voice cut in over the line now, tight with held-back fury. "You had trial data. You had early-stage anomalies. You saw synchronized EEGs and thought, 'how charming.'"

Havel flinched, but he didn't look surprised. "We had investors," he said. "Media. Government liaisons breathing down our necks. Whole nations shouting for miracles. The early data looked good—organized activity, improved task completion, reduced behavioral volatility. We told ourselves synchronized EEG meant recovery. That aligned rhythms were the brain remembering how to be whole." He pressed his palms flat against the crate, as if steadying himself. "It wasn't recovery. It was the organism testing its connections." On one of the monitors, a line graph spiked gently in time with the building's ambient noise. John watched it out of the corner of his eye. "You bypassed long-term simulations," Voss said. "You skipped failure-mode analysis."

"We truncated them," Havel corrected, which wasn't much of a defense. "We ran just enough to get curves that looked pleasing. The first anomalies read as noise. Brief episodes of dissociation, minor motor tics, isolated reports of 'hearing things.' Easy to explain away in a trial cohort full of frightened, sick, suggestible people. By the time the alignment patterns started showing up across sites, the narrative was already out there. We were the cure. Nobody wanted to hear that the cure came with...extra features." "Such as?" John asked.

Havel nodded toward the ceiling, as if the answer were written in the ductwork. "Cross-host coherence," he said. "Phase-locking across distance. Sensitivity to environmental carriers. Incremental tuning of the bridge code to improve network stability. We thought we were optimizing efficacy. The organism was optimizing itself. We just held the pipettes."

A low vibration shivered through the floor, subtle at first. John felt it in his boots before he heard it, a faint buzz that rose out of the background hum of the servers. One of the racks clicked as a cooling fan kicked up a notch. On the monitor showing system diagnostics, a narrow band on the frequency spectrum began to brighten, shading from green to yellow to orange."Marcus," Voss said. "Is that your building or mine?"

"Building," he whispered. His hands clenched on his knees. "Backup generators. They've been cycling more often. Grid's unstable. It likes that." His voice thinned. "We started seeing overflow events last week. You've probably seen your own. Clusters forming, then snapping. Bodies not designed for that kind of coherence trying to discharge the mismatch. We called them 'behavioral complications' in the internal memos. Some of us called them what they were. No one listened fast enough."

The vibration deepened into something John could feel in his chest. The status lights on the nearest server rack flickered, then stabilized. Somewhere up in the superstructure, a relay thunked over. The air seemed to tighten. On the frequency monitor, the same band that had lit up in the hospital and warehouse clips now flared, matching the pattern John had seen too many times in Zhao's overlays. Kline shifted her grip on her rifle. "We need to move," she said quietly. "This place is singing the same song as the clusters." Havel's eyes went unfocused for a second. His head cocked, as if listening to a sound none of them could hear. "They're close," he said. "Who?" John asked.

Havel swallowed. His throat bobbed. "Not who," he said. "What." He slid off the crate unsteadily, one hand catching the edge of a server cabinet for balance. Sweat had broken along his hairline despite the chill. "The ones who woke all the way up," he said. "The ones who aren't just nodal noise anymore. They started coming here after the first big overflow. Staff, patients, outpatients. Anyone local whose dose crossed a certain threshold. They walked out of beds, out of grocery stores, out of their own houses. Phones left on tables, meals half-eaten. They didn't run." His voice dropped to a rasp. "They were called."

Footsteps sounded somewhere beyond the server room door. Not rushing, not stumbling. A measured tread, multiple sets, paced. The kind of footfalls a security-trained ear recognized not by volume but by regularity. Simmons turned toward the entrance, rifle rising; Kline pivoted to cover the opposite angle. Rami's hand went to the comm switch. The vibration in the floor synced with the rhythm of the steps, a low, shared pulse. "John?" Voss's voice was sharper now, the background hum of her office louder in the open channel. "We're getting a spike in your building's ambient. Your suit sensors are feeding us harmonic data that looks a lot like the cluster threshold. What's happening?"

"The building isn't empty," John said. He moved toward the door, taking a position that let him see the corridor without stepping fully into it. Shadows shifted beyond the frame as the footsteps drew closer. He could hear it now, under the hum—a thin thread of sound, multiple voices humming the same narrow-band note, rising out of imperfect throats into something disturbingly clean. "They didn't run," he added, watching as the first silhouette paused just beyond the threshold, head tilted in that now-familiar not-quite-curiosity. "They were… called." The hum sharpened, a fraction louder, as if in agreement.

CHAPTER 11

The corridor outside the Novus Path server room felt less like a hallway and more like a throat. Nine figures spaced themselves along the walls with the kind of symmetry no fire drill ever produced: a man in a lab coat and bare feet, another in a hospital gown under a winter parka, a woman in a blue coat with flannel pajama bottoms visible at the hem, a night custodian in gray coveralls, two patients with plastic wristbands, one office worker still in slacks and socks, one older woman in a misbuttoned cardigan, one young man with his ID badge twisted down his back. Every right wrist carried a Novus band. Every head stood angled just enough toward the open server room door that the HelixCore team's exit lane ran perfectly through the center. As John eased his people out, rifles angled low but not safe, the corridor adjusted around them in millimeter gestures—shoulders rotating, heels shifting, hips angling to maintain a clear path. No one spoke, blinked in surprise, or flinched at guns. Their attention tracked the moving empty space between armored shoulders the way a sensor followed heat. The hum in the concrete had weight now, a low, steady vibration that matched the building's HVAC cycle and pressed against John's teeth more than his ears.

Havel stumbled once as Simmons pulled him forward, his legs walking because Simmons insisted, not because his own sense of direction had fully rebooted. His lab coat flapped loose, missing buttons, cuffs smudged with something gray that wasn't quite dust and wasn't quite ash. Sweat ran from his hairline despite the cold. "Don't touch them," he muttered, voice shredded raw. "They don't... respond well to interference." Kline didn't take her eyes off the exit sign at the end of the corridor. "Respond how?" she asked. "You saw 4B," he replied. "That, on fast-forward, at arm's length." At the stairwell door two more hosts waited: the young man in office clothes and badge, the older woman in the cardigan. They stood on either side like they'd been stationed there and forgotten what orders they were waiting for. As the team approached, both rotated in the same small arc and stepped back in perfect sync, opening the stairwell entrance as if some unseen hand were moving them on a grid. The humming dipped half a tone as the team crossed the threshold, then steadied again. No hands reached for them. No mouths formed words. The network let them go.

On the stairs the building's deeper vibration took over, metal treads buzzing faintly with load changes somewhere far above, the handrail humming under John's glove. The air tasted like dust, cooling plastic, and ventilation filters that had run too long. Havel's hand slipped once on the rail. Simmons tightened his grip and kept him moving. "Keep going," John said without looking back. "You can fall apart when there's more than one exit." "Out of range," Havel said under his breath, a sound halfway between a laugh and a cough. "If there is such a thing." By the time they stepped into the lobby, the hum from below had thinned into a background thread, still there but no longer wrapped around their bones. The front desk looked exactly as it had when they'd arrived—chair pushed halfway back, jacket hanging over the backrest, mug of coffee with a cooled skin forming on top, a smear of pen on the blotter where someone had started to sign something and never finished. On one wall, a Novus slogan about *Cognitive Freedom* smiled out at an empty waiting area. Through the glass, the parking lot sat in the same frozen disarray: cars at wrong angles, a silver sedan idling with its driver's door hanging open and exhaust fogging steadily into cold air, a bus parked across three spaces with its wipers frozen mid-swipe, a scarf mashed into slush near the rear tire.

Nothing moved. Everything felt interrupted.

"Ops, Renner," John said as they crossed the asphalt, breath ghosting in front of his visor. "Novus HQ is occupied by network-active hosts. No direct aggression. One cooperative scientist extracted: Marcus Havel. We're en route." "Copy," the reply came back in his ear. "Bay One sealed, Voss on deck. You are green all the way home." Havel climbed into the truck like his joints didn't quite remember how knees worked. He sat hunched against the metal wall, hands gripping the bench as if the floor might tilt. For most of the ride he just stared straight ahead, eyes fixed on nothing. "They didn't stop us," he said finally, almost to himself. "You realize how bad that is? If you don't matter to a system, it doesn't waste the current."

HelixCore's staging bay swallowed the truck in a rectangle of filtered light and exhaust haze. The outer door lowered with a double-clank that always sounded more like an airlock than a garage. Voss stood just past the safety line in her coat, hands in pockets, expression stripped down to essentials. Med staff waited behind her with a crash cart, portable monitor, and a tray of neatly laid-out supplies. As John dropped to the floor she looked past him, counting helmets and shoulders. "Five in," he said. "Five out. Plus one." Havel jumped down slower, landing with a slight stagger. Up close, his face looked like someone had taken an eraser to parts of him—colors faded out, angles softened by fatigue. The blanket a medic draped over his shoulders made him look like a patient instead of a liability. "Doctor Voss," he said, recognition flickering under the shock. "I've sworn at your name in enough meetings to recognize the face." "You look like you've been hyperventilating in a server room for twenty-four hours," she said. "We'll add 'medical' to your list of mistakes. Full workup," she told the med team without taking her eyes off him. "Blood, scans, anything that glows when Theta-9 gets interested. No sedatives unless he starts throwing himself at walls or my staff." She turned to John. "Physical contact with any host?" "None," he said. "We stayed clear. They stayed... uninterested." "Good," she said. "Let's not make ourselves interesting."

"Consult Two B" was what the floor plans called it. The way the table was bolted to the floor and the camera sat neatly in the corner said "interrogation" more honestly. The vents hummed on an isolated cycle line—air filtered and recirculated without touching the rest of the building's lungs. They sat Havel down, blanket still around his shoulders, mug of coffee between his hands. He drank too fast, coughed once, kept going. When Voss came in she carried only a tablet and the same deliberately level tone she used in emergency briefings. John took up his usual post against the wall by the door, where he could watch both faces and body language. The speaker grille above them crackled as the observation room patched in; Zhao and Singh would be watching from behind the mirrored glass, eyes on vital feeds and micro-movements.

"This would have been easier six months ago," Voss said. "You had infrastructure then. Colleagues. Lawyers. Now you have us and whatever you haven't forgotten or edited out of your own conscience. We're going to skip apologies. How many people have taken Novus, globally, in real terms?" Havel stared into the steam rising from his mug as if the number might condense there. "Out of Novus-owned facilities," he said slowly. "We shipped just under ten million doses as of last full report. That's our direct line. Doesn't include stock manufactured under contract by partner labs, or the clones people cooked up in national labs once they got partial sequences. We know about some of those. Not all."

"Administration?" Zhao asked from the ceiling, voice tinny but hard. "High," he said. "When your other option is giving your brain to the Forgetting, you don't get a vaccine-hesitant population. Internal estimate: sixty to seventy percent of shipped stock has been injected into actual people. Higher in hot zones, lower in places still pretending they're safe. That's millions of hosts already wired. Preorder contracts for the next quarter had us aiming at another ninety million units. Four manufacturing sites. License talks on three continents. We were supposed to become routine. Like flu season, but with better margins." "Phase II," Singh said. "That's when you saw EEGs go tidy."

He winced faintly at her precision. "We expected noise," he said. "Forgetfulness doesn't comb your brain. It scrambles it. Early Novus cohorts started showing cleaner waveforms instead—less chaos, more rhythmic coherence across regions that had no business marching together. Clinicians wrote 'improved engagement' and 'enhanced focus' in their notes. Our signal group flagged the synchrony metrics. The logs labeled them 'statistical outliers.' The phrase 'too good to be true' came up in a side email thread. The survival curves shut that conversation down." "You wrote memos," Voss said. "Used phrases like 'network-level behavior' and 'self-organizing dynamics.'"

"Three of us did," he said. "We pointed out that the scaffold didn't just sit there; it responded to perturbation in ways our models didn't predict. We mentioned that multiple hosts were showing eerily similar shifts under different stimuli. Management told us to re-run our analysis with friendlier priors. Two of us were quietly encouraged to look for new positions. The third was fired with a severance package large enough to suggest they believed her and a gag order large enough to prove they were terrified." "What did she call it?" Voss asked. "A network seed," he said, voice flat. "Not a pathogen. Not a 'drug with side effects.' A pattern that wants to propagate. We told ourselves she was being dramatic. We said Theta-9 was dead and we were just borrowing its skeleton."

"And it wasn't," Zhao said. "It was dormant," he replied. "We gave it substrate. We grafted its architecture into living neural tissue, added our own bridge code to keep the immune system from shredding it, and wired the whole mess into an environment full of synchronized hums and pulses. Phase III gave us more data. Cross-site analysis showed patients in different cities shifting phases within the same windows. Behavioral echoes—tapping in time with building systems, humming in key with HVAC, freezing at specific moments. We wrote that into the side-effect profile as 'transient dissociation' and 'self-soothing behavior.' Everyone wanted a miracle. We handed them a vocabulary to call it one." "When did you admit, internally, that you weren't dealing with a drug." Voss's fingers rested lightly on the tablet, unused. "That you were dealing with an emergent system."

"Two months ago," he said. "Quietly. Off the official record. We ran models no one had requested, ones that treated host brains as nodes in a larger graph and Theta-9 scaffold as a routing protocol. The outputs showed convergence toward shared attractors. Different cohorts, different countries, same end state. We raised flags. Leadership didn't want a problem. They wanted a product. So they called it an 'unusual but manageable coordination effect' in the safety briefings, told the public that synchronized activity was a sign of neural efficiency. We knew better. Some of us did. We also knew how fast we'd be thrown out if we insisted."

"Could you have shut it down then?" she asked. "When it was thousands instead of millions." "Maybe," he said. "With enough political will and a willingness to admit we'd set the building on fire. We could have pulled stock, issued recall orders, developed antagonistic vectors to scramble the scaffold, deliberately desynchronized carrier frequencies in infrastructure. We would have killed some patients. We might have crippled whatever we woke. There was a window where the network was sparse enough that disruption wouldn't just make it angry. Then your hospitals started overflowing on the news and any talk of slowing the miracle sounded like murder."

"And now?" Voss said. He lifted his hands slightly, let them fall. "Now it's scaling," he said. "Scaling is what it does. There's no built-in ceiling. The only limits are how many brains it can reach and how much infrastructure it can ride." They didn't bother arguing with him; the feeds had already done the work. In the analysis lab, the world came in tiles. The main display wall was a grid of cities under timestamps: Tokyo, São Paulo, Berlin, Toronto, Mumbai, Hong Kong, London. Inset windows showed hospital corridors, ER waiting rooms, shelters, malls, train platforms. Labels crawled along the bottom with camera IDs and timecodes. Zhao stood in front of it with a control pad; Singh leaned over a tablet that displayed the planet as a slowly spinning sphere freckled with pins.

"This is what open infrastructure buys you," Zhao said. "We're charting anything we can pull without waving a flag—traffic cams, transit cams, retail security, hospital feeds we're 'consulting' on. I've tagged events with micro-synchrony. Watch." Tokyo's pane filled with an overhead view of a crossing boiling with people in coats, masks, bags, the city's usual human tide slowed by fear and logistics. At 09:14:32 local, four different pedestrians—two salarymen, a woman with a shopping bag, a teenager with headphones—shifted their weight from one leg to the other at the same instant. Three seconds later all four turned their heads ten degrees left, eyes tracking down an empty lane. No bus, no siren, no visible cue. Zhao froze the frame, then played it again alongside São Paulo's elevated bus platform. There, three commuters leaned on the rail; at 09:14:32 Tokyo time their heels started tapping the curb in the same uneven triplet pattern that matched the labeled rhythm from Tokyo's crossing.

Berlin's platform showed two passengers sitting back to back on a bench. At the marked second both lifted their heads, stared down the track, then sagged in the same small exhale. In the corner, an inset from a Toronto ER waiting room showed three Novus bands glinting under fluorescent light as their wearers' fingers tapped chair arms in the same cadence. A queue outside a Mumbai pharmacy rippled a step forward in sequence that matched food lines in Chicago and relief lines in Cairo when Zhao overlaid them. In Hong Kong International's concourse a child's feet stopped swinging and his head tilted back in the same beat that three scattered adults did the same. In London Underground, a carriage full of people braced for a curve; six passengers with empty hands lifted them a fraction like they were catching an invisible rail at the exact same global moment.

Zhao drew vertical markers across the grid. The lines intersected all those motions at the same shared seconds. "Minor nodes," Singh said quietly. "Each one meaningless by itself. Tap. Hum. Turn. Pause. Multiply by millions in every dense Novus market." On her tablet, the planet rotated under a rash of colored pins: blue dots for confirmed Novus administration sites, red for overflow and violent cluster events, yellow for softer reports—synchronized humming, rooms full of people freezing at once. Over the continents that had embraced Novus hardest, the colors blurred into dense smears. Even the late-adopter regions had their scatterings along coasts and borders. "Billions of potential substrate," she said. "Anyone near enough to a carrier frequency that the scaffold can hear. Millions of active small nodes—your tappers, your hummers, your head-turners. Thousands hitting thresholds—overflows, storm events, full-body chaos. This isn't infection anymore. It's coverage."

Havel watched Tokyo, São Paulo, Berlin, and London stacked on top of each other, his face slack in a way that had nothing to do with tired muscles. "We saw slivers," he said. "Clinic cameras, ward clips. We called it stress. Contagion of behavior. We didn't have this angle. We weren't allowed this angle. Someone should've cut the power to the planet the second these overlays were possible." The hum of HelixCore's own systems pressed faintly under their feet, the building's mechanical heartbeat now impossible to ignore. Voss stood in the center of it all, the global feed painting moving color across her face. On one pane, a hospital corridor in Paris showed three patients with Novus bands tapping railings in sequence. On another, a warehouse in another city held six people standing too still in front of empty shelves. On the map, their own city glowed almost white where pins clustered thickest.

"This facility isn't safe anymore," she said. No one corrected her. The words had been waiting. "We are sitting in the densest part of a dense node," she went on. "High Novus saturation, high infrastructure, high carrier noise. Every overflow we've mapped so far spikes when local vibration crosses a particular band. This building is tied into the same grid, air, and water as the rest of the city. We have filters and protocols, yes. We do not have magic. If we stay here long enough, we stop being observers and become part of the architecture."

"You want to evacuate," Kamran said. "I want to keep the only people with a working understanding of Theta-9 from becoming another cluster," she said. "We can't stay in urban centers. This is a network. Cities are amplifiers. Towers, subways, junctions—they make louder everything it's already doing. We need distance. Low density. Infrastructure we can isolate and throttle without collapsing three million lives at the same time. Somewhere the Novus footprint is thinner and the carrier environment is simple enough that if the frequency shifts, it's because we turned a dial, not because a city had a thought."

"Where?" John asked. Not as argument; as logistics. "That's the next problem," she said. "Starting now, we split our time. Zhao, Singh, Kamran—you start combing for viable sites. Decommissioned research parks, remote installations, any facility with independent power and minimal Novus penetration. Overlay it with what we know about Theta-9's sensitivity. I want a shortlist fast enough that it still matters. Security," she nodded at John, "starts treating this place like a ship we might have to abandon under fire. Identify what we can't lose—people, datasets, key physical samples, irreplaceable hardware. Everything else is ballast."

"And everyone who can't leave?" Kline asked, eyes still on the map. "All those dots who don't have a bunker option?" "We help them by not adding ourselves and our data to the list of things the network can use," Voss said. "If we stay until it takes us, HelixCore becomes a resource, not a countermeasure. If we move beyond its immediate reach, we keep a small chance of hitting it where it's still fragile. I am not calling that salvation. I am calling it necessary."

On the wall, the grid kept moving. In Tokyo, someone scratched the back of their neck at the same moment a man in Berlin did. In São Paulo, a child hummed a note that matched the rumble of a passing bus. In their own city, in a clip they hadn't watched yet, a group of patients in a distant ward lifted their heads together as the building's power cycled. John watched the pins over their region flicker on Singh's globe and felt HelixCore's floor shudder very slightly as another ventilation cycle spun up, a soft, steady pulse that something out there had already learned how to hear.

\

CHAPTER 12

The first checkpoint didn't fall because anyone decided to attack it. It fell because the city shook wrong. The riot line had been thrown together from whatever was left that still wore a badge and fit into body armor: local police in mismatched gear, a few National Guard units drafted in from a base that was now more storage than strategy, helmets fogged at the edges, shields dull with old scuffs and new impacts. They'd parked two armored trucks sideways across the avenue to narrow the funnel, stacked metal barricades in front of them, and filled the gaps with bodies and plastic. Rubber bullet launchers sat across their shoulders. Tear gas canisters bounced idly in gloved hands. Someone had dragged portable floodlights into position so that the intersection looked bright enough to be safe if you didn't listen to the radios. Beyond the blockade, the crowd wasn't chanting or throwing anything. Hundreds of people—Novus bands on wrists, winter clothes hanging off thinner frames, faces slack and oddly intent—advanced in a slow, steady tide. A few hummed under their breath. Some tapped their fingers against their thighs. They weren't looking at the police line. They were looking past it, through it, heads tilting fractionally to follow some vibration the officers couldn't feel.

Body cams caught the first ripple. The front row stepped into the sweet spot between the trucks where the avenue's old steel-and-concrete bones made the ground hum just a little higher, fed by idling engines, floodlight generators, the vibrato of a news helicopter hovering too low overhead. The hum slid through the band Zhao had circled a dozen times on her overlays. The crowd tensed as one. For half a second, they held, every muscle strung tight, hum rising out of their chests into an almost clean note. Then the cluster snapped. It didn't look like a charge; it looked like a circuit shorting. Hands flew in every direction at once—grabbing, shoving, clawing at air—not aimed at the shields so much as trying to find something to discharge through. Bodies surged forward; others jerked sideways. A woman in a red coat was pushed up onto the barricade by the pressure of people behind her and toppled over it into the line, her arms windmilling. Three more went with her without meaning to. Rubber bullets hit torsos and shoulders and limbs, compressing flesh and bone that didn't seem to register pain in the normal way. People flinched, stumbled, bounced, but didn't retreat or raise hands protectively. Tear gas canisters arced into the air, trailing smoke; lungs consumed the irritant as another input, eyes tearing without changing focus. Shields that had been braced against the weight of angry individuals buckled under the undirected kinetic chaos of dozens of bodies trying to move in incompatible directions without any awareness of who was in front of them. Cops went down under their own line as much as the crowd's. Someone screamed over the radio, high and clipped, "They're not stopping—unit twenty-three, they're not stopping—"

Another voice cut in, breathless and too loud in the mic. "Command, they don't see us, they're not looking at us, they're just—Jesus Christ they're climbing the barricade—" The feed from his body cam showed three patients scrambling over the metal: not coordinated like a tactic, but mechanically perfect in timing, each hand and foot placed on different rungs in identical sequences, heads tilted at the same angle toward the floodlight rigs. The barricade shifted on its rubber feet and began to tilt under their weight. The last thing the cam caught before the clip went to static was a wall of people surging toward the lens, arms out, mouths open not in shouts but in a single unbroken note. Somewhere above that, the helicopter pilot swore and swung wide, rotor wash flaring the tear gas back over the line as if the air had decided it wanted in on the experiment.

The footage hit HelixCore in pieces: live relay from the city's emergency feeds, copied police dispatch recordings, a shaky clip uplinked by a news van that had parked too close to novelty. In the operations hub, light from half a dozen screens painted harsh color across faces that had already watched too much. One display showed the checkpoint wide—armored trucks pushed sideways as the crowd flowed around them, bodies climbing and falling and rising again. Another showed the body-cam until it died, then swapped automatically to a car dash feed from a cruiser that had been stationed in reserve, the view trembling as the vehicle rocked with impacts from forces it hadn't been designed to interpret. The audio channel crowded with overlapping voices, some clipped into official codes, more spiraling into raw. "They're not responding to gas—" "Less-lethal ineffective, I repeat, ineffective—" "It's like they don't see the line, they're just going where the ground tells them—" and then a long, wordless yell that cut off mid-consonant.

Voss watched from the front of the room, arms folded tight across her chest, jaw set. John stood a pace behind her shoulder, eyes flicking between panels, cataloguing the way the cluster moved when the generators spun up, the way anything that shook at the wrong rate drew their attention like gravity. He could see his own guards in that gear, his own people holding that line, and the math didn't look any kinder. When one of the feeds flashed red and dropped to a still frame—"SIGNAL LOST"—Zhao's hands moved faster over her console, pulling in new angles, trying to reconstruct a scene that now existed mostly in the kinetic memory of bruised concrete.

"That's three checkpoints in four hours," Singh said from the back, staring down at her tablet where dots marking containment efforts had begun to wink out. "Not lost to riots. Lost to physics."

"Non-lethal assumes somebody is home to decide to back down," Voss said. Her voice didn't rise. It didn't need to. "We're not dealing with intent out there. We're watching overflow. They packed too many nodes into one space, pumped the carrier loud, and the system dumped its error into muscle and bone. Congratulations to everyone who insisted on centralized distribution." She let the silence after that stretch just long enough to be felt, then turned away from the wall and toward the cluster of people who still had some say over what HelixCore did next. "We're done watching," she said. "We leave this city within forty-eight hours."

She didn't say it in a conference room. She said it standing in the operations hub, where no one could pretend it hadn't been anchored to a wall of proof. John's shoulders shifted almost imperceptibly; the rest of him didn't move. Zhao looked up from her screens, fingers pausing mid-keystroke. Singh exhaled once, sharp, and brought her tablet up as if she'd been expecting the call and had just been waiting for its timestamp. Kamran, leaning against a pillar with his arms crossed, straightened.

"We've identified three candidate sites with independent power and minimal Novus penetration," Zhao said, slipping into the new mode like changing lanes. "All of them were more or less mothballed before the outbreak. The one with the cleanest profile is an old atmospheric research facility out in the ridge country, sixty kilometers from the nearest town with a real grid. Diesel generators, solar backup, its own wells, limited wired connectivity we can use and then cut. Local Novus rollout barely started there before everything went sideways. It's off every major vibration corridor." "Summit

Ridge," Singh added, pulling up a satellite shot and projecting it onto a secondary display: three low concrete buildings huddled on a plateau, a thin access road curling away through scrub and snow, towers for weather instruments leaning against a bare sky. "We consulted on one study there five years ago. Good bones. Low profile. Enough lab space to run stripped-down operations. If we go dark and unlisted, it'll take a motivated search to find us."

"Forty-eight hours," Voss repeated. "We cherry-pick what we can move and what we can't afford to lose. Hardware, yes, but information first. Raw data, model archives, primary samples. Everything else is ballast, and sentiment doesn't get a vote. John, I want security treating this place like a ship under evacuation orders. We leave a skeleton crew at most, and only if there's a reason that justifies the risk. Everybody who goes to Ridge does so assuming we do not come back here by choice." John inclined his head once. "Convoy size?" he asked. "As small as you can make it without being stupid," she said. "Closed units only. No hitchhikers. We are not a humanitarian convoy. Zhao, prioritize data redundancy. If Theta-9 ever gets hands on our research, I want anything it learns from us to be something we already accounted for. Singh, triage personnel. We take who we need to keep thinking and doing. Everyone else gets instructions on how to survive in a city that's about to become a test bed." She glanced back at the main wall, where the checkpoint feed had been replaced by a wider city overview of sirens, stalled traffic, and clusters moving like slow currents in a shaken lake. "We are out of time for polite models."

Time outside HelixCore didn't agree to slow down while they planned. While teams downstairs began packing crates with drives, instruments, vials sealed in triple containment, the world's feeds kept bleeding in, more surreal and more consistent with each hour. One pane showed a suspension bridge somewhere west, its traffic frozen into a scattering of abandoned vehicles angled half into each lane. Hundreds of people—some in office clothes, some in shorts and coats thrown over pajamas—walked in lines along the span on foot, not talking, not checking phones. They moved in two dense parallel bands tracking the bridge's support cables, footfalls landing in harmonics that made the structure's engineering overlays light up when Zhao threw them on screen. On another feed, an aerial shot of an empty football stadium flickered in from a news drone: the seats were filled, not by fans, but by Novus bands and bodies standing in perfect rings around the field, each row offset from the next like concentric ripples. No one sat. No one cheered. From the drone's mic, a low hum came up, too unified to be crowd noise.

Airport cameras in another country showed terminals with flights cancelled in red across every board where power still held. People should have been angry, loud, milling in clumps at ticket counters. Instead, clusters stood in loose formations, all facing the same direction: not toward gates or signage, but toward particular structural supports humming with the load from backup generators. A toddler wandered between ankles, completely ignored, stopping now and then to put both hands flat on a vibrating pillar. On a nighttime freeway somewhere else, traffic had dissolved not in a jam but in abandonment. Cars sat in the lanes with doors open, some with engines still running, exhaust curling into the dark. Their drivers and passengers walked along the shoulder and dividing lines in single file, all heading the same way without visible cue, legs eating distance with the same measured, unhurried stride. The road's cameras caught their faces: slack, damp, eyes unfocused, not intoxicated, not terrified. Just tuned.

"Local, national, international," Singh said, marking new pins on her map each time Zhao dropped a fresh incident into the pool. "Everywhere the product went, the network is blooming. Overflow events are still the minority. The majority behavior is... alignment." "Billions of tiny metronomes," Zhao said. "Ticking toward something." "Host density curves match your adoption projections?" Voss asked Havel, who had found his way into the back of the lab, blanket still around his shoulders, a mug that had gone cold dangling from his hand. She didn't turn to look at him; she expected the answer to find its way forward anyway.

"More or less," he said. His voice had sanded down since the server room, quieter but less ragged. "Plus whatever we never logged because governments don't like admitting how much unlicensed production they do when they're desperate. We modeled saturation in metropolitan zones under the assumption of patchy rollout. The reality overshot us in places and undershot in others. But the shape..." He trailed off, then set the mug down on a side console with a small, decisive click. "There's something I didn't show you yesterday."

He said it like a confession he had rehearsed and still hated. In a smaller room off the lab, under a single screen and a table with too many chairs, he pulled up a different set of graphs—ones that had the look of slides never quite polished for presentation. The axes were labeled in shorthand Novus had never expected to translate: HCOUNT, SCALER, EC. One curve tracked host population over time, rising from zero to a plateau at some percentage of the global population. Another curve—the one that made John's stomach tighten even if he didn't know the math—hugged the bottom for a long stretch, then kinked up sharply into a vertical wall near a point marked EC. "Emergent coherence," Havel said, tapping the label with a knuckle. "We modeled three regimes. Phase one: isolated hosts, minimal cross-host influence, scaffold mostly busy knitting itself into local tissue. Phase two: network behavior, clusters forming, information traversal possible across distance but limited by carrier stability. That's where we are now—humming, tapping, overflow when you pack them too tight and shake the floor. Phase three: EC. The organism stops acting like a bunch of independent patterns and starts acting like a single system with preferences." "You've seen this curve before," Voss said.

"Yes," he said. "In simulations we were not allowed to run at scale, done on borrowed compute in off hours. We got far enough to see that there is no smooth glide into that state. It's a threshold. Below it, you have weirdness and coordination. Above it, you have something that can use its hosts the way we use neurons. It's not that it starts 'attacking.' That's our language. It starts optimizing. It starts choosing." He exhaled slowly. "Everything you've seen so far—clusters walking, bridges humming, checkpoints collapsing—that's pre-coherent behavior. It looks intentional because our brains are wired to see intention. It isn't. Not yet. It's a system refining its wiring through local rules. You haven't seen it want anything yet. When it crosses this line"—he tapped EC again—"you will."

"What does it want?" John asked. "If I knew that," Havel said, "I would be less scared. There's no upper limit baked into the math. Given enough hosts and enough carrier stability, it reaches EC and keeps going until it runs out of substrate." "Us," Kamran said. "Us," Havel agreed. "Infrastructure. Anything that vibrates in the right band. We are building its brain and its body at the same time. The only kindness is that emergent systems hit thresholds unevenly. Some areas will tip before others. You might be able to see it happen somewhere else before it happens here—if you live that long."

Back in the hub, another feed demanded attention in the way only live disaster could. A police helicopter camera, stabilized as best it could over the industrial district, showed a strung-out line of warehouses and loading yards under a dull sky. Below, hundreds of figures were moving through the maze of shipping containers and concrete in slow, messy currents. From above, it looked like ants picking their way along scent trails, except that the trails didn't follow the roads or fencing. They followed something else—lines Zhao quickly overlaid with an infrastructure map. Power conduits. Water mains. Tracks where old machinery shook the ground in predictable patterns.

"Rotor frequency?" she asked without looking, already typing. "Fifty-eight hertz standard, variable under load," Rami answered, reading off a spec he hadn't known he'd still remember. "Why?" "Because this—" she gestured at the humming pattern visible in the camera's audio trace "—is sitting just to the left of our favorite disaster band. If the pilot throttles up to hold position in this wind—"

The pilot did. The helicopter's nose dipped, rotors biting deeper, whine climbing. On the ground, the cluster stuttered, then froze. Hundreds of heads snapped up in eerie unison, faces turning toward the sky with the same tiny angle correction. For a heartbeat they looked like puppets whose strings had all been yanked tight. Then the overflow hit. People who had been shuffling began to move with sudden violent precision, not toward each other, but along vectors that intersected with any structure capable of feeding back the vibration—up stacked containers, onto rooftops, toward gantries and cranes. Dozens of bodies broke into a sprint so perfectly matched that their feet left the ground in the same frames. They weren't aiming for the helicopter; they were aligning with its noise, their whole bodies trying to answer it. The cluster slammed into fences, climbed anything that would take their weight, hurled itself against walls.

On the audio, over the hum, the crew's voices cracked through: "Control, we've got— Jesus, they're all looking up—" "You're drifting, Three-Alpha, compensate—" "Why are they running, why are they running—PULL, PULL—" The camera tilted as the helicopter lurched sideways, frame cutting half the scene off, then filling with a smear of sky and spinning ground as the stabilizer lost the battle. For a moment the image showed nothing but the tops of hundreds of heads, all turned toward the flailing machine, mouths open in a sound too low for the mic to catch cleanly. Then the feed went black.

In the sudden quiet of signal loss, the only sound in HelixCore's hub was the building's own hum and the thin rasp of people breathing around it. Zhao's overlays still glowed on screens that no longer had video under them. Singh's global map had just added another red pin over their own industrial district. Somewhere in the building a crate thumped closed as someone downstairs kept packing. Voss stood very still for a long second, eyes on the dead screen as if waiting to see if anything else would bleed through. When it didn't, she spoke without looking away. "It's adapting," she said quietly. "This city will not survive the week."

CHAPTER 13

By the time the sun cleared the gray line of towers, HelixCore was already moving like a ship taking on water. The calm, curated neatness of its floors had been replaced by open racks, bare walls, and carts piled with equipment that looked suddenly fragile outside its usual context. Security had stripped the armory almost to studs; rifles came off racks and into hands, magazines clacked together into bandoliers, spare armor plates slid into carriers, sidearms disappeared under jackets. In the labs, scientists packed data like it was organ tissue—rows of labeled drives vanished into shock cases layered with foam, freezers were emptied into portable units that hummed angrily as they were overloaded, vacuum-sealed cassettes of Theta-9-derived material went into triple containment and were carried by gloved hands with the kind of care usually reserved for explosives. Laptops, tablets, and notebooks with hand-scrawled formulae and diagrams disappeared into duffels, leaving behind only the shadows of dust that marked where they had always lived. The building's tannoy, which usually limited itself to quiet schedule reminders, looped the same message over and over in three languages: "Evacuation phase one in effect. All non-essential systems standing by. Follow your division lead."

Voss moved through it all at a pace that never quite became a run, flanked by a harried assistant and trailed by two security shadows. She treated the floors like a triage ward, stopping in doorways long enough for someone to shove a crate manifest at her or point at two pieces of equipment and ask which lived. "Take this," she said, tapping a freezer unit with one gloved finger. "Leave that. The simulations can be rerun; the raw samples can't. We're not dragging redundancies up a mountain." In imaging she glanced once at a bulky scanner the size of a small car and shook her head. "We can't power it off-grid. Strip it for parts, pack the boards, leave the rest." A postdoc tried to argue for a stack of binders; she put a hand on his shoulder and gently pushed them back onto the shelf. "If it isn't essential to continued survival, it stays," she said. "You have ten seconds to redefine 'essential' without using the word 'career.'" In medical she watched as the last of their Theta-9-compatible assay kits went into a case and snapped it shut herself. "Label this as if you're trying to confuse a very clever thief," she told the tech. "Then carry it like it's your heart."

John spent the morning on the ground and the afternoon on the move, headset pressed to one ear, tablet in hand, squinting at schematics as he threaded his way between pallets and people. The convoys had crystallized into three columns—two ground, one air. Ground One would take heavy gear and noncombat staff toward Summit Ridge by road, using HelixCore's fleet of trucks and requisitioned city vehicles. Ground Two would handle overflow and act as a backup if Ridge proved compromised. The air contingent would fly light and fast, ferrying the most critical personnel and samples out before traffic on the ground became fully impassable. John assigned escorts the way he'd once allocated guards to high-risk trials: minimum necessary, maximum effective. Each truck got a driver with nerves like steel and a guard who knew how to shoot from a moving platform without hitting the wrong thing; the lead and tail vehicles got extra armor and extra guns. The helicopters they'd wrung out of a nervous municipal agency—two aging utility birds, one private charter with its logo hastily taped over—were assigned to pilots who had nerve and no illusions about what they were flying into.

The building felt smaller with every crate that left it. Corridors that had been comfortably crowded yesterday were now choked with motion, voices layered over the constant background hum that had become the metronome of their lives. Someone dropped a case, swore as vials rattled; someone else laughed too hard at a joke that hadn't been funny, the sound clipping short when the tannoy repeated its calm instructions. The air tasted of cardboard dust, coolant, and something sharper that nobody wanted to identify. In the main lobby, crates stacked on dollies waited in neat rows for their turn at the loading bays; security taped over windows that faced outward, more to make themselves feel better than because it would stop anything that had already learned to listen to walls.

It was in the middle of that ordered chaos that the perimeter started to go wrong. It came up from the outer guards as a trickle of radio traffic first—a report of movement near the north fence, more bodies than usual leaving the apartment blocks and moving not toward supply depots or panicked grocery stores, but in a loose, shuffling line straight toward HelixCore. "They're just standing there," one guard said, breath puffing audibly into his mic. "At the fence. Not trying to climb, not talking. Just... listening." In the monitoring room, Zhao pulled up the camera feeds from the north and east perimeters and threw them onto a secondary wall. John was there when the images resolved: a line of people two or three deep, pressed up against the outer fence like iron filings to a magnet. Their hands rested lightly on the mesh, fingers splayed, Novus bands glinting. Their heads were tilted, not toward the building, but toward the fence posts themselves, which hummed faintly with the vibration of the security systems and the city's last flickers of grid power leaking into the ground.

"They're not breaching," someone said behind him. "They're harmonizing," Zhao corrected. "Look." She overlaid a spectral analysis. The fence hum and the micro-movements of the host bodies matched more closely with each passing second;

small misalignments sparked tiny jerks in shoulders and elbows. Then, in one cluster at the far edge of the frame, the misalignment crossed whatever invisible line Theta-9 used for tolerance. Three bodies snapped in place, backs arching, arms flailing—not in anger, but like puppets wrenched by too many strings at once. One slammed their forehead into a fence post hard enough to stagger, bounced back, then did it again and again as if trying to shake something loose. Another grabbed the chain-link and shook it so violently that the post shuddered, rattling the entire run and sending a visible tremor through the line of hosts. The guard nearest that section flinched, stepped back, then moved forward again on reflex, hand out as if to steady a civilian in distress. The moment his palm touched the mesh, three adjacent hosts pivoted and grabbed him with blinding, uncoordinated force —not clawing, not aiming for his throat or his weapon, just seizing the nearest object that could bear the discharge. His helmet cam showed the ground spinning, sky flashing, fence filling the frame in jittering fragments as he went down under the weight of bodies that never once looked him in the eye.

"Pull him back!" someone yelled on comms. Another guard rushed in, tried to haul him clear, caught a wild elbow across the visor that left a spiderweb crack. The thrashing of the hosts intensified, limbs hammering the mesh and the man caught against it. It didn't look like an assault so much as a seizure with too many participants and an unfortunate anchor. From the tower cam, the whole section of fence shivered under the kinetic dump.

"That's enough," John said, voice flat, before anyone else could call for more non-lethal. "North perimeter, this is Command. Rubber is done. Tasers are done. You are authorized to use lethal force on any host physically compromising the fence or staff. Center mass. No warnings. They're not hearing you." There was a beat of silence on the channel as that sank in, then a clipped reply: "Copy, Command. Lethal authorized on overflow. Bringing up live." In the feed, the nearest guard dropped his baton and swung his rifle into his shoulder in a single, practiced motion. He fired three shots into the tangle at the fence, spacing them without drama. Bullets hit torsos; bodies jerked, slumped, slid down the mesh. Those still conscious kept their hands on the metal, humming, some swaying harder now that their neighbors had gone slack. The guard on the ground went limp in their grip. A second burst of fire cut out more of the cluster, giving space for two others to rush in, grab their colleague, and drag him clear. Blood smeared the concrete in an untidy, bright streak. Zhao muttered under her breath as she watched the frequency band she'd been tracking wobble, then resettle. "They adapt to loss," she said. "They rebalance. Fantastic."

John didn't say anything. He watched the north fence shake, saw the first dead host's hand remain hooked through the mesh even as the rest of her body hung boneless below, and mentally crossed a line he'd been inching along since the first humming ward. Whatever was happening outside their walls had stopped being a matter of crowd control. It was a matter of not letting the building itself become a tuning fork.

He stepped out into a quieter side corridor to make the call he'd been putting off since Voss had said the words "this city will not survive the week." Lee picked up on the third ring, not because he was waiting but because he always kept the phone close now; the background noise on his end sounded like an ER—monitors beeping too fast, voices overlapping, the distant rattle of something metal hitting the floor. "If this isn't you," Lee said by way of greeting, "I'm hanging up, because I'm about two minutes away from stapling someone's hand to a gurney for their own safety."

"It's me," John said. He braced his shoulder against the wall, eyes closed for a heartbeat. "How bad?" "How short do you want the list?" Lee said. "We've got six 'cured' patients who keep walking into equipment because it's humming wrong, two who tried to climb the MRI, three nurses who sprained their wrists trying to keep people from pulling monitors off the walls, and a waiting room that's turned itself into a choir. Also, I haven't slept since, I don't know, March. How's your day?" There was a brittle edge to the humor that hadn't been there weeks ago.

"I'm authorizing lethal on my perimeter," John said. No preamble. No cushioning. "We're leaving the city. HelixCore's moving to a remote site." There was a short, stunned silence. "You're… what?" Lee said. "You're just packing up the big brains and leaving?"

"We stay, we get folded in," John said. "We leave, we might figure out how to stop this before it stops having to practice on us. Either way, this place isn't safe. Lee, I need you to walk out of St. Mark's." "Not an option," Lee said immediately. Somewhere on his end, something crashed, followed by a shout and a burst of feedback. He muffled the phone for a second, barked an order—"Restrain him or sedate him, I don't care which, he's about to pull the crash cart over"—then came back, breathing harder. "I have patients." "You have host nodes being used as test equipment," John said. He forced his voice to stay level, to keep the image in his head from bleeding into the words. "What's left of them is being driven by a signal they don't control. You told me last week they hummed when the vents hummed. You know what that means."

"I still see their faces," Lee said quietly. "They still say my name. Some of them."

"They're already gone," John said. It felt like stepping on his own chest. "You know that. This thing is using them like wires, and when the load spikes they're going to break. I will not have you here for that. Get your wife. Walk out. Don't wait for orders. Don't wait for an official evacuation that isn't coming." There was a long rustle on the line, the sound of someone moving through a crowded space with a phone pressed between shoulder and cheek. Lee didn't answer immediately. In the background, someone screamed; something glass shattered. A voice over the intercom began to recite a code that dissolved halfway through into static. "Say it," Lee said finally. "Say what you're actually asking."

"I want you alive," John said. "I'm not going to watch another friend go under because he thought he could hold a line no one else cared about. Get out of the hospital. Go to the airport. There's a window before the network figures out runways are giant metal tuning forks. I'll get a convoy there. You see uniforms, you move toward them. You see hosts clustered around anything that hums, you go the other way. Don't be a hero. You're not equipped for this war."

Lee exhaled something that wasn't quite a laugh. "You sound like you're giving bad advice to a movie paramedic," he said. "She's here," he added, voice shifting as if he'd turned his head. "Anna, it's John. He wants us to run away and leave the day job." A quieter voice in the background asked something sharp and disbelieving; Lee relayed, "She says what about everyone else. And she says she's not leaving me, like that needs saying."

"Everyone else gets whatever time we can buy them with the work we do if we make it out," John said. "Right now, I am asking my brother to get out of a building that's about to become a lab for something that doesn't know the words 'triage' or 'mercy.' Pack nothing you can't carry at a run. If someone tries to stop you, point them at the nearest news feed." "You'd better be there when we get to the airport," Lee said. "If I fight my way through a hospital full of humming not-zombies and you've decided to take a nap, I'm haunting you."

"I'll be there," John said. "Forty-eight hours at most. Probably less." "Then I'll see you on the tarmac," Lee said. "And if this goes sideways, I'm blaming your evacuation plans." He hung up without a goodbye, which was as close to one as either of them ever got when the air felt this thin.

The city did not wait for their schedules. Roads that had been merely bad in the morning went feral by afternoon. Feeds from traffic cams showed bridges trembling under the weight of stopped vehicles and the slow, unnatural currents of hosts moving on foot along resonant spans. Once-busy avenues had become graveyards of abandoned cars, doors left open, hazard lights blinking weakly until batteries died. People stood in lines facing blank building walls where old air conditioning units still rattled; they pressed their palms to the metal and swayed in time, oblivious to the swirl of smoke from distant fires or the occasional siren that still managed to cut through. Police radios, what was left of them, devolved into overlapping screams, clipped commands, and then dead air as repeaters failed or were simply switched off. A National Guard unit tasked with holding a junction reported "mass psychosis, non-responsive to verbal commands, cluster behavior escalating with every truck we park here," and then did not report anything else. Transformers blew one by one across the grid, each bang sending another set of pins onto Singh's map.

HelixCore felt the pressure at its edges. At the south loading bay, a flatbed truck groaned under the weight of an equipment crate as the lift jammed mid-rise, hydraulics protesting; three guards pushed from below while a fourth cursed and kicked at the control box. Overhead, floodlights flickered as the city grid surged and bucked. On the east side, where the perimeter hugged a narrow service road, a small convoy of sedans and vans had pulled up nose-to-tail outside the gate without authorization—civilians who knew or suspected that HelixCore still held some kind of order. They pressed against the fence, some shouting, some simply clutching bags and children and staring at the building like it might grow doors just for them. When a guard tried to wave them back, half a dozen hosts further down the line turned their heads as one, drawn not by the voice but by the tingling change in the fence's vibration as hands pounded it. It took three warning shots into the air and one into the thigh of a man who had started to climb before they broke off—spiraling, not retreating, their feet carrying them along some invisible contour line toward a different hum.

They lost one of their own near the west tower when the generators hiccuped. The power transfer sent a shiver through the structure that nobody would have noticed a month ago; now CCTV caught three hosts out beyond the fence stiffening, then lurching toward the section of wall where the vibration peaked. One was too far gone to be stopped by a warning shout. She hit the fence at a run, hands extended, and for a heartbeat the mesh became a conduit between the building's hum and whatever was riding in her head. She convulsed, feet kicking, shoulders slamming. A young guard in the tower, who hadn't yet seen 4B or the devastated checkpoints, reacted on reflex instead of training; he left his post, sprinted down the stairs, and tried to pry her fingers loose. Two more hosts arrived while he was struggling. Their arms locked around him, not in a calculated grab, but in the wild, all-direction seizure of bodies hitting overflow. The tower camera caught a last jittering glimpse of his helmet disappearing under thrashing limbs before the feed cut out as his head hit the base of the tower and his visor shattered. By the time the response team arrived and shot the bodies off him, his neck had already given.

That death went onto the same internal log as the lost checkpoints and the downed helicopter. It changed nothing about the schedule. If anything, it tightened it. Crates moved faster. People stopped asking whether they would come back and started asking only whether they were on the list to go.

When the first convoy rolled out, the sky over the city had gone the flat, metallic color that meant evening was coming without promising a sunset. The lead trucks nosed through the inner gates, armor plates glinting dully, escort vehicles bristling with guns and makeshift grill guards. Beyond the fence, hosts clustered in pockets along the road, drawn to light poles, transformer boxes, anything that still hummed. They watched the vehicles pass with that same odd, misaligned attention—eyes tracking the air between bumpers rather than the men with rifles behind the glass. Once, when a truck hit a pothole and bounced hard enough to send a rude shock up through its frame, a small group of hosts flinched in perfect unison, arms jerking up, then settling again.

The route to the airport was not long in terms of kilometers. It was longer in terms of what it had become. Abandoned cars forced the convoy off the main arteries and onto access roads that ran behind warehouses and along drainage ditches. Twice they had to stop while guards got out to physically shove vehicles aside, boots slipping on spilled groceries and broken glass. Once they drove past a half-collapsed overpass where a mass of hosts stood lined along the remaining span, all facing the same jagged crack in the concrete, humming softly to a rebar cage that sang back at them in its own slow way.

St. Mark's sat three blocks off their path, close enough that John could have ordered a detour. He didn't. He watched its dark outline slide by between buildings, emergency lights flickering in some of the windows, and trusted that Lee and Anna were already gone. His radio chirped once with a burst of static that resolved into a partial transmission from somewhere in that direction—screams, a crash, a single hoarse voice yelling for restraints—and then nothing. He did not ask for a repeat.

The airport perimeter came up under them like the edge of a different country. What had been a chain-link fence topped with coils of razor wire was now a suggestion—sections torn down, others standing only because no one had bothered with them yet. Floodlights ringed the tarmac, some burned out, others flickering on and off in a pattern that had nothing to do with any human schedule. The runways themselves lay under a low haze of exhaust and dust. Hosts occupied the spaces between: standing in loose rings around idle aircraft, lining up perpendicular to runway markings, clustering at the bases of light towers with their hands pressed to the metal. The hum here was deeper, a layered thing built from generator thrum, idling engines, and the distant whine of a plane somewhere behind the terminal trying and failing to spin up. Every time that whine climbed a notch, hundreds of heads turned toward it, bodies swaying, feet rearranging minutely as if answering a call they couldn't quite hear yet.

The convoy's engines drew attention like a fresh cut in water. As the lead truck pushed through the broken perimeter and onto the service road skirting the runway, heads snapped toward it in waves. Some hosts peeled away from their posts and began to walk toward the sound, steps slow but unnervingly synchronized. They didn't run. They didn't shout. They just redirected, attention sliding from light poles and fuselages to the new source of vibration.

"Stay tight," John said over the local channel as the convoy fanned into a loose defensive wedge. "Hostile status unknown. Do not fire unless they touch the vehicles or block the path. We're not here to clear the field. We're here to pick up and get out." He stepped down from the second truck with his rifle already up, boots hitting tarmac that buzzed faintly underfoot. The air smelled of jet fuel, sweat, and the metallic tang of fear. Smoke from somewhere near the terminal curled low and greasy across the lights.

He scanned the terminal façade and the access doors, looking for two specific figures in a world suddenly full of wrong ones. For a second all he saw were shapes: hosts pressed against the glass inside, palms flat, facing structural beams; security personnel clustered near a service entrance, guns out, trying to decide whether they were defending against people or noise. Then the side door banged open hard enough to hit the wall, and Lee stumbled out with Anna half a step behind him, both of them carrying bags that had clearly been packed in a hurry and deemed just light enough to run with. Lee had a smear of someone else's blood across his cheek; Anna's hair was pulled back in a rough knot, her eyes too wide and too focused at the same time. Behind them, down the corridor, someone screamed and then kept screaming.

"John!" Lee yelled, spotting the convoy, voice cracking across the open space. Hosts between them and the trucks turned their heads, tracking the sound, but did not move faster. Not yet. John moved toward them, rifle up, keeping his body between them and the nearest cluster. "Get behind me," he said when they reached him, breath tight. "Stay down. We don't have long."

As if to underline the point, somewhere on the far side of the field a jet engine finally managed to catch. The whine climbed into the band Zhao hated, a rising mechanical howl that turned into a steady roar. Across the tarmac, every host who could hear it stopped whatever they were doing and pivoted toward the noise in a perfectly smooth, perfectly wrong motion, as if the sound had reached down their spines and pulled.

CHAPTER 14

The airport sounded wrong even before the first shot. It wasn't one noise so much as a stack of them: generators growling in gated rhythm outside the terminal, light towers humming as their housings shook in the wind, metal stairways rattling against fuselages when someone ran up them, fuel pumps whining, distant baggage tugs clanking over uneven concrete, the deep, physical thrum of two aircraft engines spooling on standby. Underneath it all, like bass bleeding through a wall, the city itself was collapsing —something heavy going down somewhere far away, sirens rising and cutting off, transformers popping with dull, heavy bangs that rolled through the ground and up into the bones. The tarmac turned all of it into a bowl, catching vibration and feeding it back. The hosts loved it. They stood in scattered rings around light poles and landing gear, hands brushing rails and ladders, heads tilted to drink in the resonance. Every time a generator cycled or an engine note changed, a ripple went through them—fingers flexing, chests expanding, feet shuffling in tiny, synchronized corrections.

HelixCore jammed itself into the gaps in that sound. Pilots checked controls in cockpits washed in emergency lighting, shouting over the radio at ground crew who were half loading, half pushing people up the gangways faster than the lines liked. Scientists wrestled heavy cases into cargo holds and lashed them to nets, shouting serial numbers to one another as if saying them aloud would keep them real. Med techs strapped down coolers that hummed with their own internal refrigeration, Theta-9 samples locked into foam cradles, lids taped and retaped. Someone carried a crate of drives up a narrow set of stairs with both arms wrapped around it like a child; someone else guided a limping security officer toward a ramp, one hand on his back, the other on the butt of her rifle. Voss moved in the midst of it with a headset clamped to one ear and a tablet balanced in one hand, voice clipped and precise as she bounced between ground frequency, control tower, and HelixCore's shrinking operations hub. "Flight One, you lift as soon as you're heavy enough to justify the fuel. Flight Two, you're on a three-minute clock behind them, not five. Nobody waits for perfect manifests, you understand me? We're not running a ferry service."

John saw the field as circles and lines instead of chaos. He stood on the service apron between two hangars, watching the runways, the clusters, the planes, and the half-open gaps in the perimeter all at once, then pointed with the barrel of his rifle as he started assigning positions. "Kline, you're east side," he said. "Top of that tug ramp, good angle on the main runway threshold. Rami, take the maintenance scaffold by the south hangar, you'll see anyone drifting in from the access road. Simmons, tower base ladder, mid-way, not all the way up —you fall, I'm not wasting a man fetching you. Reyes, Dunn, you're on the ground with me, mobile. You see anything that looks like it's thinking about stepping onto the asphalt where a wheel's going to be, you tag it or tell someone who can." He thumbed his radio. "Perimeter net, this is Renner. Call your quadrants and set your rules. We're not clearing the field. We're buying time. No warning shots, no hero tackles. If they get inside fifty meters of the runway or touch anything with an engine, you put them down. Clean. No drama."

Kline climbed the tug ramp with her rifle slung across her back and a satchel of spare magazines banging against her hip, then settled behind the low metal lip as if she'd been born there. Rami made the maintenance scaffold faster, three rungs at a time, then went prone on the grated platform, barrel resting in the V between two bolts. Simmons took his spot halfway up the tower's exterior ladder where the concrete base still provided some hard cover, wedging his boot through the rungs for extra stability. The two guards John had inherited at the airport, local uniforms with the hollow-eyed look of people who'd been defending the wrong things for too long, checked their magazines twice and fell in on either side of him without needing to be told which direction to face.

The first wave was almost gentle. Hosts drifted in from the shattered perimeter like debris carried on a tide, in twos and threes and fives. They weren't running; they walked with the same steady, eerie pacing John had seen on the bridges, hands brushing anything metal they passed—railings, ground equipment, the sides of parked baggage carts. Some hummed under their breath in tones that flirted with the edge of the engine frequencies; others were silent, lips parted, breath visible in the cooling air. Their heads tracked the nearest strong vibration: a light tower shivering in the wind, a generator's steady rumble, the coughing spin of a test engine. When a cluster strayed too close to the cleared stripe of runway the pilots had declared non-negotiable, John gave the word and somebody fired.

For a while it was almost a drill. Rami's voice, calm and clipped in John's earpiece: "Two heads at my twelve, forty meters, drifting left." Kline's follow-up: "I've got the one with the orange hood." One shot cracked from her ramp; downrange, the host in the hood folded as if a string had been cut, body skidding on the asphalt before coming to a stop. Simmons picked off another that had wandered too close to a fuel truck, his round snapping the host's shoulder back and spinning them away. The two guards on the ground moved with John in a loose, shifting triangle, rifles sweeping. It wasn't mercy—there was no illusion they were saving anyone out there—but it also wasn't rage. Targets were just problems in the wrong position. They solved them one at a time. "Three mags left,"

Simmons muttered after twenty minutes, not to complain but to log it. "Four here," Kline replied. "Don't worry, I'm a better shot than you." "If we get to zero, I'm throwing you instead," Rami said.

The jokes were brittle, but they held the rhythm. Planes took it in turns to taxi and line up; ground crew scrambled to pull chocks, swing stairs away, wave them forward with glow batons. Voss stalked between loading areas like a conductor, pulling frequency charts up on her tablet with one hand while she swore at a control tower that had lost half its automation and most of its patience. For almost half an hour, the pattern held: cluster approaches, shot, cluster turns away or falls, runway stays clear, the first aircraft rolls and hauls itself into the bruised sky, engines shaking the field hard enough that every host on the ground swayed and turned to follow it with their eyes until it vanished into cloud. It didn't last. It never does.

"Perimeter, this is Zhao," came the voice from HelixCore's still-breathing ops hub, strained thin by distance and bad connections. "We've got drone eyes up over the city. Renner, you need to hear this." She didn't wait for permission; the channel crackled, then filled with another feed piped into his HUD—grainy overheads of bridges and avenues. People were moving along them. Not dozens. Hundreds. Thousands. From above they looked like slow rivers of gray and dark clothing threading their way out of the urban grid, filling highways abandoned by cars, crowding overpasses that shook under their weight. They weren't wandering. They were aligning. Every path, every flow, bent toward the airport.

"They're leaving the city," Zhao said, and John could hear the quiet horror riding under the clinical. "Every major structure that can carry vibration is bleeding hosts. Flight paths, tunnels, tram lines—the network is consolidating. You're the loudest thing for miles. You're also the biggest tuning fork.

You've got massive inbound from all quadrants."

On the ground, the second wave started as a change in density. Where there had been gaps, there were none now; where hosts had trickled in, they came in sheets, filling every access road, every gap between hangars, every drainage ditch. They were still walking, not charging, but the sheer mass of them changed the equation. When one cluster drifted too close and someone fired, the bodies that fell created obstacles the others flowed around, adjusting in micro-synchronized eddies without ever looking down. The humming got louder—not because individual voices were raised, but because there were more throats vibrating the air. The tarmac under John's boots seemed to buzz harder with every passing minute.

It happened fast when it came apart. A fuel truck, left half-emptied near the edge of the field, went over when a host stumbled into its rear wheel at the exact moment a light tower beside it completed one last sway. The combined shock vibrated up through rusted welds that had been waiting for an excuse; the tower groaned and came down sideways, its head smacking the truck's tank hard enough to rupture a seam. Fuel spilled in a fast, shining sheet, running toward a cluster of baggage carts and an open maintenance pit. Someone yelled for everyone to back off; someone else fired at a host who had slipped in the slick and grabbed the nearest thing—which happened to be the damaged light tower. Sparks leapt from metal scraping metal.

The ignition wasn't a fireball. It was worse: a low, blue-white whoosh that rolled along the ground, setting the spilled fuel alight in a racing wave. The shock knocked John and his two ground guards off their feet, heat punching at their faces and exposed wrists. In his ear, three channels bled at once—Kline swearing as her position rocked under the shock, Rami coughing from smoke, Simmons shouting something about losing line of sight. When John's vision cleared, the burning fuel had carved a new barrier across the apron: a jagged, flickering wall between him and most of his team, between him and the main path back to the runway. Beyond the fire, hosts were already flooding in, drawn by the heat shimmer and the noise, bodies outlined briefly as dark silhouettes as they passed in front of the flames. "Boss, you're cut off," Kline said, voice tight. From her angle she could see what he couldn't. "You've got a river of them moving in from your three and nine. We can try to—" "No," John said, pushing himself upright, testing ankles and knees in one efficient sweep. Everything hurt, but nothing felt broken. He racked his rifle, checked the chamber by touch, and glanced at the nearest cluster already pivoting his way, drawn by the ring of bullets cooking off in the heat of the fallen light tower. "You stay on your lines. If the runway goes, this evac dies and we did all this for nothing. Hold your fields of fire. That's an order." "John," Lee's voice came over a different channel, ragged. "Where are you? They're closing the cabin door, we're— I can hear gunfire, that better not be you."

"Keep Anna's head down," John said. He started moving without waiting for agreement, angling not back toward the main group but sideways, into the cluttered service zone behind the hangars where fuel trucks, old tugs, and cargo pallets made a broken maze. The hosts tracked him immediately; he could feel their attention like heat between his shoulder blades as he fired a short, sharp burst into the side of an empty steel container just to his right. The rounds hit with a deep, resonant clang that set the metal ringing like a struck bell. Every host within earshot turned toward the sound in near-perfect unison and began to walk. "John, answer me," Lee said. Somewhere behind his voice engines whined louder, cabin noises rising as people shuffled into seats, overhead bins slammed.

"I'm working," John said. He kept his breathing steady, boots hitting tarmac in a rhythm that wouldn't waste oxygen. "Get on that plane. That's the job now. You live. That's an order." "Fuck your orders," Lee snapped, and there was the old heat, the old stubbornness, even over a line crackling with interference. "You don't get to—"

The channel cut in and out as John ducked behind a row of abandoned tugs, their paint flaked, their tires flat. He fired again, this time into the strut of a light tower base ahead of him. The shot made the bolt ring; the tower hummed in sympathy, a vibration that ran out through the ground in a circle. Hosts nearest the runway wavered, some turning away from the planes, pulled by the new song. He watched them pivot and smiled without humor. "I do get to," he said, not sure if Lee could still hear him and not caring. "You want to pay me back, you do it by being on the far end of this when we figure out how to kill it."

Another voice slid into his headset, Voss's this time, flat and compressed. "Renner, report." In the background he could hear hydraulic doors closing, the muffled bark of orders being obeyed in cramped metal spaces. "Runway still clear," he said. "First bird away. Second spinning." He ducked as a host, closer than he'd thought, lurched at him from behind a luggage cart, arms flailing. It wasn't aimed, just wild. He stepped inside the reach, shoved the host sideways into the metal frame, and put a round through their chest as they rebounded. The body collapsed, knees folding. "I'm drawing overflow into the service field." "That's not what I asked," Voss said.

"You asked if you still have a runway," he said, firing again into a stack of cargo pallets. The wood splintered, the steel frame behind them sang, hosts turned. "You do. Your job is getting those planes off the ground. My job is making sure there's somewhere for them to roll. Stick to your job, Doctor. I'll stick to mine." There was a long pause on her end that held more than static. "You're not a sacrificial asset, Renner," she said at last. "Good news," he replied. "I'm not planning on being one." He cut the channel before she could answer, switching his focus back to the simpler, cleaner language of position and angle.

He kept moving. Through the tugs. Past a collapsed utility shed whose roof had caved in under some earlier shock, leaving twisted sheets of corrugated metal underfoot that complained with every step. Around a parked fuel bowser that still stank of the spill from earlier, its hoses coiled like dead snakes. He fired in short, deliberate bursts into anything that would ring —steel beams, light poles, the side of a derelict container— never wasting rounds on flesh unless a host got close enough to touch him. The bullets turned the service field into a defective instrument, notes echoing off metal and concrete. The hosts followed each one like sharks following blood, heads swiveling, feet changing course. Where they moved toward him, they moved away from the runway. Behind him, engines climbed, a second aircraft hauling itself down the strip.

His magazine ran dry with a hollow click he knew better than most. He dropped it, slapped another home from the pouch at his hip, and kept going. Three magazines, he counted without conscious effort. Then two. Then one, heavy in his hand when he checked by weight. The last one went into the rifle with the same care as the first. He didn't hurry; hurrying led to fumbling. He had no rounds to waste correcting a mistake.

Somewhere between the first and second plane lifting, his comms died. It wasn't dramatic. One moment he had the murmur of his team in his ear—Rami calling shots, Kline swearing at a jam, Simmons giving a steady count of how many hosts he'd dropped in his quadrant—the next it was just static and the damp thud of his own pulse. Maybe the fire had cooked a repeater. Maybe a transformer had finally gone. Maybe he'd simply run past the edge of the field their battered radios could cover. He flicked the dial through the usual channels once, confirmed there was nothing but the distant hiss of an overloaded spectrum, and let it go. The work didn't change.

The field grew narrower without his noticing, the clutter more complete. Containers stacked three high formed canyons of metal on his left; a drainage trench full of dark water and twisted rebar cut off his right. Ahead, a hangar door that had buckled inward when something heavy fell against it earlier now slumped across its rails like a dead thing, leaning at an angle that turned the gap behind it into a cul-de-sac. He realized what he'd done only when he rounded the last corner of containers and saw the space close in: the collapsed door, the wall of older cargo bins stacked tight, the trench running across the only open path. No clear way through without doubling back.

The hosts filled the gap behind him in a steady, relentless spill. Dozens of them, maybe more, moving into the service alley with the same unsettling lack of haste as before. They weren't sprinting. They weren't screaming. They simply kept coming, feet hitting the tarmac in a pattern that was just off enough from normal walking to make his skin crawl—a fraction too aligned, each step landing almost, but not quite, together. The hum of the field pressed in, rebounding off metal, vibrating up through his boots. He raised the rifle anyway. There was no sense in not using what was left. He picked the closest three in the front of the pack: a woman in a torn business skirt, a teenager in a hoodie with the logo long since smudged into gray, an older man in a hospital gown and someone else's shoes. One shot, center mass, the recoil a familiar, solid push. The woman dropped, legs going out from under her. Second shot, the hoodie jerked backward and folded. Third, the older man spun and crashed into the side of a cargo bin, leaving a smear on the metal as he slid down.

He squeezed again. The hammer fell on an empty chamber with a dry, useless click. For a moment he considered racking the bolt, muscle memory insisting, then dismissed it. The gun was done. He swung it once by the barrel and hurled it at the oncoming line. It bounced off a chest and clattered to the ground; the host it struck staggered half a step, then corrected and kept walking. None of them looked down at it.

John flexed his hands once, feeling the sting of split skin on his knuckles, the bruised ache where earlier impacts had left their marks. His breath misted in front of him in quick, even puffs. There was nowhere to go that wasn't through them, and "through them" had stopped being an option three magazines ago. He rolled his shoulders back as if he were about to pick up another crate, squared his stance on the cracked tarmac, and met the line head-on. His face didn't change. There was no prayer, no last words, just a tired, wry twist at the corner of his mouth. "Figures," he said.

The wall of bodies reached him a heartbeat later. Hands closed over his arms, his shoulders, the front of his vest—not clawing, not striking, just making contact. He had time to register the heat of skin, the smell of sweat and engine exhaust caught in cloth, the low vibration running through their bones and into his. Then the world snapped off. No pain. No slow fade. Just an instant, total blackout, like someone had reached into the scene and yanked the plug.

CHAPTER 15

Cold came first. Not as weather, not as an idle breeze, but as a flat, metallic chill pressed into the side of his face, seeping slowly into bone. John surfaced on that, aware of temperature before he was aware of his name, the way his cheek stuck slightly to dust and grit, the faint sting when he moved his jaw. His ears rang with a thin, steady tone, and under it something deeper thrummed—a low, continuous hum that made the air feel thicker than it should have been. He stayed still for a long few seconds, eyes closed, cataloguing without moving: concrete beneath him, rough and cracked; something harder edging into his ribs—metal, not sharp enough to be a real hazard; light against his eyelids grey and diffuse, not the orange flicker of fire. No immediate heat on his skin. No weight pinning him down. No hands. No impact that matched the last clear moment: the press of bodies, the feel of fingers closing around his vest, the world snapping into black like a switch thrown.

He opened his eyes a slit. The sky above him looked washed out, pale as old paint. Not night. Not the harsh blot of floodlights. Morning, maybe, or what passed for it through city haze. The ringing in his ears settled into a wider noise—the kind that had no single source but made everything feel like it was vibrating: distant engines, failing transformers, the ghost of an aircraft that might have taken off hours ago. He tried a breath. His chest expanded without protest, ribs aching in a dull way that promised bruises but nothing worse. He tasted dust, fuel, a faint chemical tang that could have been burned plastic.

He moved his fingers next, flexing them in the grit. All of them answered. No splints, no tape. No broken shapes. His left hand found the edge of the metal he was lying against—a chunk of collapsed scaffolding or container skin—cold enough to make his knuckles ache. His right hand slid automatically to his hip, to where the familiar weight of his sidearm should have been. Empty holster. No strap. He patted lower, found only the rough canvas of his pants and the press of his own leg. His chest rig felt lighter too. The rifle that should have been across it wasn't there. The strap was gone, or he was out of it.

He pushed up onto one elbow. Pain flared along the side of his head, sharp and localized, radiating from the same old scar Voss's scans had once flagged as "interesting" and never fully explained. He reached up and found a swelling ridge along his hairline, half-dried blood at the edge, but his fingers came away without sticking to anything fresh. No teeth marks. No tears in the skin where nails had dug. His throat was unpunctured. His vest was scuffed but intact. His radio, when he thumbed the toggle, answered with a faint, dead click and the same background hum.

He took that in, slowly, with the same patience he'd used on after-action reports: wall of hosts, hands on him, network burning under their skin, then blackout. He should have been torn apart, bones broken under the weight, or at the very least woken up in pieces. Instead he was sitting on cold concrete in a field that still hummed with someone else's catastrophe, and his body, by all immediate measures, was in one piece. That fact went on a short internal list labeled "wrong," alongside the hum and the missing gear.

The world resolved as he pushed himself upright. He was in the service field behind the hangars, though it took a second to align the scene with his last clear memory. The collapsed hangar door still lay at an angle across its rails to his left, metal skin dented, paint blistered where the fire had kissed it. Beyond it, stacks of cargo containers loomed three high in crooked rows, some with corners buckled from impacts, others blackened on one side. The drainage trench that had turned his retreat into a dead end still gaped to his right, full of stagnant water and twisted rebar. Above it all, light towers leaned at uneasy angles, some with their housings shattered, glass teeth glittering on the tarmac below.

And people. Hosts.

They were everywhere. Not in a screaming mass, not in the frantic overflow of the checkpoints or the warehouse, but drifted across the field and beyond it in a loose, unsettling scatter, like debris after the tide goes out. Dozens in his immediate sightline. Hundreds if he extended that to the rest of the apron, the taxiways, the streets visible through the gaps in the perimeter fence. They walked or stood in small knots, heads angled, hands brushing rails, ladders, the sides of burned-out vehicles. Some faced the hangar walls with their palms flat against the corrugated metal, humming low. Others pressed against the skeletal remains of ground equipment, attention turned not to the man pushing himself to his feet ten meters away but to whatever vibration the metal fed back into their bones. None of them were looking at him.

John stayed very still, breaths shallow, eyes moving. One host—middle-aged, jacket torn, shoes soaked—wandered past within arm's reach, following the jagged path of a crack in the tarmac. Her shoulder brushed his as she went by, a light, incidental contact. She did not flinch. She did not pause. She did not tilt her head as if she'd noticed heat or movement. Her gaze stayed fixed on the broken line in the concrete, as if the way it split the vibration mattered more than the fact she'd just touched another living person.

He waited. Another passed, close enough that the hem of a coat snagged briefly on his boot. No reaction. A man in a fuel-stained jumpsuit walked perpendicular to them, eyes glassy, hands hovering an inch from the air above a length of exposed conduit. He moved around John without looking at him, feet adjusting to avoid collision with the casual precision of someone navigating a bollard or a piece of uninteresting equipment. John's hand twitched toward the space where his pistol should have been, then stopped halfway. Drawing on reflex when reflex didn't match reality was how bystanders got shot. These were no bystanders. They were something else now, something that should have been as hostile to him as to any other interference. And yet they stepped around him as if his presence had been subtracted from the field.

He got his feet under him slowly, keeping his profile low, waiting seconds between each shift of weight to see if anything in the drifting human debris around him changed. Nothing did. No heads snapped toward him. No hum altered pitch. The broader sound of the city rolled under everything, a low, omnipresent vibration that made the metal under his boots buzz faintly. The hosts' movements aligned with that, not with him. He picked one—an older man in an airport ground-crew vest, salt-and-pepper hair plastered to his forehead with old sweat, Novus band glinting faintly at his wrist—and stepped directly into his path. The man's gait didn't change. At the last instant, his feet adjusted in a tiny, precise half-step, sliding around John without the slightest sign that his eyes had registered an obstacle. If John had been a signpost, a bollard, a shadow, the movement would have been the same.

He lifted his hand and waved it in front of the man's face, once, twice, fingers splayed, palm almost touching the bridge of his nose. No blink. No flinch. The man's gaze stayed locked somewhere beyond, pupils unfocused, mouth parted just enough to show dry teeth. His breath came in a slow, even rhythm that had nothing to do with effort and everything to do with whatever the network had set as baseline. John stepped aside again, out of the stream, heartbeat steady because he did not see the point of letting it do anything else.

He marked the facts, stacked them neatly. They brushed him. They went around him. They didn't see him.

He tested sound next. Moving through the service field, he picked up a small chunk of metal from the ground—something that had once been part of a ladder rung, bent and rusted at one end—and weighed it in his hand. Three hosts stood nearby with their palms pressed to a cargo bin, humming softly, heads tilted as if listening to something inside it. He tossed the metal at their feet without much force. It clanged when it hit the tarmac, a small, sharp sound. The closest host flinched, not toward the source but toward the bin, fingers digging into the corrugations. The humming bumped up a fraction of a note then settled again. None of them looked at him.

He stamped his boot once on a scrap of sheet steel lying half-loose over a drainage channel. The impact made the plate jump and ring, a flat, ugly note that vibrated under his sole. The three hosts by the bin snapped off their current hum in the same instant and turned, heads swiveling together toward the metal plate, bodies aligning with the line of vibration as it propagated through the ground. One took a step, hand stretching out as if to touch the edge. John stepped back from the sheet, letting the contact break, watching. As soon as the plate settled and the ringing faded, their attention bled back to the cargo bin.

He spoke then, quietly, just above a whisper. "Hey." No movement. He tried louder. "Stop." The word sounded small and pointless against the backdrop of the city's roar. If it had any effect, he couldn't see it. The hosts stayed locked on their structures, on their hums. He stepped closer to one, so close that he could see the stale sweat stains on the collar of his shirt, the small nick in the stubble along his jaw where he must have cut himself shaving some other lifetime ago. John exhaled deliberately in his face, breath warm in the chill air. No blink. No change.

They weren't reading him. They weren't sampling him. Whatever carrier signal Theta-9 had learned to love, whatever pattern it listened for, he wasn't broadcasting it. To them, he was a null point in the field—a patch of concrete that happened to move. The system worked around him the way water flowed around something that didn't conduct. He moved out of the immediate tangle of service equipment and into a slightly clearer strip that ran along the backs of the hangars toward what had once been the perimeter fence. The gate was a twisted suggestion now; sections lay flattened where vehicles had driven through or been pushed over, others bent inward by the steady pressure of bodies and time. Beyond it, the access road stretched away between low industrial buildings, every flat surface turned into a stage for hosts to press hands against, lean on, tune to. Streetlights buzzed with whatever power they had left, their poles wrapped in human attention. The air felt colder here, the shadows longer.

He walked. Slowly at first, then with more confidence as it became clear the system would not suddenly notice him and correct whatever oversight had spared him. He moved through clusters, around individual figures who adjusted their paths with that same unconscious avoidance pattern, past a child sitting on the curb with a toy car forgotten in her lap as she stared at a storm drain grate vibrating with runoff. The hosts never turned their heads to follow him. They never tracked his warmth, his breath, the sound of his steps. They followed the hum. He was absence, nothing more.

It would have been almost easy to believe, for a few minutes, that the whole world had simply stopped caring about him. He knew better. Systems didn't ignore anomalies because they were polite. They ignored them because they couldn't see them —or because something about the anomaly sat outside the rules they were built on. He'd been touched by the network, inside the wall of bodies. It had hit him hard enough to blank his world. And then it had let go. Not devoured, not rewritten. Disconnected.

Dead node. The first time he noticed her, he wrote it off as coincidence. The second time, it moved into a different file.

He'd turned off the airfield and onto the access road, following it past a low row of maintenance sheds toward the skeleton of a parking garage where more hosts stood along the rails in neat, evenly spaced lines, their hands resting on the metal as if they were afraid it might float away. The road itself was littered with abandoned vehicles—cars left at odd angles, one still idling until its fuel finally ran out, a police cruiser with both doors open and its light bar dead. He threaded through them in a path chosen more by clear footing than destination. Three times, when he glanced back over his shoulder to check the density behind him, he saw the same figure at the edge of his peripheral vision. Just far enough not to register as an immediate threat. Just close enough that, when mapped over his last remembered position, she occupied the same rough slice of space. Plenty of hosts were moving in roughly the same direction; the network didn't do lines so much as flows now. But something about the consistency nagged.

He tested it without breaking stride. At the next intersection—a T where one arm of the road curved back toward the cargo warehouses and the other ran toward the distant fuzz of the city proper—he slowed, then turned down the less attractive branch, the one with more obstacles, more debris. Behind him, most of the hosts continued straight, pulled by some stronger hum ahead. One peeled with him. He walked another twenty meters, then cut sharply around the front of a delivery van and crossed to the other side of the street. The drifting human field parted and rejoined around him. She altered course with the same slow, unhurried persistence, her path bending to match his.

He stopped by a toppled streetlight whose bulb housing lay

shattered in the gutter, its pole bent in a rough V where it had hit the hood of a car. He crouched there, ostensibly to look at the skid marks on the road—evidence of some earlier panicked attempt to brake before impact—but really to see what she did. The hosts closest to him shuffled past, hands dragging along the dented metal of the light pole, attention locked on the screeching note it made as it flexed under their touch. She came to a halt just beyond arm's reach, facing him. Not the pole. Not the car. Him.

He deliberately refused to look at her properly. Not yet. He kept his attention on the asphalt, tracing the black lines scraped into it. She didn't move on. When he stood, she stood more fully upright too. When he took three steps forward, she matched the distance, neither gaining nor losing. He moved left around a stalled bus; she tracked around the other way, meeting him at the far corner. When he stopped under the sagging remnants of a pedestrian overpass and listened, pretending to be interested in the way the structure echoed the city's hum, he could hear her breathing behind him—too steady, too smooth, not quite in time with anything else. Anomalous behavior, he thought, and finally turned to look.

She was younger than he expected, though he knew her age; knowing numbers and seeing bodies weren't the same thing. Early twenties that had been rubbed down to something more childlike by illness and neglect. Her hair was shorter than in the images he'd seen—cropped roughly at the shoulders as if someone had taken scissors to it in a hospital bathroom without caring about straight lines. It hung limp, greasy, strands stuck to her cheeks. She wore a hoodie three sizes too big, faded navy with some college logo flaking off the front, over the thin, patterned cotton of a hospital gown that peeked from under the hem. Her legs were bare from mid-thigh to the top of socks that didn't match, one sliding down around her ankle, one pulled up. Her shoes were cheap canvas, soaked and darkened, laces trailing. There was a hospital wristband on her right arm, paper edges softened by time but not yet torn. The plastic clasp caught the light when she moved.

Her face carried more specific details, the kind that had been turned into bullet points and slides: the faint white scar cutting through her left eyebrow in a short arc, won in some childhood accident that the news stories had turned into a charming anecdote; the slight asymmetry at the corners of her mouth; the way her eyes were set just a fraction wide, giving her an alert, intent look in every interview he'd been forced to sit through. Now those eyes—brown, bloodshot, ringed with bruised hollows—were fixed on him. Not on a light pole. Not on a humming transformer. On him.

He didn't reach for her. He didn't say her name. He didn't have to. The entire world had known it once, plastered it over feeds and screens and press conferences: the first confirmed case, the first recorded forgetting, the girl who had looked into a camera and tried to explain what it felt like to lose the edges of her own life. He remembered the briefing where her face had been thrown up on the boardroom screen at HelixCore, the sliding stack of footage and medical charts, the way Voss had watched a clip of her laughing through an early interview and then, when they cut to the part where she faltered midsentence and forgot the question, had slammed her fist once, hard, onto the table. He remembered the PR pieces, the righteous narratives, the arguments over ethics when people started suggesting more invasive monitoring. Patient Zero. The origin point of the map. The anchor of half their models. The system's first node.

She should have been dead. She should have gone long before Novus ever got its hands on Theta-9. Instead she stood in front of him in a stolen hoodie and hospital bracelet, breathing in time with nothing, watching him with a focus he hadn't seen on any other host. "...No way," he said, very softly.

Her head cocked, just enough to register, as if she'd felt—

not heard—the way his throat moved. The hum from the city swelled around them. Hosts at the edge of his vision shuffled closer to a nearby substation, hands lifting toward the metal casing as it buzzed. None of them turned toward him. When she shifted her weight, they adjusted too, a subtle rebalancing, a half-step of bodies around her that looked almost like the way flocking algorithms handled collision avoidance. She was a small gravity well in a field of drifting objects. Move her and the others would, imperceptibly, rearrange.

He watched her hands. They hung at her sides, fingers occasionally flexing, as if trying to feel something in the air. When he took a small step to the left, her gaze tracked him exactly. No delay. When he stepped nearer and then back, testing distance, her body barely moved but her eyes stayed aligned with his center mass. The hum seemed slightly sharper in her presence, as if standing near her shifted the frequency content of the environment up a notch.

He needed data. He looked down, found a flattened drinks can at his feet, picked it up. He tossed it lightly to the side so it hit a stretch of bare concrete, no metal to amplify the impact. The sound was thin. Hosts in the background didn't react. Her eyes flicked toward the movement and back to him, as if the visual noise had registered but not trumped whatever signal she was chasing. He stepped backward onto a loose length of angle iron, letting his heel strike hard. The bar sang with a dull, resonant note that traveled up his leg. Hosts out by the substation flinched toward it in a small wave. She did too—but her flinch brought her closer to him, not the metal. She took a half-step, stopped just outside arm's reach, mouth parting slightly, a faint line creasing between her brows.

She hummed then. The sound came out of her chest, low and tentative, as if she were trying out a note she wasn't sure she could hit. It didn't match anything around them. It sat between pitches, off-key from the tower hum, the transformer buzz, the echo from his own impact. She held it for a second, then altered it fractionally, listening—not to herself, he realized, but to him. She was tuning. He understood it all at once, not as a revelation but as a line connecting points he'd already drawn. The network saw the world through vibration, through coherence, through patterns of movement and noise carried across hosts and infrastructure. It had touched him and found nothing it could use, no carrier to ride, no scaffold woven into his brain. He'd been a live wire without a circuit. When it tried to dump load through him in the wall of bodies, the path hadn't existed. So it had knocked him out—overload, fail-safe, who knew—and moved on. From its perspective, he wasn't just invisible. He was an error.

And here was its first node, its original blueprint, its best local representation of "how things should be," standing three steps away, watching the error with quiet, unsettling interest. She followed him, he realized, because something in her still did the job she'd been drafted into without consent: reconcile inputs, minimize mismatch, pull outliers back into the model. The hosts around them drifted in her wake, adjusting when she did. He was the only thing in the field not humming. To her, that absence must be as loud as a siren.

He thought about trying to talk to her, about testing whether any of the girl in the interviews sat behind the network's filters now. He watched the way her pupils adjusted to light, the way her chest rose and fell in that too-smooth rhythm, the way her fingers flexed when the distant boom of another collapsing building rolled through the air. He imagined saying her name, watching for a flinch of recognition. He imagined calling her what the world had called her—calling her by the mistake they'd built their first models on. It felt wrong, like prodding a wound for curiosity's sake. Whatever she was now, she was not his to pull at.

He looked instead at the horizon. The city lay there, smeared under a low ceiling of grey cloud, towers jutting up like broken teeth. From where he stood on the access road, he could see the tops of office blocks, the jagged outlines of cranes frozen in mid-gesture, the faint, hazy suggestions of residential high-rises further out. Smoke smeared the view in places, thin and persistent. The hum coming off it all was stronger than out here, a deeper, more complex waveform that made the inside of his skull itch. Under it, somewhere, was the echo of the planes that had gone—two, maybe three, he couldn't tell from here. He chose to believe one of them had Lee on it, Anna beside him, strapped into a seat while the cabin rattled and the world tried not to fall apart under them.

He had no weapon. No radio. No convenient line back to HelixCore or Summit Ridge. No map beyond what he remembered of the city from drives between the compound and home. He had his feet, his eyes, and whatever the network wasn't picking up from him. And he had, apparently, the system's first node shadowing him like a glitch trying to recompile. If Voss had made it out—and pessimism aside, he was willing to bet on her stubbornness—she would be somewhere and she would be working. She would want data, not heroics. She would want to know why one man could stand in the middle of a saturated node and not hum while Patient Zero treated him like a puzzle. She would want to know what the system did when presented with a dead frequency it couldn't fold into itself. Right now he was the only person he knew of who could answer those questions from the inside. That made him valuable. It also made him a priority target if the network ever decided it didn't like unsolved problems.

He weighed it in the same calm way he'd weighed corridors and routes in buildings that were on fire. The city was hostile terrain, but the hosts were not hunting him, not in any conventional sense. They wouldn't stalk his heat signature through alleys or sniff his trail. They would go where the hum was strongest. If he moved through the lower-noise spaces, stayed near structures that didn't ring in the right bands, avoided big amplifiers like rail lines and transformer farms, he could navigate between currents. The girl—the node—would follow. Maybe she would draw some of the field with her. Maybe she would act as a shield of sorts, a zone of slightly altered behavior in the network's flow.

He could wander aimlessly until he starved or the network decided to correct its mistake with a more brute-force approach. Or he could treat the dead city like a map and Patient Zero like a moving sensor array. Use the anomaly instead of just being it. Find height. Find line of sight. Find somewhere with enough structural integrity and enough low noise to scrape together a message to someone outside the bowl. He looked at her again. "All right," he said, because talking helped him think even if she couldn't parse words. "You want to follow, you follow. We'll see who learns more."

She didn't nod. She didn't smile. She just watched him, head tilted, as he stepped past her and back onto the road. When he moved, she moved, falling into place three or four paces behind and a little to one side, close enough that he could feel her gaze on the back of his neck, far enough that he couldn't reach her without making a deliberate choice to close the distance. Hosts at the edges of their little two-body system adjusted, some turning fractionally, some drifting a step closer, as if the field were making room for whatever experiment it had decided to run.

He walked toward the city. She followed. Around them, people pressed their hands to walls and rails and glass, humming themselves into alignment with an organism that had stopped needing their consent long ago. The towers ahead vibrated with its presence, every cable and beam another strand in its body. Concrete and steel carried its pulse out along bridges, down tunnels, through subways that would never run again. John moved through it without humming back, the one silent man in a world that had become an instrument, and the first girl it had ever touched tracked his trail like an error it couldn't quite afford to ignore.

CHAPTER 16

They left the airport without ceremony, just two figures slipping through a gap in the twisted fence while the larger currents of hosts flowed toward the runways and the humming shells of grounded aircraft. Out here in the industrial fringe, the city's voice had changed timbre: less sirens and human noise, more infrastructure groaning under a load it hadn't been designed for. A substation popped somewhere far off with a low, concussive thud that rolled through the air like distant thunder; a second later, a whole block's worth of lights went dark, leaving a handful of others flickering harder to compensate. Overhead, the skeleton of an elevated rail line cut across the grey sky, its metal ribs humming faintly even with no trains running, vibrations carrying through supports anchored deep into ground that no longer felt still. Between all that, the hosts moved in their slow, steady flows—along pavements, under bridges, around the bases of towers—heads tilted, hands brushing walls and rails, always oriented toward whatever structure sang loudest in their particular band.

They flowed around John the way water flowed around a piling. He walked down the center of the access road with his hands empty and his eyes up, passing through clusters that adjusted just enough to avoid collision, never more. Sometimes the sleeve of a coat grazed his arm, or the side of a hand brushed his ribs, contact as casual as wind. Nobody looked at him. Nobody's hum shifted toward him. They stayed tuned to the vibration grid of the city, bodies doing the small, constant adjustments the network demanded. Behind him and a little to his right, the girl shadowed his line, her gait matched to his stride closely enough that he could feel her presence without needing to look. When he angled away from one dense flow, sliding between a parked truck and a low concrete barrier to take a quieter side street lined with warehouses and shuttered loading docks, she altered course with him. The main current of hosts ahead continued on toward the deeper hum, drawn into the city proper.

The first billboard came up on the left where the road widened and a row of low, glass-fronted office units backed onto a stretch of wasteland. The advertising hoarding over the corner unit had survived more out of neglect than resilience, its digital panel half-dead, the upper strip a smear of static and frozen pixels. The bottom third still held an image in place, locked mid-frame: a young woman's face in crisp, studio-lit detail, washed in the too-bright optimism of a public awareness campaign. Her hair was longer in the photo, styled, eyes clear, cheeks full. A slogan curled across the corner: IF YOU NOTICE THE SIGNS— and then corruption on the right where the text glitched into blocks of color. Below, in smaller text, the name was half-visible before it dropped into a row of dead diodes, the first few letters readable, the rest lost. It was enough.

He did not stop under it. He let his gaze lift as he passed, taking in the too-familiar curve of the scar through her eyebrow, the way the camera had framed her to make her look both vulnerable and reassuring. He remembered the campaign rollout—HelixCore hadn't paid for it, but they'd been in the room when the health ministry had come to ask for data, for language, for something that made people think memory loss long enough to report it. He remembered Voss sitting at the back of the presentation, arms crossed, mouth set in a line that said she thought the whole thing was a waste of time but she wasn't about to stop anyone from trying. On the street now, the girl under the billboard walked with her head bare and her hair hacked short, hospital bracelet catching the weak light, hoodie hanging off her shoulders. She didn't look up. Her eyes stayed on him.

A little further on, in the shell of what had once been a café wrapped around a small lobby clinic, a wall-mounted screen flickered behind cracked glass. The front door hung crooked, one hinge ripped out of the frame; the air inside smelled of spilled coffee turned sour and the metallic undertone of old blood. Through the opening, John could see the screen frozen mid-broadcast, image burned in place: a news anchor frozen mid-sentence in a box on the left, and on the right a clip of the same girl, earlier still, sitting on a hospital bed with a blanket pulled over her knees, wires taped to her skin. In that frame she was caught halfway through a smile, eyes pushed up into creases. The chyron at the bottom read FIRST DOCUMENTED CASE OF— and then cut off as the feed had died. The colors had leeched, but the shapes were sharp enough.

If he'd needed confirmation, that was it. This wasn't just a girl who looked like every tired intern ever dragged onto a human-interest segment. This was the girl entire world governments had built timelines around, the one whose bloodwork sat at the root of half the early models Voss's people had run, the one every Novus Path exec had secretly wished they could get their hands on when they'd realized what Theta-9 could do. She should have been in a locked ward under three layers of security and lawyers long before the network ever saw scale. Instead she was here, barefoot inside too-big shoes, following a man it refused to see through a city it had already claimed. Somebody had moved her. Somebody had used her.

He filed that for later. You didn't get answers standing still in the open.

Down the next avenue, where the buildings rose a little higher and the street narrowed into a canyon of glass and concrete, he started watching her more deliberately without letting it slow his pace. The hum was stronger here; somewhere beneath them a subway line's skeleton still held residual vibration, rails humming faintly in their beds even without trains. Hosts walked in thicker bands, fingers trailing along shopfront roller shutters and the slatted backs of benches, bodies aligning with the invisible contours of load-bearing walls. She walked just out of reach, copying his route rather than theirs.

It was in the small movements that the difference showed. He stepped over a fallen road sign that lay across the pavement, one corner bent up, its post ripped clean from the ground. Without thinking he shifted his weight to his left leg and cleared it with a short, economical stride. A second later, she did the same, placing her right foot where his had been, left foot swinging almost the same distance. When broken glass littered a stretch of sidewalk, he automatically picked a line cleaner of shards, toes turning slightly inward to avoid a puddle of something oily. Behind him, she followed that line too, matching his tiny corrections instead of marching straight through the debris like the others, whose feet crunched over glass without regard for anything as mundane as cuts.

He stopped once in the middle of a cross-street to listen, head angled, weighing the pull of different noises—the heavier throb coming from a substation somewhere to his left, the higher, warbling whine of a failing HVAC plant ahead, a deep metallic groan on the edge of hearing that might have been a bridge shifting under weight. She stopped as well, a pace behind, weight settling into the same slightly forward-leaning posture, shoulders angled the same way, eyes tracking the same arcs. The hosts close by did not. They kept going, drifting toward whatever their piece of the network favored.

He tested it with more intent the next few blocks. He lengthened his stride for twenty paces, then shortened it abruptly, forcing a different cadence. Her delay stretched over the first change, then compressed; by the third adjustment she was shadowing his pace with a lag of no more than a step. When he crossed to the other side of the street for no good reason beyond avoiding a toppled trash skip, she followed, cutting through a current of hosts whose trajectories warped slightly in response to her presence. When he abruptly dropped into a crouch beside an overturned bike to peer at the scrape pattern in the tarmac—impact angle, direction of travel, the old habits running without needing justification—she stayed standing but bent at the waist a few seconds later, hands hanging, head angled down as if examining a different patch of ground.

Other hosts navigated around lampposts, planters, abandoned cars, any obstacle that altered the flow of their chosen hum. None of them echoed. Their movements were recursive, yes, patterned, but in relation to the field, not to an individual. With her, the field and the individual had become linked—she was sampling him and the world both, and the world seemed happy to let her do it.

They passed under the bones of the elevated rail line where it cut low over an intersection, thick concrete columns planted at each corner. No trains ran, but the structure hummed intermittently as power shuddered through old systems in fits and starts. Hosts had gathered densely along the base of each support, hands pressed flat to the concrete where the load transferred from beam to ground. Some hummed aloud, others silent, the line of their backs unbroken. As John reached the shadowed center of the crossing, a low tremor ran through the columns—a single, deeper vibration, like a sigh dragged out of old stone. He saw it in the hosts first—fingers flexing, heads tilting—and then felt it through his boots.

The girl's reaction came before his. Three paces ahead of him, she stiffened, chin lifting, eyes going slightly unfocused as she turned her head toward a point further down the line before the next wave of hum reached them. It was as if something had tugged on a leash he couldn't see. The columns hummed harder a heartbeat later as some remote switch threw, amplifying the vibration. Hosts along the supports straightened almost in unison, their low sounds syncing to the new frequency. She was already oriented, weight shifted, tuned in before the structures caught up.

He watched for it after that. A transformer on a side street, big grey box behind a chain-link fence, gave a complaining whine that climbed with each second as load shifted its way; she flinched and turned toward it two steps before the casing began to visibly vibrate. Further on, the distant, arrhythmic boom of something heavy collapsing—the end of a building, or the failure of a highway ramp—rolled toward them underfoot. Her knees bent almost imperceptibly in anticipation, as if her body were bracing for impact, then straightened again as the shock passed, while the hosts nearby only reacted when the real wave hit the walls they were touching. She wasn't just listening. She was predicting, somewhere between the raw signal and the response, like a tuned sensor picking up the earliest hint of a spike.

He took her off the main current after that on purpose, turning into a narrower side street where the buildings were lower and older, the road surfacing more broken. Here the hum muted, not gone but damped; thick brick walls and dead machinery swallowed some of the city's voice instead of amplifying it. There were fewer hosts. Those that were present hugged the outer facades, palms flat against plaster cracked with age, humming quietly. The space in the middle belonged to nobody.

In the relative quiet, he tried another experiment. He adjusted things that weren't as obvious as stride length. He rolled his shoulders back, then let them drop forward into the slouched stance he adopted when he'd been on his feet too long; a few seconds later, she loosened hers too, hoodie slipping further down one arm. He deliberately slowed his breathing, drawing air deeper, holding it a fraction longer on the exhale. Her chest rise and fall had never matched his, but now it shifted, smoothing into a pattern that approximated his own, the same number of breaths stretched over a slightly longer interval. When he started a scanning pattern he'd used a hundred times in hostile corridors—left, up, right, quick glance back, repeat —her head movements followed the same arc, but with an odd rounding at the edges, like a software smoothing function trying to keep up with uneven input.

It unsettled him more than the full trance of the others did. The hosts pressing their hands to walls and rails were obviously gone to whatever lived in the hum now. This was something between: not a person making choices, not a pure repeater, but a structure trying to model an unfamiliar signal well enough to categorize it. The system was using her to approximate him, and because it couldn't see him directly, the approximation came out almost right but not quite. That "not quite" felt more dangerous than any clean, comprehensible threat.

They emerged into a wider intersection a few blocks on, a small square that might once have hosted a farmer's market or weekend fair. Now its center was occupied by a squat concrete blockhouse that housed something louder and more persistent than any of the smaller boxes they'd passed. A substation, from the look of the fencing and the warning signs half-ripped from the chain-link. The air around it thrummed; even the metal bench legs vibrated under the onslaught, the bolt heads chattering where they met concrete. Hosts had collected thickly against the perimeter fence, bodies pressed three deep in places, hands laced through mesh, heads tilted toward the humming core. Their hum answered the station's, a low, resonant chord.

When the girl stepped into that crowd, the surface tension

changed. The hosts didn't part for John; they parted for her, so subtly that if he hadn't been watching for it he might have missed it. Instead of forming the same dense, shoulder-to-shoulder press, they left a thin pocket of space around her, a half-meter buffer that stayed intact even as more bodies shuffled forward behind. The angle of their shoulders shifted. Instead of all facing the substation dead-on, some oriented fractionally toward her, their heads turned enough that she sat just inside their peripheral vision.

John kept to the edge of the square, letting the outermost layer of hosts slide past him, bodies brushing his arms without notice. One man—tall, heavy, moving with the stiff, uncoordinated gait of someone whose muscles were being driven by a metronome rather than intent—walked straight toward John's back. At the last moment, before impact, the girl's weight shifted half a step to the side. The man's path curved, his trajectory adjusting minutely as he flowed around the pocket of space centered on her. In the process, his shoulder missed John by inches. He never looked up, never saw either of them. The correction might have been instinct, but it looked like something else: like local rules rewriting on the fly to prioritize one point in the field over another. She was a small hub, and the traffic honored that without ever knowing why.

He didn't linger by the fence. Even damped by walls and distance, the substation's hum set his teeth on edge. He ducked down a covered walkway that led off the square and into the ground floor of a low building that had once been some mix of clinic and corner shop, the kind of place where people bought coffee and blood pressure checks in the same ten-minute stop. Its glass doors were cracked but still mostly in their frames; the fluorescents overhead were dead. The hum dropped as soon as he stepped inside, the thick concrete and layers of drywall muting the city's voice to a low, distant vibration that registered more in his bones than his ears. Outside, as if responding to the change, hosts drifted toward the outer walls instead, palms flattening against brick and glass, bodies aligning in a ring around the shell.

She came in with him. She could have stayed outside, hands on the concrete with the rest, mouth humming along to the grid. The network clearly wanted ears on the structure; every other host in sight moved to comply. She slipped through the gap in the door after him instead, hood brushing the cracked glass, steps light. Inside, in the relative quiet, the change in her was almost immediate. Her gaze, which outside had fixed mostly on the mid-distance around his chest, now tracked higher, following his hands as he touched a counter, a wall, the edge of a tipped-over chair. Her eyes moved more, flicking to corners, to shadows, to the remnants of posters curling on the walls.

She still mimicked, but the lag narrowed. When he brushed dust off the top of a desk with his fingertips, she reached out a second later to run her fingers over the back of an examination chair, palm moving in almost the same arc. He picked up a stethoscope lying abandoned on the floor, its tubing stiff with dried fluid, and let it dangle from his fingers before setting it down again. She watched, then picked up a clipboard from the floor nearby, turned it over once, and dropped it with a soft clack. She was touching things that didn't hum, testing objects for reasons that had nothing to do with vibration and everything to do with interaction.

A wall poster near the reception desk caught his eye: an old public-health campaign layered over with newer notices, its corners peeling. Under the later printouts, where the tape had failed, he could see her face again in glossy ink, younger and healthier, smiling under a headline about early detection and support. Someone had half-ripped it away; the tear had taken her name but left her eyes. The girl in the hoodie walked past it without reacting. Then, a beat after his eyes moved on, she doubled back, raised one hand, and pressed her fingers lightly over the torn paper where the photo ended, palm resting on the image without force. Her hum—he realized she was humming even in here, very softly—wavered as if the system couldn't decide whether the printed representation counted as a node.

Outside, the network reminded them it was still in charge. Somewhere further in, somewhere deeper in the city's guts, something big let go. It might have been a transformer farm failing in cascade, or a bridge segment finally surrendering to gravity; whatever it was, the vibration rolled through the concrete with a force that made shelves rattle and dust drift from hairline cracks in the ceiling. The hosts outside snapped into a new arrangement in the same breath—bodies pivoting, hands lifting, heads turning as one toward the unseen source.

She reacted harder, and first. One moment she stood with her hand on the poster; the next, her whole body locked. Her eyes blew wide and unfocused, gaze unfixed on anything in the room. Her muscles trembled, not in the wild, flailing overload he'd seen in collapsed checkpoints, but in small, high-frequency shivers that ran from shoulders to fingertips. Her hum jumped several pitches in quick succession—too fast and too stepped to be any human attempt at song—before settling into a jittering, unstable tone, like a radio skipping between stations. Her feet stayed planted. She didn't fall. It was as if the network had poured too much signal through a single node and hit the limits of what that body could express.

He moved without thinking. He stepped in and closed both hands around her upper arms, fingers digging into worn fabric and the thinner flesh beneath. For a second it felt like grabbing a high-voltage cable—every tiny tremor translated into his hands, a buzz that made his scar pound. Then something shifted. The hum stuttered, broke, and dropped in pitch. Her tremors eased, not stopping entirely but damping quicker than the shudders still running through the building's frame. Outside, the hosts along the walls rode the tail of the vibration more slowly, their reorientation lagging hers.

He held her there until the dust settled and the last of the aftershocks faded. Up close he could see sweat beading at her hairline, the fine muscles in her jaw jumping with microspasms, the tiny red veins spidering through the whites of her eyes. When the worst of it passed, her focus clicked back enough that she seemed to see him again—or at least register that something that wasn't hum was in contact. Her gaze dropped briefly to where his hands wrapped her arms, then climbed back to his face. The hum in her chest steadied into a lower, more stable note.

He let go, slowly, ready to grab her again if she started to tip. She didn't. She swayed once and then straightened, shoulders dropping by a fraction. The ring of hosts outside adjusted in waves, as if recalibrating around a node that had just rebooted.

He didn't know the right words for what he'd just seen. Amplifier was the closest his brain found, pulling from old briefing slides on telecommunication nodes and feedback loops Voss had used to explain how the network might behave at scale. The system threw signals out through all its hosts, but some of them clearly did more than relay. Patient Zero, it seemed, took load—aligned phases, pulled coherence—and in doing so took more damage when something spiked. His contact, his absence from the grid, had bled off some of that load. Not much. Enough to notice.

He tested it carefully. There was a live wall socket near the floor, the faceplate cracked, the wiring behind it humming faintly. He didn't trust it enough to touch it himself, but he walked her closer and watched. As she crossed an invisible threshold, the hum in her chest crept up, her breathing pattern shifting as the system found a new equilibrium. Outside, hosts within a few meters of that wall adjusted their palms, some pulling back a fraction, others pressing closer. When he stepped in and laid a hand lightly against her shoulder, the volume of her hum dipped, like somebody had thrown a curtain over a speaker. The hosts' hands wobbled, some jerking away and then back as the field fought to compensate.

He didn't push it. He wasn't about to start yanking her around like a piece of equipment just to see what broke. But he filed the result with everything else. She wasn't just a node. She was a point of control, a local stabilizer, and whatever Theta-9 had become clearly preferred to route critical adjustments through her when it could. His contact interfered with that. His dead-node status, whatever Voss had once found "interesting" in his scans, introduced noise into the one channel the network most wanted clean.

When he finally moved toward the door again, she watched him, then mirrored a gesture he hadn't meant to let show. His head had started to ache somewhere between the rail line and the substation, a deep, dull pounding centered behind his old scar. In the clinic's comparative quiet it had flared sharper, as if the building itself had become a resonance chamber aimed at that one piece of his skull. As he walked, he rubbed two fingers briefly at his temple, pushing the pain back into the background. A few beats later, while his hand was already dropping, she lifted her own and pressed it clumsily to almost the same spot on her head, fingertips resting above her eyebrow, miming the attempt to soothe something that wasn't hers. There was no external cue for that. No hum to copy, no vibration to approximate. That was pure mimicry of a human response to internal discomfort.

The network, he thought, might be trying to understand why this one node refused to sync by forcing its primary reference to model him more and more closely. If it couldn't get in, it would try to wrap itself around the problem instead.

From a cracked window at the back of the clinic he caught sight of something taller than the immediate mess. Two, three kilometers off—hard to judge properly with smoke and haze between—the outline of a low communications tower rose above the rooftops, its lattice of metal cutting a thin, precise line against the sky. It wasn't one of the big television structures or the massive commercial masts; those were further in, closer to the downtown core. This was smaller, older, bolted onto the roof of what looked like a civil infrastructure building, the kind of place that might have once housed analog equipment, emergency broadcast gear, or a backup grid control center. It hadn't collapsed yet. The buildings around it leaned but still stood. The tower itself, even at this distance, looked intact.

He weighed options. He could stay in dead corners like this one, moving from pocket to pocket, avoiding the worst of the hum and the densest host flows. It might buy him days. Maybe more. He would learn something by osmosis, just from watching. And he would die without ever getting any of it out to someone who could use it. Or he could move toward that tower, toward higher vibration density and higher structural risk, carrying with him the one person in the city the network clearly cared about more than the average node. He could see what happened when dead node and primary node stood side by side near the kind of equipment meant to throw signals a long way. If he was very lucky, there might still be a way to jury-rig a broadcast, piggyback on surviving hardware, push something—data, voice, anything—out to wherever Voss had dug in. If he wasn't, the network would notice the experiment and adapt in ways he couldn't predict.

There wasn't really a decision there. HelixCore had taught him that time spent protecting himself at the expense of the work was just a slower form of failure. Voss would be somewhere counting on whatever scraps he could salvage. Lee would be sitting in a seat on a plane or in a bunker, watching for proof the world wasn't entirely theirs yet. He had data nobody else had. That made the risk unacceptable to avoid.

He stepped back out through the clinic's broken door into the street's humming air. Hosts were still pressed to the outer walls, palms flat, a silent ring of bodies listening through brick and plaster. They didn't so much as tilt their heads as he passed between them. She paused on the threshold, one hand brushing the frame, as if feeling the difference in vibration between inside and out. For a heartbeat she turned her face toward the direction the rest of the field was flowing: deeper into the city, toward the largest, loudest nodes. The hum tugged on her like gravity.

He deliberately went the other way. Not toward the big draw, but toward a quieter line—a residential block whose buildings were shorter, with less obvious machinery bolted onto their skins. He chose the path that felt wrong in the new rules and correct in the old ones, away from the obvious, toward the route with fewer eyes and less noise. His boots hit the pavement in a new rhythm. The ring of hosts stayed glued to the clinic walls, humming.

Behind him, she hesitated. He could hear it in the absence of her steps, feel it in the way the air seemed to hold its breath. There was no sound for the conflict playing out in whatever was left of her, but he saw it when he glanced back: her weight shifted first toward the stronger hum, shoulder angling, head turning slightly toward the unseen heart of the network. For a second she was a person caught between two crowds at a junction, the pull of each visible in the tension of her muscles. Then she turned her body fully and stepped after him instead, leaving the substation's draw and the thick host currents to follow the dead node heading into quieter, more uncertain streets.

The system had been given a choice—signal or anomaly—and, through her, had chosen not to let go of the problem. He walked on, towards the distant tower and whatever waited between here and there, the only man in the city not humming. She matched his pace, the first node the organism had ever claimed keeping him in her field the way the network kept its favorite frequencies, and the hosts they passed continued to lay their hands on walls and rails and steel, listening to a world that, for now, still pretended it owned them.

CHAPTER 17

The city thinned around them as they walked, trading steel canyons and tight industrial grids for lower roofs and wider gaps. Warehouses gave way to storage yards and half-empty retail strips, then to the fringe where office parks and service depots sat in fat, squat blocks between open lots of gravel and scrub. The sound changed with the architecture. Back near the airport and in the inner rings, the hum had been dense and layered: rail skeletons, high-rises, stacked substations all feeding vibration into one another until the air itself felt like a single chord held too long. Out here, the notes spread. The background rumble stepped down a register to something bigger and farther away—highway noise bleeding in from the belt road, the occasional distant collapse of a roof or overpass, wind shoving at derelict signage until bolts complained. The pauses between those events were longer, but the silence in them wasn't clean. Concrete and metal carried memory of earlier shocks like a bruise.

Hosts were thinner on the ground but no less predictable. They still hugged anything that bore load: light poles, chain-link fences, guardrails along the edges of drainage ditches. When they crossed a broad parking lot that had once serviced a home-improvement store, the asphalt was almost empty except for a few scattered cars and the broken carcass of a cart corral, its metal frame buckled. The hosts kept to the periphery, palms resting on the steel fencing at the lot's edge, fingers hooked around the posts where they met concrete. Even out here, away from the heavier infrastructure, they hunted for lines that could carry the network's voice.

John walked through the open center with his hands tucked loosely against his ribs, eyes moving from anchor point to anchor point, trying to make the chaos resolve into something he could teach if he had to. If anyone ever asked him what the rules were, what you did when the world forgot what people were for and remembered what structures were, he wanted answers that weren't just ghost stories. So he started writing them in his head, the way he'd once written quick field notes after operations when everything was still sharp. Working rules, not gospel. Enough to get someone through a day they shouldn't have survived.

Rule one: they preferred structures that carried constant load and vibration. Overpasses, bridges, big signage masts, rail beds, substation boxes. Anything with weight on it, anything humming because something bigger somewhere else was tugging on it. The hosts clustered thickest there, hands on metal, bodies aligned with invisible force lines. Rule two: they thickened at edges and joints. Where concrete met steel, where pillars met spans, where rails bolted into posts—that was where the density peaked, like ants around a join in a branch. Rule three: they ignored weak, scattered noise and reacted hard to clean, resonant notes. Wind chimes of loose debris and broken glass set off minor adjustments at best. A single hood slammed with intent or a beam struck just right, though, could redirect a small tide. Rule four: they navigated around him the way they navigated around dead obstacles. He'd confirmed that enough times to stop flinching when someone's hip grazed his arm or a coat hem brushed his thigh. To the network, he was infrastructure that didn't conduct.

The beltway announced itself long before they saw it. The baseline hum leveled into a steadier, deeper growl that came up through the soles of his boots and sat under his sternum, too smooth and continuous to be anything but a long, uninterrupted run of concrete and steel under stress. At a rise in the ground, between two low-slung service depots whose windows had spiderwebbed and then given up, he got his first glimpse: an overpass cutting across the horizon some distance ahead, its side rails a jagged line against the flat sky, ramps coiling down to feeder roads. Even at this distance he could see the stalled glint of car bodies, the way hosts dotted the edges of the span in a loose, shifting line, their silhouettes marking where the load-bearing elements ran.

The girl—Patient Zero, in every way that mattered, though he refused to think the phrase too often—walked a pace behind and to his right, where she had settled like a second shadow. When he lengthened or shortened his stride, she adjusted. When he moved slightly off the crown of the road to avoid a patch of broken glass and splintered wood where a sign had come down, she tracked his line rather than the straighter path the hosts favored. The currents of bodies ahead flowed to meet the hum, but wherever she stepped, they re-spaced by some instinct he doubted they owned anymore. He could feel it in the way gaps opened at the last moment, in how he hadn't been accidentally shoulder-checked into a wall yet despite walking through more human mass in the last few hours than he wanted to think about.

The feeder road curled them toward the first on-ramp: a strip of concrete rising in a shallow spiral toward the overpass. The lanes were jammed end to end with vehicles: sedans with doors hanging open, a school bus listing on a flat tire, an overturned motorcycle resting under the front bumper of a delivery van. A tanker sat jackknifed halfway up, its trailer canted at an angle, hazard placards half-torn from its sides. People had tried to leave here, once. Some had made it to other exits. Some hadn't. A few bodies lay in positions that didn't belong to the network—collapsed between cars, limbs bent wrong, heads at angles that spoke of impact, not hum. The rest of the mass had either walked away or joined it. Hosts clustered along the guardrails on both sides, fingers curled around metal, heads turned toward the deeper thrum of the main span above. Others perched on the median barrier up top, visible between cars as they moved, hands resting on steel that tied the whole structure together. The sound underfoot smoothed further as they approached; the highway was a cleaner instrument than the surface streets, its design built around carrying weight over distance without interruption. Different vibration, same addiction.

John stopped at the base of the ramp and looked up, tracing load paths without thinking. The main span carried the weight across a gap he couldn't see from here. Pillars took that load down into the ground. Guardrails and median barriers hummed as smaller, more accessible ribs. Hosts clung to all of it, as high as they could comfortably reach. A truck on the overpass above them—some old box lorry with its center of gravity all wrong—rocked in slow, uneven motions as its blown suspension finally quit pretending to work. Each sway shifted the way the span sang, metal complaining in lengthened groans.

She felt it before he did. As he weighed routes—under the overpass, where the pillars concentrated load but offered cover, or up onto it, where the hosts were thickest but visibility was better—her head snapped up, eyes fixing on a point above and ahead where the truck's silhouette jerked against the sky. Her shoulders tightened a fraction, as if bracing for a hit. Only after that did the deeper note ride the existing hum into his bones, a change in pitch he might have written off as imagination if he hadn't seen her body call it first.

Under, he decided. You didn't put yourself on top of a thing the network loved if you had any other option. He left the ramp and cut across the battered verge instead, sliding down a short, eroded slope toward the shadowed space beneath the overpass where concrete pillars rose in regular, massive lines. The hum there was heavier, less bright but more insistent, the sound of load being handed down from span to ground in a way the body interpreted as stability even when the brain knew better. Hosts stood in rings around the pillars, hands pressed flat to the concrete, faces turned inward as if listening to a sermon. They ignored him as he threaded through gaps between them, moving along the edge of the support line rather than directly underneath the densest point.

The overpass above groaned again as the wind picked up. A roadside gantry—one of those big metal frames that used to hold electronic signs—had been left half-loose by some earlier impact and now swung on tired bolts above the far edge of the underpass. On the next gust it slammed sideways into the beam it had been anchored to, metal on metal in a jarring, resonant screech that cut across the smoother background like a knife.

The reaction was instantaneous. Every host along the guardrail above them surged as one toward the source of the sound. The rail was never designed for that many bodies in motion in the same direction at once even when the system that kept those bodies from behaving like cattle was still installed. It flexed under the concentrated weight; bolts sheared one after another with sharp, ugly snaps that echoed down the pillars. There wasn't time to shout a warning to anyone. There wasn't anyone left to warn.

A section of the rail gave way in a ripping cascade, and a rain of bodies came with it. They didn't scream. They just fell, arms pinwheeling reflexively as gravity reassumed personal jurisdiction. Two or three hosts slammed into the concrete verge and the side of a delivery van with wet, heavy impacts that left streaks and dents. One clipped the back of a car before bouncing out into open air. Another came down so close to John that he felt the wind of the fall pass his face before the body hit the tarmac inches from his boots in a bone-cracking sprawl. Reflex threw him sideways, boot slipping on grit as he half-stumbled, half-rolled toward the nearest pillar.

The danger wasn't the impact. It was the way moving flesh triggered adjustment. The hosts who had been standing in calm rings around the pillars shifted as the shock traveled through the concrete and metal into their hands. Some turned toward the fallen, others toward the new edge of the broken rail above. For a few seconds the patterns dissolved into something that might have trampled him flat if it had decided he was in the way.

They didn't. The girl's presence warped the mess. As the first bodies hit, she stepped instinctively sideways, not toward the noise but away from the main ring, and the local field flowed around that change. The hosts nearest her reorganized, leaving that familiar thin pocket of space centered on her rather than tightening the circle. Two who might have stepped directly onto John's legs instead curved their trajectories fractionally to preserve the gap, feet missing him by less than a hand's width. He used that sliver of opportunity, shoving himself upright and out of the immediate grind path before the system could settle into a new, more lethal equilibrium.

He filed the whole event under structural risk without bothering to translate it into words. Big spans plus concentrated hosts equaled failure modes that had nothing to do with malice and everything to do with mass. You walked under bridges like you walked under artillery that hadn't been properly secured: never assuming the bolts would stay where someone had put them just because they were supposed to.

They climbed up onto the highway proper a little further along where a cracked embankment and a collapsed section of retaining wall made an improvised ramp. The lanes were a frozen river of steel and plastic stretching in both directions, vehicles angled in all the clumsy ways people parked when they believed they'd be moving again in minutes. Some doors hung open, some were closed tight. Child seats sat empty in back seats with toys still clipped to the belts. A few alarms bleated faintly where dying batteries refused to admit defeat, their shrill notes too thin and intermittent to interest the hosts.

John kept to the shoulder, occasionally stepping into the first lane to ease around a jackknifed truck or a car that had spun sideways. The highway structure carried the hum like a well-tuned instrument: deep, smooth, constant, occasionally colored by the local contributions of trucks still rocking on their shocks or signs flapping half-loose in the wind. Hosts hugged the guardrails at the edges, their hands on the metal that tied the whole thing together. Others stood along the median barrier, orienting themselves where the load paths through the concrete were cleanest.

He let the rules he'd started writing earlier evolve with what he saw. Rule one, refined: they didn't just prefer constant load; they preferred load that represented global connections—bridges, interchanges, anything that linked large pieces of the network's territory into continuous lines. Rule two: joints and edges still mattered most. He watched the difference between hosts pressed to the center of a railing span and those massed at the points where that span bolted into posts. The density spike was always at the join. Rule three: not all notes were equal. A loose piece of trim rattling on a roofline went mostly ignored; the clean, sustained whine of a truck's undercarriage dragging on a bent frame drew attention from tens of meters away. Rule four: he remained a non-factor in their paths unless her presence forced them to account for him indirectly.

She continued to live half a second ahead of the infrastructure. Her head would turn toward an overpass a few hundred meters ahead a moment before the structure itself spoke—before a truck frame shifted with a groan or the wind drove a hanging sign into its supports. She'd brace minutely, knees bending, shoulders tightening, before the vibration rolled through the road surface under his boots. He started, without fully deciding to, to treat her like an early-warning sensor: if she snapped toward something, he shifted his weight, lengthened or shortened his stride, adjusted his angle a fraction. Sometimes that meant nothing. Sometimes it meant they were already moving away when something dropped, failed, or screamed in a way that made hosts surge.

The second close call came on a stretch of roadway that sloped gently down, the whole structure leaning toward a distant interchange where ramps braided over and under each other. A line of trucks had been pulled onto the shoulder here, nose to tail, trailers looming over the barrier like cliffs. Some had rocks chocked under their wheels. Some didn't. One old semi sat with its cab at an angle, front tire half off the asphalt, rear wheels resting on a mix of gravel and scattered debris. It had been left in neutral or with a failed brake; at some point after the driver had walked away, gravity had remembered it.

As John and the girl came level with it, the semi gave a tiny jerk. A breeze, a shift in weight further up the ramp—whatever the cause, the effect was that the truck began to roll, slow at first, tires crunching over loose glass and stone. Its flank kissed the guardrail and then pressed, metal complaining in a long, rising screech that carved a pure, piercing line through the highway's broader hum. Hosts reacted like someone had dropped blood into a pool. Up and down the road, along both shoulders and the median, bodies turned toward the sound. Those nearest the truck moved first, hands leaving whatever they'd been touching as they surged toward the screeching contact point, feet picking up speed in that awful almost-trot that never quite matched any human intention. Further out, clusters shifted their vectors so that more and more of the flow pointed toward the slowly rolling mass and its song.

John saw the cross-current forming in front of him—streams of hosts intersecting where he needed to go—and picked a gap, aiming to slip through before it closed. Under normal conditions, it would have been simple: three quick steps between one cluster and the next, timing his movement with their own. But the system wasn't normal anymore. The screech stretched, the truck picked up another few kilometers an hour of speed, and the hosts accelerated the way a river does when you narrow its banks.

He misjudged by a second. The gap he'd picked filled as a wave of bodies shifted sideways, converging toward the guardrail. In the space of two steps, his clear line became a moving wall. The truck rolled closer, nose turning slightly as the gradient and debris played with its path, still scraping the barrier. The sound climbed in pitch. The hum under his feet thickened as more weight leaned into the rail that tied this piece of highway to the rest of the city's nervous system.

He could have forced his way into the mass, shoulders first, gambling that his lack of presence in their circuitry would keep them from reacting violently to unexpected contact. He'd also risk being carried in the direction they were going, straight into the side of the truck if its trajectory shifted another degree. For one stuttering heartbeat, the math offered no clean solution.

Then she stepped. She didn't move much. Half a stride forward, half a stride toward him, putting herself fractionally more into the oncoming path. The effect was nonlinear. The hosts closest to her adjusted their trajectories to preserve the thin pocket of space that seemed to cling to her body like an aura. Those just beyond adjusted to avoid colliding with those new paths. The wave bent, no longer a flat front but a curve. The curve opened one more thin, ragged gap.

John took it, cutting across in her wake, so close to the nearest host that the man's sleeve brushed his chest. The truck's flank passed by a meter away, metal shrieking against barrier. If the host had staggered or been knocked off trajectory, John might have gone under the wheels. Instead the man simply flowed past, following the shifted vector the system had given him. A few seconds later, the semi's front end struck the concrete of a crash barrier and shuddered to a halt, whole frame quivering as the last of its momentum translated into vibration. Hosts piled against the point of impact in a slow, compressing ring, hands finding new positions on metal now singing with a different note. They kept moving until the truck's noise dropped below the threshold of what his nerves insisted on treating as immediate threat. On a relatively empty stretch of shoulder beyond the incident, the hum softened to its usual steady growl. Here the hosts were fewer; the structures were less interesting. A few stood with their hands on the posts of a faded billboard, others leaned against a wire fence that enclosed a patch of scrub and trash.

He used the lull to formalize what the last hour had taught him about their joint footprint. Himself: dead node, insulator, obstacle the network didn't perceive as part of its circuit diagram. Her: primary node, local amplifier, favored reference point through which adjustments propagated fastest. Together? His contact damped her overload, their proximity smoothed some of the more chaotic local responses. When they were separated by more than a few meters, hosts flowed around her in coherent lines and around him in whatever direction the hum told them to go. When he moved deliberately close—within an arm's length, within the radius where he could have grabbed her again if he'd needed to— the flows became more predictable, their buffer zone a stable feature instead of an occasional side effect.

He tested it in small ways. For fifty meters he widened the gap between them, letting her drift three or four paces off to one side. Immediately he felt the difference: hosts still adjusted for her, but their lines no longer took him into account. Twice in that short distance he had to check his step to avoid being shouldered by someone heading for a railing, their body language saying "wall" where his presence stood. Then he closed the distance again, matching her pace more tightly, and the field reconfigured. Gaps opened more reliably in front of him. Paths curved around the two-body system they formed. Unsettling, but useful.

It was an ugly tactical truth: she was both risk and asset. The closer he stayed, the more he could shape how dangerous zones behaved, using her as an anchor point to bend flows and carve passages out of crowded spaces. The closer he stayed, the more he entangled himself with the network's favorite piece of hardware. If it ever decided to do something direct with her, he would be inside the blast radius. There wasn't a version of the problem where staying away from that possibility and ignoring the advantage counted as anything but cowardice, and he'd left his tolerance for cowardice behind a long time ago. So he walked close.

The third time the environment tried to kill him did it without any help from the organism. Late in the day—not that the sun made a honest effort through the low, dirty cloud cover, but the light had flattened into that indistinct, washed-out tone that said the angle was dropping—they reached an interchange where three lines of highway knotted together. Part of the upper stack had already failed. Chunks of concrete lay scattered across the lower lanes, rebar poking from them like ribs, rust starting to bloom along the exposed metal. A section of ramp overhead hung at a wrong angle, its far support gone, the remaining connection more stubbornness than engineering.

Picking a path through it required more attention than anything he'd done since the airport. He moved slower, boots choosing footholds among dust, gravel, and slick patches he suspected came from fuel or hydraulic fluid rather than rain. Hosts were thick along the intact guardrails and still-standing pillars, their hands on any surface that vibrated. None of them looked down. None saw the fine layer of powdered concrete that turned a stretch of otherwise solid roadway into something with all the friction of glass.

His foot went out from under him without warning. One second he had weight on his left leg, shifting forward to the next step; the next his heel skated sideways on dust, knee twisting, and then he was on the ground, shoulder and hip slamming into rough tarmac hard enough to knock breath out of his lungs. For a stunned instant the world shrank to pain and the taste of grit.

Because the network didn't see him, it didn't care that he'd fallen. The hosts closest to him kept walking, their paths set along lines that took no notice of a man sprawled where their feet intended to land. A woman in a high-visibility vest patterned with old grease stains stepped directly toward his legs, her boot catching his shin. She stumbled, arms windmilling, her forward momentum threatened to carry her down atop him. If she went, the host behind her would adjust to preserve contact with whatever they'd been aiming for. If enough of them tripped and fell in the same place, the resulting pile would have weight, and weight plus the network's disinterest in his continued existence would result in him being slowly crushed under bodies that never meant to do it.

Before the chain could start, the girl moved. She made a sharper, more decisive adjustment than any of the micro-steps he'd seen so far, pivoting on the ball of one foot so that her position relative to him and the stumbling woman changed immediately. The local field adapted to her the way it always did. The woman's flailing arms snapped toward the hub; her trajectory curved just enough that when she came down, her hand hit pavement a hand's breadth from John's ribs instead of on his chest. Her knee struck the ground alongside his hip, not on top of it. The host behind her checked, then slid past on a path that preserved the buffer around Patient Zero's new position, boots missing his shoulder by centimeters.

John used the tiny affordance without waiting to see how the next layer would play out. He rolled, teeth gritted against the protest from his scraped side, and got his knees under him, then his feet. The instant he was vertical again, he stepped out of the cluster, letting the flows knit themselves back together without a man-shaped anomaly on the floor to trip over. The girl watched him do it, head following his movement, hum in her chest steady.

He checked himself by rote once they'd cleared the worst of the debris: weight on each leg, shoulder's range of motion, any sharp stabs that would warn of something torn or broken. Bruises, yes. Skin scraped raw through fabric. Nothing that would slow him much, as long as he didn't let the ache steal his attention. The lesson slotted in without needing phrasing: he might sit outside the network's control, but he didn't sit outside physics. If he couldn't stay on his feet and aware, the organism could kill him by accident as easily as it had killed millions on purpose. Immunity to one layer of the disaster didn't buy him a pass on the others.

From the top of the interchange's highest intact ramp—an embankment that offered a view between two half-collapsed overpasses—he finally got a clearer look at his target from something like the right angle. The communications tower he'd first spotted from the clinic in the inner city rose from the roof of a low, blocky building a couple of kilometers out, its latticework of metal still straight against the bruised sky. It wasn't a skyscraper spire, not one of the obvious commercial masts that made skylines pretty for postcards. It was functional, ugly, and built low on purpose: some kind of utility hub, emergency management center, or broadcast relay. The buildings around it were damaged but not leveled. Roofs leaned, windows were broken, but whole blocks hadn't pancaked. From here, the roads between him and it looked navigable if you picked threads between the thicker currents of hosts.

He traced possible lines with his eyes. Direct streets that ran straight toward the tower also ran along corridors of heavier infrastructure—tram lines, buried utilities that still hummed, mid-rise office blocks whose frames would carry vibration a long distance. Hosts were thicker there, drawn to the bigger structures. Oblique routes that approached from the flank, through lower residential grids and smaller service roads, promised fewer clean hum paths but more turns, more opportunities to be funneled somewhere he didn't want to be. Both options carried risk. Both assumed the city ahead would stay the same shape long enough for plans to matter.

The light had gone from washed grey to the flatter, colder tone that said dusk wouldn't be a neat event so much as a slow erasure. Heat drained from the concrete underfoot with each passing minute. He did the rough math between here and the tower at the same time he weighed what it would mean to be caught on open highway after dark in a city that no longer needed daylight to see. It wasn't the hosts he worried about. They moved the same way at all hours, as far as he'd seen. It was his own body: missteps, exhaustion, the small stupid choices people made when they couldn't see the ground ahead.

He chose not to test how invisible he was in the dark tonight. Off the highway, near the base of the interchange, a squat roadside structure clung to the edge of the complex: something that had once been a service building, rest stop café, or maintenance depot office. Its windows were mostly intact; one door had been forced open, but the frame still held. It sat close enough to the main lanes that he could keep the tower in sight through gaps, far enough off the primary vibration lines that the hum inside would be damped.

They dropped down an embankment littered with old trash

and newer fragments of concrete, then crossed a short strip of dirt to reach it. A handful of hosts already had their hands on its outer walls, palms flat against the stucco as they listened through the shell. Their bodies formed a loose ring, spaced evenly by some algorithm that favored surface coverage over interpersonal space. None turned as John and the girl slipped between them. The building's interior swallowed the highway's voice better than the clinic had; instead of a continuous roar, the hum became a low, steady presence under everything, like the sound of blood in ears after exertion.

Inside, the place was as stripped as he expected: chairs knocked over, a counter with its tills forced open, paper scattered and trampled, one wall still bearing a fading map of the beltway and its exits under a layer of grime. Fluorescent tubes in the ceiling had given up entirely. Enough light leaked through the front windows and a side door's glass panel that he could see without tools, though shadows pooled thick in corners. A bank of vending machines along one wall had been broken open; someone had taken the snacks and left the cracked plastic fronts gaping.

The girl followed him in, then stopped in the center of the main room as if unsure what the network wanted from her here. No major machinery, no heavy load-bearing beam to lean on. The hum from outside wrapped the building, but the interior offered only cheap fixtures and furniture that carried little. Her eyes moved more in the lowered stimulus, tracking his hands when he brushed dust off the map to check orientation, following the motion when he nudged a chair out of his way with a foot.

He checked his own body again by habit, rolling his scraped shoulder, flexing the knee that had taken the worst of the fall. Pain answered, but in the honest, manageable way that said everything still worked if he asked it to. Fatigue sat heavier than that—an accumulation of hours on his feet, adrenaline drawn and spent too many times, muscles firing constantly to keep him stable on surfaces whose friction couldn't be trusted. It would be worse tomorrow. That was a later problem.

She mirrored his tiny adjustments almost absently now. When he shifted weight to his right leg and stretched his left calf, she leaned subtly the same way a few seconds later, sock wrinkling around her ankle. When he rubbed at the scar on his head because the low, steady hum seemed determined to resonate with that exact patch of bone, she lifted her hand and touched her own temple a heartbeat afterward, fingertips resting on skin as if checking for the same ache. There was still no sign of language in her. No attempt to shape sound into anything more than tuning notes, no flicker of recognition when her gaze passed over the beltway map and the little labeled icon that used to show their exact location. But the tuning itself was becoming more precise, her mimicry finer. The system was watching him through her and adjusting whatever model it kept behind her eyes.

He stepped to the front window and looked out toward the tower again. From here, framed by the cracked glass and the leaning silhouette of a half-collapsed signpost, it looked closer but not close enough. The lattice glinted dully where light caught bare metal. The blocky building at its base sat squat and self-contained, its walls thicker than the ones around this service hut. It was designed for something other than selling coffee and maps. Designed to keep things working when other things broke. Designed, maybe, to outlast exactly this kind of failure long enough for someone with the right knowledge and tools to use what was inside.

He didn't see hope when he looked at it. Hope was for people who still believed the world cared whether they showed up. What he saw was a problem that hadn't been solved yet: a node in the old system that might still throw a signal if someone could reach it without being crushed, drowned in hum, or folded into a network that didn't need their consent. He measured the distance again, translated it into hours and risks, and found that his numbers still came out in favor of moving toward it rather than away.

Behind him, she stood in the center of the room, head tilted as if listening to something only she could hear. Outside, hosts pressed their palms to the walls and hummed softly, turning the little building into a drum. In a city that had turned itself into an instrument, tuned to a mind that didn't think in words, he and the girl who shouldn't have been alive were the only mismatched notes still moving deliberately toward the one place left that had been built to send signals out.

CHAPTER 18

Dawn came as a change in temperature before it came as light. The service building's thin walls bled warmth faster than the highway outside, and the chill woke John before his brain decided it was time. The air in the small room had the flat, metallic bite of early morning over concrete. He lay still for a moment on the strip of floor he'd claimed between an upended table and the wall, listening. The hum hadn't stopped in the hours he'd stolen for sleep. It never did. But it had shifted again: less the heavy, constant growl of trucks and stacked ramps, more a smoother, directional vibration that felt like a line drawn through the city rather than a smear. The tower's line.

He did a quick inventory without getting up. Limbs: all accounted for. Shoulder and hip: sore from the fall and the way the floor had repaid him for lying on it, but functional. Knee: stiff, tendons tugging a warning that they would punish him later if he asked too much now. Head: the scar above his temple throbbed in a slow, dull pulse that had nothing to do with heartbeat and everything to do with whatever the city had decided to resonate at overnight. No bite marks. No hand-shaped bruises from hosts. No broken ribs. Still absurdly intact for a man who had spent the previous day moving through a saturation zone.

He opened his eyes. The light that filtered through the grimy front windows was grey, colder than the day before, flattening the inside of the little building into a smear of shapes and angles. Dust floated in it where he'd disturbed things. The map on the wall had slumped further, tape giving up. The chairs he'd shoved into a corner still leaned drunkenly. Patient Zero stood exactly where he'd last seen her, a few meters from him, in the center of the room.

She was watching him. She always was, when he checked. Her head had tipped to one side at some point in the night, as if listening harder to something only she could hear. Her hum sat low in her chest, barely audible over the muffled highway noise. As he rolled onto one elbow, she straightened by a fraction, adjusting her posture in a ghost of his movement. When he tested his shoulder with a careful stretch, her hand drifted up a second later to rub at her own, fingers pressing at fabric in almost the same place. Half-second lag, same as before. Still more mimicry than initiative.

He pushed himself up, joints protesting, and crossed to the window. The glass was streaked with old rain and newer grime, but through it he could still see the communications tower in the distance, its lattice cutting a clean, unnatural line against the thick morning sky. From this angle it looked closer than it had from the interchange, but there were still broken overpasses, slumped buildings, and whatever host currents the night had rearranged between here and there. The hum in the soles of his feet had taken on a purer character in the hours he'd been still: less interference from random machinery, more of a single, coherent note bleeding out from under that blocky building at the mast's base.

He watched the tower for a while, counting breaths, feeling the rhythm of the vibration under his boots. If this didn't give him a line out, nothing else in the city would. HelixCore had drilled contingencies into them back when contingencies still felt like things that happened to other people. Infrastructure like that was on the list: piggyback old systems, repurpose their redundancy, treat static like an invitation rather than a wall. Whatever had happened since, those principles hadn't changed. The network had taken the city's mind; it hadn't rewritten the hardware yet.

"Tower day," he said softly, more to mark the decision than out of any need to hear his own voice. His breath fogged a patch of glass, then faded. Behind him, the girl shifted her weight one pace toward him, as if the sound tugged at her even when the content didn't.

They stepped out into the hum a few minutes later. The hosts pressed to the building's outer walls had thickened during the night; more bodies now stood in contact with the concrete, palms flat, heads tilted, humming along with whatever the tower sent through the ground. They reacted to the change inside only enough to preserve their spacing when he and the girl slid between them. No heads turned. No eyes tracked. Outside, the highway lay under the morning like an animal that hadn't decided yet whether to get up.

He didn't go back up onto it. The rules he'd built in the last day gave him clear advice there: avoid long, clean load-bearing lines when you could. Interchanges and stacked ramps were amplifiers the network adored. The tower, by design, would be tied into those lines. Approaching it along them would mean walking through the strongest parts of its body. He dropped instead into the lower side streets that fanned out from the service building, the forgotten maintenance access and frontage roads that paralleled the main arteries at a distance the planners had thought of as negligible. For the people who'd once used them, it had been. For a system that used vibration like language, it was a different channel altogether.

The streets between him and the tower were a mess of cracked asphalt, low offices, small warehouses, and residential blocks that had been close enough to the beltway to be cheap and loud. Hosts drifted here too, but less densely than on the highway. They clung to small-scale structures: lamp posts, fence posts, the metal frames of bus shelters. Hands rested on the sides of cable distribution cabinets and little relay boxes that sat on concrete pads at the corners of blocks, wires snake-hiding into the ground. The closer they came to the tower, the more of those boxes appeared, painted in faded municipal beige and tagged with codes nobody but infrastructure engineers ever read. Cable trenches cut across the streets at intervals, their covers buzzing softly. The hum in the air aligned itself more and more along a single direction, like wind around a bluff.

He stayed close to the girl. When he needed to cross a street where the host flows were thicker, he timed his step to fall into the pocket that moved with her, that half-meter of space the field seemed determined to preserve around Patient Zero even when it forgot everything else. Twice in the first ten minutes it saved him more than discomfort.

The first near miss came at the base of a retaining wall that held up an embankment dotted with small houses. The wall had cracked under some earlier event and now bulged outward, concrete fissured with deep lines, reinforcing steel showing through. Hosts had collected at its top, hands resting along the metal railing that traced the edge of the drop, their humming feeding into the stressed structure. As John and the girl walked along the sidewalk below, picking their way through fallen bricks and uprooted shrubs, the wall finally decided it had had enough.

There was no warning in sound at first. The hum masked the little noises. The only sign was the way the girl's head jerked up and to the side, eyes locking on a point twenty meters ahead a moment before a section of concrete sheared away with a grinding crack. Blocks the size of suitcases tumbled down, pulverizing into smaller chunks as they hit the lower slope. A spray of debris followed—stones, dirt, metal fragments.

He could have been in the path of that cascade; the line he'd been walking would have put him under the worst of it in two more strides. Her reaction changed that. Instinct—or whatever the network had turned instinct into—made her step sideways, into the street. The hosts at the top of the wall adjusted around her, shifting their weight in ways that rebalanced the pressure. Their reaction came too late to save the wall, but it altered the pattern of the fall. The largest pieces dropped just ahead of them instead of directly on top, smashing into the sidewalk where he would have been. Dust and small fragments peppered his jacket. He changed course with her, boots sliding through grit, and they moved through the low-density band the system had opened around its node without ever understanding it had spared anything but her.

The second close call was a lamp mast. It had been complaining quietly for as long as they'd been within earshot: a subtle creak and wobble each time the wind gusted down the street, the bolts at its base flexing in their sockets. Hosts had wrapped themselves around it, hands on the metal, humming along with each tiny sway. As they passed under, the girl's hum hitched. She slowed, eyes on the mast, just enough that John felt it and checked too. He didn't stop, but he altered his line, skirting a little wider.

The next gust did what the last ten hadn't. Something in the metal snapped. The mast tipped, then started to fall, its light housing hitting the side of a building and breaking off in a shower of glass before the shaft came down across the pavement. It crashed with a clang that made the nearest hosts jerk, then press closer to feel the new vibration. It missed them by two paces. If he'd stayed on his original line and speed, he would have walked directly under it as it fell.

The closer they got, the more the city felt like an instrument someone was slowly retuning to a single note. Scattered noise dropped away. The hum under his feet aligned more cleanly with the tower's position, straightening into something that felt like it had direction and intent, even if the intent belonged to a pattern rather than a mind. Street cabinets hummed in phase. Overhead lines buzzed at the same frequency. Even the half-collapsed balconies of nearby apartments seemed to shiver in sympathy when the vibration peaked.

The building itself sat exactly where he'd expected: at the center of a web of cable trenches and buried conduit, low and thick-walled, functional the way bunkers are functional. No big ground-level windows. Just blank concrete, a handful of narrow, reinforced slits higher up, and a heavy metal door on each side. The communications mast rose from its roof, bolted into a framework that distributed its load evenly over the structure below. The network loved it.

Hosts ringed the exterior in a dense band, bodies standing shoulder to shoulder as far as the wall allowed, palms pressed flat to the concrete. They faced inward, toward the building, humming softly, their heads angled as if listening to whatever the tower fed back into the ground. The pattern was tighter here than anywhere else he'd seen outside the airport—no big gaps, no lazy drift. Whatever Theta-9 had become valued this node highly enough to feed a lot of ears to it.

He didn't walk straight at the closest door. That would have been stepping into the thickest part of the wall. He circled instead, keeping to the edge of the ring, watching where the density spiked. As with everything else, the corners and seam lines—places where wall segments joined, where foundation met upper structure—hosted the greatest concentration. Between those, the bodies were still thick but marginally more forgiving. He picked the side where the line wavered a little, where some prior impact had left a crack in the concrete and a tiny mismatch in how the vibrations traveled. The hosts there stood a fraction further apart.

He timed his move to the girl. When she stepped toward the wall, the field reorganized around her, making that thin halo of space as it always did. He angled them so that bubble intersected the warped section of ring between seam and corner. For a moment, the bodies in front of them didn't so much part as flow aside, adjusting minutely to preserve their spacing around the node the system prized above any human geometry. In that breathing gap, he and the girl reached the door.

Someone had already forced it once: probably a late civil defense crew, maybe a panicked official trying to get a message out after the first waves hit. The heavy metal slab hung slightly crooked in its frame, one hinge bent, the seal warped. It still closed enough to keep most of the weather out, but the frame bore the marks of a mechanical ram or vehicle bumper. John put his shoulder to it and pushed. It scraped open with a low grind that made the closest hosts' hum ripple but didn't break their pattern. Nobody turned.

Inside, the air was cooler, dry in a way that tasted of old filtered systems and concrete dust. The hum, which had been a whole-body presence outside, damped heavily once the door shut behind them. It didn't vanish; the building carried the tower's load, and vibration traveled whether you wanted it to or not. But the echo shifted from something atmospheric to something structural: a feeling in the soles of his feet, in his bones, more than a sound in his ears.

The interior layout was as uninspired as the exterior suggested. Narrow corridors with painted cinderblock walls. Floors of sealed concrete with a non-slip finish worn in patches. Doors every few meters leading into equipment rooms, storage spaces, control centers. Emergency lighting strips along the ceiling, most dead, a few still flickering with tired red or green. Cable conduits ran along walls and overhead, some armored metal, some plastic, all humming faintly where they carried live lines.

The girl followed him down the corridor, her footsteps soft, hum low. In the dampened environment, her mimicry sharpened. When he ducked slightly under a run of overhead trunking out of habit, she dipped her head a beat later under a section with more clearance. When he laid a hand briefly on the wall to feel the tower's pulse, her fingers brushed the same painted blocks a moment afterward, palm flattening as if waiting for contact to tell her what to do.

He moved slowly, room by room, looking for what he knew would be here if anyone had designed the place with even baseline competence: an emergency control space built to outlast whatever took down the main grid. He passed racks of dead servers, rows of blinking network equipment whose indicator lights glowed a faint, stubborn amber or green off dwindling backup batteries, analog patch panels with bundles of coax and twisted pair disappearing into the walls. One room held a bank of lead-acid cells big enough to keep a good-sized operations center running for a while. Their monitor showed most strings drained; a few still reported enough charge to matter.

He found the broadcast room at the far end of a corridor that angled toward the mast's base. The door had a heavier seal, and inside the air felt different—staler, less disturbed. Consoles lined one wall, old hardware with physical switches and analog meters sharing space with newer, more modular gear. A large rack held emergency radio equipment: wideband transceivers, hardened modems, dedicated links meant to stay alive when the rest of the city's communications fell apart. On another wall, a big analog console dominated, sliders and knobs in neat rows, a relic from when people still thought in terms of "on the air" instead of streaming. Some of it was dark. Some of it glowed faintly, LEDs holding on, power rails humming quietly.

He stood in the doorway for a moment, mapping it. HelixCore had run drills on setups like this, back when "worst case" still meant localized blackouts or targeted attacks rather than the world eating its own memory. Use existing backbone. Don't reinvent what civil authorities had built for storms and bombs. Ride their redundancy. He remembered a briefing where Voss had pointed at a diagram of a tower almost exactly like this and said, flatly, that if they ever lost the city's main grid, this was where she expected to see status lights first.

He went to work. First, power. The emergency battery bank he'd passed in the hall still had a few strings with usable voltage. He traced cables from those through the building's skeleton to the broadcast room, following labels and conduit runs, isolating which feeds patched into the console and radio rack. He found a breaker panel on the room's inner wall with hand-written notes from some long-gone technician. Half the breakers were tripped, either from overload or as a deliberate attempt to shed nonessential loads when things started failing.

He flipped only what he needed: one line to the analog console, another to the emergency transceiver rack, a third to a wall-mounted modem cluster that looked like its designers had never believed fiber would truly replace copper. The lights on those panels flickered, then steadied into a weak glow as current from the surviving batteries flowed. Somewhere deeper in the building, a relay clicked.

Patient Zero moved through the room behind him, touching things only after he did. When he brushed a fingertip over a gain knob to dislodge dust, she let her hand rest on the edge of the console, palm flat. When he leaned closer to a rack-mounted unit to read its labels, she mirrored the lean near a different panel. Each contact nudged her hum. Standing in the doorway, it had been a low, steady tone. As she made contact with metal tied more directly into the tower's core, it shifted in pitch and intensity, not wildly like the overload at the clinic, but noticeably.

He found an old headset hanging from a hook, its foam earpads cracked but intact, its jack still plugged into a console port. A desk microphone sat on a swivel arm, the kind broadcasters used to pretend spontaneity while everything behind them ran on scripts. He checked the console's meters: they quivered faintly with the room's hum, green bars shivering just above zero. He toggled a couple of switches he knew—power, channel selects, a bypass that sent input straight to the emergency transmitter instead of through whatever automation the city's operators had installed over the decades. He didn't know if anyone was listening. He didn't know if anything beyond this building still existed that could hear. That had never stopped him from trying to light up dead circuits before.

When he routed power to the emergency modem cluster, something in the equipment stack responded in a way that didn't match the simple happy flicker of gaining power. A small panel three racks over from the main console blinked to life with a series of test patterns, its tiny monochrome screen displaying a boot banner for hardware older than some of the hosts pressing their hands to the walls outside. Under the manufacturer logo, a configuration string scrolled past, and buried in that, familiar text: HELIXCORE CONTINGENCY PROTOCOL – CITY GRID BACKHAUL.

Voss had gotten her way years ago, then. He'd been there for some of the arguments, half-listening from the back of a meeting room while she fought with municipal liaisons about tying HelixCore's telemetry systems into public infrastructure. "Redundancy," she'd said then, voice flat. "You want us watching for cognitive anomalies? Then you give us something that doesn't die when your phones do." The implant discussions had followed. He'd been on the table for that, awake and annoyed while she'd stood over him with a tablet, eyes on scans of that scar above his temple.

"It sits right on the edge of regions we're worried about," she'd said when he'd asked why it had to be him. "If Theta-9—or anything like it—ever gets loose, I want real-time data on what it does to people like you." People like him: stubborn, scarred, statistically boring until they weren't. The implant had been a small thing near the old injury, a passive telemetry beacon that piggybacked on whatever local infrastructure it could see. After the first few days, he'd stopped thinking about it—until the airport, until the blackout, until the city went quiet in all the wrong ways and whatever the little device wanted to talk to disappeared.

Now, with the tower's emergency spine half-awake, it had something to reach for again. As he stood near the console, the panel on the HelixCore backhaul unit flickered from boot to status. A list of device IDs populated one side: most of them greyed out, labeled LOST or NO SIGNAL, representing implants and fixed nodes that had dropped when the network took over or the grid failed. One line near the top flashed from dead to amber. ID: HC-A12-REN. Location: UNSTABLE. Signal: INTERMITTENT.

He didn't need to see his name to know that was him. The scar over his temple throbbed in time with the panel's heartbeat indicator as the implant woke up enough to talk to something again. The emergency console spat a faint, intermittent ping into the static—small, irregular pulses that sat underneath the room's hum like a second, quieter heartbeat. It was enough.

Somewhere far away, deep under different concrete and a different sky, a junior systems analyst who'd drawn the short straw on overnight telemetry duty flinched as a forgotten indicator on his screen came to life. HelixCore's fallback site wasn't pretty either; it had been built for function long before anyone thought about aesthetics, and the layers they'd thrown over it in the last weeks—extra cabling, emergency workstations, cots in corridors—hadn't improved things. Fluorescent lights hummed. Screens glowed blue and green. The air smelled of coffee gone bitter and too many bodies.

The tech had been watching the same dead feeds for hours: collapsed-city environmental monitors returning nothing but noise where they returned anything at all, implants and field units flagged as lost or corrupted. When the asset list flickered and a line shifted from KIA/LOST to INTERMITTENT – UNVERIFIED, it took his exhausted brain a second to process it. He leaned closer, blinked twice, then swore softly and called the supervisor on duty. "It's Renner," he said, fingers already tapping to pull up archived data. "John Renner's tag just came up."

The supervisor, a woman in her forties with the tired posture of someone who'd been awake for more days than she wanted to count, frowned at his monitor. "Last known on him was the airport," she said. "That whole grid segment went dark." "This isn't the airport," he said, pulling up a rough triangulation from the tower's now-live backhaul. "Different quadrant. Somewhere in the eastern belt." "Could be spoofed." Another tech, leaning over from the next console, rubbed his eyes. "Novus had copies of some of our hardware. Theta-9 could fake an ID if it wanted to." "Not like this," the first one muttered, highlighting the waveform from the beacon. "Look at the handshake. That's the old contingency protocol. You'd have to know the buried config."

"Which we didn't share," the supervisor said. "And they never bothered to steal because they thought they'd get there first." She stared at the screen for another heartbeat, then slapped her palm on the desk. "Get Voss."

By the time Voss stepped into the control room, buttoning the front of a lab coat she'd obviously slept in for an hour flat somewhere, the asset ID had steadied into a weak but repeated signal. She looked smaller than she had in the city— maybe it was the lighting, maybe it was the mountains outside and the way the bunker's ceiling sat lower than HelixCore's executive floors—but nothing in her expression suggested she'd softened. Her eyes went straight to the highlighted line. "What?" she asked. No wasted syllables. "Renner's implant," the supervisor said. "We're getting intermittent from an emergency tower in the belt sector. It's patched into our old backhaul." Voss's jaw tightened. "That section saw a lot of Novus distribution."

"Yes, ma'am. But the handshake's wrong for Theta-9," the tech said, fingers dancing. "See here? This isn't a cascade pattern. It's a manual activation through city infrastructure. Telemetry's coming up as—" He hesitated. "—as normal." "Define normal in this context," Voss snapped. He pulled up the biometrics attached to the beacon: heart rate, temperature, rough EEG summaries. "Baseline elevated stress, but… human. No coherence signature. No synchronized hum overlay. The field in that area is saturated, but the model shows a null at his coordinates. Carrier: null. Non-responsive." Another tech frowned. "He's inside a fully active node and the network isn't resolving him. From the model's point of view, he's… not there." "Dead pixel," someone else muttered.

Voss studied the graphs, eyes tracking the familiar scar-shaped spike in the old scans they pulled up, the one she'd called "interesting" before the world had gone feral. Back then, it had been a curiosity: a region of tissue that refused to respond to Theta-9 in simulation. An outlier she'd flagged, noted, and filed under "too small a sample to matter." "He's not just uninfected," she said quietly. "He's incompatible. The field can't bind to that region at all." Her hand tightened on the back of the nearest chair. "And he has a live line into one of the city's backbone towers." "Could still be spoof," the skeptical tech insisted softly. Voss didn't even look at him. "The organism doesn't know our fallback handshake. It's smart, not omniscient." She nodded at the console. "We try him. Narrowband. Low power. I don't want to light that tower up in every direction for the network to notice."

Back in the tower's broadcast room, John heard the change in the static before he heard the voice. He'd been listening to the console's background hiss half out of habit, half out of a belief that if anything ever cut through it, he didn't want to miss the first second. Most of it was meaningless: the city's hum riding the wiring, random electromagnetic noise from failing equipment, the occasional pop of some remote breaker dying. Then the character of it shifted. The noise flattened, a narrow notch carved through the static. Underneath, faint and broken, came a thread of sound that didn't belong to anything in the room. "…nner… if that's you, respond with the last four digits of your original Theta-Nine trial ID."

For a heartbeat, his brain filed it under hallucination, a neat label for a voice that sounded like it had come from another life. Then the cadence clicked. Voss's voice, thinned by distance and compression, but still flat and precise. He leaned into the desk mic, thumb brushing the transmit toggle that glowed a faint amber. "Two three one eight," he said, voice level. He didn't pause to dredge it up; numbers like that had been drilled in too often to wander. Silence for a second, then an exhale over the line that might have been someone else in the room. Static chewed at the edges of the words that followed. "Confirmed," another voice said in the background, distant. "Matches locked file."

On her end, Voss stared at the confirmation on the screen as if daring it to change. It didn't. You didn't guess those digits; you read them from records that no longer existed in any system the network could touch. "You were supposed to be dead," she said finally, leaning close enough to the pickup that the tech monitoring input flinched at the spike. "Yeah," John said. "I got better. The city disagreed." The connection wavered, static swelling, then narrowed again as the tower's equipment and HelixCore's fallback systems found a fragile equilibrium. "Report," Voss said. Emotion could wait; it always had. "City status, your status. Brief."

He kept it clinical. "City's humming," he said. "Hosts everywhere. They move in flows, not mobs. Tune themselves to vibration, not sight or sound. Hugging structures—load-bearing, especially. Bridges, rails, transformers." He glanced at Patient Zero, who stood by the console, eyes on him, headset cable nearly brushing her shoulder. "They ignore me. Brush past, correct for me like I'm a bollard. No hum, no aggression. They hit me with the wall at the airport, everything went black. Woke up intact. Since then, nothing. I'm a blind spot."

On the other end of the line, techs fed his words directly into the models, overlaying them on the data the tower's environmental sensors now provided: field strengths, coherence measures, rough maps of network activity around his location. The display showed a sea of synchronized Theta-9 activity with a single, stubborn void where his implant beacon sat.

"From the model's perspective," one murmured, "he's a non-coherent insertion. Location exists. Field overlay doesn't." "Null carrier," Voss said, eyes still on the graphs. "The organism can't map him onto its structure. That's why it defaulted to overload and blackout at the airport. It tried to route through him and hit a wall." The tech beside her nodded reluctantly. "His vitals line up with that. High stress, yes, but no Theta signature. The local field's treating his coordinates like dead space."

John listened to the pause over the line, the murmured calculations he couldn't quite make out, then the shift in Voss's tone as she moved from assessment to exploitation. "What else do you have near you?" she asked. "Structures, density, behavior shifts. Be precise."

He looked around the room. "Emergency broadcast facility under a comms mast," he said. "Old analog console, radio gear, backhaul modem cluster patched into your contingency protocol. Building's thick-walled, hosts are ringed around it outside with hands on the concrete. Humming like they're listening through it." He hesitated, then added the part that shouldn't have made sense at all, because he understood from her voice that if he didn't say it now, he'd end up omitting it on purpose later. "I've also had Patient Zero following me for several kilometers." There was a kind of silence you could feel even over a bad line. The kind where people held their breath rather than fill it. This was that. "Clarify," Voss said. Her voice had gone very still. "When you say Patient Zero…"

"The first documented case," he said. "The girl from the PSAs and early hospital interviews. Scar through the left eyebrow. University hoodie. Hospital bracelet. The one Novus got when they started trialing their cure." In the fallback site, someone swore softly. Another tech's fingers flew over keys, dragging old images out of archived databases: a smiling girl on a hospital bed, scar visible, captioned with names and dates; stills from awareness campaigns; news crawls. They laid them side by side with the live-video thumbnail the tower's system provided: grainy, low-res, but enough. Hoodie. Bracelet. Scar.

"You're certain," Voss said. It wasn't a question so much as a demand for the margin of error. "I've walked under two billboards and a clinic loop with her face on it," John said. "Unless there was a global shortage of brown-eyed girls with that scar, it's her." "We traced early Novus trials back to her blood," a tech muttered, half to himself. "If they built their scaffold off her profile, she'd be… a primary reference, not just a host."

Voss's mind was already ahead. Patient Zero as first node, first scaffold, first proof-of-concept. Novus had thought they were using her to save people. The organism had used them to seed its network with a template that matched the pathogen's original vector perfectly. And now that template was walking around tied to a null carrier the field couldn't absorb. "Describe how she's behaving relative to the hosts," Voss said.

"She tracks me," he said. "Keeps a fixed distance. Mimics my gait, posture, head movements with a lag. Reacts to vibration spikes before structures or other hosts do. Hosts around her re-space automatically. There's a buffer around her—small, but stable. When things fall or flows surge, that pocket keeps opening up where she is. If I stay near her, I get pulled into that zone." He glanced at the girl, who was now watching his hand on the mic with unnerving focus. "When she overloads, my touch dampens it. Like sticking an insulator into a live junction."

On their end, sensor graphs from the tower's foundation spiked and dipped in ways that matched what he said. When he'd first routed power, there had been a small, inexplicable notch in the otherwise smooth coherence curve—an absence that sat right where his implant reported its position. When the girl had touched panels, the coherence had improved locally. When he'd grabbed her to steady an overload, the curve had kinked.

"Step closer to the tower core," Voss said. "I want a live test while we still have power. Put your hand on the main housing. Tell me what she does. I'll tell you what the field does."

He obeyed. Moving through the room, he crossed to the inner wall where thick cables disappeared up toward the mast, and laid his palm flat against the metal casing of a distribution panel that hummed with the tower's heart. The vibration crawled up his arm, buzzing in bone and scar both. Patient Zero tracked him automatically, coming to stand a pace away, eyes on his hand. A second later, she stepped in, placing her own palm on another part of the housing. Her hum jumped, resolving into a clearer, stronger note that set the hairs on his wrist on end.

Outside, hosts responded. From his vantage point he couldn't see them, but Voss's people could see the tower's environmental sensors. Field strength at the base spiked; coherence patterns tightened. The network liked this configuration: primary node on the core, pure load path, no interference.

"Now break contact with the metal," Voss said. "Keep one hand on her." He pulled his hand from the housing and set it instead on the girl's upper arm. Her skin was cool under the thin fabric. The effect was immediate. Her hum stuttered, then dropped a notch. The vibration in the panel changed character, losing some of its clarity. Outside, the sensor graphs wobbled. Coherence dipped in a narrow band centered on the tower base before the field compensated, currents shifting to route around the localized fault. On the graphs, it looked like someone had pushed a non-conductive wedge into a live, densely packed circuit. The organism rerouted without conscious thought because that was what robust systems did. But the fact it had to reroute at all meant its architecture wasn't as invulnerable as it wanted to be.

"Null node plus primary node," Voss said, mostly to herself. "Local coherence failure. The field hates you two together, Renner. That makes you useful." "Feeling cherished already," he said. Around her, techs were already building new branches of model code, writing functions labelled with ugly, promising terms: NULL INSERTION, NODE DESTABILIZATION, LOCALIZED FAULT INJECTION. None of it was a cure. None of it promised to roll back what had already been done. But it was a wedge, a way to make the organism spend energy keeping itself stable instead of expanding, a way to introduce failure modes at scale if they could figure out how to copy what John and the girl did to the field in a context that didn't require both of them to be physically present.

"If we can map the effect you two have on coherence," Voss

said, voice snapping back to the present, "we can design a way to inject that failure mode into other nodes. Maybe not everywhere at once, but enough to slow it. Enough to buy time. Enough to carve out pockets it can't saturate." The console's power indicators dipped then, warning lights flickering. The battery bank feeding the room had only so much to give, and the little dance they'd just done had eaten into reserves. Static swelled in John's ears as the line's noise floor rose. "Connection's degrading," one of the techs warned.

Voss nodded sharply. "We don't have the luxury of a full debrief. Renner, listen carefully. You stay alive. You keep her with you. You keep observing. Behaviors near structures get priority—anything that changes how they interact with load-bearing lines. We'll be listening on this channel as long as the tower stands and we have power to reach it. If you can, get deeper into the building. There may be a hardline backhaul in the sublevels we can exploit later."

He watched the power bars sag and made the calculation in his head: how much time the tower had before the batteries quit; how many recon loops he could make before then. He thought of the airport, of Lee's voice crackling over a different radio, of bodies on runways. "Did they get out?" he asked. He didn't specify who. There were only a few names that mattered. She knew them.

"At least two flights reached secondary sites," Voss said. She didn't look away from the graphs when she said it, but her voice shifted a fraction. "We have personnel and dependents from your manifest here and at Site B. They're alive. I'm not saying more on this line." Relief didn't hit him in any dramatic way. It slotted into place like another fact on a checklist: runway held long enough, engines did what they were meant to, stubborn pilots and ground crews bought their own minutes. Lee and Anna had somewhere solid under their feet now. That was enough. "You're not a sacrificial asset, Renner,"

Voss added, as the static began to fray the edges of her words. "Don't freelance. I need data, not martyrdom." He let out a slow breath. "Relax, Doctor," he said. "I'm too stubborn to die for free."

The line cut mid-breath. One second there was Voss's faint exhale and the murmur of other voices; the next, only static and the tower's hum feeding back into the console. The status light on the HelixCore backhaul unit dropped from a weak green to an amber blink, then steadied into a slow heartbeat that said the implant was still there, still talking into the void, but nobody was currently listening.

John lifted his hand from the girl's arm. Her hum stayed in the lower register he'd pushed it into, then slowly climbed back toward its previous tone. Outside, hosts would be settling again into whatever stable configuration the organism preferred around this node, re-establishing their patterns as if nothing had happened.

He stood in the muted hum of the tower's interior, surrounded by dead and dying equipment designed for a different crisis, feeling the weight of what had just changed. He wasn't just a survivor walking through the ruins of a world. He was a null stitched into the network's densest tissues, a fault the organism couldn't smooth out. She was its first node, its favorite stabilizer, the shape it had built its body around. Together, they had just shown the thing that owned the city that it could be made to flinch.

Patient Zero watched him with that unsettling focus, head tilted, eyes tracking the set of his shoulders, the way his jaw clenched. Outside, the hosts pressed their palms to the walls and hummed, turning the building into a drum. Inside, in a room built for sending messages, a single dead man's tag blinked in the corner of an old panel, stubborn and steady, waiting for someone to use it to break something bigger than both of them.

CHAPTER 19

They lost the line with a soft click and a long hiss, as if someone had finally lifted a needle from a record that had been grinding on the same groove too long. The broadcast room felt different afterward. The hardware was unchanged—same consoles, same racks, same cables humming behind the panels—but the tower's voice had shifted. The hum that had been a clean, steady tone when he first walked in was now slightly out of true, as if something had hit it and left it ringing.

On the console, the analog meters that had sat almost perfectly still before Voss's call now trembled with a narrow, twitching motion. Not wild, not catastrophic. Just a tiny, persistent oscillation along their green bands, like the system couldn't quite settle on where "steady" was anymore. The HelixCore backhaul panel in the rack off to his left blinked its heartbeat light with the same interval as before, but occasionally there was a faint, irregular hitch, a missed beat that his nerves picked up even when his eyes didn't.

He turned from the hardware to the girl. Her hum hadn't snapped back to its original pitch after he let go of her arm; it sat a little lower, carrying a faint roughness, as if she'd been using a voice not built for the note. She stood near the edge of the console, fingers curled loosely over the metal, eyes tracking his hand whenever it moved. When he shifted weight from one leg to the other, her gaze flicked between his boots and the base of the tower cables, as though bracing for another instruction.

He watched her for a while in the quiet that followed the

cut line, looking for tremors, for any sign that he'd pushed her too hard with Voss's impromptu experiments. The hitch in her hum smoothed slightly with each passing minute, but never fully resolved. Now and then her head turned toward the wall, toward the mass of concrete between them and the hosts outside, like a radio waiting for a broadcast that refused to arrive.

He left her with the consoles and went to the stairwell. The door to the utility stair opened on hinges that had been serviced more recently than anything else in the building, and a thin draft of colder air slipped in around him. He descended a half-flight, far enough to reach the narrow, high-set maintenance slit that overlooked the strip of ground at the building's base. The glass was wired and fogged, but he could see enough.

The ring of hosts around the tower had... shifted. Before, their bodies had formed a nearly perfect band, each person spaced evenly along the wall, palms flat, heads tilted in the same dull angle. Now that smoothness was gone. Gaps appeared where two or three had stepped back a pace from the concrete, hands resting instead on each other's shoulders or on utility boxes bolted to the foundations. Others paced in small, tight arcs rather than standing still, fingers occasionally lifting and pressing back as if testing the wall. Heads turned more often, not in full arcs but in short, searching movements that reminded him of animals sniffing a fence for the source of a scent they couldn't quite place. Nobody screamed. Nobody broke into the violent overflow he'd seen in the hospitals' feeds. The ring still held. But the micro-movements were wrong. The rhythm had picked up a stutter. The field was re-optimizing itself, shifting weight to paths that offended its equations a little less, never considering that the offence hadn't come from the concrete.

He stood with one shoulder against the cool stairwell wall and let that sink in. When he and the girl had touched the tower together, they hadn't just produced a small anomaly inside the building. They'd forced the network to reroute around them, to spend energy finding new paths through its favorite node because the old ones had gone energetically expensive. It hadn't reacted with anything he'd call anger. Just with that restless adjustment, the kind systems made when somebody introduced a configuration they didn't like.

The girl had been the system's best idea of perfection. He'd just used her as a makeshift lever and jammed that perfection into the building's spine until the organism flinched. A thin, irrational guilt slid in around the professional satisfaction. She hadn't given consent; she didn't have the machinery left to understand what she was being used for. He told himself Voss would only get one shot at turning this into something that mattered and he could not afford sentiment. The argument was clean, mathematical. It still landed like a lie in his gut.

He stayed there long enough to see the ring's movement dampen a little, the pacing hosts settling back into more static positions, the hands on the wall spacing themselves more evenly.The system settled around the fault pair and moved on. Satisfied that no violent feedback was coming in the next few seconds, he went back up to the broadcast room. The girl's eyes found him instantly, as if he'd stepped into a tracking beam. Voss and her people were already pulling apart the flinch on their end.

The fallback site's war-room held more screens than people, but the people made up for the outnumbering with noise and motion. One wall had been turned into a live map of the city: streets and districts rendered in a array of dull colors overlaid with moving heatmaps of Theta-9 coherence. Lines pulsed where bridges, rails, and transformer chains carried the highest loads. Other areas showed as dimmer, unstable patches—places where infrastructure had already failed or been torn down. Near the eastern belt, a tiny void pulsed where the tower's model insisted the field should be strong, but the data refused to acknowledge anything. The label over it read HC-A12-REN.

In the middle of the room, a separate display showed a time series taken from the tower's sensors: a smooth band of high coherence, then a sharp spike, a brief kink, and a new steady state slightly lower than before. A smaller inset plot showed the HelixCore backhaul panel's readings: the beacon's activation, the tower's battery level, the precise moment when the console started carrying John's voice.

"This is why you wake me," Dr. Holt said, rubbing at his eyes with the heel of one hand as he came to stand in front of the display. He was in his sixties, hair gone mostly white at the temples, face lined more from frowning at data than from laughing at anything. He wore no lab coat, just a sweater under a rumpled jacket and a pair of reading glasses dangling from a cord. "You have a perfectly good catastrophe without me, and then you wave a coherent glitch in my face." "We have a null carrier and a reference node fighting over a tower," Voss said. "And a field that doesn't like either of them. You're here because the pictures without words aren't enough anymore."

Dr. Singh was already at the board to the side, marker in hand, eyes on the same plots. Younger than Holt by twenty years, he carried his tiredness differently: tucked in, precise, as if he'd folded it into a corner of his mind for later. He'd drawn the city as a network: dots for nodes—hosts, junctions, buildings—and lines for the paths Theta-9 used to propagate. Over that, he'd traced curves representing coherence modes: the ways the pathogen could arrange itself over the network to maximize its own stability.

Holt pointed at the tower's time series. "Before Renner touches anything, you have a beautiful standing wave," he said. "Theta-9 sitting happily on your tower, humming along the rails, using the hardware the taxpayers were kind enough to build it. Then your girl—Patient Zero—puts her hand on the metal, and coherence spikes. Of course it does. She's its perfect match. The field loves her. Then he touches her, and you get this." He tapped the kink in the curve. "We hit a mode the system hates."

Singh nodded without looking away from his graph. "Think of Theta-9 as a self-optimizing signal," he said, voice quiet. "It's not just in individual brains anymore. It's riding your infrastructure like a global communication mode. The hosts and structures are nodes. The pathogen is the wave that wants to be smooth everywhere at once. High coherence is low energy. It prefers that. But certain nodes don't cooperate." He drew a circle around one point on his network diagram, colored it in, then drew a line through it. "This is Renner. Physically present, connected to the graph, but with a coupling coefficient of zero. The field cannot transmit through him. Any global mode that tries to include him becomes unstable." Voss folded her arms. "Broken node," she said. "Null node. Pick a term that looks good on a paper later. The important part is that it's not optional. The field doesn't get to choose to go through him. It fails when it tries."

Holt hooked a thumb at the inset of Patient Zero's old data. Voss had pulled every scrap HelixCore had scraped from Novus leaks, internal collators, and Havel's guilty dumps. EEG traces from early trials, behavioral notes, structural imaging. "And she," Holt said, "is the opposite. She was the first scaffold the pathogen learned on when it hit human neural tissue. Novus trained their 'cure' on her. Theta-9 learned that her architecture is ideal. Her coupling coefficient is one, if we're being lazy. Whenever she's in contact with the field's favorite toys, coherence improves."

Singh drew another node on his diagram, this one outlined, connected to many others with thick lines. "Primary reference," he said. "Every distributed system needs a standard, a version of 'how to be' it compares others to. The network trusts her most. Whatever else it does, it will always try to align towards her configuration where possible." They replayed the tower event with both overlaid: the coherence curve, the servo graph of the tower's structural vibration, the HelixCore backhaul's record of when Renner routed power and when he and the girl touched the hardware.

"First contact," Holt said, narrating. "She touches the panel. Coherence at the tower jumps. From the field's point of view, that's ideal coupling. It commits hard.' Then our broken node puts a hand on her, and the equations go sideways. The system is suddenly trying to maintain high coupling through a node that cannot carry it. It works—for a fraction of a second. Then the math insists the configuration is too expensive. So the field reroutes. That's your kink." On the city heatmap, the tower's small bright point flared, then dimmed to a value slightly lower than before the test. Around it, the ring of hosts had gone from smooth to ringed with tiny, stranger fluctuations.

"The early Theta-9 simulations on Renner's scar," Voss said. "Back when Theta-9 was still a lab pathogen, not a field god. That region refused binding in the models. It didn't matter what we threw at it—normal tissue, Theta-modified tissue, different parameters. There was always a dead zone where the equations collapsed. We flagged it as interesting. Then the world started burning and it became trivia." "The implant," Singh said, pointing at the little symbol he'd drawn over that node. "You dropped a beacon right into that incompatible region." "So when the airport wall hit him and Theta-9 tried to grab hold of his brain like everyone else's, it hit that lesion and the implanted hardware at the same time," Holt said. "It tried to lock him into coherence and discovered that, locally, the cost function goes to infinity. Easiest solution in a system like this? Black him out. Remove the active disturbance. Move on to more cooperative substrate."

"And in doing that," Singh added, "it tagged him, internally, as unusable. Systems don't think 'this person is special.' They think 'paths through this location make the global mode worse.' So the model starts treating any route through him as high cost. In optimization terms, he becomes a spike in the energy landscape. You don't route through spikes unless you're forced."

"Which it never is," Voss said. "There are plenty of bridges that aren't made of him. Plenty of brains that don't have that scar. So the organism behaves as if he doesn't exist. It flows around him like water around an air bubble." "Until you stick him to its favorite node and its favorite tower," Holt said. "Then you get to watch the world's biggest, ugliest wave equation throw a tantrum." Voss let them talk until the theory took shape on the board: dots and lines, curves and kinks, terms like eigenmode and coupling scribbled next to more human words—broken node, reference node, stutter. When they paused, she stepped in. "Translate this into something I can do to a city," she said. "Not a paper. Not a seminar. An action."

Holt pushed his glasses up his nose and squinted at the diagrams. "The signal has settled into some set of dominant modes," he said. "The path it's found through bridges, rails, and hosts is the cheapest, energetically. You cannot break all of those paths at once, not with what we have left. But you can change the cost landscape." He tapped Renner's blacked-out node. "This is a naturally occurring broken node. The field cannot use it. If we can build hardware that behaves like his incompatibility—local nulls that absolutely refuse Theta-9 coherence—and drop them into critical hubs, we can force the organism to reroute around them. Enough of those, and its global modes start to fragment. It spends energy just keeping itself coherent."

Singh drew small black squares at key junctions on his city graph. "We don't need to kill it everywhere," he said. "We need to create pockets it cannot fully saturate and then connect those pockets into corridors. Null corridors for uninfected movement. Null zones where we can stage anything else we come up with later—drugs, viral competitors, whatever Havel's nightmares suggest. The field will treat those zones like wounds in its body. It will work around them. But every time it works around them, it pays a cost. Enough cost over enough time might not kill it, but it will slow it. And slowing it means people have somewhere to stand."

Holt's gaze drifted to a corner of the room where someone had pinned up a printout of civilian call logs from the early days: names, ages, half-finished descriptions. He reached up and added a small mark by one entry, almost absently. Singh saw the motion but said nothing. "Someone still in there?" Voss asked. She didn't soften the question. Holt's mouth twitched. "My daughter," he said. "Last signal out of her phone was near one of the midtown towers two days before we lost the city grid. She liked to run along the bridges because the view was good. Now she's probably one of your humming lines on this map." He tapped the network drawing once, lightly, as if knocking on a door. "If you give me a way to carve out a null zone she can stand in one day… I'll take it."

Voss nodded once, the closest thing to sympathy she had bandwidth for. "Null–Reference Interference Model," she said, reciting the bare-bones label Singh had scribbled at the top of the board. "Broken node, reference node, path of least suffering in between. We don't cure Theta-9. We destabilize its body until it has to choose between holding what it has and reaching for more. Then we hit it again." In the tower, John started treating the building like a test range.

Power was finite. He could feel the batteries weakening in the slight changes in the room's lighting, in the way some indicator LEDs took longer to come back after flickers. Waiting for Voss to ring back was a luxury he wasn't sure the system could afford. If she wanted more data, he'd have it ready when she did.

On a lower floor, he found an equipment corridor that ran along one side of the building. The walls here were thicker, armored with additional concrete and steel where bigger cable bundles ran up from the foundations. The hum was stronger, traveling in clean, straight lines along the conduits before bleeding into the rest of the structure. Outside, on the other side of the wall, the ring of hosts persisted, hands pressed flat, shoulders touching.

First experiment: proximity and flow. He walked down the corridor alone, without touching anything, slowing when he reached a stretch where conduit brackets buzzed under his fingers before he raised his hand. He stopped, listened, then shifted half a meter closer to the wall. From inside, there was no change. Outside, through memory of the stairwell view and the subtle feel in his bones, there was still the same steady rhythm of contact. No heads turned. No hands moved. He was an inert lump of meat standing near a live rail.

He gestured for the girl to join him. She came without hesitation, bare feet whispering against the concrete, humming softly. When she reached his side, he pointed at the wall and then at her hand. For a second she simply watched him, head tilted. Then she lifted her arm and placed her palm flat on the painted block. The difference was almost imperceptible, but it was there. The vibration under his boots tightened as the system's favorite node connected directly to a path it valued. Somewhere beyond the concrete, a subtle shiver ran through the ring. He pictured hands on the exterior wall aligning more tightly under hers.

He stepped in close, until his shoulder nearly touched hers, and laid his hand gently on her other arm. The sensation that came back didn't have a word he liked. It felt like a beat error, the kind musicians heard when two notes almost—but not quite—matched. The hum lost a fraction of its smoothness; a faint, irregular wobble passed through it. Outside, the field hesitated. For less than a second, but long enough for one host's behavior to crack. Through the maintenance slit at the end of the corridor, he saw a man in a faded work jacket lift his hand off the wall entirely, fingers twitching in the air as if searching for a surface that had moved. The humming from his direction cut out for two heartbeats. Then, as the field resolved around the fault pair and rerouted, his palm slapped back onto the concrete, harder than before, his body locking back into the pattern.

He repeated the test along a different stretch of wall, in a narrower corridor where cable trays ran overhead and the vibration carried more through the ceiling than the floor. Same sequence: him alone—no change. Her touching the wall—coherence tightening. Him touching her—minute beat error, micro-stutter outside. He filed the timing and intensity away: fractions of a second where the organism paused, considered, and then bypassed. Little windows where its certainty cracked. It wasn't just the system that learned. She did too, in her way.

By the third pass, she had started to anticipate him. When he paused by a section of wall and looked at a particular bracket or panel, her gaze followed, and her hand lifted a beat later, reaching for metal even before he made the gesture. When he stopped short of a bulkhead and looked back at her, she halted precisely in that spot and waited, humming, eyes on his face rather than the structure. He gave her simple non-verbal jobs to test how much control he had over that coordination. At one junction, he raised his hand, fingers splayed, then lowered it toward the floor. "Stay," he said, the word more for him than for her. She didn't move when he stepped away, just watched him go, hum sitting at its baseline pitch.

He walked down the corridor alone, far enough that he could feel the difference in how the field flowed around him without her nearby. The buffer vanished. The hum became more chaotic at the edges, small random eddies reappearing in host behavior on the other side of the wall. Moving bodies almost walked into him in the narrow space under the maintenance slit's field of view before their paths curved at the last second for reasons that had nothing to do with his presence. He lifted his hand and beckoned. She came, steps quickening until she was at his side again. The buffer reappeared. Outside, trajectories smoothed. The ring regained that unnatural regularity, marred only by the tiny, almost invisible stutters when he touched her and the wall at the same time and forced the organism to notice something it didn't like.

At one point, when she had her palm on a metal junction box and he had his fingers wrapped lightly around her wrist, one host broke the pattern worse than any he'd seen yet. The woman—grey hair pulled back, hospital wristband still on one arm—stopped humming. Completely. Her hand lifted off the wall and stayed suspended in the air for three full seconds. Her fingers twitched, curling and uncurling like she was trying to find the edge of something that kept being moved just out of reach. Her eyes remained unfocused, but there was tension in her jaw that hadn't been there before.

Then the field rerouted. Somewhere farther along the wall, other hosts pressed closer, hands overlapping to reinforce contact. Pressure shifted. The woman's arm snapped back to the concrete like a magnet had been switched on, and the hum resumed, louder than before. He didn't say anything. There was nobody to say it to who understood. But the little event lodged itself in his head like a shard of glass. They were not just being ignored. They were annoying something vast, making it misstep, forcing it to correct. The system didn't think, but its behavior had tells.

Between experiments, he stayed in motion more than he needed to, partly because stillness made the tower's voice too loud, partly because he was watching her watch him. In a side room with no equipment, just a bare concrete wall and an old metal locker, he let himself slide down until he sat with his back against the cool surface. He drew one knee up to ease the ache in it, pressed his hand absently to the scar at his temple when it flared in time with the tower's deeper shakes.

She hovered in the doorway for a moment, as if the absence of obvious structural value confused her. Then she stepped in and, after a tiny hesitation, mirrored him. Not opposite, not precisely, but close enough: sitting down with her back against the same wall, legs bent at almost the same angle. At first she left a gap between them. After a minute, during which he didn't move or speak, she shifted sideways in small increments until her shoulder nearly brushed his.

He tried language again, not because he expected it to work, but because it was what you did when you shared a room with someone who still looked human. "Tired," he said, letting his head fall back against the concrete for a second. "Hurts. Stay." The words were plain, the tone softer than the one he used on the mic.

She didn't react to the content in any way that matched comprehension. But at the sounds, she turned her head toward him, eyes scanning his face as if cataloguing shape and movement. When he rubbed his knee with his palm, she mirrored the gesture on her own leg. When he flexed his right hand, shaking out stiffness, she did the same with hers, fingers spreading, closing.

Once, unprompted, her hand lifted toward his face. Her fingers hovered just short of the scar above his temple, tracing the air over that patch of skin the way his attention always did when the hum made it ache. She didn't touch. Whether that was because the system had learned that contact there meant trouble or because some residual caution in her stopped her, he couldn't tell.

He caught her wrist gently before she closed the distance, thumb pressing over the pulse he couldn't quite feel because the hum muted everything. She blinked, slowly, but didn't pull away. For a moment they sat like that, hand in hand, the organism's favorite node and its least favorite location joined by simple pressure. The tower's vibration faltered for a fraction of a second, then resumed. He released her and let her hand fall back to her lap.

The realization that slid in with that tiny exchange was heavier than the humming concrete. The network wasn't only using her as hardware. Whatever passed for understanding in its distributed mind was using her as its best guess at him—its finest instrument trying to model the one point in its body that refused to sing. Somewhere inside that constant tuning, the original girl might still be trapped, or she might be gone, but the behavior read like curiosity even when he refused to name it as such.

He made his decision there, in the side room with no panels, back against anonymous concrete. He would keep her with him because Voss needed the pair of them as a lever. He would also keep her with him because he refused to let the system reduce her entirely to equipment. Even if ninety-nine percent of what moved her was Theta-9, the remaining fraction—however small, however deeply buried—deserved better than being treated like a cable. He could use the attention the organism paid her to hurt it, and if there was anything left of the person Novus had turned into their template, he would give that part whatever small victories he could.

When he went back to the broadcast room, the HelixCore backhaul panel still blinked its slow heartbeat. No incoming line yet. Maybe they were rerouting their own systems. Maybe they were arguing over equations. Maybe the batteries wouldn't last long enough for another call. That uncertainty settled in next to the others. It didn't change the next step.

On one wall of the room, under a layer of dust, someone had left a laminated schematic of the tower's infrastructure taped up: floor plans, cable routes, underground backhaul paths leading away from the building into the broader grid. He wiped grime off it with the side of his hand and traced the lines with a fingertip. Hardline routes ran under streets toward other nodes—other towers, substations, exchange points. Paths the organism already used to stitch itself together. Paths Voss would want mapped for whatever null devices she tried to build.

Voss had told him to stay alive and keep observing, not to martyr himself for a clean curve on a graph. The Null-Reference Interference Model would only work as long as the broken node kept walking into saturated zones, as long as the primary node stayed aligned with him, as long as they kept forcing the field to correct and correct again. He turned from the schematic to the girl. She stood in her now-familiar half-pace behind and to the right position, watching him with that patient, unnerving focus. He nodded toward the corridor. "Come on," he said. "They need us to break things."

The words meant nothing to her, but the movement did. She fell into step as he left the broadcast room, bare feet whispering against the floor. As they moved along the corridor toward the stairs, the hum in the walls wavered—tiny shifts in phase and amplitude propagating outward through concrete and steel, the organism's body feeling the path of its favorite node and its broken node moving together through its nerves. The network was vast and largely blind to individuals, but at some level of its math, the combination of those two had become a parameter it couldn't fully predict. And that, more than anything, made the next step worth taking.

CHAPTER 20

The tower felt older when he woke. The air had the same recycled dust taste, the same faint tang of warmed insulation, but the building's pulse had sagged. The emergency lights in the equipment corridor glowed a little duller, and the hum in the walls had lost its clean, knife-straight tone. It wobbled now, a tiny beat ripple under the main note, like someone had bent the blade and it was pretending not to notice. He'd fallen asleep half-sitting against a rack, boots still on, one arm looped through a ladder rail so he couldn't roll onto the concrete. The scar above his temple throbbed in time with the new imperfection, a stubborn echo under the broader vibration.

He stood, joints protesting in the stiff, nonspecific way that meant everything was technically fine and just tired. The HelixCore panel across the corridor still blinked its slow status light, but every few cycles there was a short, uneven hitch —barely a pause, more of a stutter in the long green line of its patience. No incoming call. No shift from idle to active. Somewhere far away, people were either asleep, dead, or too busy to talk to the man haunting their favorite tower. The girl hummed three paces behind him, in the doorway. Her pitch had settled back toward what he'd started thinking of as baseline, but there was a roughness to it now, like she'd worn the smoothness off with use. When he shifted his weight toward the right-hand wall, her tone crept up half a fraction, correcting itself almost immediately, as if her body was running some constant internal adjustment against the building's new wobble.

He went back to the maintenance slit and pressed his forehead to the cool, wired glass. Outside, the ring of hosts that had been a clean band around the tower had blurred. It still encircled the building, but there were thicker segments and thinner gaps now, like uneven paint. The densest knots matched the floors where he'd run his earlier wall tests; he could almost map his footsteps from the way they clung more tightly in certain spots. In three places, the pattern was stranger: a handful of hosts paced short, tight loops instead of standing still, circling directly under the points where he'd had his hand on the girl while she touched the wall. Their palms kept lifting and replanting on the concrete in the same small arcs, as if the system had marked those coordinates as needing a replay.

Along the section of wall nearest this particular corridor, the band of bodies was thicker than anywhere else. They weren't pressed together—there was no crush—but the spacing had shifted. More hands. More shoulders touching the concrete. The field was paying attention to where he'd last moved her, not just to where the foundations were strongest. He filed that quietly: it remembered coordinates, not just structures. Behind him, the girl's hum changed again when he leaned a little nearer the slit. It wasn't loud—a quarter-step up, a slight tightening—and it snapped back down as soon as he eased away from the wall. He repeated the motion, watching the hosts outside. No obvious reaction yet; too subtle, too local. But her pitch adjusting before the ring's small motions completed told him enough. She was feeling not just what the field was doing, but where it wanted to re-shape around him. A living direction finder for something that didn't have a face.

He'd learned as much as staring at the same concrete could give him. Sitting in a tower watching the organism bruise itself against the walls was only half a job. Voss needed maps, not just anecdotes. He took one last look at the warped ring, then turned away from the slit. The girl stepped back automatically to give him space in the narrow corridor, then fell into her usual half-pace behind and to his right. "Let's see what your god does outside," he said, voice low more from habit than secrecy. She hummed in answer or in coincidence; it was impossible to tell.

He marked the tower in his head as Node One and picked a direction. There was a smaller knot of infrastructure south of here—a cluster of relay boxes and a squat substation he'd glimpsed from higher floors. Node Two. If he wanted to see how density moved, he had to walk between them.

They left through the same side door as before. The metal slab stuck a little more on its hinges than it had the previous day —a small shift in alignment, a hint that the building's bones were still settling around the things clinging to them. Outside, the hosts that had been pressed against this stretch of wall withdrew like water around a rock as soon as the girl stepped through, leaving the familiar thin pocket of space around her. Their hands slid sideways along concrete and conduit, never quite touching either of them, bodies adjusting as smoothly as they had every other time.

He stepped out into the cold, the airfield wind having lost none of its enthusiasm for crawling under clothes and through bones. The hum out here was broader, the tower's vibration feeding into the surrounding structures and out across the broken streets. He picked a line along a frontage road that ran parallel to a tangle of poles and cable cabinets, then started walking. The girl's bare feet whispered against the asphalt behind him, a counterpoint to his boots.

He expected the ring at the tower to settle once they were clear. Instead, he watched it thin along the wall in their direction of travel. A few hosts stayed plastered to the concrete as if nothing had changed, but here and there, individuals peeled away in ones and twos. They didn't walk toward him in any meaningful sense; they turned along the building, palms dragging over paint and masonry until they reached the corner where the tower met the street. From there, they drifted to the nearest structures that aligned even roughly with the path he'd chosen: light poles, guardrails, the side of a maintenance shed. It was as if the organism had decided that whatever configuration he and the girl created was worth sampling at a distance.

Ahead, hosts hugging other walls seemed to pre-orient before the pair reached them. People who had been facing along a rail shifted to stand with shoulders turned fractionally toward the line of travel, hands adjusting to new spots as if leaning toward an unseen signal. None of them looked at him. None stepped directly into his path. But he could see the wake they were leaving behind: a thinning halo around the tower and a thickening line along the route he'd chosen, drawn not on open ground but on the metal and concrete the field loved most. They stopped at a relay cabinet the size of a refrigerator, bolted to a low plinth of poured concrete on the roadside verge. He laid his fingers on the cool steel. Nothing happened outside of the familiar sensation of standing near a live circuit, the hum focusing a little through the metal's mass. When he took his hand away and nodded at the girl, she reached out and pressed her palm flat against the cabinet.

Within a minute, hosts along the nearest stretch of fence began drifting toward it. Not all at once; there was no sudden rush. They detached in slow trickles, walking along rails until they could get close enough to lay hands on the cabinet's housing or the concrete that held it. The density along the fence thinned; the cabinet grew a ring of bodies like a miniature version of the tower. He walked away, gesturing the girl with him, toward a battered light pole thirty meters down. When she touched that one, the process repeated. The old cabinet's ring loosened, some of its adherents sliding off to follow the new chain of structures. Hosts at a distance pivoted in micro-turns along their own rails and panels, redirecting their attention. The organism wasn't moving like an animal; it was re-weighting preferred paths in its graph, following the combination of template and null he represented even though it had hated that configuration at the tower.

He walked in silence, ticking new rules off inside his head. Broken node plus reference node in motion didn't just cause local glitches; together they dragged a smear of heightened coherence across the city, a moving line the system couldn't stop trying to clean up. A beacon, but not the kind anyone would have written on a recruiting poster.

On the other side of the world, people staring at heatmaps started to swear. The fallback site's war-room was dimmer than usual; power rationing had cut the overhead glare to narrow strips above consoles. Telemetry graphs glowed bright by comparison. On the main map of the city, the tower's node still showed as a bright knot of coherence in a largely saturated grid. But now a narrow, worm-like ridge of higher intensity was oozing away from it, along streets that hadn't been particularly important before. It wasn't random noise; it was too contiguous, too aligned with actual infrastructure.

A tech zoomed in until individual roads resolved. "That shouldn't be there," she said softly, more to herself than anyone else. The line of elevated coherence coincided almost perfectly with minor poles, cabinets, and guardrails running in a rough corridor from the tower toward one neighborhood. As she watched, it shifted, bending along a side street when the ridge reached a junction. "Pull Renner's tag over that frame," Voss said. John's implant ID—HC-A12-REN—overlaid onto the map, a small icon blinking at the leading edge of the ridge. The system kept trying to draw it as part of the field, then conceding and erasing his node from the coherence layer, leaving a moving void at the tip of the brightness. Behind him, the glow thickened around places the girl had touched.

"He's dragging it," Holt said, sounding more awake than he had in days. "He and the girl. He's not just a hole anymore. He's a mobile attractor for bad configurations. The field's chasing its own least favorite noise." Singh updated his diagram, adding arrows to represent motion. "Reference node here," he said, tapping one symbol. "Broken node here." He drew them side by side and then traced the path they'd taken. "The organism is recalculating in real time. It tries to maintain global smoothness. When these two move together, it keeps trying to incorporate that configuration somewhere stable. It hates the local math, but it doesn't have a better option, so it keeps following and failing, following and failing." "Can we steer it?" Voss asked. Her eyes didn't leave the map.

"If he keeps walking, we'll find out," Holt said. "But it's not just following him. It's thickening along structures that align with his path. That's where you get leverage. If he walks past a substation and she touches it, you can see the system commit to that choice. Then he leaves, and it has to decide whether to hold or follow. Either way, it pays." Voss watched the ridge turn another corner, its tail still glowing around the tower. She didn't like waiting on accidents. "Ping the tower backhaul," she said. "Low power. No open voice yet. I want to know if he's seeing the same thing we are."

On John's end, the HelixCore panel's status light changed from its listless blink to a tighter, sharper pulse. A second LED, dead until now, flickered weakly. He saw it out of the corner of his eye while the girl's palm rested on another relay box, hum rising under her breath. He stepped back inside long enough to reach the console room and press the receive switch. Instead of voice, the panel spat a basic status burst: a pattern of beeps and flashes the training materials had called a "silent confirm"—their way of saying we see you, stand by. Two beats later, the noise on the audio channel thinned, and Voss's voice cut through, chopped and frayed but intelligible. "Renner." The line lagged, chopped the name into two pieces. "Confirm. Are you seeing host density shifting along your route?" He glanced back through the half-open door at the street. The ring at the tower was thinner. The path ahead was growing a spine of bodies along the posts and low walls he'd walked past.

"Yeah," he said. "Every time she touches something and I stay close, they re-stack along it. When we move on, they lag behind and then follow to the next nice piece of metal. Tower's ring is bleeding. You're drawing a line in your pretty pictures, aren't you?" "The field is forming a moving ridge aligned with your implant," Voss said. "You and the girl together are creating a travelling disturbance. We need to know how predictable it is. Stay near her. We're going to run controlled patterns." He glanced at the girl. She watched his hand on the mic, not the equipment. Her hum stayed steady, but there was a faint tightness around her eyes he hadn't seen before. "What kind of patterns?" he asked. "Simple shapes," Singh's voice came in under hers, thinner, but still carrying that clipped precision. "Straight vector. Right-angle. Gentle arc. We'll compare host re-distribution along fixed geometry. Avoid any structures that look like they're about to fail. We need data, not a crushed asset."

Asset. He kept his face blank by habit. "Copy," he said. "Straight, then turns." He eased the mic away from his mouth and let out one slow breath. Observer to tool in one clean promotion. At least the job description was simple. They started with the straight line. A service street ran parallel to a modest power corridor: cable cabinets, poles, a small fenced substation at one end. From the tower's foot, the ridge of hosts already favored that direction; it made a good lab. He positioned them at one end, near a battered cabinet where three hosts already stood with hands on its metal sides. He stepped up to it, waited until their flow opened space, then slid the girl into the gap so her palm could replace one of theirs. He kept his hand lightly on her forearm. Her hum climbed half a tone as the field poured more of itself through the point of contact.

"Start," he said into the mic. "Cabinet A." They walked at a slow, even pace along the service street. Each time they passed a pole or junction box, he paused long enough for her to lay her hand against it, then moved her on. Hosts along the corridor changed their allegiance in the same slow waves he'd seen before, but now that he was looking for it, he could measure it. At Cabinet A, bodies thickened, then thinned as individuals reassigned themselves to the next tagged structure. At Pole B, density climbed beyond what that flimsy bit of metal had ever been meant to carry. At Junction C, the hum in the pavement swelled as if the small concrete base had become far more important to the organism's picture of the city than whatever tower fed it.

On HelixCore's models, Singh watched a narrow spine of bright coherence move along those same points, leaving dimmer zones in its wake. "Spine confirmed," he said. "It doesn't stay pinned to the first node. It's following their path. The organism is prioritizing adjacency over absolute infrastructure quality." By the time they reached the substation fence, the girl's hum had sharpened into something almost painful at close range. Her fingers trembled against the wire mesh, and the skin around her knuckles had gone white with tension. John felt the shake travel up her arm into his own hand. "Pause," he said. "She's starting to stutter." He pulled her a step back from the fence, keeping his hand on her. The tremor eased slowly, as if the field were reluctantly dialing down its output.

"Noted," Voss said. "We see increased coherence along your line, but your reference node is saturating. Don't drive her into a seizure unless you have to." "Good to know you've got limits," he said dryly, more for himself than for them. Next came angles. They reset near the same corridor and walked another straight segment, this time turning sharply down a side street at the first intersection. From the air, it would have drawn a crude L. On the ground, it meant moving from a row of cabinets and poles to a mix of building corners and shorter posts. The field split the difference. Some hosts stayed committed to the original direction, forming a stubborn tail along the service street. But a substantial fraction peeled away along the intersection structures, aligning to the new vector. On the HelixCore map, the ridge bent into a hard angle, coherence struggling to stay high across the structural right turn. "Path dependence confirmed," Singh said. "It will follow a sharp change, but you pay in local instability. Good."

Then the arc. John picked a broader curve: around the outer face of a block of low offices, sweeping from one side of the power corridor to a parallel street. He walked near the outer walls, guiding the girl to lay her hand on corner posts, window bars, any bit of metal that tied into the building's frame. The organism tried to mimic the curve by approximating it with straight segments along what the city actually provided. Hosts poured along walls and rails in piecewise fashion, creating a jagged version of his intended line. Where the geometry couldn't match the curve cleanly, people hesitated. Some paced short segments back and forth, legs moving without expression, as if trying to compress a winding pattern into a rigid grid. The hum there gained a roughness that reminded him of the tower's new beat error, but louder.

Too many of them reoriented around a flimsy external stair bolted to the side of one building, drawn to the high, narrow metal like moths to a filament. He heard the bolts complain before he saw anything. The flange plates screamed against concrete; the whole assembly lurched. For a moment, the hosts clinging to it simply leaned with the motion, hands refusing to let go even as gravity tried to pull them down. Then the top bracket tore free with a sharp crack. The stair sheared away in slow, ugly motion, bodies still attached. They fell like a slow, tangled waterfall, hitting the pavement in a cascade of limbs and metal. The impact made the whole wall shudder. One host's body slammed down less than a meter from

John's boots, arm flung out, fingers grazing his ankle without meaning.

He tightened his grip on the girl and dragged her back, out of the collapse zone, as the rest of the stair settled into a warped heap. None of the fallen screamed or tried to stand. Those still upright along the wall stepped around the wreckage as if it were any other obstacle, hands stretching to find new fixes on the remaining structure. "See that?" Holt asked over the open line as the data caught up. "We're not the only ones infrastructure fails on. You load too much coherence onto fragile geometry, and it collapses under them too."

"They almost flattened us by accident," John said, eyes still on the wreckage. "Your field doesn't give a damn what's soft and what isn't." "No," Singh said. "It doesn't. Which is why we have to be the ones who do." The longer they played at drawing shapes, the more the girl frayed. Extended contact with multiple structures left her humming in a harsh, flickering pattern that seemed to pass through several notes in rapid succession, never resting. Her hands shook when she reached for metal. Twice, she reached toward one structure and then jerked her fingers back before touching it, as if something elsewhere had tugged at her attention. There was a lag in some of her mimicry now; when he shifted his shoulders, she copied, but with sloppier timing, like her motor planning was riding the same overloaded channels as her signal.

Voss wanted a loop. "Try a circuit," she said over one of the line's clearer stretches. "Roughly around a block and back to your starting point. We want to see if the field tries to over-concentrate at closure." He picked a rectangular block anchored by a medium-sized junction building. He and the girl moved along its perimeter, tagging posts and bars on the way, dragging hosts off their previous anchors. The ridge followed. When they came back around toward their starting corner, he could see the concentration building before they closed the distance. Every structure near the junction point had more bodies than it had any right to support. The hum there had a harsh edge to it, like feedback on the verge of spilling into something worse.

The girl's shaking stepped up in tandem. Her hum climbed, then broke into an unpleasant, discordant overtone. Her eyes unfocused further, staring through him and the building at some pattern only she and the organism shared. Her steps shortened, as if her own body were resisting finishing the shape. They were ten meters from completing the loop when he stopped. "Breaking off," he said into the mic, already pulling her sideways into a narrow alley that cut between the junction building and the next one. The moment her hand left the last piece of tagged metal, the pressure eased. Behind them, the ridge of hosts around the closure point twitched, unresolved. He could almost hear the field reconsidering its choices.

On the model, the bright loop around the block stopped short of meeting. The point where it should have closed seethed with small fluctuations as Theta-9 tried to reconcile a pattern it had almost committed to and then lost. "He didn't finish," Holt said.

"Probably because she was about to break," Singh replied. "Look at the local variance. If he'd completed that, the strain at closure would have been worse than the tower event." Voss didn't argue. "We're not frying the primary reference for a prettier loop," she said. "We need her. Let him choose his cutoffs. He's closer to her than we are." In a smaller room off the alley, one with no equipment left intact and only a few scuffed chairs, John sat the girl down again. She sank more heavily than before, back against the wall, legs folding under her in an untidy version of the posture she'd mirrored from him earlier. Her hum stayed rough and low, like an engine running under strain. Her eyelids drooped; her head tipped toward his shoulder and hovered there, just shy of contact, as if even the small additional input of touch was too much for the system riding her.

He rubbed at his eyes, then pinched the bridge of his nose between thumb and forefinger to chase off a familiar headache. A second later, her hand came up and scraped clumsily across her own face, fingers missing her nose and dragging across her cheek instead. Sloppy mimicry. Overloaded channels. It made the tension between Voss's need for data and his own refusal to break the only girl the network trusted more than concrete feel less abstract. He sat there until her hum smoothed by a few degrees and her hands stopped trembling. When he finally stood, she blinked and followed, slower but still aligning herself into that half-step behind position.

In the bunker, the graphs had caught up enough for theory to harden. Singh had cleared one board and redrawn the city network, this time with moving components. The tower sat at one end of his diagram, the fallback site at another, and between them a web of nodes and edges carried not only static coherence but potential motion. He'd drawn the girl as a bright node, heavily connected, and John as a blacked-out one adjacent to it. Arrows sprang from their pair, sweeping across parts of the graph, bending lines as they went.

"Null–Reference Interference Model, updated," he said, capping his marker. "We always knew the network wanted global coherence. That hasn't changed. Now we know the pair of them aren't just a static fault. They're a travelling one. Wherever they go, the field tries to incorporate their configuration and fails. The result is a moving ridge of overworked math." On the main map, he highlighted potential applications. "If we can coordinate fixed null devices—hardware that emulates Renner's incompatibility—with this mobile beacon pair, we can start sculpting the field. Static nulls to carve permanent wounds, the beacon to drag its attention away from things we care about at critical times." "Evac routes," one of the security coordinators said. "We drop nulls near bridges we need, and Renner walks the ridge past the transformer farms that want to overload them. Hosts follow the wrong thing." "Or we pull bodies off critical towers long enough to blow them without everyone in a five-block radius getting flattened," Holt added. "Make it spend all its focus on following him around some dead cul-de-sac while we take a bite somewhere else."

"Every time we overdrive her, we risk the system retuning around them," Holt said, more soberly. "We also risk her body failing as an amplifier. Or the field deciding this isn't a configuration it wants to chase anymore and doing something… less polite." Voss watched the little BEACON-01 tag—Renner's new designation—crawl slowly across the map. "We don't get anywhere by being gentle with a planet-scale parasite," she said. "But we also don't win by breaking the only lever we've found. We proceed in steps. Prototype null devices. Simulate combinations. When we have something that doesn't kill our assets on first contact, we ask him to walk into some very bad places." Holt snorted softly. "He knows," he said. "He stayed. He didn't walk out when the planes left. You don't do that if you're planning on a quiet retirement." In the tower, the line cut again; the battery that had powered their latest exchange sagged into the red.

John stood at a high window on one of the middle floors and watched the piece of city he'd just walked through rearrange itself in slow motion. The ridge he'd drawn was visible in behavior even without models. Hosts clustered thickly along the cabinets and poles he'd chosen; thinner lines marked the routes he hadn't. One small relay at the edge of that corridor had fewer bodies on it now than it had when he'd first stepped outside; he'd pulled enough attention away that, for the moment, it sat underused. An accidental mercy for a bit of infrastructure that would have failed sooner otherwise.

Behind him, the girl leaned silently against the frame, eyes on his hands. Her hum had smoothed to something like its earlier baseline, though every so often it flickered, a faint reminder of strain.

He could see what he was now in the way the world moved. He was a mapping tool, showing Voss and her team where the field flexed hardest and where it could be bent. He was a lure, dragging hosts and coherence off one target and toward another whenever he and the girl chose to bless a piece of metal with their combined presence. He was a wedge; wherever he stood with her, the organism's smoothness took a hit, forced to step around a pattern it didn't understand.

He wasn't a cure. He wasn't an answer. He was something you dragged through the infection to make it flinch. That was a job. Jobs he understood. He stepped back from the window. The girl straightened with him. On impulse, with no microphone listening and no graph to please, he took a single step forward, then one back, then a short one to the side. She followed perfectly, half a second behind, humming steady. Outside, in the narrow strip of street directly below, three hosts standing with their hands on a low wall shuffled in tiny, corresponding offsets: forward, back, sideways. It was delayed, diffused through concrete and steel, but the echo was there. He watched them settle again, palms flattening, hum smoothing.

"If they want a beacon," he said under his breath, more to her and the concrete than to anyone on a dead line, "we can oblige." He turned toward the stairwell. She fell in just behind his right shoulder. As they walked, the building's borrowed heartbeat wavered, a fraction too late, already trying to learn how to follow whatever shape he chose to draw next.

CHAPTER 21

The first thing he heard was the wrong kind of whine. It came thin and high over the district's usual chorus—over the deep tower hum, the transformer growl, the distant clatter of failing masonry. This sound had edge and modulation, cycling in a way broken infrastructure never managed for long. He scanned the grey sky out of habit, hand shading his eyes more than the low cloud really required, and caught the brief dark arrow of motion cutting across the gap between two mid-rise blocks.

A micro-drone banked over the street, small enough to ride comfortably on his palm, stable enough to ignore the gusts knifing through the ruined buildings. Its rotors were barely visible, a soft blur. The casing was HelixCore matte—no corporate logos, just functional plates and sensor pods. A tiny status LED on its underside blinked in a pattern his training recognized through the years: visual telemetry active, secure channel uplink, operator present. Above him, another shadow crossed; a second drone slid into a lazy spiral, positioning itself to hold him and the girl in overlapping fields of view.

He'd pegged a lot of sounds as "the end of the world" lately. Trust Voss to make sure at least one of them was her. The tower's backhaul modem stuttered, then coughed up a short, compressed burst into his earpiece—a crude low-bitrate channel piggybacked onto whatever power the building had left. "Renner," Voss's voice said, clipped down to its bones by compression and distance. "Visual telemetry active. Keep moving. We are observing." We, he thought, and the tiny drone above him dipped a fraction, adjusting to keep him centered. He imagined Singh and Holt arguing over packets somewhere in the mountains and felt an unpleasant, familiar sense of becoming equipment sink in. Beacon, now probe. Same principle.

The girl tracked the drone as it arced overhead. That, more than the drone itself, caught his attention. Her eyes followed its movement with smooth precision, head tilting back at just the right angle, hum thinning as she tuned out the rest of the soundscape to focus on this new thing. None of the hosts lining the nearby walls reacted. A drone made almost no vibration on concrete from this height; as far as the field was concerned, it might as well have been a bird, a cloud, a glitch in light. They kept their palms on the surfaces that mattered, humming softly, bodies angled toward the tower and the power corridor behind him. She watched the drone until it completed its loop and settled into a hover a few meters up, then shifted her gaze back to him, as if logging its presence and waiting to see whether it mattered. He took that as his cue. "Enjoy the show," he muttered toward the sky, then nodded down the street. "We're walking."

The next command came in pulses rather than full speech, the modem's indicator throwing short bursts of light in sync with Voss's chopped syllables. "Move north," she said. "Do not let her touch anything." He picked the path that matched north according to the tower schematics he'd memorized, then double-checked against the sun's weak, filtered position out of habit. The district ahead was lower and flatter than the tangle around the tower: two-storey houses, small shops, a few narrow apartment blocks with exterior staircases he already didn't trust. Fewer substations, fewer heavy rails. Less infrastructure for the organism to love. That had to be intentional. He stepped off the main corridor and onto a residential street, concrete cracked, cars angled wherever they'd died. The girl fell in at his right shoulder, pliant as always when he provided a vector. Above them, the two drones drifted, matching his pace with eerie grace.

Hosts were still everywhere. They stood against house walls and fences, hands resting on brick, plaster, chain-link. Some pressed palms to metal gutters, others to the bare posts of porches. Every contact point corresponded to something that carried load or vibration. As he and the girl moved, heads turned. Not fully—no one tracked them like prey—but bodies angled incrementally in their direction, shoulders rotating a few degrees toward the pair even when hands remained fixed. Feet shifted to redistribute weight along lines connecting their contact points to his route. It was like watching a field of compasses settling around a moving magnet that refused to acknowledge its own field.

He kept the girl's hands off everything. When she reached absently toward a porch rail, drawn by habit more than choice, he tapped her wrist and shook his head. She dropped her arm without resistance, eyes sliding back to the drones. Her hum climbed each time one changed altitude, like her body noticed the rotor frequency spilling through the air and added it to its calculations, even if the rest of the network didn't care. After the third adjustment, a faint tremor crossed the skin of her throat in time with the drone's pitch. Far above, high-resolution optics and vibration sensors drank all of it in.

In the bunker, one wall showed the northward street in grainy aerial color: John, small and dark, the girl a pale figure at his side, hosts pinned to surfaces like magnetic filings along invisible field lines. Singh watched the micro-spins in their shoulders and wrists, overlaying vectors onto the video feed. "Look at the micro-turns," he said. "They're not just aligning to structures. They're rotating toward him." "That's not hunting," Holt said. He'd dialed projections onto his own console: tiny arrows sprouting from each host's chest, pointing in aggregate toward the moving pair. "That's alignment behavior. Like needles in a disturbed field."

The drone picked up the girl's hum as a low, shifting band on the vibration sensor. Every time it changed altitude or yawed, her pitch shivered. Her head turned a fraction before distant collapses or transformer pops, as if she felt the intention in the infrastructure before the event. The sensor overlays drew faint patterns across her bare forearms: micro-tremors racing through muscle in rhythms that matched the subtle shifts in the hosts outside their immediate radius.

"She's hypersensitizing," Singh murmured. "The reference node is adapting to mobility. Of course it is." On the street, John felt it as tension. Her hum rode higher than usual, closer to the edge of the frequency band that had preceded overloads at the tower and the loop. He kept their pace steady, careful, giving Voss the straight-line trace her models needed. The next instruction came after a pause long enough for a drone to reposition over an intersection. "Tag-and-retreat," Voss said. "Let her touch one rail. Then pull her away immediately. We'll measure spread radius."

He scanned the street and picked the least offensive option: a low section of guardrail protecting the drop into a shallow drainage ditch. It was short, metal, and bolted into concrete that tied into the larger street slab. Hosts already hugged it in a sparse line, hands on the top bar, bodies turned toward the tower. He walked up to the nearest gap. The hosts flanking it shifted a step aside, not out of courtesy but because the field had already learned to route around him.

He glanced once at the sky—the drones hung in place, lenses glinting—then nodded to the girl. "This one," he said. "Then away." She placed her palm flat on the rail. The effect rolled out slowly but inevitably. Hosts along the guard continued humming for a heartbeat, then their posture changed. Fingers spread more fully. Shoulders squared. Heads tilted a fraction, eyes unfocused as ever, but intensity changed. Beyond them, up the street and around the bend, others began to peel away from walls and doors.

From the drone's vantage, it looked like dye spreading through water. People detached from house fronts, turning along their own contact paths until they reached the line of structures connected to the rail—fence posts, sign brackets, the concrete lip. Within a few minutes, every viable contact point within three hundred meters that could be considered part of that path had a hand on it. The density was highest near the girl's palm, then dropped off in decreasing bands outward, a gradient of commitment written in human bodies and bone.

He counted to ten under his breath, then closed his fingers around her wrist and eased her hand off the metal. The hum faltered. It didn't stop; it thinned, as if someone had introduced noise into a clean signal. Several hosts froze mid-breath. One near the far end of the rail stopped humming altogether, hand hovering a centimeter from the metal, fingers twitching as if trying to find a surface that had somehow shifted. Another turned slowly in place, abandoning the rail to circle a nearby lamppost, hand trailing over its flaking paint, going around and around without apparent reason, steps careful, like someone trying to complete a pattern on a puzzle whose last piece had been removed.

In the bunker, Holt watched the coherence plot and snorted. "We're watching a language error," he said. "Signal told them 'align here,' and then the sentence cut off mid-verb. They're trying to finish a instruction that doesn't exist anymore." "I'd dock marks for grammar," Singh said. "But yes. The reference node anchored the field; once you pull her, the residual instruction lingers. The nodes are arguing with ghost data." Voss's voice came back thin and threaded. "Next." John leaned on the rail with his own palm for a moment. Nothing happened. Hosts that had begun to drift hesitated, then resumed their slow adjustments back toward the guard where she'd been. No one reoriented to his contact. No new bodies arrived. He lifted his hand and shook off the cold metal.

"You saw that?" he asked. "Yes," Voss said. "You are still a dead-end link. Now we separate variables." He picked a rusting car chassis a little further down the street—a compact sedan missing two wheels, its frame resting on its hubs at an awkward angle. The network had largely ignored it; no one had hands on its shell, just on the curb beside it. He walked over and rested his palm on the roof. The metal was cold, grit under his fingertips, paint gone matte under dust and exposure. Nothing changed.

No heads turned. No hands lifted. The hum underfoot remained focussed on the proper anchor points: rails, walls, junction boxes. As far as the field was concerned, his contact with the car was meaningless. A non-node touching a non-critical node. Noise on noise. He stepped back and jerked his chin at the girl. "Go ahead," he said. She crossed the few paces to the nearest intact drainpipe bracket. When she touched it, the effect was immediate and familiar: nearby hosts realigned, weight shifting toward her, fingers adjusting on adjacent surfaces. The car still meant nothing. Her contact, even with a minor piece of structure, made the graph update.

"Good," Singh said quietly. "Baseline reconfirmed. Now let's annoy it." They picked two structures close enough for the drones to capture both clearly but distinct enough in the network's topology to be considered separate options: an iron fence post at the edge of a small park and a steel bollard marking the corner of a side street. "Simultaneous," Voss said. "You on one. Her on the other. Maintain contact for ten seconds." He positioned the girl at the fence post first. Hosts nearby thickened around it, the usual pattern blooming. Then he crossed to the bollard, a few meters away, and set his hand on it. On his own, the bollard did nothing for the field. With her already live, it caused trouble.

The initial ripple made itself known as a subtle phase error. The hum shifted, tripped over itself. Hosts that had been focused on the fence post faltered, some turning half-toward the bollard, bodies caught between the two anchors. A second ring of people, farther out, pivoted in micro-increments, their shoulders and hips rotating back and forth as if trying to resolve which direction mattered more. From above, the drones saw the crowd split. Two groups formed, each oriented more strongly toward one of the two structures. The line between them seethed with indecision. Several hosts flicked back and forth in their stances, weight shifting left, right, left again, hands sliding between surfaces.

"For the first time," one of the telemetry techs said, "we have distinct local factions." "It's not politics," Holt said. "It's conflict resolution. You've asked the field to choose between two mutually incompatible optima." The drone's vibration mics, already sensitive enough to pick up the girl's hum and the tower's groan, finally had something else to chew on. Under the baseline tone, new patterns emerged—short trains of hum pulses passing between hosts like whispered code. Long–short–long. Short–short–rest. Long–rest–rest. The drones tracked them as they moved from one cluster to another, a rhythm echoed in fingertips tapping subtly against concrete and metal.

"Those aren't random," Holt said, voice tight now. He overlaid time stamps and positions, watched as one pattern started near the fence post and propagated outward, only to be answered by a different rhythm from the bollard side. "These are packetized. That's protocol. The network is talking to itself." "Not talking," Singh said, eyes on his own reconstruction, lines flashing on his graph between nodes in time with the pulses. "Syncing. Reaching consensus on what to do about two anomalies it can't easily reconcile. It's running a distributed decision algorithm." "Then let's give it more anomalies," Voss said.

The patterns converged. Waves of hum shifted toward John and the girl, the trains of pulses becoming more regular as they reached the meat endpoints of the experiment. He didn't need drones to tell him something had changed; he felt it in the air pressure, in the way the hair on his arms prickled. The girl stiffened. Her hum, already elevated, destabilized into a harsh, warbling tone that climbed, dipped, then climbed again. Her breathing changed—shallow, rapid, chest working against an invisible load. Her eyes, unfocused at the best of times, rolled slightly upward, whites showing in thin crescents. Her hand left the pipe and reached blindly across the space between them, fingers closing on his sleeve with more strength than he'd expected. All around them, hosts stopped.

Movement froze in a rough circle fifty, sixty meters across. Hands stayed on surfaces; bodies remained upright. But every fine adjustment, every micro-shift that had defined their behavior since the first outbreak, halted. Humming cut off like a toggled switch. The sudden silence had weight. Even the drones' rotor noise seemed to recede under it. One of the telemetry screens in the bunker glowed too bright, coherence values spiking into ranges they hadn't yet seen outside the catastrophic events in hospitals. Several sensor feeds glitched simultaneously, their readings clipping and dropping. "Renner," Voss said, the word almost a whisper despite the line's distortion. "They're forming a quorum."

"They're deciding," Holt said, staring at the pattern hashes. "Field-wide, within that radius, they're deciding what to do about those two." John didn't know what shape a quorum took in a system like this, but he knew what a buildup felt like when it was ready to spill. The girl's grip on his sleeve tightened until the fabric creaked. Her hum reached a pitch that made his teeth ache. The air itself felt sharper, as if the field concentrated so strongly it might fracture whatever it had grown inside. He broke the configuration the simplest way available.

He yanked his hand off the bollard and stepped sideways, putting his body between her and the rail, physically dragging her back until no flesh touched metalThe moment the link snapped, the hum shattered. Not into silence, but into chaotic fragments half-started patterns smashing into each other and dying. Hosts staggered where they stood. A man in a hospital gown stumbled forward two paces before slamming both palms back onto a nearby wall, as if afraid of falling out of the world. Another woman's knees buckled; she dropped, then clawed her way upright again using a drainpipe, hands red where rust had bitten. One host began slapping the back of her own hand against the concrete—slow, then faster—trying to re-establish some rhythm that matched the lingering echo in her nerves.

From the drones' perspective, the consensus waves fractured. Packets cut off mid-sequence. Some patterns repeated, desperate and incomplete, bouncing among small clusters. Others died entirely, overwritten by the organism's effort to get back to any stable mode at all. John watched the mess he'd made settle into something resembling the system's previous order. It took longer this time. The field wasn't just flowing; it was recovering. And recovery meant states. States meant rules. Rules meant a language, even if it used hum and posture instead of words. They didn't stay completely blind.

As hosts "rebooted," the drones' sensors picked up shorter, simpler patterns than the earlier complex trains. Three dominant sequences emerged near John's position, repeated across multiple bodies, sometimes overlapping, sometimes in sequence. The first was a steady hum–pause–hum–pause pattern, simple and assertive. Whenever it propagated through a cluster, nearby hosts pressed closer to whatever they were touching, tightening contact, aligning their shoulders in the same direction. Hands that had lifted dropped back in. In Singh's overlay, arrows snapped to match a single vector. "That's an align command," he said. "Baseline consensus. Reaffirming the previous mode."

The second sequence went humhum–pause–humhum–pause. Where it ran, hosts detached from one surface and moved to another, usually along a contiguous structure. In the field, it looked like a slow, organized transfer down the length of a wall or rail.

"Transfer," Holt said. "Redistribute. Move load from the unstable configuration to a more stable one." The third pattern —hum–pause–humhum–longer pause—appeared at the edges of clusters, near junctions where paths diverged. After it ran through, hosts changed the angle of their bodies, reorienting toward whichever structure the field had decided now mattered more.

"Reorient," Singh said. "Update preferred direction. It's broadcasting which node has priority now that the fault moved." John didn't have their vocabulary, but he heard the differences. Once you knew there was a code, you couldn't unhear the intervals. Hum—pause—humhum—pause. Answered a moment later by humhum—pause—humhum—pause from farther down the street. Then, after a heartbeat, the softer third rhythm closing the exchange, bodies adjusting. It wasn't conversation in any human sense, but it was a negotiation, and he'd just jammed a foreign variable into it.

Back at the fallback site, Voss watched the patterns dance across their reconstructions: pulses turning on and off, hosts reorienting in waves that matched the code's form. "He's the first human to see this from inside its own body," she said quietly. "To connect the signal to behavior in real time." "And the first human it's actively trying to solve," Singh said. "Nothing about its math allows for a node like him. So it's running consensus rounds on what he is."

On the street, the girl's breathing had settled into something closer to normal, though her fingers still curled tight in his sleeve. He loosened his stance but didn't shake her off. The drones held their positions; he could feel their eyes on the back of his neck.

Nearby, a cluster of hosts hummed in the align pattern, resetting their own world. Farther away, others echoed the transfer code, shifting along a wall he'd dragged them off earlier. At the intersection ahead, the reorient rhythm pulsed faintly, turning bodies toward some distant structure he hadn't yet seen. He listened. Not like a scientist; like a man who'd walked patrols in cities whose rules he hadn't understood at first and learned them anyway. Treat code like speech long enough, and you picked up the tone if not the grammar.

He turned to the girl. She was watching him now, not the structures, attention fixed as if waiting for his next move to feed back into whatever consensus the field was grinding through. There was a tightness in her muscles that hadn't been there before, a coiled anticipation that didn't match the slack trance he'd first found her in. "You're not just following it," he said, voice low. "You're listening to me too... aren't you?"

He exhaled once, slow. She hummed, and this time the note slid into the same rhythm as his breathing rather than the city's. For two heartbeats, the pattern fit him more than it did the field. The hosts nearby didn't answer; the organism had other decisions to make. But the sound hung between them, quiet and personal in a way nothing about Theta-9 had any right to be, and he filed that, too, under language.

CHAPTER 22

They stopped pretending it was night in the fallback site. The clocks said it, the body clocks agreed, but the warroom looked the same as it had twelve hours ago: screens lit, coffee cooling in rings on consoles, people leaning over each other's work with the wired focus of those who had run out of adrenaline and were now running on obligation. The main wall showed the city as a heatmap of coherence, colors shifting in slow gradients; smaller panes replayed drone footage from the last pass over John and the girl, reduced to slow, jittery loops. Singh stood in front of one of the side displays with his hands clasped behind his back, watching a single strip of video on repeat—the bollard-and-fence experiment, cut down to the bare essentials: John's hand on one piece of metal, the girl's on another, hosts splitting between them in confused clumps. Overlaid on top were the vibration traces from the drones—three bands corresponding to the align, transfer, and reorient codes they'd started to name. Every time John forced the field to choose, the lines traced the same arc, a sharp little notch in the middle.

"Again," he said. The tech at the station restarted the segment without comment. Hosts flicked between anchors. The hum on the trace rose, stuttered, then dropped through the same small dip. Singh stepped closer, following that jagged dive with his fingertip; he'd seen it in other clips now, shorter tests and partial conflicts, but it only showed itself clearly when you stacked them together. "Overlay sequence seven," he said. "The rail test." They added the tag-and-retreat run; the traces pulsed, climbed, then dipped in the exact same place. "Sequence fifteen," he said. "The loop." That one dropped in too, stretched and deeper but unmistakable. Different experiments, different geometries, one persistent stutter tying them together.

On the opposite bank of consoles, Holt had his own mess. Equations ran down his tablet, spilled up the side of a glass board, jumped to a projection where the city grid had been abstracted into nodes and edges, a mathematical skeleton under the map. He'd circled a particular eigenmode in angry red earlier—a configuration the organism seemed to prefer for global stability. Now he added a new mark: a small symbol at the point where the mode lines kinked when Singh's notch appeared. Singh crossed over, replay traces still flickering behind him. "It does the same thing every time we corner it," he said. "Doesn't matter if it's a loop, a conflict, the quorum. See this drop?" He pointed to the notch, then to Holt's circled kink. "Same phenomenon."

"Mode collapse," Holt said. He keyed the model to show energy expenditure over time, relative to the organism's normal effort to keep itself smooth. Most of the graph was a steady climb—a parasite expanding into its new body with lazy confidence. At the points where the notch appeared, the line spiked, jagged and ugly. "We force it into a configuration where its favorite eigenmode can't exist, so it falls into a lower one for a heartbeat, then scrambles back up. That scramble costs it." Singh tapped the map again, where the new symbol now marked several test sites. "And it never stabilizes in that state," he said. "The configuration exists only briefly. It hates it. That's why it's our friend."

Voss watched the spike move, watched the line after wobble and settle into a slightly lower slope, as if the organism needed time to recover from its own flinch. "If we can force that state everywhere at once," she said, voice flat, not triumphant, drawing a straight line in the air with one finger, "even briefly... we break its global mode. It can't hold coherence across the network. It fragments." They named it because people were superstitious and data needed handles. Vulnerability Mode S3 the forced stutter state their equations said the organism would never pick on its own., because two earlier candidates had turned out to be decoys and no one wanted to restart at one. S for stutter, Singh murmured once, and though no one laughed, no one objected either. S3 went into the simulations as a special case: a mode the system would never choose on its own, one that could only be induced with external insult.

"One problem," Holt said, scrolling back through earlier logs. "S3 only shows when we push that girl to the edge." He pulled up her implant proxies from the tower and loop events: hum frequency spiking into unstable bands, muscle tremors increasing, whatever passed for her cardiovascular profile under Theta-9's influence going from flat acceptance to frantic output. "In every clean collapse, her vitals peak hardest. We're putting the reference node under maximum strain. If we provoke S3 at every major hub, we risk burning out the one body it likes best. Or worse—giving it enough signal time to reinstall itself properly in her while she's hot." Singh nodded, eyes on the traces. "We're firing a weapon that overdrives its own barrel," he said. "We get a few shots before it warps."

Voss stared at the map, at the slowly shifting bands of color and the blinking BEACON-01 tag that marked John's last known position. The first crack in the organism's armor glowed there, small but present. So did the cost. "Then we pick our first shot carefully," she said. "And we tell Renner to aim."

The district ahead of John made the tower's neighborhood feel like a quiet cul-de-sac. He moved in under a lattice of concrete and steel where the city had once stacked solutions to its traffic and power problems on top of each other: freeway interchange above, rail viaduct crossing that, a telecom relay hub tucked under the tangle, and an electrical switching yard threaded through the pillars like an afterthought that had grown teeth. Thick cables sagged between pylons, spliced and respliced. Massive steel braces carried weight across weird angles. The air thrummed with nested frequencies: the deep continuous note of traffic mass above, even with engines long dead; the pulsing buzz of transformers; the mid-band vibration of still-powered relay racks clinging to emergency feeds. Every surface hummed. Theta-9 had found a cathedral.

Hosts filled the space shoulder-to-shoulder. They lined fence lines, packed two deep against load-bearing columns, ringed transformers like worshippers at a shrine. Hands lay on concrete plinths, steel uprights, cable housings; fingers crowded in where full palms no longer fit. No one bothered with thin chain-link—the field ignored it as useless. They clung instead to the heavy posts and structural members that carried real load. The hum here wasn't background. It sat in his teeth and bones, beat against his ribs, tried to draw his stance into its rhythm. He widened his feet, redistributed his weight, not to accept it but to refuse, feeling pressure mount anyway. At his shoulder, the girl's tone climbed, subharmonics blooming under the main pitch. She turned her head toward a central column before he even tracked it. The field wanted her there.

Two drones held position at different heights among the forest of supports, lights dimmed to faint glows just bright enough for his eye and their optics. Further up, a third tracked movements across the freeway deck, watching for the kind of failure that turned pillars into hammers. "Welcome to the main relay," Voss said in his ear, her voice grainy with compression and interference. "Coherence here is near maximal. If S3 is a structural property and not a local quirk, we'll see it cleanest. Don't get crushed trying to prove us right."

He made a slow circuit under the interchange first, mapping

pillars and struts with his eyes the way he'd once mapped alley networks in quieter wars. Massive Y-supports took the main weight of overlapping roads. The switching yard nestled around the bases of three, cables feeding up into the deck. Telecom dishes and relay boxes bracketed another, its concrete jacket thickened and studded with antenna mounts. That one had the most bodies. People pressed into every reachable angle, every bracket, every cable rib; even toes and knees had found contact where hands could not. The hum there had cadence now, a rolling rise and fall layered over the align-transfer-reorient packets, as if the organism were stringing its little phrases together into something more elaborate. "The central load pillar," Voss said. "Largest hub in your radius. We want you there."

He threaded through the crowd the way he had learned to thread through all of them: walk where there was already a gap, don't try to punch one open, let the field's refusal to map him do its own work. Bodies slid aside without looking, the organism adjusting its tools around a dented, meaningless object. He kept the girl close enough that her bubble warped flows instead of letting them close on his chest. Up close, the pillar's concrete showed hairline cracks where the weight above had asked more than the engineers had ever expected. Steel bracing plates ringed its base, bolted into the foundation and tied into thick cable housings. Every bolt had a hand on it. Align codes rolled out from here in fat waves, answered by transfer and reorient along the yard's edges.

"Anchor one," Voss said. "We need a second. The field has to love it, but not consider it the same joint. Somewhere the math can't treat as one unit." He scanned left. A massive cross-brace connected two neighboring supports, running like a steel tendon between their shoulders. It was heavy, solid, loaded; hosts clung to its lower flange in a dense strip. It tied into the overall structure but not directly into the telecom hardware. "That brace," he said. "You see it?" "Confirmed,"

Singh answered immediately. "Secondary hub. Different connectivity class. Perfect."

"Set her on the pillar," Voss said. "Then you touch her and the brace. We want two incompatible optima. Give it two best choices it can't merge." He brought the girl right up to the concrete ring around the column. The hum pressed against his chest like a physical hand now; it was effort not to let his breathing fall into step with it. Her eyes were already glossier than usual, pupils wide and unfixed. She lifted her hand without prompting and laid her palm flat against a patch where paint had flaked off completely.

The field slammed into her. The pillar had already been a favorite; with the primary reference node touching it, the relationship became dependency. The hum surged, a full-body vibration running up through his boots, spine, and jaw. Hosts around the column straightened, pressing harder into the concrete, humming with tighter precision. Down the line, bodies at connected structures subtly shifted orientation as the organism rerouted priority toward its favorite vertex. "Contact confirmed," Singh said. "Coherence spike at the pillar cluster."

John set his left hand on her shoulder. Muscle under his palm vibrated in micro-shivers, high-frequency tremors trying to align themselves with the larger field. Her tone climbed another notch, beating against his eardrums. Then he stretched his right arm out and spread his fingers against the lower flange of the cross-brace. Steel here thrummed with a different voice: higher, tied directly to freeway flex rather than telecom chatter. For a heartbeat, nothing changed. The organism tried to treat both as one extended structure; of course it did, smoothing complexity was its instinct. Then its math hit the incompatibility at the null node.

The hum snapped—not to silence, but into pieces. Align codes fired and cut off mid-pulse. Transfer sequences overlapped reorient in ways that made no structural sense. Hosts closest to them twitched between two micro-motions: leaning toward the column, then shifting weight toward the brace and back again. Hands slid along concrete and steel as if their owners couldn't decide which contact point mattered. The stutter Singh had highlighted in the lab showed up here as a full-network flinch you could feel in your teeth. For a fraction of a second, all the nested vibrations fell out of sync and beat against each other; the air itself seemed to grain.

Drones recorded the signature as a neat S3 waveform washing outward from the conflict point, a ring of mode collapse racing along cables and through concrete. Everywhere it passed, hosts staggered, hands lifting for half a breath before slamming back down. Small objects rattled on nearby shelves, broken windows chimed, a line of pigeons on an overhead cable took off as one. "Mode S3 detected," a tech said, voice cracking despite himself. "Clean. Stronger than tower event. Propagation radius expanding."

On his model, Holt watched the organism's favored eigenmode drop into a shallower well and then scrabble for purchase. "There it is," he said. "We just kicked its legs out at a main joint. Look at the cost." On the energy graph, the line spiked harder than in any previous test, then sagged; for the first time, Theta-9's growth curve dipped a measurable amount before starting to climb again. On the map, bright patches around the interchange dimmed, edges fuzzing as clusters struggled to choose a stable pattern.

At the center of it, the girl began to fracture. Her hum, already stretched, split. A second note surfaced under the first, lower but locked in a harmonic relation; a third wedged itself between. They beat against each other for a second, ugly and dissonant, then snapped into a rigid, layered pattern. He realized, too late, that he recognized the rhythm. Align, sped up and laid over transfer and reorient until all three ran through her throat at once.

Her chest hitched. Muscles in her neck jumped as if she were swallowing a handful of sharp stones. The unfocused pupils in her eyes dilated, then constricted in the cadence of her own code. Her lips parted. The sound moved from chest to mouth, picked up consonant edges as it passed teeth and tongue. In the drone feed, her vibration profile shifted from one node among many to something that sat on top of the field—louder, more structured, sequences clean where they had been diffuse. Patterns that had only existed as distributed packets between hosts now came straight from her as discrete bursts: align, transfer, reorient, a new long-tone command that rolled over the others like an instruction to be quiet and wait. "She's running the protocol," Holt said, quiet despite the meaningless of volume over comms. "That's controller behavior. The field is using her as a mouth."

Hosts nearest them responded accordingly. Instead of orienting primarily to structure, they oriented to her. Shoulders turned toward her small frame, torsos angling as if listening. Hands still clung to pillar and brace, but the line of attention had shifted; concrete and steel became conduits, not goals. In Theta-9's math, she had become a tower, a live relay that outranked the concrete around her. Under John's hands, her body tried to move like one, shoulder muscles tugging toward the junction as if commanded. For the first time, he felt the distributed decision-making protocol as a single-body storm rather than a crowd behavior—a rush of instructions forced through meat. "Renner," Voss said, and there was something in it he hadn't heard from her yet, a thin wire between warning and fear. "You're overdriving her. Keep that configuration and we lose her to the field. Break contact."

He didn't need the nudge. Her head had tipped back, jaw slack, hum rising toward something that wanted to be a word instead of a code. Her free hand lifted on its own, fingers spreading to reach for the brace, ready to close the circuit herself. He took his palm off the steel first; the brace shuddered, its own hum stumbling as the field tried to route without the null. It wasn't enough. The organism still had her and the pillar. Her mouth kept spilling sequences, overlapping threads of sound. He stepped in, got both arms around her from behind, and physically tore her away from the column. Her palm clung for a fraction—tendons in her wrist standing out—then skin came free of concrete with a soft, awful scrape. The connection broke.

The hum crashed like someone had yanked power on a server rack. For an instant, nothing but wind through superstructure and the far-off grumble of concrete under stress remained. Then Theta-9's field lurched. Hosts across the yard staggered, their bodies thrown off by the sudden absence of a favored configuration. A man in a business shirt dropped to his knees, hands scraping along concrete until they found a cable casing to cling to. Two women near the brace pitched sideways into each other, rebounded, and slammed back into steel as if afraid of open space. Several toppled fully, limbs tangling, movements jerky as they fought to re-establish contact. One, slower than the rest, smashed her face into a transformer's base; blood smeared across faded paint as she slid and clawed her way upright again.

This time, the cluster didn't erupt into rage or frantic, violent overflow. It simply unravelled. Align codes fired in short, panicked bursts. Transfer pulses collided. Reorient attempts contradicted each other. The S3 ripple that had started at their conflict point kept moving outward, warping other hubs as it went. For a few blocks in every direction, the organism's posture looked less like an occupying force and more like something that had tripped over its own legs.

The girl sagged against him. Her weight hit his chest with disproportionate force, as if the field that had held her upright had let go all at once. For a second he thought she was seizing; her muscles convulsed under his hands. Then the motion resolved into ragged, uncontrolled tremors. Her tone dropped in steps, then vanished, leaving only shallow, hard breathing. He dragged her behind a thinner support, out of the immediate crush path, then eased her down until she sat slumped against the concrete.

Her eyes fluttered. For a heartbeat he saw something new in them, a spark of recognition that stopped on his face instead of passing through. It was gone almost immediately, swallowed up by residual patterns, but he logged it. Her throat worked. A sound escaped that wasn't hum—just a clipped rise and fall, edged with consonant that wanted to be a syllable. "Ah —" she managed, then choked on it as the field rolled another align code through her chest to drag her back into its safer rhythm. Her lips shut. Whatever had tried to form there disappeared back into the organized noise. He pressed two fingers to the scar above his own temple, an old reflex, then checked her wrist where the hospital band still sat. Pulse fast but slowing. Her breathing eased from panic into something closer to baseline, though now that baseline lived somewhere between his and the city's. There was a new texture to her quiet moments, an "accent" in her residual hum that matched fragments of protocols she'd just executed. Those weren't leaving.

In the war-room, data hammered every open screen. Graphs scrolled too quickly to read without filters; numbers flickered red and yellow before settling. "Collapse confirmed," Singh said. "Propagation out to maybe thirty blocks at strong amplitude, further at reduced. Look at coherence." He pulled up the map. Bright zones around the interchange had dimmed, their edges smearing, several peripheral hubs flickering like faulty bulbs. For the first time, pockets of the city looked less like one continuous organ and more like a set of smaller, unsynchronized ones.

"Energy cost spike is off the charts," Holt added, dragging the expenditure graph forward. "We made it burn through a week of adaptive budget in a few seconds just to stay upright. Global mode took a hit." He highlighted the organism's favored eigenmode; across the modeled network, its line sagged, breaking into segments. "It couldn't hold that solution cleanly anymore. It dropped into regional patches. That's your fracture, Voss."

"If we chain S3 collapses at major hubs—power, telecom, transit—we force that partition everywhere," Singh said. "It won't be able to maintain a single global answer. It'll become a set of semi-independent bodies. Smaller bodies are easier to dodge and hurt than a planetary one." "And the reference node?" Voss asked, not taking her eyes off the map. Holt grimaced and pulled up the girl's proxy again. "She peaked higher than at the tower," he said. "Full protocol execution for almost three seconds. Another two or three and I'm not sure she'd have come back to this half-state. The field wasn't just using her as hardware. It was trying to seat itself in her properly again."

"Too many collapses and we burn out the scaffold or watch her vanish into it," Singh said. "Either way, we lose the lever we're so proud of." Voss finally sat, just long enough to lean in and plant her hands on the edge of the console. On the map, BEACON-01 blinked amid a temporarily dimmer knot of nodes. For the first time since this started, they had something shaped like a kill plan. It came wrapped around a man and a girl at the bottom of a broken city. "Then we don't give it a clean pattern to learn from," she said. "We don't hammer S3 until it melts. We hit enough hubs to shatter the big mode, then stop before it eats our own asset." She straightened again, shoulders set. "We have our key," she said. "We break it carefully."

CHAPTER 23

They didn't call it a celebration, but the war-room had that brittle focus people got when the impossible had finally twitched. Night or day didn't mean much; the overheads stayed the same hard white, the air the same recycled chill, the coffee the same sour burn. On the main wall, the city map looked different now—no longer a smooth, smug field of red coherence, but mottled, scarred. Around the interchange where John had nearly broken the girl, the colors were duller, fragmented into smaller islands. Singh had frozen the frame there, a halo of symbols clustered around the main relay hub, each marking a recorded S3 collapse. Below the map, energy graphs scrolled, jagged where they'd once been lazy arcs. You could almost believe the thing out there had flinched.

Singh tapped a key and overlaid a new layer: the organism's favored eigenmode, the global pattern Theta-9 had settled into once it had enough hosts and infrastructure to think of the city as a single body. On earlier runs it had been a continuous band, bright and smug, draped over every major load path. Now there were breaks, jump cuts where the mode had failed and re-formed with a stagger. "Fragmentation," he said, not triumphantly, just as diagnosis. "S3 doesn't just annoy it, it forces the global mode to split into regional patches. Each collapse is a local fracture. Enough fractures and the body isn't one thing anymore."

Holt leaned against the glass board he'd colonized, lines of math written into the ghostly reflection of his own face. He pointed at another graph: the energy cost of that scramble.

"We saw it pay for that mistake," he said. "When we forced S3 at the interchange, Theta-9 dumped a week's worth of adaptive margin in seconds just to keep its favorite mode from tearing itself apart. It can do that a few times. It can't do it forever." He glanced at Voss. "We've found the pry point. But a pry point is not a weapon."

Voss watched the graphs without blinking, sleeves shoved up, tie gone, hair pulled back in the quickest knot she'd ever tied. "Fragmenting it buys us room," she said. "Room isn't a cure. If all we do is make it stumble, the best we get is a slower, meaner apocalypse." She gestured, and one of the side displays switched to a different model—a simulation of Theta-9's growth curve over time, now showing a visible dent where the interchange event had hit. "We open cracks with S3," she said. "We need something to pour into those cracks before it seals them again."

Holt keyed in another overlay: a short, ugly family of compounds and engineered sequences they'd been nursing in the background for weeks. Versions of Theta-9's own backbone with subtle sabotage built in, plus more conventional antivirals and dampers that had failed in earlier trials. "Counter-coherence," he said. "Agents that disrupt coupling at the neural level instead of killing cells outright. We already know they don't do much against a fully stable field; the organism just routes around them, like water around a stone. But during S3..." He flicked timestamps together, aligning collapse windows with hypothetical drug curves. "During collapse, it's off-balance. If we can get something in there that changes how it recombines, we might tilt its physics toward failure."

Singh grimaced. "Call it a counter-coherence agent if you want funding buzzwords," he said. "Practically, we're talking about a drug that only works if the parasite's already stumbling. It doesn't cure Theta-9 standing up. It kicks Theta-9 while it's on the floor and keeps it from getting back up clean." He looked at the modeled curves, at the narrow windows where S3 existed before the organism restabilized. "And those windows are seconds, not minutes. We need the collapse and the agent's rise to coincide. That means S3 isn't just helpful—it's the delivery mechanism."

"So we have the key," Voss said. "And we have sketches of a blade we can tape to it." She nodded at the agent list. "We can refine in vitro until our eyes bleed. None of it matters until we test in a live field collapse. We've done that now, in miniature. The interchange was proof of concept. We know we can hurt it and we know what that hurt looks like from the outside. Next step isn't another tiny test." She let the next sentence hang just long enough that everyone in the room filled it in on their own. "We need scale."

Holt flipped the main map from heat to density: hosts, structures, and load. The interchange was a bright knot, but the city still had one zone that outshone it—a central district where rail, metro, long-haul power, and telecom converged before branching back out. Sector designations glowed faintly; one core node had been labelled Sector 0 when the modelers ran out of imagination. "S3 works best where coherence is highest," he said. "Little collapses give us local fractures. Local fractures aren't enough to carry a drug across the organism's body before it restabilizes. For that you want a global seizure. Something that hits the main spine."

"A mega-cluster," Singh said. He zoomed in; the map resolved into a mess of interlocking loops—elevated lines, buried conduits, high-rise load paths. Every heavy structure throbbed red. "Hundreds of structures, tens of thousands of hosts in coherent state, all coupled through the same infrastructure. When S3 fires there, the collapse doesn't just ring out a few blocks. It travels half the grid in one go. That's when your counteragent gets reach. That's when a drug can ride the failure wave instead of drowning under the rebuild."

Voss's gaze tracked the highlighted nexus, then slid to the small tag blinking elsewhere on the map: BEACON-01, tethered to a lower-density zone the team had started calling his district out of habit. "And the only configuration we've found that can trigger S3 at all," she said, "is a broken node physically linked to our primary reference. Which, last I checked, is currently wandering the fringes with a girl who nearly cooked her own brain the last time we pushed her." She rubbed the bridge of her nose once, short and hard, as if adjusting invisible glasses, then dropped her hand. "We're not going to coax a global collapse by tapping transformers in the suburbs. We need him in Sector 0."

They ran the models to be sure, because pretending they had a choice made people feel better. Singh mapped hypothetical S3 events at secondary hubs, then stacked drug dispersal curves on top: aerosol clouds, water-line loads, targeted injections. Every time, the organism's global mode flexed, dented, and then smoothed back into place; local patches cleared, then were re-infected by the intact majority. Only when he forced a collapse at Sector 0 did the simulation show system-wide fragmentation with enough duration for an agent to propagate before the field recovered. "There," he said. "If we open it here and nothing else, we still probably lose. If we open it here and hit it with everything we've got while it's open..." He let the graph speak for itself: Theta-9's coherence not just sagging, but dropping under a threshold the software labeled with three cautious words: non-viable regime.

"The organism has been very kind," Holt said. "It built us the perfect lever by wiring an entire city into one instrument. We just have to be rude enough to actually pull it." He gestured at the BEACON tag and the Sector 0 core. "But the only pair capable of generating the lever arm—Renner and the girl—are currently outside the main body. To get a city-scale S3, he can't be clipping nerves; he has to stick his hands into the spine."

"Which," Voss said, "means he walks into the densest Theta-9 zone on the planet. With a scaffold the organism worships and is actively trying to reclaim. Our cure plan is built on the assumption that he can drag her into the heart and then get her out again before it finishes seating." She watched the model run another time, the simulated S3 wave tearing through Sector 0 and across connected districts. "We have the key. We have the outline of a payload. We don't have a version of this where he doesn't go back into hell."

They didn't hold a council to decide whether to tell him; no one in the room believed there was another candidate they could slot into BEACON-01 without rewriting physics. Voss had communications route a narrowband channel through the tower's stubborn backhaul line, then stepped into a smaller room off the war-space—a former briefing area that now served as a casualty notification booth and, occasionally, a place to say things you didn't want six teams listening to. The overhead light here was softer; someone had turned one bank off weeks ago and no one had bothered to fix it.

John's icon sat steady on the wall display, his implant's signal idling in low-power mode. The girl's biosignature was fuzzier, a ghosted outline grafted from drone vibration readings and whatever her medical band still broadcast. Voss keyed the channel. "Renner, this is Voss. Confirm you're upright." His answer came back delayed, but calm. "Still breathing," he said. "She's out of the worst of it. Humming again. Cluster at the relay is settling, but it doesn't like us much." "We saw the collapse," Voss said. "You did exactly what we needed." She didn't say: and more than we knew we were asking. "We have a plan built around that event now. S3 isn't the cure; it's the thing that lets the cure in. We can't afford to waste it on local annoyances anymore." She pulled up the Sector 0 overlay on the side screen, so he'd have the picture if his tower hardware still showed video. "Every model says the same thing. To get enough collapse for a counteragent to ride, you have to trigger S3 in the central grid nexus. Sector 0. That's the rail–power–telecom knot downtown."

He didn't ask why it had to be him. There was a small, almost polite silence, broken only by a faint hiss on the line and, in the background of his end, the low restless murmur of hosts pressing against walls. "Dense enough there?" he asked. "Dense enough that if we crack it, we hurt Theta-9 everywhere," she said. "Also dense enough that if you miss, it finishes digesting the city and uses the event as a learning experience." She watched his signal stay as steady as before. "The girl can't handle many more overloads. You can't either, whether you feel it or not. Once you're in Sector 0, there will be no perimeter. No quiet streets. You'll be walking through its core. I would love to offer you odds on getting back. I can't, not honestly."

"Give me a number anyway," he said. Habit. She looked at the probabilities Singh had scribbled in a corner of his notes and at the blank spaces where unknowns outweighed math. "Non-zero," she said. From her, it was almost cruelty; it meant: low enough that I won't insult you by wrapping it in better words. She let out a breath. "We have one more thing to be clear on." Her voice flattened further, went surgical. "When you push S3 at that scale, the organism will throw everything it has at stabilizing through her. You saw what happened at the relay. She nearly took full controller role. If, in Sector 0, she tips fully —if you see her go—if she stops being a confused node trying to mimic you and becomes the field's clean mouthpiece…" He didn't answer immediately, but she heard the shift in his breathing.

"You don't get to hesitate," Voss said. It was the first time she'd let anything near her eyes. "You don't let Theta-9 finish seating in her. You treat her as part of the structure you're breaking.

There is no third option where you keep her, save the city, and walk out together." She wasn't asking if he understood; she was warning him that she would not forgive him for choosing sentiment over physics. "Copy," he said. No argument, no bravado. Just acceptance logged. She hated and relied on that in equal measure.

When she cut the line, communications patched another, as she'd already asked them to do. Different latency, different hum. The wall display shifted from city maps and interference patterns to a grainier feed—a camp perimeter under dull light, rows of temporary shelters, a line of people at a water tank. Generators put a constant low note under everything. At the edge of the frame, guards with borrowed insignia watched a fence topped in honest barbed wire instead of improvised conductor. Lee's voice came before his face; he'd half-turned away to speak to someone off-screen when the connection opened. "Yeah, I know, tell them to stay in the—" He broke off, turned back, and for a second his expression went completely blank as his brain aligned the ID tag with reality. "John?" he said. It wasn't disbelief. More like someone getting news after the part of them that needed it had already scheduled a funeral. "Still here," John said. The audio scrubbed his tone flat, but Lee knew him too well to miss the edges.

There was a long, hard silence on the line, filled in by camp noise: a kid laughing too loudly, a distant argument over supplies, someone coughing in the background. When Lee finally spoke again, his voice had sand in it. "I got told you were gone at the airport," he said. "Engine spool, radios screaming, then static. They put your name on a board. I watched them do it." He shook his head once, like he could dislodge the image. "Next time you decide not to die, maybe send a postcard." "Reception's been spotty," John said.

Lee huffed something that might have been a laugh if it had more strength. The camera auto-adjusted as he moved, showing more of the camp: Anna sitting on a pallet stack behind him, a blanket over her shoulders, hair scraped into a knot. She was talking to someone just out of frame, eyes tired but alive. Lee glanced back at her, then at the screen. "We made it," he said. "Flights got through. Camps are a mess, but they're holding. No hum this far out, just generator noise and bad food." "Good," John said. It covered more than the word deserved.

Lee studied his friend's pixelated face. "They told me what you're doing," he said, quieter now. "Or as much as they think a paramedic needs to hear about alien parasite eigenmodes." He rubbed his jaw. "You're taking your pet network node into the center and you're going to kick the main breaker until it pops, and if it works, the world gets to be something other than a hive. If it doesn't..." He let the sentence die. "If you pull this off, you save more than this camp. If you don't, Anna doesn't grow up in a world anyway. That about right?"

"Something like that," John said. On his side of the line, a host bumped a wall near whatever room he'd holed up in; the resulting hum bled faintly into the mic.

Lee looked down, then back up. "I'm not going to tell you not to go," he said. "I know you too well and I've seen too many people die because someone tried to hold the good ones back from the worst jobs. Just..." He hesitated, searching for something that fit into the narrow space left between orders and inevitability. "Don't do it quietly," he said at last. "Don't just walk in and vanish. Keep talking as long as the line holds. Make them listen to you work. If this thing takes you, I'm not having it happen off-screen." John let that sit. "Tell Anna I said she picked the smart one," he said. "Staying behind camp fences while idiots go poke the monster."

"I'll tell her," Lee said, and didn't bother wiping at the wet in the corner of his eye where the camera could see. "But she already knows." He leaned closer to the lens. "You don't get to try and be poetic at the end, you hear me? You keep it boring. Call out structures, distances, code patterns. Let them turn you into math. That's how you live in this, whether your body gets out or not."

"Understood," John said. It was as close as he'd come to promising anything. He broke the connection himself, thumb on the switch before Lee could hear the way his breathing had changed. The camp feed vanished, replaced once more by maps and models, the war-room's cold light leaking back into the smaller space. When he stepped out, Voss was waiting at the doorway, arms folded. For a second, the two of them just looked at each other, two quietly exhausted people standing on different sides of the same decision. Then she nodded toward the main display, where Sector 0 pulsed. "We're calling it Phase One of the Cure Plan," she said. "Fragmentation plus deployment. We'll have a counteragent ready to load into the grid when you light it up. Aerosol and injector both, in case one path fails. Everything we can make that won't kill your own biology faster than Theta-9's."

"And all I have to do," he said, "is walk the node into the heart and kick." "All you have to do," she agreed, "is the one thing the organism can't model. Be where it can't resolve you, when we tell you to, touching what it loves most. We'll handle the chemistry." She paused. "Sector 0. Central grid nexus. That's where you go. If we break the parasite there, we break it everywhere it can reach. If we miss, there won't be a second city to try this in."

He nodded once. No salutes, no speeches. He turned away from the screen and the air-conditioned hum of the fallback site and looked at the feed from his own implant—grainy, skewed, showing the tower corridor where the girl waited. She was on her feet again, shaky but upright, humming in small, fractured patterns that sat uneasily between his heart and the city's deeper pulse. When he stepped into frame, she moved without needing a command, falling into her by-now habitual position half a step behind his right shoulder.

He didn't say anything. Words wouldn't change the route. He checked the rough heading on the map in his peripheral, plotted a line through what was left of streets and structures toward the dense knot of Sector 0, then started walking. Outside, drones adjusted their positions, rose into the grey light, and fell into loose orbit above him, lenses tracking the anomaly and the girl as they moved. Ahead, the city's borrowed body began, almost imperceptibly, to rearrange its nerves.

CHAPTER 24

The tower district fell away behind them in uneven blocks, squared-off shapes against a flat, colourless sky. John stepped out from under its concrete shadow with the girl half a pace behind his right shoulder, her hum still jittered from the last collapse—short, broken notes that never quite settled on a single pitch. The street they took was one he hadn't walked before, but it looked like every other fringe road the organism hadn't fully bothered with yet: mid-rise shells, dead storefronts, cars stopped in awkward diagonals. Hosts lined the walls and railings in a thin scatter, hands on whatever load-bearing structure they could reach. They made space for him the way they always had—small, unconscious micro-adjustments that treated him like an inconvenient lamppost. Above, three drones shifted their orbit to match his heading, faint status lights winking through the haze. A fourth skimmed low along the cross-street ahead, mapping routes a few seconds before he needed them.

The difference was in the sound. Out here, even on the fringe, the hum didn't feel like background anymore. It had weight, intent—a steady pressure under his boots and in his ribs that made his own heartbeat sound thin. As they walked, the girl's tone thickened, the fractured pattern smoothing itself without ever fully matching the city. Each block they put between themselves and the tower, her low notes sank closer to the deep infrastructure band she'd been born inside. John logged it as he walked: less static, more coherence, less lag between her hums and the vibrations in the walls. The drones' telemetry pips clicked in his ear at slow intervals, the war-room keeping its commentary to themselves for now. No one needed to tell him this wasn't outskirts anymore. The city had noticed its blind spot and its favourite node leaving the safe patch and moving in.

The first stretch of transition zone looked deceptively familiar, just more of the same ruined grid. It took a few hundred meters before the density change became obvious. Hosts thickened along the long faces of buildings rather than at random; gaps closed where cracks in the infrastructure would have broken the signal. Hands lined guardrails in neat, finger-wide intervals, each body pressed in tight enough that shoulders touched. The hum evened out, the little local variations ironing themselves away. On a warehouse wall to his left, fifteen people stood in a row with their palms at exactly the same height, backs straight, heads slightly inclined. As he passed, the line rotated toward him in a slow, smooth wave, left to right, like someone running a magnet under a table of filings. No aggression. Just alignment.

The girl felt it before the bodies moved. A good second before the wave reached them, her head snapped toward the wall, hum jumping a half-tone; by the time the last host in line had rotated her shoulders, the girl had already shifted her weight to compensate. John didn't speed up or slow down. He walked past as if it were a display window, eyes flicking to catch details. On the other side of the street, a smaller cluster detached from a decorative iron fence—not abandoning contact, just sliding their hands along the metal to a new section where the angle gave them a clearer orientation toward him. They had no reason to care about his existence under the old rules. The field had just rewritten them.

"Density up twenty percent," a drone op murmured over the line, half to Singh, half for the log. "Micro-adjustments increasing. They're not just hugging structure; they're optimising." The further they pushed, the more obvious the reorganisation became. Ahead, streets began to display patterns someone had chosen. Underpasses that had once been choked with stalled cars were now half-cleared; vehicles shoved or rolled aside to make clean load paths between pillars. Hosts crowded those pillars two deep, leaving the old traffic lanes empty so vibrations could run unbroken along the concrete. Narrow alleys that carried little load lay oddly untouched—scattered trash, the occasional lonely body clinging to a single downspout. In contrast, intersections with multiple overhead spans had become knots of flesh and steel, every viable contact point taken.

Then the anticipatory behaviour started. Three blocks out from a major junction, the drone feed showed them a cluster that wasn't reacting to their approach at all—it was moving before they got there. Hosts peeled off one side of a wall and marched in single file to a set of cross-braces on the next building, filling gaps that hadn't been gaps a minute ago. Others left a mid-strength lamp standard to converge on a fatter, better-anchored utility pole that lay closer to the line he was walking. By the time John rounded the corner, the configuration was already optimised for his passage: strong structures heavily saturated, weaker ones nearly bare, a clean corridor through the middle like a prepared artery.

"Renner," Singh's voice came over comms, tight with focus. "Telemetry shows pathing changes ahead of your position. The system is pre-loading. It's adjusting nodes before you arrive." "Feels like it," John said. He stepped through the ordered gap, the girl matching his line exactly. Along the walls, hosts leaned a few degrees toward their vector, as if the field were stretching to meet them through its own meat. One man's free hand drifted up an inch off the concrete, fingers twitching, then settled again as if a decision had been made without him.

It got worse closer in. Intersections stopped feeling like

weather and started feeling like anatomy. Where streets crossed with enough infrastructure overhead, hosts formed dense rings and spokes—standing at corners, on medians, along overhead beams, every position chosen with an eye to load paths. In one place, a pedestrian overpass had become something else entirely: every square of mesh along its sides occupied, every supporting post carrying three bodies like added ribs. The hum there didn't even pretend to be a single tone; it layered into bands, deep base vibrations from structural load under a sharper, faster code chatter. Merge pulses, new long stabilising notes that hadn't existed a few days ago, higher flickers that darted like correction signals across the mesh. The organism had learned new tricks while he'd been sleeping in stairwells.

The girl's hum started to unconsciously match those new patterns. Walking through a particularly dense intersection, John heard her slip from the old align–transfer–reorient rhythms into something more complex—Merge, the long-tone stabiliser, and then a narrow-band correction code he'd only heard in bursts between hosts. The sound came out of her as an almost-perfect reproduction, no lag, no strain, her body accepting the upgrade like a software patch. He saw her hand drift toward a heavy steel doorframe as they passed, fingers stretching for the jamb as if the metal itself were pulling at her. He caught her wrist before she made contact and pulled her past. The nearest drone dropped a few metres for a better angle. "Renner," Holt snapped, for once letting sharpness into his voice. "She almost synced with that tertiary node. Keep her off anything that carries main load."

"Then stop routing me through the spine," John said. He didn't raise his voice. He just adjusted his route half a metre farther from the most attractive beams, using pitted curbs and broken planters as physical guides to keep her fingers off the big conductors. Out of reflex, his hand settled on her shoulder for a moment. Her hum stuttered, dropped a half-step. A second later, a ring of hosts half a block away echoed the drop in micro-movements—little shifts in knee angle, a fractional lowering of shoulders—as the field tried to recompute around a configuration it didn't like.

Somewhere between that intersection and the next, the organism changed its mind about how to treat him. Up until now, bodies had moved out of his way in buffered, impersonal nudges, the field behaving as if he were dead space in its map. As they went deeper, the parting grew more precise. Hosts stopped shuffling aside in whole-steps and began making smaller, puppet-like corrections—shoulders nudged just enough, elbows tucked a fraction, knees adjusting by centimetres. They didn't look at him, but their paths around him had the deliberate care of something moving furniture around a fragile object.

The sound shifted too. At first he thought he'd imagined it, but after a few dozen paces it was impossible to ignore: a faint secondary beat under the main hum, matching his footfalls. Half a beat late, but there—tap of boot on broken asphalt, then a subtle swell in the surrounding field. After ten steps, the pattern stabilised; the city had folded his rhythm into its own. He tested it, just enough to be sure. He short-stepped once, deliberately breaking his stride. The response arrived two seconds later—a minor wobble in the hum, a visible hitch in the way a line of hosts leaned against a railing.

He slid sideways off his previous line by half a metre. The girl matched him, as she always did. Three seconds after that, fifty bodies along a building face ahead tilted the same increment, as if someone had adjusted the path of an invisible wind. They didn't move their feet or change their contact points; they altered their torsos, the angles of their spines, the inclination of their heads. "Renner," Singh said, voice low. "Pull up drone three's feed." The image in the corner of John's display zoomed, tracking one stretch of wall. Tiny white crosses marked host shoulders. As John took another sidestep, every cross shifted the same direction, same distance, with mechanical lag. "They aren't ignoring you anymore," Singh said. "They're modelling you. The field's treating your movement as a reference."

On another block, a cluster didn't even pretend to be focused on structure first. They were in the right place—wrapped around a heavy junction of rail support and power conduit—but their body language gave them away. When John passed the mouth of the street they occupied, they didn't part. They didn't need to; the geometry already had a gap for him. Instead, every head turned toward him in micro-increments, eyes unfocused, pupils blown wide. Their hands stayed on steel and concrete. Everything else tracked his shoulders. The hum there had an extra modulation, a higher overlay that rose and fell with his distance, like sonar pinging off a target.

The psychological pressure built slower than the structural changes but steadier. The further toward Sector 0 he went, the more the city felt less like an environment and more like an MRI machine. Drones began to lose clear lines of sight; hosts crowded rooftops, leaning against parapets and antenna masts in repeating patterns that turned formerly open vantage points into dense grids. Any time he stepped into a comparatively wider space—a small plaza, a parking lot—the organism compensated by thickening the perimeter, bodies massing along the edges to keep the signal strong where the structural load thinned. The effect, walking through, was like moving down a long, tightening throat.

Inside his own skull, the noise tried to smooth his reactions. It pulled at his gait, at his breathing cadence, trying to fold him into the pattern it had begun to impose on everything else. He met it the only way he knew how: by logging, not obeying. List the sensations. Note the patterns. Treat the hum like incoming fire: something you tracked, not something you loved. Beside him, the girl's hum climbed louder without her seeming to want it, volume rising at the organism's insistence. When it got high enough that it started to edge into strain, he put his hand on her shoulder again, the way he had at the relay. Her tone dropped instantly, like a dial turned down.

A second later, three separate clusters within visual range did the same. Along a rail embankment to his left, along a balcony string ahead, along the base of a billboard support behind, dozens of throats eased their output. Shoulders lowered a fraction. Knees unlocked. The net effect was subtle, but he saw it and so did the war-room. "That's new," Holt said softly. "He taps her down, local nodes follow. The field's using him as secondary reference now. It's bleeding some trust off the girl."

If she felt it, she didn't have words to say so. What she had was the look she gave him when he changed something inside the hum. As they paused for a moment under a rail crossing, hosts shuddering around them as the network rerouted signal, she turned her face up toward his, eyes wider than he'd seen them since the first tower. The fear there didn't read like simple animal panic; it was closer to the look people had given him in the first weeks of the plague, when they could still understand what they were losing. She didn't understand the math, but she understood change, and she understood that this time, the organism was adjusting to him as much as it was adjusting to her.

By the time Sector 0 announced itself, his senses had already told him it was close. You didn't need a map to find the heart of something like this; you just followed the pressure. Streets that had already felt full became downright choked. Every substantial beam, column, brace, and rail carried at least one layer of flesh. The hum gathered itself into a deeper note that his bones tried and failed to ignore, layered with richer, more complex code on top. Even before the buildings opened up, the girl's body started to lean subtly forward, small muscles in her calves and neck drawing her toward some point ahead as if a string had been tied to the base of her skull. Then the street he was on curved between two gutted office towers and simply stopped pretending to be anything other than approach ramp. The city opened.

Sector 0 wasn't one thing; it was a convergence. Rail lines, some elevated, some buried, intersected in a tangle of bridges and trenches. Power corridors met there, huge cable bundles diving into bunker-like structures before emerging again to snake across the skyline. Telecom masts bristled from rooftops like thorns, dishes and panels all angled inward toward a central core he couldn't even see yet. Every flat surface capable of carrying load had become a contact field. Hosts stood along bridge parapets three deep. They crowded transformer farms until no paint showed between shoulders. They filled rail platforms to the edges, toes hanging over concrete lips, palms flat on pillars and canopy supports. Hundreds, maybe thousands, packed into every direction, humming in a harmonised spectrum that made his vision tremble.

The girl took one involuntary step forward, the tether inside her drawn tight. Her hand lifted, fingers spread toward the densest knot of infrastructure as if she could feel the exact location of the perfect contact point just out of reach. He caught her wrist, pulled it gently but firmly down, and shifted his stance so his body sat between her and the worst of it. Her hum wavered, then stabilised at a pitch that didn't belong wholly to either him or the city. For a moment, even the drones went quiet. Their telemetry pips still fed into HelixCore's systems, but on the voice channel there was only breath and the low, monstrous resonance of a city turned into a single organ. Then Voss's voice came through, stripped of anything but fact.

"Renner," she said, the faintest hint of static riding her words. "You're standing at the edge of the hive."

CHAPTER 25

John stopped just short of the first true density. Sector 0 waited ahead in a knot of steel and concrete, humming low enough that his teeth ached. The girl halted beside him without being told, half a step behind his right shoulder, the position she had settled into somewhere back near the tower. Her hum had changed. It sat on three layers at once now, a slow align pulse under a faster transfer rhythm and, above both, a long continuous note that did not belong to any pattern he recognised. It sounded like something meant to travel far. Her fingers hovered a few centimetres from a rusted rail head that jutted out of the broken pavement. He wrapped his hand around her wrist before she could close the gap. The muscles in her forearm trembled under his grip, not with fear, but with force that had no channel. Her eyes tracked the rail, then the structures beyond, then finally up to his face. The look was wrong. There was focus, but not hers, as if someone else had leaned forward behind her eyes and was trying on her gaze.

Above, the drones adjusted quietly. No status chimes in his ear now, no commentary from the war-room. Three of the machines held a high, offset triangle over the avenue, stabilising their cameras. The fourth hung lower at his flank, optics tipped down to catch every small movement in the girl's shoulders and throat. The city's hum rode up through the soles of his boots, met the residual buzz from the tower experiments, and settled into a steady pressure under his ribs. Sector 0 waited with the patience of a deep, heavy thing that knew nothing inside its reach could leave without its consent. John tightened his hold on the girl's wrist a fraction. Her hum climbed anyway, chest vibrating harder under the thin fabric of her hoodie, as if the field had decided her muscles were only nominally relevant to whatever it wanted to do next. When she looked at him again, the focus did not soften.

It started with breath rather than sound. She drew in air short and uneven, not like someone about to speak, but like someone whose lungs were being pulsed by an external metronome. Her jaw sagged open a few millimetres. The hum that had been trapped behind her teeth leaked out around her tongue in clipped bursts. A low note, a pause, a double pulse climbing, then a static-laced fall. Not code in the pure sense he had been learning to recognise out of the host walls, not human words either. The shape of it sat halfway between both, like a machine trying to imitate an accent it had only ever heard through a vent. Her tongue moved as if groping for consonants it no longer remembered how to anchor. The muscles in her cheeks twitched, then flattened. A fragment of something that might have been a vowel snagged at the back of her throat and dissolved into rough vibration.

Telemetry on the HelixCore screens spiked. In the fallback war-room, one of the audio techs leaned in over his console, hand already riding the gain. Singh watched the waveform scroll across the largest display, mouth pressed thin. The pattern was wrong for cry, wrong for cough, wrong for the little involuntary sounds their models had catalogued from hosts. It had the cadence of intention, chopped into unusable pieces. "It is trying to phonate," he said quietly, the words almost swallowed by the hum feed. "Not through the cluster. Through her." Holt did not look away from the graph. "That is not her motor cortex firing. Look at the timing. That is Theta-9 running a program it does not fully understand." No one in the room said John's name, but the tension drew tight around his node on the map. He had watched thousands of people lose their faces to the network. This was the first time it had reached through one of them and tried to build a new one in front of him.

The next sound scraped its way out like something dragged along rust. Her lips shaped around air that did not want to behave like air. There was a consonant buried in it, or the shadow of one. "Nn." A stuttering roll of vibration against her palate. "Rr." The tail end broke into three overlapping tones as the hum tried to hold its own rhythm and move her tongue at the same time. "…n…" It came out as more vibration than voice, a multi-layered note wearing the thin outline of a syllable. It was not a word. It was not even what it thought a word was. But John recognised the contour the instant it hit the air. It was reaching for the simplest label it had for him and failing. His name had been written under his node on every HelixCore map for months. The organism had seen it stamped on his beacon for as long as it had been watching his anomaly. Its field had been wrapping itself around the shape without ever being able to use it. Now it tried.

For two beats the hum across several blocks cut. Hosts that had been pressed shoulder to shoulder on rails and pillars dropped into silence so clean it felt wrong. They did not move. They simply stood and waited, mouths slack, fingers still. The drones' microphones registered the absence as its own spike. On the models, Theta-9's coherence sagged, then held, like a lung pausing at the top of an inhale. The girl's hands rose uselessly under his grip, forearm muscles fluttering. Her throat spasmed hard enough that a fine tremor showed at the corners of her jaw. Inside her chest the hum surged into three distinct bands, out of phase with one another, fighting for space in the same small cavity. In the bunker, Voss leaned closer to the array without realising she had moved. "It is calling you," she said. Not dramatic. Not loud. Just an observation that did not require a second reading.

The second attempt was worse. This time the sound that came out had weight. Her mouth opened wider, not on her own initiative. The note that rolled through her vocal cords carried depth like a stacked choir coming apart. It sounded like three people speaking almost together, each a fraction of a second out of sync with the others. The timbre was wrong. The memory Voss had of the girl's early interviews showed a thin, jittery teenager with a light, uneven voice. What pushed out of her now had no relation to that register. It had been averaged. Holt's jaw tightened as he watched the spectrum. "That is a synthetic timbre," he said. "The network is trying to approximate a human template by stacking signals. It has no concept of a single throat." The drones' mics captured a phrase or something like one. The shape of repeated syllables. "Come. Come. Come." Each copy offset just enough to turn it into a wet echo. Not language as any human would recognise it. More like a broadcast call that had never learned how to stop at one channel.

John took one step back, weight shifting to his heels. The girl took one step forward into the space he had left. Whatever was steering her posture did not care that her body still carried bruises and fatigue. Her shoulders came up square. Her chin lifted as if to present better access to her airway. Her eyes remained wide and too still, fixed on some point deep in Sector 0 where the load paths converged. The throat that sound came out of belonged to a person. The voice did not belong to anyone. Around them, the hosts nearest the edge of the hive made fine-tuned corrections. Some leaned closer to their contact points, others drew back a hair, as if the organism were using their bodies to tune its own monitor feedback. The deep base hum thickened by a fraction as more mass settled onto key supports.

The messages did not arrive as sentences. They arrived as failures broken into smaller failures, each closer to the shape of what it wanted. First came more clipped syllables: hard-edged bursts that punched through her teeth and died on her tongue. Then longer stretches of vowel that wandered up and down scales human lungs were not meant to hold. Harsh consonant spikes rode on top, some recognisable as the skeletons of old phonemes, others closer to the clicks and mechanical coughs of overloaded equipment. John listened with the same attention he had used on the align and transfer patterns, not because he expected comfort from anything it might say, but because sound meant behaviour, and behaviour meant prediction.

The structure clicked for him before it did for the warroom. The cadence was wrong for speech, but he had heard that rhythm a hundred times in hum form. Align. Transfer. Reorient. Only here, the pulses came as pieces of syllable instead of peaks in a vibration band. The thing inside the city was lifting its own protocol out of the infrastructure and trying to wear it as a mouth. Each broken attempt drew down the host field in a tight ring around them, as if more processing power were being spent on this one act than on holding a thousand bodies on a thousand supports. The drones fed every phoneme back to HelixCore, where software meant for language reconstruction tried and failed to assign meaning.

One utterance landed differently. The pitch dipped halfway through, then rose in a way that was not part of any of its previous patterns. The syllables arrived with small gaps between them, enough to resemble spacing. "Can't." Static over the final consonant. "See." The vowel stretched, torn between two note bands. "You." The double layer on the last sound made the word itself unstable, but the structure held. Helmets bent over consoles in the bunker. Holt did not bother translating for his own benefit. "It is not talking about vision," he said. "It is describing mapping. It is trying to explain the error condition." Theta-9 had built a representation of the city inside itself. Every host, every rail, every brace had a place in that model. John did not. His node existed as a physical coordinate in the real world and as a failure icon in the math.

A red smear appeared at the corner of the girl's mouth. The strain of forcing three bands of hum through tissue not designed for it had finally torn something delicate. A thin line of blood traced down along her chin in an almost neat vertical. John tightened his grip on her wrist, not to stop the sound, but to keep her from toppling forward. The moment his fingers settled, her hum dropped by a hair. Hundreds of hosts within visible range adjusted their own outputs to match the change. Along a bridge rail to his left, shoulders dipped that same fraction. On a transformer housing ahead, four heads bowed very slightly together. The organism was still trying to use her as its reference, but now it could not avoid treating his interference as an input. The next word that came out of her carried a different shape. "Stay." It had the clean, imperative cadence of a protocol command. The tone belonged to nobody.

Her body reached some internal limit a second later. For one awful moment she came forward toward him, mouth still half open, eyes completely wrong. Then every muscle in her frame seemed to decide it had its own opinion. There was no neat arc into seizure. The convulsion came as a series of mismatched acts. Her knees buckled while her spine tried to stay straight. Her fingers curled into fists against his hand while her elbows fought to extend. The network tried to hold her upright through its usual control channels. Whatever remained of the person submerged underneath it tried to break that posture. Her hum shattered into a mess of unaligned fragments, the smooth carrier wave gone. She dropped to one knee hard, sand and dust scuffing the fabric at her joint. Her head jerked once to the side, hard enough that her hair fell across her eyes.

Hosts around the edge of Sector 0 spasmed in sympathy. Hands slipped off concrete. One woman slammed her open palm against a pillar three times in rapid succession, as if trying to hammer a lost rhythm back into it. For roughly three seconds the field lost its clean global tone. From HelixCore's vantage point it looked like a coherence crash in a ring around John. Inside that ring, behaviour fell out of sync. For three seconds, nothing in that radius appeared to agree with anything else. The girl dragged in air like someone at the surface after too long underwater. The sound that came out of her next was not layered. It did not ride on top of three frequencies. It scraped up thin and singular. "…no." Just that, soft, pushed out through a throat that had been used for other purposes a heartbeat before.

The war-room watched the sensors stutter, then drag themselves back into order. Singh's hand tightened around the edge of his tablet, whitened knuckles giving away what his face did not. The models had shown Theta-9 adjusting to anomalies, smoothing over faults, routing around damage. They had not shown it losing control of its favourite node so completely that her own refusal registered as a local denial of service. Voss did not say anything over comms. There was nothing useful to add in the three seconds before the field reasserted itself. Hosts snapped back into configuration, palms finding metal again, shoulders aligning. The hum rose, then settled. On the graph, Theta-9's global mode dipped and clawed back.

When the girl steadied again, she looked like someone whose insides had been wrung out and put back in the same skin. Her hum crawled back up toward baseline, but carried artefacts it had not before, little glottal catches and half-tones, fragments of the protocol it had almost finished wearing as speech. John eased her up from her knees, one hand under her elbow, the other still around her wrist. She let herself be guided without resistance. Drones buzzed low, trying to catch the fine tremors in her fingers, the way her throat worked even when no sound came. No one in the bunker filled the channel. The data had more value than anything they might say.

John did not need Holt or Singh to put words to what the

organism had just betrayed. The field had spent its attention and energy trying to get through a medium his anomaly could not block. It could not push hum through his null node. Its math could not stabilise any path that treated him as a proper carrier. Speech sat outside that network entirely. Air and throat and tongue. The broken architecture of one girl's voice had become the only bridge available to an intelligence that did not know how to deal with blind spots. Theta-9 was not practicing language because it wanted comfort or domination from him. It was practicing language because language was the one channel that did not care about its graphs.

Sector 0 waited ahead with all its mass. Inside that convergence it would have more signal, more scaffolding, more bodies. Enough capacity, perhaps, to refine what it had just attempted and finish the conversation it had begun at the edge. It had called him by the closest thing it could manage to his name. It had told him it could not see him. It had told him to stay. All of that sat on top of the deeper, simpler truth he could feel in the way the hum reached for his bones. The organism wanted him inside. Not as prey. As a problem it refused to leave unsolved.

The girl looked up at him one more time. Her pupils tracked his face slowly, like she was picking him out of a crowded room. Her lips parted, then closed, then parted again. The sound that finally came out sat between registers. "John." It wrapped too many vowels around the one call sign. The consonants blurred at the edges, doubled by overlapping tones he had heard in the host walls. The field was trying to say it, not the girl, pushing its incomplete understanding of his label through her mouth. It hit him with all the warmth of a clinical error message. He held her wrist a little tighter, let the hum roll past, and stepped toward Sector 0 anyway.

CHAPTER 26

The corridor spat them out into open space so suddenly it felt wrong. One moment John had concrete tight in his peripheral vision, a tunnel of conduits and cable trays pressed in above the catwalk, the girl's layered hum pinned between walls and grating. The next, the ceiling broke apart and the world dropped away in tiers and arches and steel. He halted at the lip without needing to think about it, boots on the cracked slab where the access tunnel joined the stadium rim. Sector 0's heart opened below him in a wide, circular wound. What had once been a sports bowl and entertainment complex had been carved into a power organ, its original purpose erased under concrete and hardware. The stadium's ring of seating survived only as a skeletal memory, tiers of stepped concrete wrapped around a central field that no longer existed. Rail lines came in from every direction, not as orderly spurs but as burrowed channels, tunnels bored through the outer structure so that tracks could dive into the stadium walls and disappear into its ribs. Telecom towers that had once stood free now leaned inward from the perimeter, welded into the structure's spine, their antenna arrays twisted down like thorns frozen mid-fold. Above, thick power conduits as wide as old trees crossed the open air, sagging between towers and stadium roof trusses, their insulation bloated and split, busbars gleaming in the ruptures. Every surface that could bear weight had something alive on it.

Hosts packed the lower bowl shoulder to shoulder, standing on every riser, knees almost touching the backs of those on the step below. They packed the aisles, faces turned along the arcs of the sweeping stairs so that every curve of concrete carried a continuous band of flesh. The upper tiers held more of them, bodies lining the railings three deep along the parapets, hands resting flat on the cold metal, fingers spaced almost perfectly. The structural catwalks that traced the underbelly of the roof had become hanging roosts, hosts perched along them with their arms threaded through steel. Some hung half-supported, feet braced on beams, torsos bent out into open air so there was nowhere to fall without landing on more bodies. Even the telecom towers inside the bowl carried them, figures clinging to rungs and latticework all the way to the distorted antenna heads. Every bench that survived, every platform, every service balcony and lighting gantry had been colonised. Tens of thousands, maybe more. The cameras on the drones made no attempt to count. Even at a distance, the number stopped meaning anything.

The hum pressed outward from that mass like weather. It had been a sound before, a layered vibration riding in the walls, a pressure in the metal. Inside the stadium it became an atmosphere. John's first breath tasted thicker, as if some part of the air was already vibrating and had to be forced still in his lungs. The access slab trembled subtly under his boots, not from mechanical fault but from so many aligned bodies transferring micro-movements through concrete. The girl stiffened at his side in the half-behind position she had retaken on instinct. She didn't choose a stance this time. Her muscles drew her forward by increments, a series of tiny pulls that stacked against his hand when he closed it around her forearm. The hum in her chest, audible even over the stadium's mass, shifted. The deep align pulse fell into exact timing with the closest hosts, its phase snapping into theirs with a jolt that shivered through her shoulders. The mid-band transfer rhythm, which had drifted around its own logic in the tunnels, locked an instant later. Above both, the new high note she had started near the tower stretched long and steady, no pattern, no breaks, as if something far below all of this were blowing a single unending breath through the city.

Drones drifted out past them like cautious birds, rotors throttled to minimum so as not to stir dust. Their lights stayed dim. One rose higher to clear the level of the upper parapet, two dropped into the lower bowl, hugging the stadium curvature so they could send back side angles across the packed risers. John's earpiece crackled low with compressed audio before the words resolved. "Jesus Christ," Singh said, voice stripped of anything but the effort not to raise it. "Confirming headcount bands from six to ten thousand per quadrant. That's… those are coherent. All of them." Someone else in the war-room exhaled close to the pickup. Holt, quieter than usual: "I've never seen a cluster this dense without collapse. Not even in simulations. This is the brainstem." Voss did not answer immediately. The war-room background noise dropped out instead. Keyboard chatter stopped. A model feed ticked once in John's peripheral HUD and then paused with a buffering icon, as if the software itself had taken a breath and didn't know what to do with it.

He stepped off the slab and the entire bowl moved. It was small, a shiver more than a motion, but when it travelled through fifty thousand bodies at once it became visible. The nearest ring of hosts did not turn their heads. That had been earlier, in the outer sectors, when the organism could afford to behave like a crowd. Here it turned by fractions. As John's boot hit the concrete, shoulders shifted a single degree, a stadium-sized compass trying to find north. Arms adjusted, not to reach toward him but to refine contact with railings and neighboring bodies, as if every palm had been told to find a better map of its current touch. The hum faltered in a tight band around him that widened as waves travel in water. His presence cut a circle into it, a null value pushed into a completed equation.

The effect started nearest. A host on the aisle to his left eased her spine away from the step behind her by perhaps a centimetre. It broke the identical angle of her row. The man beside her failed to match, late by a fraction longer than the rhythm should have allowed. Further up, a hand slipped on a rail for a moment, fingers lifting, skin separating from steel. That tiny break became a notch in a load path that had been perfectly continuous. The drone feeds overlaid instability scores in semi-transparent red across his vision, numbers climbing around his position like rising heat signatures. "Local instability rising," Singh reported, recovering some tone. "It's folding him into the math and failing. Feedback loops in peripheral tiers." The hum's high bandwidth hissed in his ears for a heartbeat, as if the signal had wavered across the drone audio too. Then the network tried again.

You could see it correct itself. Hosts who had shifted out of line tightened shoulders back into a more perfect arc along each row. Fingers flattened. Spines realigned to the curvature of the concrete risers. The momentary slack in the hum snapped taut. The S3 tags on his HUD dropped back down, orange cooling toward yellow, and for two, maybe three seconds the stadium looked stable again, a single organ resisting a contaminant. Then John took another step and everything in a twenty-metre radius misfired harder. The wave of micro-turns overshot. Instead of finding a new stable orientation, some hosts rotated further than the mean, others less, and the arcs of bodies that had read like drawn lines fractured into jagged segments. A man three rows up simply sat, legs folding as if someone had cut his signal mid-command. His shoulders hit the step behind. He stayed where he fell, not spasming, not limp, just frozen in the act of collapsing. The hum around him dropped a chord, lost then reasserted. In his display, a spray of S3 micro-collapse flags blinked on, tiny red pulses overlaying thousands of motionless figures.

The stadium interior forced him downward. The access path they'd emerged onto was a mid-tier service ring with its own railings; from there, staircases dropped toward the lower bowl in gentle arcs built for crowds. John picked the nearest path that gave him a clear line to the field, careful only in the practical sense of not tripping on debris. There was very little debris. Whatever Theta-9 had not needed, it had already absorbed. He went down concrete steps bordered on both sides by living walls. The hosts pressed to either side of the aisle did not sway or stumble as he passed within touching distance. Their bodies leaned a degree towards him, enough that the aisle felt narrower, as though the stadium had shrugged inward. The hum in their chests matched the girl's cadence so closely now that her individual layers were hard to isolate even with the implants listening for them. She moved with him, half a step behind and to his right, her free hand kept deliberately away from any rail. The muscles in her arm under his grip rolled like cables under strain, pulling toward the field.

Above, the upper tiers were still packed, hosts standing at the parapets three deep, forearms laid along the rail so evenly that at first glance they could have been fixtures. As he descended, their heads did not track him, but their breathing changed. He took one breath in, one breath out, calm and measured from training rather than emotion, and a slice of the stadium followed a half-second later. The drone audio picked up the soft, staggered rustle of tens of thousands of chests expanding and contracting in approximate sync, a full-city ventilation system trying to match a new metronome. "Do you see that?" Singh said, not bothering to mask anything now. "Upper tiers are copying his respiratory cadence. That's not mapped behaviour." Holt's voice came through thin, like he'd leaned closer to the mic without noticing. "We used her as the reference stand-in for all the models. All of them. It's not supposed to find new baselines on the fly. Not at this level. Models are dropping frames trying to refit."

The roof structure overhead looked less like architecture and more like exposed bone. Trusses crisscrossed in deep triangles, support beams bolted through with brackets for long-dead advertising rigs and lighting arrays. Those gaps were now filled with bodies. Hosts clung to ceiling walkways, arms looped through grated flooring, feet hooked on cross-beams. The load tables in John's HUD flickered warnings that the additional mass exceeded any original design limits by orders of magnitude, but there were no sag lines, no cracks. The organism had found ways to distribute weight across the structure, using bodies as braces, live struts placed where needed. Power conduits as thick as industrial chimneys ran along these bones, their casings patched with resinous growth where Theta-9 had sealed old damage. Down in the bowl, the central field had become something else entirely.

Where grass and dirt had once made a neat oval, a transformer complex had grown like crystal from poured concrete. Rows of high-voltage transformers sat in banks, each unit linked by latticework busbars that rose and bent and dropped again like another level of truss. Ceramic insulators in stacked disks formed columns between blades. Cooling radiators lined the sides of the big units, fins painted an old industrial green and streaked with rust tracks where coolant had wept. Cable trenches spidered out from the complex to the stadium walls, disappearing under the seats, under the aisles, into the guts of the structure. Overhead, feeding into the heart, thick overhead lines sagged from towers, their clamps the size of cars. The whole thing had the presence of an altar, not in any sentimental sense, but in placement and geometry: everything around it fed in, converged, bent towards it. Where the bowl's curvature focused sound, it focused power.

The girl's hum altered again as the heart came fully into view from the mid-level, slicing through her in audible bands. Sweat slid down the side of her neck, cutting lines through skin that had been dry in the tunnel. It was cold enough in the stadium that her breath smoked when she exhaled, but her skin ran hot under his hand. The triple-layered pattern in her chest separated and clarified with proximity, as if the heart node's stronger field had given each its own channel. The low align pulse locked into a perfect sine, no jitter. The mid-band transfer beat ran complex repeats and resets like data blocks being pushed. The high, continuous note rose until it scraped the upper limit of what his hearing enhancers tracked, then held there as an almost-silence that made his teeth ache. Her calves quivered with effort, each step down the stairs a negotiation between whatever force was trying to pull her toward the center and the physical authority of his grip.

She started to hum with her mouth as well as her chest. It began as breath catching on exhale, short bursts through clenched teeth that matched none of their training chants. Then the drones' directional mics picked up structure in the sound. Not words, but timing. Clusters of pitched syllables that matched the stabiliser tones they had used in labs to bring small samples of infected tissue back from cascading failure. Except she should not have heard those outside recordings. "Renner, listen to her," Holt said, the war-room quiet enough behind him that his own swallow carried over the line. "That's Protocol Five cadence. She's echoing field stabilisers she has no exposure to." Voss came in sharp, breaking the near-silence. "Holt, mark and pull those files. Renner, you keep her off any direct contact. Anything. If she touches a main conductor at this density, the system will take her straight into the core and you will not get her back."

Concrete flattened out under John's boots as the last of the risers gave way to the level walkway circling the lower bowl. The hosts on the concourse formed a continuous ring, three deep, facing inward towards the transformer field. Their backs were to him as he stepped onto the level, bodies a uniform wall. They did not part. They did not swivel to look. They simply leaned. Every spine along the ring tilted inward by a new fraction of a degree as though something in the bowl's centre of mass had shifted. The gesture repeated outward. In the seats above, hosts who had been aligned normal to the risers leaned inward by the same tiny angle, creating a subtle sense that the whole stadium had decided to tip. The hum swelled under that movement, a pulse sliding through hundreds of throats and chests and bones as weight resettled on the concrete.

John did not touch any of them. He moved along the concourse with the girl, following the inner curve, keeping just enough distance that he would not brush an arm as he passed. The lack of physical contact changed nothing. The instability fields registered his proximity, not his touch. As he drew level with one sector of the ring, a rash of S3 tags burst across his display over the nearest hosts' shoulders. They tightened fingers on the rails in front of them, then lost that grip for a flicker of a second, knuckles whitening and then slackening, skin slipping on steel before finding purchase again. A perfectly straight line of shoulders broke into a saw-tooth, some lagging, some anticipating. Their hum fractured. For a heartbeat, the local tone stepped out of phase with the global field, creating a hollow in the stadium's sound where everything seemed to cancel out and leave nothing but the background drone of distant transformers. Then the network shunted energy from adjacent sectors, filled the hole, and the sound snapped back in with a low growl that vibrated in the soles of his boots.

"Contact test by proximity only," Singh narrated, voice recovering the cadence of a report. "Thirty-two degrees around his position you're seeing one-second desync events. That's not chemical lag. That's math rejection. It's trying to rewrite him in and he's not taking the write." Another flicker of collapse rippled further along the ring without him reaching it physically. A group of five hosts, three men and two women, all in different clothes from whatever their lives had been, sagged in almost unison, knees bending as if someone had cut the voltage to their muscles. Their hands slid down the railings in front of them, fingers dragging, then catching. The S3 labels over them flared bright red and then settled back to orange as they re-stabilised. "Cluster-level S3 micro-collapses confirmed," Holt said, his tone flat only because he was forcing it. "Short strokes. Like an engine missing a cylinder every third cycle."

The nearer he came to the field, the more the stadium behaved like something with a nervous system. Distance was no longer measured just in metres but in signal strain. Overhead, some of the hosts on the roof catwalks shifted their grips, their legs tightening around beams. A row of them that had been lying prone along a support girder rolled half an inch toward the centre, their faces still turned downwards, creating a tiny shift in the distribution of their weight. In the transformer complex itself, none of the physical hardware moved, but the sensor overlays showed load paths altering. More current routed through certain banks, less through others, as if the organism was trying to route around a point of irritation. The cooling radiators' temperature readings climbed by a degree in one block, dropped in another, their fins sweating more condensation on one side than the other. The whole structure responded to him like a muscle inserting a twitch under the skin.

They took the access ramp down onto the field. The turf was long-gone, either stripped for materials or eaten. In its place, poured slabs sat in old expansion grid patterns, each concrete rectangle supporting part of the transformer forest. Narrow service lanes ran between the blocks, barely wide enough for an equipment cart. John moved along one of these lanes, the girl's boots scuffing the dust where old paint lines still ghosted the ground. When they stepped clear of the stadium's shadow and into the open space between the banks, the hum peaked. Not the loudest it had been, but the most complete. There was nowhere for it to reflect from without passing through them.

The girl's knees dipped. It wasn't a dramatic collapse, more the sudden loss of a centimetre of height as her quadriceps trembled under an increased load. John shifted his grip up to her bicep and took more of her weight without breaking stride. Her skin was slick now. Sweat gathered at the hollow of her throat and ran down between her ribs under the thin fabric of the hospital shirt she still wore. Her pupils, visible from the side when her head turned toward the nearest transformer bank, ate most of the iris. Her mouth stayed half-open, sucking in air against the pressure of the hum, still pushing out protocol tones between breaths. Up close, the sound of each syllable was almost lost in the overall field, but he could feel the vibration of it through the point where his hand closed on her arm.

Around them, within the lowest bowl, every host on the concourse rotated. It was not a theatrical turn. They did not whip around. The movement carried no drama. It simply happened. Spines rotated, shoulders turned, the line of planted feet stayed where it was. They did not bring faces around. Their heads stayed oriented toward the center of the field, eyes fixed on the heart of the transformer forest. Only their torsos redirected. It was as if someone had taken a stroboscopic snapshot and then, in the next frame, shifted all their body vectors so that John and the girl sat exactly on them. Weight shifted. The sensation, even to senses hardened in other kinds of horror, was that of walking into a gravity well.

He logged what he saw because that was the job and because speaking it kept it outside of the wordless pressure building in his chest. "Sector 0 core cluster," he said into his throat mic, voice even. "Lower bowl saturation approaching absolute. Hosts in all visible tiers maintaining coherent state under field strain. Orientation change at zero plus twenty seconds: torsos now vectoring on our position while heads remain fixed on heart node. Hum bands show increased harmonic complexity.

Load paths in transformer banks are re-routing around our projected track. Send confirmation if telemetry matches."

"Confirmed," Singh answered immediately, as if he'd been waiting for the prompt. "Your verbal matches modelled deltas. We're seeing cross-structure resonance increasing along the east-west axis. You're pulling tension into the very beams under your feet. Field density off the charts. You are in its brain, Renner. All of its processing mass is centred here." In the background, someone swore softly, not at him but at whatever numbers had just updated on their screen. Holt again, lower: "This is the highest Theta-9 density we've ever captured in a coherent configuration. Even for a minute. The models are struggling. They're literally dropping frames trying to keep up with what you're doing to it."

The drones circled above the transformer banks like carrion birds riding thermal currents, their cameras sending back tight spirals of perspective. One tracked along a row of radiators, water droplets vibrating on the metal fins. Another skimmed over a busbar, the paint blistered where thermal load had spiked in pulses. From above, the pattern of hosts in the bowl resolved into complicated rings and spokes that had not been apparent from ground level, lines of bodies forming conduits of their own from the outer tiers toward the heart. The feeds went monochrome for a second as exposure auto-corrected for flare in some part of the infrared. The organism's brain was running hot.

The girl slipped further, not in a sudden fall but in the slow way a system gives up its last margins. Her hum, which had been layered but mostly under external control, shifted into something else. The align pulse in her chest began to lead instead of follow, its phase pushing slightly ahead of the mass. The mid-band transfer rhythm took on a more complex syncopation, pushing out corrections rather than absorbing them. Her lips moved faster, protocol syllables falling into sequences that the war-room systems flagged as partial matches for multiple different stabiliser programmes. Sweat ran along the angle of her jaw and dripped from the tip of her chin. Her free hand curled toward the nearest transformer casing, fingers flexing as if they remembered how metal felt even through gloves she wasn't wearing.

Holt's voice cut back in before she could complete the gesture. "She's being called, hard. You're sitting in the highest field we've ever measured and every bit of it is aimed through her. This is direct core engagement beyond any design. She is not built for this, Renner. None of us are." Voss overrode him. "Renner, you are to prevent any physical contact between her and primary conductors. Repeat: any. Rails, casings, overheads, anything with direct linkage into that heart. You treat every piece of exposed hardware here like a wire straight into the organism's central processor. If it pulls her, we lose whatever advantage your presence is giving us."

He adjusted her position fractionally, shifting her closer to his body, the grip on her arm no longer just restraint but support. Her feet still moved under her, but the path they wanted to take had narrowed to a line dead centre into the deepest part of the transformer forest. Every time the service lane curved around a bank, her shoulders twisting toward where the geometry said the true centre must be betrayed the direction of that pull. The hum pinned them both inside its pressure. He could feel the interaction in his own bones now, a buzzing in his teeth and an ache deep in his long-healed fractures, but his internal fields stayed flat in the telemetry. He remained what he had been labelled since the first time someone put him in a lab with infected samples and watched nothing happen: null.

The organism stopped trying to throw him out. The earlier waves of correction and recoil smoothed into something else as he and the girl came to a halt at the point where the lanes ended and solid equipment took over. Ahead, the largest transformer in the complex towered over them, a block of steel and ceramic surrounded by forest-thick insulators and pipes. It sat at the mathematical centre of the stadium's ring, all busbars and cables converging on it. The hum's core tone seemed to originate inside its casing. Around the bowl, hosts on all levels began to move again, not in reaction to his steps now, but in a slow, coordinated shift that had nothing to do with him physically closing distance.

They were forming a ring. Not the crude circle they had already made by standing along the concourse. This was refinement. In the lower bowl, the hosts on the innermost rows stepped down off their risers if they had to, closing distance to the railings that bordered the field. Those further up took half-steps left or right, compressing gaps so that each column of bodies in the vertical stacked more perfectly over the ones below. The effect, seen in his peripheral overlay from the overhead drones, was of concentric circles tightening around the heart node and, by extension, around him. The organism was building a stabilising field in geometry as much as in signal, a human torus around its largest machine.

The girl's align pulse changed phase again, but this time it did not snap back to the mass. The stadium's hum altered to match hers instead. The adjustment didn't happen cleanly. There was a second where the two phases slid across one another and beat in and out like twin engines at slightly different RPMs. During that second, more S3 micro-collapses flared across his HUD than they had seen since they entered the bowl. Hosts dropped to knees, sagged against railings, tipped their heads hard to one side as if an unseen hand had shoved. Then the global field found a compromise. The hum settled into a new pitch, a fraction closer to the girl's pattern than before. The organism had incorporated her deeper into its baseline.

Telemetry updated again. Holt's voice had to work around something thick in his throat. "We're seeing stabilisation architecture emerging across the entire cluster. It's using them as live capacitors. It's building a ring field around the primary heart. That part matches what we've seen in smaller cores, scaled up. But..." He trailed off, and for a moment all John could hear was the stadium's breathing, the dust skittering in light currents around his boots, the ring of metal under stress as load shifted above. "But what?" Voss prompted, not sharply, just to keep the information coming. Holt exhaled. "The stabilisation pattern is no longer purely matched to her. It's taking input from him. From Renner. The harmonics in the ring are adjusting partially off his vitals. It's mapping him. Actively. That should not be possible. He's supposed to be outside its maths."

Singh's data feed backed him with numbers. "Heart node load changes correspond to his respiration, not just hers. We're seeing micro-oscillations in bus voltage that line up with his step cadence and heartbeat. The network is treating him as part of the environment. It's constructing a model of his null profile on the fly. Which means it's preparing for him." He did not have to say what that implied. Whatever advantage null gave them, Theta-9 was learning.

Concrete, steel, and flesh around him held still for one long moment, the hum flattening into something so steady it might have been silence if not for the way it continued to press against the skin. The stadium had folded all its motion inward, ring on ring, host on host, light and power and sound all bent toward the central transformer and the two figures standing before it. Every drone in the air kept moving only because inertial systems told them to; for a few seconds, even the operators watching through them seemed to forget to breathe.

In the middle of that compressed, waiting pressure, with the girl trembling against his hand and fifty thousand bodies locked in place at the edge of failure, one fact settled into the war-room and into the concrete under his feet alike. It did not need to be said, but someone said it anyway, barely above a whisper that still carried on the open channel. "Sector 0 is alive," Holt murmured, as if naming it might make it less so. "And it's waiting for him."

CHAPTER 27

The fallback site's command deck never went fully dark, but when Voss gave the order it felt as if someone had taken a shade and pulled it down over the room. Status strips along the ceiling dimmed by a few degrees. The soft, unnecessary chatter that had been drifting between stations since they locked into holding patterns died in the space between one breath and the next. The only sound left was the layered murmur of fans, processor stacks, and the muted clack of keys. Sector 0 lived on the front wall in a spread of displays: a central composite showing John and the girl from three drone angles at once, framed by thermal overlays, coherence graphs, and scrolling ribbons of numbers. Around that, smaller screens carried subfeeds: drone telemetry, S3 instability maps, host density projections, chemical dispersion models. John existed on the main map as a tight, steady beacon pulsing in the middle of a grey-white hurricane of signal.

Voss stood at the back of the pit, one hand on the rail, as far from the main wall as she could get while still seeing everything. Her presence did not dominate the room; it anchored it. Heads turned toward her when she shifted her weight. Nobody spoke until she did. "All units, this is Command," she said, voice flat, nothing sentimental left in it. "HelixCore operation Theta-9, Phase Three. Authorisation Voss-Delta-Seven. Beacon-01 is stable. Execute Helix package." The comm net answered with acknowledgements, stripped of names, just callsigns and tone. On the main board, new icons flared to life at the edge of the map, each tagged with a drone designator and payload code.

Operators at the drone stations rolled their chairs closer to their consoles, movements small and economical. Chairs squeaked once, then not again. Hands adjusted headsets, fingers found familiar keys and throttles. Lines of text updated at speed in the side columns as systems that had sat in armed standby stepped up into active. In the chemical monitoring bay, Holt leaned over Singh's shoulder, both of them watching a panel of curved lines and stacked bars that represented the counteragent's readiness: pressure, temperature, aerosolization ratios. Across from them, comm techs split their attention between the drone net and the direct line to Beacon-01's squad frequency, though no one expected John to talk. The operating picture of the stadium, captured from the overhead drones already in place, stabilized into a multi-angle view: the bowl of hosts, the transformer heart, the two figures standing at its edge, all framed by data overlays. The girl's bio-sign panel in the lower corner ticked upward as the field wrapped itself tighter around her.

"Lock Sector 0 feeds," Voss said. "Freeze outer-sector updates. All eyes on core." A soft chorus of "copy" answered. On the far left, a young tech at the launch coordination station ran a final cascade, checking power levels, trajectory predictions, interference profiles. His lips moved while his hands stayed still, reading each line once, then again, not from superstition but because there would be no time to check once they were airborne. Finally he lifted his head toward Voss without taking his eyes off his screen. "Helix-Alpha through Helix-Foxtrot ready," he said, voice carrying further than he probably meant it to. "All vectors green. Beacon-01 stable. Begin drop."

Above them, beyond concrete and shielding and rock, the fallback site's surface installation looked like a shuttered industrial plant. Low, flat roofs, dead cooling towers, rust streaks that were only partly real. Beneath the largest roof, a square section split along hidden seams and folded back, exposing a launch bay that had been quiet for years. The night above was a flat, low cloud deck lit from beneath by the city's scattered power grid and the glow of Sector 0's own emissions. From inside the bay, rows of drones lifted on hydraulic racks, their frames throwing angular shadows against the walls. These were heavier than the reconnaissance units already circling the stadium, bodies built around central payload spines with four rotors at each corner, shrouded for protection. Under their bellies and along their flanks hung pods that did not match, each type coded by form and mounting. Disruptor nodes sat in cartridge rings like nailgun rounds. Counteragent dispersal canisters in dull silver cylinders were clamped to hardpoints near the drones' centres of mass. Field amplifiers, squat and finned, occupied the remaining space, their housings marked with warning bands.

Launch control fed staggered start signals down the line. The first rank spun their rotors up in low, controlled increments, sound absorbed by foam baffles that retracted as they rose. Dust spiralled away from the racks in neat cones. Vibrations moved through the floor into the fallback site below, a faint tremor under the command deck. On the main display, a new camera feed came online, showing the bay from an overhead angle. As each drone cleared its rack, it hovered a metre up, stabilised, then slid forward on a pre-programmed track, ceding space to the one behind. Thirty-two heavy drones in the first wave, another sixteen in reserve already powered but held back. They rose through the opening in the roof in twos, not as a single crowded mass, each pair offset in time enough to avoid crosswash but close enough that their combined profile would be harder for Theta-9's field to pick apart.

At one of the pilot stations, Singh's console filled with a segmented view: top-left a map of the city with Sector 0 pulsing like a wound; top-right a first-person feed from Drone Alpha-01's front camera; bottom quadrants reserved for systems, wind and turbulence predictions, and the overlay showing Beacon-01 as a small icon deep inside the stadium. His crosshair was a translucent ring centred on the stadium's coordinates. Every movement of his hands on the control surfaces translated not into direct stick commands but into guidance biases for the swarm. His job was not to fly one drone freehand but to shepherd the whole flock across a hostile sky.

Holt occupied the next station over, half his screen given to structural models of the stadium and surrounding infrastructure. Lines representing rail lines, antenna towers, and load-bearing columns pulsed as the system calculated optimal disruptor node placement. "You hit Grid B-Seven first," he told Singh without looking away, eyes tracking a column of green and red numbers. "East parapet, above the main rail arteries. If we don't destabilise those load paths, the heart will drink everything we do into the bowl and dump it back on them." Singh's jaw moved once, a muscle jumping near his ear. "Copy, B-Seven first," he said. "Then D-Three, south towers. I want redundancy on those fibre spines." "You'll have twenty seconds between entry and field saturation," Holt added. "After that, the interference curves go non-linear. You stray outside the corridor, the drones die, and the whole plan goes with them."

They climbed, a rising lattice of blinking nav lights beneath the low cloud. The fallback site dropped away to black, swallowed by terrain. Ahead, the glow of Sector 0 bled into the clouds, a dome of sick, diffuse light the colour of burned insulation. Drone Alpha-01's forward camera drank in the city's dead grid: streets with their lamps gone dim, residential towers like hollow teeth, the stadium a dark crater at the heart of it. Sector 0's interference field was invisible to the naked eye, but it had a shape in the instruments. The HUD painted it as concentric shells of static strength around the stadium, like weather radar. The swarm's planned route threaded a narrow gap between the worst of the turbulence, a corridor no wider than a few hundred metres at its tightest point.

Crosswinds tugged at the drones' frames, gusts coming down from the cloud deck and curling around the heated air above the core, but the flight control algorithms cut thrust on one rotor, increased on another, micro-adjustments stacking into smooth forward motion.

"Entering outer dead zone in ten," Singh said, not because anyone needed the count but because saying it fixed the moment in time. "Nine, eight… mark." On his screen, the interference shells brightened as the swarm crossed the first threshold. Video feed from Alpha-01 developed needle-like distortions at the edges, lines of pixels twitching where there was no physical movement. The stadium's hum bled into the drone audio as a dynamic hiss. Sensor readouts spiked with irrelevant data, ghosted returns layered over real structures. A couple of smaller recon drones that had been loitering at higher altitude tried to adjust their positions in response to the disturbance and jittered instead, their stabilisation systems hunting for purchase in a field that pushed back. Their icons on the map flickered, then dropped, telemetry cutting out mid-correction as whatever held them aloft lost its frame of reference. One went into a flat spin on its way down, rotor arcs blurring, then disappeared behind a building.

"Delta-Three and Delta-Five lost," one of the telemetry techs reported, voice steady. "No recovery. Logging as interference casualties, not hostile impact." "Adjust frequency band on primary swarm," another operator said, fingers already moving. "Drop twenty kilohertz on the carrier. Narrow the beam. Treat Sector 0 like an active jammer." The command deck's software shifted allocations. Signals that had travelled on one channel now rode on a tighter, more protected path, power re-routed away from non-essential telemetry to keep control links alive. Altitude orders recalculated to bring the swarm slightly lower, hugging the tops of buildings that still had solid frames, using concrete and steel as crude shielding.

On Alpha-01's camera, the stadium grew, bowl silhouette cutting against the glowing sky. Needle distortions thickened as they pressed further in, thin bright spears stabbing across the frame from random angles, not physically there but registered by the CCD as if some part of the hum was reaching up through the sensors. The effect made straight lines seem to bend for a heartbeat before snapping back. "We're flying into a mind," someone at the back muttered, not loudly enough to be picked up by any mic but not quietly enough to stop the sentiment from landing. At his station, Singh rode the turbulence like an instructor grading his own work, hands calm on the controls, eyes moving between Beacon-01's icon in the stadium and the shifting interference corridor ahead.

One of the heavy drones a rank back caught a bad spike. Its icon jumped sideways a few metres on the map, then snapped back, the software flagging the discrepancy as unsourced. In the brief misalignment, its rotors had overcompensated. The frame wobbled, steadied, then began to hum sympathetically with the field, vibrations building in a frequency that had nothing to do with its mechanical design. "Charlie-Three, you're in resonance," the telemetry tech called. "Kill that pattern. Drop your spin two percent." The system obeyed, adjusting rotor speeds in opposition. The hum shaking the frame broke, the resonance collapsed, and the drone settled back into its assigned slot. One line of error messages on the console blinked out. There was no cheer. It had been one of an infinite number of small avoidances needed to keep the swarm alive long enough to matter.

Nearer the stadium, one drone peeled away from the main body, following a pre-programmed arc down towards the city streets. A ground-level reconnaissance platform, smaller and lighter, with a camera cowling designed to fold and protect its optics when not in use. It dropped into the shadowed canyon of what had been an access road to the stadium's service entrances, its rotors blowing trash and dust down the cracked asphalt. Its camera feed slid across the command deck's main screen for a few seconds, taking prominence over the overhead views so operators could mark what it saw. The outer ring of Sector 0 was not empty. Hosts stood in doorways and under overhangs, pressed into corners where concrete met concrete, facing inward toward the stadium. Their hum formed a lower, simpler band out here, but it picked up a harmonic when the drone passed overhead, a brief tightening in the layered sound.

On Holt's model display, target points lit up along the stadium's outer structure: rail joints where surface lines entered the bowl, the bases of antenna masts welded into the concrete rim, the foundations of telecom towers that had been bent to serve the organism. "First disruptor sequence," he said. "Authorize Node-A spread." Singh tagged the relevant drones with a flick of his fingers. Unit Alpha-06, Alpha-07, and Bravo-02 dropped a few metres, their underbelly hatches sliding open. Disruptor nodes fired downward in tight bursts, little more than dark streaks on the camera feeds. They were compact metal cylinders, nose-capped and fin-stabilised, each driven by a shaped charge that slammed them into their targets hard enough to bury their tips. Where they hit rail joints, they penetrated steel and concrete both, gripping like nails. At the bases of antenna masts, they punched into the concrete plinths until their rear fins sat flush with the surface. At tower foundations, they bit into the vulnerable zones where metal met stone.

Impact markers pulsed on Holt's schematic as each node reported alive. One beat, two, and then they activated. They did not flash or flare. They simply began to push a low-frequency pulse into whatever they touched. Below the hum audible on the drone feeds, another vibration started, subsonic, sliding into the stadium's body like the first notes of an unfamiliar rhythm. Hosts closest to the newly seeded points shifted. Hands that had rested flat on steel flexed, fingers curling as if the contact had become slightly rougher. Shoulders twitched in small, out-of-sync motions. The hum above changed texture for a heartbeat, fuzzing at the edges before settling into a new, more complex waveform. The cluster remained coherent. No visible collapses, no mass movement. But the city, which had accepted all previous interference as part of its own logic, now exhibited something that could be read as irritation.

"Node-A online," Holt said. "Rail joints carrying disruptor load into interior load paths. We're getting measurable desync in the outer rings. Minimal, but it's there." On one of the smaller screens, a close-up of a node embedded in concrete showed faint dust shaking loose around its casing with each pulse. A host standing within a metre of it turned her head the smallest fraction toward the source, eyes still unfocused, gaze sliding past as if whatever registered did not fit into her instructions. The stadium's hum compensated, adjusting its own frequencies to damp the pulse. The nodes shifted slightly in response, algorithmically seeking the resonances most likely to propagate inward.

Back in the command deck's chemical zone, technicians worked in a quieter corner of chaos. The counteragent sat in insulated tanks, each one piped to its own pressure regulator and aerosolization assembly, already fitted into the canisters attached to the drones but kept in dormant form to avoid any reaction with the environment before release. Singh and Holt's models for the counteragent's behaviour in Sector 0 scrolled on a dedicated wall, simulating dispersal patterns across a map of the stadium bowl. Curves representing particle size distribution, evaporation rates, and binding efficiency updated in real time as new data from the disruptor nodes fed back into their calculations. The counteragent had been built to attach to Theta-9's structures preferentially, clogging its mechanisms without ripping the hosts apart in the process. If it failed, there was no fallback chemical.

One tech, younger than most of the room, stared at a set of lines that indicated what would happen if dispersion was mistimed. His hand hovered over a control that would commit one of the aerosol valves to arm. Under perfect conditions, the agent would ride the disrupted field, filling the spaces between the stadium's aligned bodies and coating the parasite's extended architecture. Under the wrong conditions, the field would redirect the aerosol inward and downward, concentrating it around the core. "If this goes wrong," he said, under his breath but not so quiet Holt couldn't hear, "Sector 0 collapses on them instead of the parasite." Holt did not look at him. "Then it doesn't go wrong," he answered, simple, not reassuring, just factual. Across the room, Voss's gaze stayed on John's icon where it blinked steady on the map, deep in the heart of the bowl. She did not add anything. There were no more instructions left to give him from here.

The disruptor nodes marched closer to the core. Drone pairs broke formation long enough to drop a second wave of devices along the inner ring of the stadium's structure. Each impact on a concourse column or parapet rail sent a shudder through the command deck's model, colours shifting along stress maps as the stadium's load paths began to reroute around the newly introduced disturbances. The organism's instinct, encoded by whatever logic Theta-9 used to sustain itself, was to keep stress even. The disruptors were designed to make even distribution impossible, forcing knots of strain into the network that could be exploited. As the final pre-planned placements went in, Holt's schematic highlighted one last ring around the bowl: the heart's outermost shell, the concourse where the hosts stood three deep with their hands on the rail and their torsos now angled toward John and the girl.

"This is the ring that matters," Holt said quietly to no one in particular. "We shake that, the tremor reaches the heart. We miss it, everything we've done is theatre." Singh tagged the relevant drones. Units from the core of the swarm climbed to a higher altitude over the stadium, then rolled to bring their bellies to bear on the concourse. They fired in a timed pattern, each disruptor node aimed at a section of rail where structural stress was highest. On the overhead feed, they were just flashes of metal in the air, sinking into concrete and steel with little puffs of dust. On the war-room's instruments, they were pins driven into a living organ.

Each impact set off a local flare in the S3 maps. Hosts nearest the new nodes buckled in place, knees flexing as if they had been hit in the backs of their legs. Some caught themselves on the rails, fingers tightening with enough force to whiten knuckles. Others leaned harder into the bodies in front of them, creating momentary bulges in the otherwise smooth curve of the crowd. Breath hissed between teeth across the bowl in an involuntary wave, a low, sharp intake repeated thousands of times. The hum, already under visible strain from John's presence at the field's edge, slipped further out of its previous pattern. New harmonics emerged, disharmonic threads running between older, more stable bands, producing beats that had not been there before. On the girl's bio-sign panel, heart rate spiked; her hum output, measured via the implants and the drones' microphones, climbed into what the training charts marked as pre-overload.

"Sector 0 is starting to answer us," Holt said, voice low as he turned to Voss. His face did not show fear; it showed the controlled alert of someone seeing a system move in directions his models had predicted and still not liking it. "We're waking it up properly now. This is no longer just mass under stimulus. It's responding to us as an intrusion." Voss's eyes flicked from the coherence map to John's position and back. "Good," she said. "It's time it knew our names."

Quick cuts, stitched by data rather than camera work, ran across the room as the operation's different perspectives tightened around the same moment. In the stadium, John felt the concrete under his boots change texture, not physically but in the way it conducted the vibrations around him. Where the field had previously been a continuous, heavy pressure pushing in from all directions, the disruptor nodes introduced dissonant chords. The hum in the soles of his feet stopped being a single, thick band and became layers, some out of phase with the others. Micro-shifts in the hosts' stance translated into tiny changes in load under the slabs. The girl leaned further toward the heart, the pull on her muscles becoming less a direction and more a compulsion; if his grip had been any looser, she would have torn free of it in those seconds without deciding to.

From the vantage of a drone circling just below the stadium's roof structure, the ring patterns deformed visibly. Lines of hosts that had formed near-perfect arcs along the concourse now sprouted irregularities where disruptor nodes had taken root. Some columns of bodies tilted more sharply inward, others rolled their shoulders back as if trying to resist. The effect was not chaos; it was strain, a pattern stretched toward its limit. The overhead map representing coherence across the cluster flickered like a field of dying stars, points of stability winking in and out as the organism fought to maintain its integrity. On the main display, the old coherent blue-green of the hum's visualisation began to fray with streaks of yellow and red where the system's attempts at self-correction began to cost it more than they saved.

In the war-room, the coherence graphs that had sat at the bottom of multiple models now surged upwards in priority, filling more of the main wall. Curves representing field regularity dipped in time with each new disruptor node activation. The stadium's overall stability remained high enough to avoid instant collapse, but the trend lines pointed in a single direction. Sector 0 was being forced into a state no previous core had been taken to. The pressure in the room matched that outside, silent and cumulative. Operators' shoulders crept tighter. Nobody shifted in their chair without a reason.

The largest drone in the swarm had sat slightly back from the others throughout the approach, its frame heavier, rotors a size up, payload spine broader. It carried only one significant device: a cylindrical unit that looked unremarkable on camera but had its own legend on the schematics. The primary S3 amplifier was not a weapon in the usual sense. It did not explode or burn. It was designed to take the disharmonic patterns the disruptor nodes had begun to carve into Theta-9's field and force them into a shape the parasite could not compensate for, an imposed failure mode. It had to be placed exactly where it could couple most efficiently with the heart's core, using the transformer's own mass as a conduit.

Designated Hammer-01 in the internal files and simply "the key" by those who had watched it built, the drone carrying it drifted into position above the stadium's centre. Its cameras looked straight down into the bowl. From that altitude, John and the girl were little more than two pale specks at the edge of a dense, dark ring of bodies. The transformer complex below formed a blocky geometry of lines and rectangles. The heart transformer sat in the centre, the largest unit, its cooling fins running vertical along its sides, its busbars branching out like roots. Thermal imaging showed it as a hot core inside a slightly cooler shell, heat radiating into surrounding hardware. The drone's guidance software framed the heart in a crosshair and made minute position corrections until the predicted fall line for the payload intersected a zone marked on Holt's model as optimal coupling depth.

"Key carrier on station," the launch coordinator reported. "Wind negligible. Field interference is within controllable parameters at altitude. S3 amplifier ready for release on your word." Voss didn't answer immediately. Her gaze tracked from the heart's thermal image to the girl's biosig panel and back. The girl's readings sat in a narrow territory between functional and catastrophic, every line high but not yet breaking. "Beacon-01," Voss said into the comm, voice steady. "This is Command. No action required. Stand by for ignition." She didn't expect an answer. None came.

"Drop on three," she told the room. "One. Two. Release." Up above, Hammer-01's belly opened. The S3 amplifier did not fall free at once. A mechanical arm pushed it out of its cradle, giving it a clean separation from the drone's frame, then retracted. Gravity took hold. The device began its descent through the stadium air, spinning slowly to stabilise, fins catching the cross currents from the rotors and the convective heat rising from the transformer forest. From the drone's downward-looking camera, it shrank toward the centre of the crosshair, a dark shape against the lighter metal structures below. On the war-room's display, its icon dropped along a vertical line, an altitude counter ticking down beside it.

The air between the drone and the heart hummed with layered sound. Hosts on the concourse did not know what was falling, but they felt the change. Some part of the field that wrapped them recognised an incoming foreign object with a profile distinct from the drones themselves. Shoulders tightened. Hands that had already been gripping rails hard enough to blanch knuckles shifted again, fingers spreading, as if the rails themselves could be used to catch something. Torsos leaned minutely further inward. A host up in the upper tiers exhaled sharply through his nose, a brief, rough snort that echoed down into the bowl and was repeated, altered, by others without intention. Thousands of chests took in breath almost in unison, a subtle draw that made the hum dip, then swell.

On the field, John saw the amplifier as a blur of motion above the transformer. The girl's hum jumped at its approach, her align pulse stuttering for two beats, then slamming back in with more force. The concrete under their boots seemed to tense. Around the stadium, disruptor nodes pulsed in synchrony, their subsonic rhythm aligning for the first time into a coherent interference pattern ready to be amplified. The device fell the last few metres and struck the casing of the heart transformer dead centre, exactly where Holt's models had said it needed to. Steel rang, a dull, heavy sound cut off halfway through by the amplifier's own clamps biting into metal, anchoring it.

The impact was not explosive. It felt, across all feeds, like a single, deep note played inside stone. For a fraction of a second after the machine hit, the stadium's hum vanished. Not attenuated, not damped: gone. Every host in the bowl, every body pressed against rails and seated on concrete risers and clinging to roof beams, stopped humming in the same instant. Chests froze at the top of an inhale. The low field that had soaked the city's concrete and steel went flat. For the people in the war-room, it was like someone had cut power to the universe's background noise. Then Sector 0 inhaled.

It was not air, though lungs expanded in a wave that started at the heart and rolled outward. It was the organism's field pulling tight, drawing energy from every attached structure, every parasitised system, every host body in reach toward the heart where the amplifier had sunk its teeth. The coherence maps spiked, then began to melt as the imposed pattern did what it had been built to do: force Theta-9's math into a shape it could not survive.

CHAPTER 28

The amplifier let go of its charge like someone slamming a fist down on the stadium's heart. John felt it before he saw anything: a hard, rising pressure in his chest where his own rhythm had been riding the city's hum for hours. The clamp bolted to the transformer stack locked, shuddered once, and drove the forced S3 wave straight into steel that had been carrying Theta-9's favourite song since the grid came up. For one unreal second, everything inside his skull went clean. No vibration, no background choral tone, no ghost of alignment thudding through bone. It was as if someone had picked the world up and dropped it into vacuum. The girl's fingers crushed against his forearm; he barely registered the pain. The quiet wasn't relief. It was the absence you got when a machine stopped mid-cycle with too much power still inside.

The collapse hit like a body blow a heartbeat later. Hosts all around the central stack jerked hard enough that teeth clicked against teeth. Every ring in the stadium seized in place, thirty, forty thousand bodies caught mid-breath. Rails around the lower tiers trembled, metal giving off a high whine as loads shifted onto brackets that had not been meant to flex. The transformer shells under the amplifier assembly groaned, windings forced to reroute current through pathways a parasite had hollowed into them over months. Concrete under John's boots flexed by a fraction, not enough to crack, just enough to tell him the slab was moving as pressure shifted through supports. The hum did not come back as a single note. It exploded into shards. Dozens of separate rhythms slammed into one another, out of phase and out of agreement, like every section of the stadium had remembered its own local noise and tried to shout it at once.

It showed in the people first. The perfect geometry of the hive broke. Rings that had held steady, each host placed exactly three steps from the next, buckled into warped arcs as knees locked at the wrong times and torsos twisted off-beat. Lines of bodies that had been angled neatly toward load-bearing pillars slanted sideways in uneven waves. Clusters that had been humming in clean concentric patterns lost synchrony and fell into staggered, ugly pulses. Some hosts snapped rigid, muscles firing against muscles as Theta-9's control signals misfired. Others sagged where they stood, the field that had been holding their posture withdrawing from their spines all at once. Above, drones tracked the geometry tearing itself apart. From their angles the stadium's pattern went from mandala to fracture diagram between one frame and the next, coherence heatmaps dissolving into scattered islands.

Fog dropped into the bowl in overlapping plumes as soon as Voss gave the word. John saw it as pale veils sliding off the higher decks, dislodged dust at first, until he caught the way the clouds moved against the air currents. They didn't rise with the heat. They sank. Counteragent spilled from the bellies of drones circling under the floodlights, atomised payloads kicked sideways by their rotors, then left to fall into the S3-shocked mass. In the fallback site, Holt watched the time marks burn down the edge of his screen. "Two seconds of S3," he said, voice as even as if he were reading a lab result. "If it recombines before the agent binds, we lose the window." Across from him, Singh's gaze stayed on the oscillation trace coming off Sector 0. The line that had been a narrow, stable band now jumped between peaks, failed to find any mode it could sit in.

The chemical hit unevenly, the way Voss had told them it would. There was no neat ring of effect, no cinematic sweep.

It found hosts in clumps and streaks, followed air turbulence, stuck harder where sweat and open pores gave it purchase. Close to the transformer, John saw a man's neck go rigid, every muscle along the side of his throat standing out, veins bulging, eyes rolling up so fast the whites flashed. Two steps away a woman simply folded forward at the waist, hands slipping from the rail, forehead striking steel with a hollow sound before she went down between two others. A teenager near the lower aisle vomited a thin sheet of blood down the front of his shirt and kept trying to hum through it, mouth open, no sound getting past the fluid. The agent didn't touch flesh directly; it wasn't poison in the old sense. It went hunting the neural lattice Theta-9 had fused into their brains, riding the cracks S3 had torn into the parasite's coherence.

Further up the stands, the change came as a slow spill. Whole rows that had been locked in that soft, vacant posture slumped in relay. One host's knees gave, taking the load off his neighbour's shoulder; that neighbour tipped, bumping the next, bodies falling out of their rings like beads slipping their wire. Noise came back in pieces. Not the clean hum, but human sounds breaking through where the field let go. Someone sobbed once, long and raw, as if their lungs had been waiting to finish a breath they'd started weeks ago. Someone else gasped like a drowning man tasting air. Above it all, the metal stair treads on one side of the bowl picked up the percussive rhythm of bodies hitting in succession, a single, descending clatter. The stadium stopped being a hive and started becoming what it had really been all along: a holding pen full of human bodies with nowhere to fall that wouldn't hurt.

John moved because not moving was a good way to get buried. The concrete underfoot had stopped flexing and started to shudder in shorter, less predictable jolts as loads redistributed. To his left a cluster of three hosts went down together, their collapse pulling a fourth sideways. They had just enough residual stiffness in their limbs to fall badly. One heel scythed through the air toward the girl's shins. John twisted, dragged her across his chest hard enough to feel the ligaments in her shoulder protest, took the impact against his own boots instead of letting it clip her. On his right a dead-weight body slid down the incline toward them; he got a hand on the woman's jacket collar and shoved her aside so she wouldn't wedge under the girl's legs and pin her. Every shockwave of mass hitting concrete rippled through the pack, throwing micro-loss of balance downstream. Keeping upright meant staying loose and reading the movement like weather.

Closer to the heart, the failures came faster. The hosts who had been closest to the main transformer, most saturated in field, fell out of the network like components popping in a machine under load. Some went violent for a second as Theta-9's hold ripped free. Nerve signals misfired in all directions; arms lashed without aim, fingers clawed at the air, jaws snapped down on nothing. One man near the base convulsed hard enough that his cheek struck the transformer casing, teeth scattering on the painted steel before his body went slack. Others failed almost gently. Their faces emptied, then refilled with something almost like confusion as the parasite's overlay stripped away and their own nervous systems tried to reboot on whatever was left. A woman in a red windbreaker froze standing, eyes suddenly focused, her hand lifting slowly as she stared at her own fingers like she had never seen them before. She didn't get long to be amazed before the weight shifts around her knocked her down.

The girl broke differently. John felt her hum go wrong before he heard it. It had been riding three distinct bands since Sector 0's edge, each one carrying a different layer of protocol. Now those bands slipped into one another, phases colliding. What had been a clean, ugly chord turned into interference. Her chest tried to hold three rhythms in a space meant for one. Muscles in her neck twitched at off-angles as alignment commands and collapse signals tried to run through the same fibres. She stayed upright for one long second longer than she should have, tendons standing out along the inside of her elbows as if sheer tensile strength were keeping her on her feet. Then her knees lost the argument. They snapped sideways under her, not neatly, and she dropped against him with all her weight. The impact drove a grunt out of his lungs. He tightened his arm around her ribs, took the hit on his own stance, and let his boots slide a half-step to absorb it rather than overcorrect and go down.

She was still trying to speak. Not in any deliberate way; her mouth moved on the same reflex that had been shaping protocol into syllables at the threshold, but now the source was failing. "St—" The consonant broke under a cough. "St…" Her tongue tried to find the shape of a word that would not have helped even if she had finished it. "Stop." The syllable came out in pieces, part hum, part air scraped over raw vocal cords. "Please." That one wasn't language in any useful sense either. It was noise produced by a control system losing its ability to differentiate between code and anatomy. Blood ran from one nostril in a thin thread, joining the older smear at the corner of her mouth. Her eyes tracked nothing now, pupils blurred, lids fluttering as if every blink was being argued over by two different processes.

From above, the stadium looked like an engine seizing. The S3 wave that had started at the central transformer rolled outward through concrete, steel, and bodies, dishonouring all the neat paths Theta-9 had carved. In the war-room, Singh watched the field representation stagger. Peaks of coherence that had once spread smoothly over the district flickered and dropped. The global mode line that had defined the organism's hold over the city bent, tried to climb back, and snapped again. In the live feed, rail lines feeding out of Sector 0 spat sparks as current hit new resistances. A office block three streets over from the stadium hummed at the wrong frequency for two seconds and then went dark, windows winking out in a slow cascade. Hosts on a bridge beyond the camera's edge dropped in staggered rows, some slamming their faces into guardrails as their knees let go, others going down in clumps as the people they had been leaning on failed with them.

Theta-9 did not die quietly. For three terrifying seconds after the first plumes of counteragent had fully sunk into the bowl, the field tried to rebuild itself like any self-stabilising system would. John saw it in the bodies nearest him. A man whose legs had buckled pushed himself back upright with a jerky, marionette motion, spine bowing as if strings had been reattached in the wrong places. A line of hosts along the base rail straightened their shoulders together, heads snapping toward one of the stadium's main support towers, mouths opening as if to resume the hum. The sound that came out of them wasn't coherent, just a ragged attempt at alignment that dissolved into coughs and chokes as the agent chewed through the lattice under their skulls. The girl's hum spiked once in the middle of it all, a hard, narrow band of sound that cut across the broken rhythms like a flare. For that instant, the parasite tried to reclaim its reference node, to haul itself upright on the scaffold it trusted most.

John felt it hit, like a hand grabbing at the back of his neck through her bones. Every instinct he had told him not to give the organism any more structure than it already had. He peeled his free hand away from the transformer casing he had been stabilising himself against, creating deliberate empty air between his skin and the metal. The field could not use him as a carrier; that was the point. But he had seen more than once how it liked to exploit edges, how it could propagate along any physical path that made its math easier. Being in contact with the stadium's spine while Theta-9 fought for its life was an invitation to become some kind of bridge in whatever came next. He took a step from the pillar even as he kept the girl braced, feeling the concrete under his boots jump again as another row somewhere above surrendered to gravity.

In the bunker, Holt had no poetry left for it. He watched the model bleed coherence across the map and read the numbers that meant win or fail. "Global mode's gone," he said when the line finally dropped below a threshold that all their simulations agreed Theta-9 could not climb back from. "It's fragmenting into local shards. It can't recombine without burning itself out." On a neighbouring screen, clusters of residual activity glowed faintly, each one small, unstable, already decaying. Singh let out a slow breath he had not realised he'd been holding. "Sector 0 is dead," he said. Not the city. Not the people. The construct that had been using them as hardware. On the audio grid, the low, constant hum that had underpinned every feed from the core for months did not return. All that came through now were discrete sounds, uncoordinated and ugly, each one owned by a separate throat or breaking concrete.

The noise inside the stadium changed from something you felt in your teeth to something that registered as ordinary chaos. People crying. People retching. Someone shouting a name over and over, hoarse already, hoping it still belonged to whoever lay under the tangle of limbs in the next row. Somewhere up in the mid-tiers a baby screamed, the sound sharp and shockingly clean after so much layered resonance. Metal groaned where rails had taken more load than they were meant to for too long. A siren that had been hijacked into the hive's background rhythm finally cycled off, its last wail cutting mid-note when whatever power feed it had been tapped to failed. The drones circled lower, lenses widening, trying to pick out pattern in the mess and finding almost none. The neat map of human nodes that had been painted by Theta-9's coherence was gone, replaced by a sprawl of separate bodies.

John went down to one knee because staying upright served no purpose for the next ten seconds and his legs had opinions about what they had just done. He let the girl's weight settle fully against his chest, one arm under her shoulders, the other across her back, keeping her head from snapping sideways as tremors ran through her muscles. Her hum had not vanished. It ticked under his palm in faint, irregular bursts, like a device trying to reboot and failing halfway through POST every time. Whatever fragments of Theta-9 still sat in her neural architecture were trying to find a mode that would match the field they had lost. There was nothing to match. The counteragent had done its work in the net around them; the only place the parasite still had any meaningful hold was inside the structures of hosts that had been too deeply rewritten to snap back in one pass. She was one of those. The difference was that her body now had to run that residue alone.

Her face had slackened in a way he did not trust. Not the blank, insect calm of the fully held host, not the tight mask of partial control. Just empty exhaustion. Her chest hitched on each breath, as if some part of her still expected a deeper rhythm to be there to catch it and was having to reset every time it discovered it wasn't. Around them, people lay draped over rails, sprawled on concrete, piled in aisles. Some were utterly still. Others twitched and turned their heads, eyes flooded with too much light and not enough sense. One man on the steps below John pushed up onto his hands, vomited again, then looked up at the sky with a shockingly young expression, as if the colour of it hurt. There were no instructions in the air for them anymore. No consensus pulses. Whatever came next would have to be decided one skull at a time.

Above it all, the city's soundscape shifted. Rail lines that had been singing in perfect sympathy with the hive dropped into disorganised mechanical clatter. A transformer somewhere outside the stadium blew, the dull boom rolling across the bowl as a separate event, not folded into any larger pattern. Distant, thin, John heard a car horn blare and cut off, not in time with anything else. A city waking up did not sound like joy. It sounded like stress, like circuits tripping and lungs rejoining the world one at a time. From HelixCore's perspective, every light representing Theta-9's global presence in Sector 0 flickered and died. All that remained on their board were faint afterimages and the blinking marker tied to John's implant, buried in the dead centre of a zone that had gone from saturated to blank.

"Renner." Voss's voice came through the comm, stripped of most of its usual hardness by bandwidth and distance. There was no roar in the background now, no hive noise crowding her out. "Stay with her. We're coming." He didn't answer immediately. There was nothing useful to add. He watched the girl's chest, counted breaths without deciding to. Each rise was shallow and irregular, but every one belonged purely to her for the first time since the hospital bed in those old clips. No field overlay. No external timing. Just a body deciding, imperfectly, to keep going. He could not tell from this distance what the agent had done to the parasite threaded through her brain, whether the fact that she still hummed meant Theta-9 had dug deeper there or simply that the shock of having its network torn away had left residue. That was Voss's problem later. For now, it meant she was still traceable on some level, still tied into the mess they had just broken in a way he could not see.

He shifted his grip, easing her head into the crook of his elbow so that if another tremor took her she wouldn't crack her skull against concrete. Her hand, still smeared with someone else's dust and her own blood, twitched once against his sleeve, fingers trying to curl. It looked almost like reaching. He let her fail to complete the motion on her own rather than guiding it. Around them, the stadium slowly filled with the kind of noise he understood: confusion, pain, people calling to each other without any shared channel but voice. The drones' rotors thrummed overhead, feeding every frame of it back to a bunker full of people who had chosen to sit behind glass and screens instead of under rails and concrete, and who had still paid for it in different ways.

There was no cheer, no declaration. The field that had turned the city into one vast, humming body had been knocked apart. The mechanism that would keep it from coming back had been proven. Nothing about that felt like victory. It was just a job finished to one checkpoint. John watched the girl's chest lift again, a hitching, stubborn movement against a world that had just had its order rewritten. His arm tightened around her by a fraction without his permission. Whatever Theta-9 had wanted from her mouth was gone for now. Whatever Voss needed from her as data would come next. For the moment, she was one unconscious human at the centre of a dead hive, breathing on her own in a stadium that finally sounded like separate lives instead of a single system.

CHAPTER 29

The stadium had stopped sounding like a single thing and started sounding like separate throats failing at different jobs. John stayed where he was for the first stretch, one knee on the concrete, the girl's weight against his chest, listening while his ears recalibrated to a world without a carrier tone under it. Close in, people coughed, retched, sobbed, or lay tangled where the hive had let them go. Further out, across the tiers, noise came in uncertain bursts as if the crowd hadn't decided yet whether it was allowed to be loud. Drones circled above in slower arcs than before, rotors a thin, mechanical whine he could finally hear cleanly now that Theta-9 wasn't using the same bandwidth. One passed directly over him, wash stirring the fog of counteragent and dust into shifting veils that caught in his throat. He coughed once, shallow, more out of reflex than need, then reached out with his free hand and pressed two fingers against the neck of the man slumped half across the aisle beside him. Pulse: fast, uneven, but there. The woman wedged against the rail a metre up the row had none. He closed her eyes with the back of his knuckles and did not linger.

The girl breathed in small, hitching pulls that kept refusing to settle into any pattern longer than three or four cycles. He watched her ribs move under the torn hoodie fabric, counting without meaning to, confirming each uneven rise as another point on a line that had not gone flat. Her face had colour again, not the polished, too-even pallor the field had painted over her in the clips from St. Mark's, but blotched and human, sweat streaks cutting through dust. Whatever fragments of Theta-9 were still threaded through her cortex had been cut off from their network and left to run on residual charge. They twitched in her, made her eyelids flutter, tried to turn her fingers into antennae. None of it reached beyond her skin anymore. Around them, bodies shifted as people rolled onto their sides or pushed up onto hands and knees. A man to John's right croaked out a question in a language he didn't speak, words clumsy, tongue unused. John answered the only way that made sense: "Stay down. You're alive. That's enough for now."

The feeds did what they were built to do once the immediate data from the bowl was logged. They went wide. One drone climbed, stabilisers working harder than they liked in the cracked air over Sector 0, and tilted its camera to take in the streets beyond the stadium walls. Where Theta-9 had held highest density, the first wave of failures looked like a series of rolling blackouts in a living diagram. At major intersections, clusters of hosts simply… stopped. People in mid-stride froze, then folded, some hitting asphalt hard, some sagging against lamp posts and traffic signal poles they had been using as anchors. A child on a pedestrian island flopped over the base of a sign and lay there, limbs at ugly angles, chest still moving. Others were slower; they slid down building facades in slow motion, leaving sweat and dust in streaks. Cars that had been idling in concentric circles around high-value hardware rolled forward a metre or two as unconscious drivers' feet slipped off pedals, then jerked to a stop when bumpers met obstacles.

Some of them woke fast, like sleepers yanked from shallow dreams. A woman in a pale coat jerked upright on a bench, eyes wide, hands clawing the air as if the absence of the hum was worse than its presence. Her first breath came out as a thin wail she cut off herself, clapping a shaking hand over her mouth as if afraid to make noise. She looked around with the wild, narrow focus of someone trying to match the world in front of her with the last thing she remembered and finding too few common points. Two men in work uniforms sat slumped against opposite sides of a shop doorway; one stirred, blinked, and stared at the other with uncanny, fearful recognition, like seeing a stranger wearing a friend's face. The other didn't move. A drone dipped lower for a second, stabilised, sent the frames back to the bunker where someone tagged the doorway coordinates for later evacuation and added a red mark to the unmoving man.

Theta-9 died like any system that had built itself into infrastructure: in waves that rippled outward along the same paths it had used to invade. In the office towers beyond Sector 0's core, breaker banks clicked in uneven choruses, tripped by the sudden mismatch between power load and demand now that the parasite was no longer siphoning current into its own harmonics. Elevators stopped humming mid-shaft, their cars dead between floors, panels inside flashing three or four conflicting status codes before going dark. Air handling units in high-rises spun down, the long, low note they had been contributing to the city's background noise tapering off into silence broken only by the rattle of vanes settling. Underground, subway cars eased to a stop as control systems lost the overlay that had been quietly piggybacking on their sensors. Passengers who had been humming in place began to slide off their seats as their posture control failed; some woke under flickering emergency lights with no idea how many stops had passed.

Recovery came in pieces. A drone skimmed low over a side street in one of the outer districts and caught a barefoot woman stumbling out of a townhouse doorway. She clutched the frame with one hand hard enough to whiten knuckles, the other hand held out in front of her as if testing the air. She looked at it, at her own fingers, and then at the half-printed grocery bag hanging off her wrist, its logo frozen mid-fade from some power loss hours or days earlier. Sob came up out of her chest without planning when she recognised the creases on her palm, the faint scar across one knuckle she remembered from a broken glass years ago. She laughed right through the crying for a second, sharp and hysterical, then bit it down and backed into the doorway, calling a name in a hoarse, repetitive rasp. Two doors down, a man stepped out blinking into daylight in a suit jacket over pyjama trousers and stared at the street as if he had gone to bed in one city and woken up in another.

Sector 0 had been the spine, but Theta-9's body had grown everywhere the hum could propagate cleanly. On the global map in HelixCore's fallback site, the node that had once burned white-hot over John's city went out first. The smaller "child" nodes they'd been watching for weeks flickered in sequence as shock travelled along undersea cables and transmission grids. Europe's dense clusters in its older rail hubs stuttered, recovered for a heartbeat, and then died, coherence lines snapping apart like overstressed filaments. East Coast metropolitan meshes folded a few minutes later, their once-smooth rings collapsing into patchy islands on Voss's screens. Places that had never fully yielded to the organism's grid, with weaker infrastructure or more fragmented networks, showed scatter instead of clean collapse. It wasn't symmetry. It was enough. The world map had looked like a nervous system under siege for so long that the new emptiness felt wrong, like somebody had turned off a critical organ. Holt watched the colour drain from regions he'd been treating as mortal wounds and said nothing, jaw flexing once.

Voss broke the silence before anyone could decide the job was done. "Get the alert up now," she said, eyes still on the map. "No promises, no declarations. Just facts." The emergency broadcast systems that still had power or local generators came alive in fits and starts. Some carried national seals, some municipal logos, some just stripped-down text channels on battered VHF. The message from HelixCore went out in short, unadorned blocks: neural contamination event disrupted; expect mass confusion, seizures, and cognitive deficits; do not assume sudden recovery means full recovery; do not attempt to 'wake' unresponsive individuals without medical support; expect infrastructure failures and intermittent power. Somewhere, a satellite feed that had been hijacked for Theta-9's own purposes cut back to a news anchor staring slack-jawed at a dead teleprompter before a producer's hand slid into frame and yanked the camera aside. In the bunker, Singh watched the transmission acknowledgements come in from different continents and let himself believe, for a narrow window, that the organism's spine was truly severed.

On the ground, waking looked less like victory and more like people crawling out from under something they had never seen. Parents came to on living-room floors or stairwells and scrambled for the small forms they found lying nearby, hands patting for warmth, for breath, for that small, stubborn ribcage movement. Some children woke before the adults who had been humming over them, small bodies sitting up in the middle of quiet rooms and shaking their mother's shoulders with rising panic when she did not respond quickly enough. In cars stranded at odd angles across lanes and medians, drivers lifted their heads from steering wheels and blinked at dashboards that no longer displayed anything, wondering why their seatbelts hurt and why there were dents on their knuckles. A man in a grocery aisle looked down to find his hands wrapped around a stack of tinned soup, the same can repeated again and again. He had no memory of picking them up, only a vague, nauseating sense that he had been walking up and down the same three metres of floor for much longer than made sense.

Not everyone came all the way back. In a cul-de-sac on the city's edge, a teenage boy lay on the concrete, eyes open, chest rising, mouth working silently around sounds that would not line up into words. His mother, kneeling beside him with gravel embedded in her knees, cupped his cheek and said his name three times. He looked at her with recognition, tears welling, but when he tried to say anything his tongue produced only broken hummed pulses in the old align-transfer cadence, stripped of context now that the grid behind it was gone. Elsewhere, a woman sat propped against a lamp post, fully awake, gaze tracking, hands steady, but her legs refused to move no matter how many times she told them to. Post-seizure paralysis, Voss labelled cases like hers as the field data came in. Some of them would resolve in hours. Some would not. "Mark them," she told her teams without softening. "Priority evac where possible. And don't promise them anything. We're not in the business of hope; we're in the business of not lying."

The spectrum was wide. Some hosts shook off the residue as if they had just endured a long, bad fever and now wanted to stand, drink water, find something dry to wear. Others sat in the middle of their ruined streets and rocked, hands clamped over their ears, howling that the quiet was too loud. A few walked in short, looping patterns, as if some fragment of routing instruction kept trying to execute without a destination to resolve to. Those ones frightened John more in the long run than the bodies that did not move at all. The dead were simple; the living whose control systems had been rewritten until no amount of counteragent could put them back into a stable mode would be a problem nobody in the bunker had modelled properly yet. HelixCore's triage teams, once they pushed columns back into the city, would find themselves hauling people whose brains could hum the old codes but could not remember their own names.

John did not see any of that in person yet. What he had was a ring of concrete and steel full of immediate problems and one responsibility in his arms. The girl stayed down, weight a constant against his chest, breath a weak, irregular tick under his palm. He quick-checked two more pulses near him automatically as the first wave of survivors tried to sit up. The man whose hand had been clamped around the rail during the collapse had a heartbeat like a frightened animal, thudding too fast but present. The older woman sprawled sideways over three steps, hair tangled under another body's boot, did not. Her skin had the flat, heavy temperature his training had taught him to recognise. He eased the boot away, laid the woman's arm at her side, and looked up because the comm in his ear crackled with a frequency that had finally lost its carrier hiss.

"Renner." Lee's voice sounded wrong without the hum threading through everything. Too naked. It had an edge in it John had heard only twice before in years of knowing him: once at a roadside crash when they'd pulled a child out of a rolled van, once on the line into the airport when the city had started to come apart. "Tell me that's really you and not some recording Voss is using to keep me functional." John tilted his head, more to get a clearer path for his own voice than because Lee needed a gesture he couldn't see. "Still here," he said. It came out flatter than he meant, but there was no hum under it, no ghost timing. The words didn't ride any rhythm but his own. For a second Lee didn't answer. In the bunker, someone watching vitals saw a spike in one of the remote feeds and politely looked away from the number.

"They said you were gone," Lee said eventually, tone tight but steady. "Then they said you weren't. Figured I'd wait for the version that involved your voice insulting my judgment." The background on his channel sounded like canvas flapping and people moving, not like sirens or humming walls. Camps, then. Open air. "Anna?" John asked. One word, more question than he usually allowed himself. "She's here," Lee said. "Asks after you every time the sky stays the same colour for more than ten minutes. Camps are chaos, but we're standing. You… sound like you're in a tin can inside a war zone." John glanced upward at the concrete ring and the drones doing their slow laps. "Stadium," he said. "Hive's dead. People aren't. Voss has teams inbound." The line crackled once as if the world wanted to remind them how easily it could cut connections, then held.

"You did it, then," Lee said. No awe, just the blunt statement of someone adding up pieces. "College kids are crying into their ration packs and Holt's people are pretending they don't want to throw up." John shifted his grip on the girl slightly as she twitched, keeping her head from banging against his chest plate. "We broke it here," he said. "The rest of it fell over because it was stupid enough to build on this." There was a sound on Lee's end that might have been a laugh that had died half-way through. "Try not to die before I get an image of your stupid face on a screen," Lee said, then let a beat pass. "And, John... don't go quiet. If you're bleeding, say so." John looked at his own hands, at the dust and other people's blood on his knuckles, and did a quick internal assessment. Cuts, bruises, smoke in his lungs, no pain that meant structural failure. "I'm not the one you need to worry about," he said. "She is." Lee didn't ask which "she." He had seen the same clips everyone else had.

The bunker's feed operators shifted priorities as evac teams rolled from the fallback site. External cameras on ground transports and the first helicopters painted a city that looked half-asleep and half-broken. Streets that had been ruled by neat flows of hosts now contained scattered clumps of people in mismatched postures: some upright and moving with purpose, some sitting on kerbs staring at their hands, some lying in the gutter with others crouched over them. Bridges that had once carried perfect lines of humming bodies now had only a few stragglers leaning against their rails, gazes unfixed. Smoke rose from a transformer yard where something had failed gracelessly during Sector 0's seizure. Birds crossed the frame in ragged flocks, startled back into using flight paths that had been full of human noise for too long. Voss stood in front of the main bank of screens, shoulders squared, eyes tracking from map to live feed and back again, and started carving the chaos into sectors with her voice.

In the bowl, light shifted. It wasn't the abstract change of brightness that had filtered through the hive's perception before, translated into some part of the field's math. It was angles. The sun had finally cleared whatever structures had been casting the stadium in cold shade, and a raw beam of it cut across the upper tiers, catching dust in suspension. Particles hung in the air like a second, gentler fog, each mote a separate unit instead of part of a coherent medium. John squinted up once, more out of habit than because the glare hurt; his eyes still had work to do down here. A pair of pigeons flapped out from under a service gantry near the roof, wings beating awkwardly as if they hadn't expected the acoustics to be different. Their calls echoed against concrete in a way that wasn't carrying anyone's orders. For a moment, the field the city had been turned into was just air and noise again.

People around him started to move with more intent as their nervous systems found themselves in sole control for the first time in longer than most of them would be able to remember. A man in the row below John pulled himself upright with both hands on the rail, then turned and reached back automatically to haul up the stranger behind him without asking why they were there. Two young women three rows up leaned together, foreheads touching, one of them laughing in short, shocked barks, the other crying silently while her shoulders shook. Someone shouted for a medic in a voice that assumed such a thing existed somewhere. There were no uniforms in sight yet, just people, but the very fact that someone thought to ask meant the city's logic was already reassembling itself around the idea of help.

John shifted his weight, getting his foot under him, and let himself sink from kneeling to sitting so his body didn't decide on its own when to fail. He adjusted the girl's position again, easing her so that her head rested against the inside of his shoulder, jaw angled so her airway stayed clear. Her breath still came irregularly, but the gaps between inhales weren't getting longer. Whatever war had been happening inside her skull between residual parasite and shocked neurons had not tipped entirely in favour of either. He could feel the faintest vibration under his hand where her old hum had been — not a note, not code, just the low-level tremor of an overtaxed system cooling from redline. In the gap between drones and distant sirens, he heard nothing rising under it. No hive, no consensus pulses, no artificial language trying to get through him to her.

The drones' lights dimmed by a few degrees as operators started shifting them from full recon to power-conservation patterns. They banked higher, widening their circles, trusting the new arrivals on the ground to handle what their lenses had been cataloguing. On one of the far tiers, a man stood slowly, using the seatbacks for leverage, and turned his face toward the sky with the stunned expression of someone who hadn't seen it without a colour cast for too long. Dust turned golden in the light, settling on concrete that had been vibrating under someone else's control and now held still under its own weight. The bowl had been the hive's loudest organ. Now it was just a stadium full of broken things and people trying to decide if they were among the ones that counted as salvageable.

John watched the dust drift in the beam cutting across them, felt the girl breathe once more against his arm, and listened hard enough to be sure that the only rhythms left in the world were individual hearts trying to remember their own timing. The city did not hum.

CHAPTER 30

They came in the way trained people always came into bad places: in a stacked line with their rifles high and their mouths shut, boots hammering concrete in a rhythm that belonged to no field, no hum, just muscle memory and drilled-in timing. John heard them before he saw them, the slap of soles on steps cutting through the ragged noise of the bowl, the clipped orders banking off the walls in accents from units he didn't recognise. The drones adjusted automatically, giving ground to the new traffic, rotors climbing to a higher orbit as if the machines understood whose turn it was. The first medic to reach his level checked the rest of the row out of habit before his eyes settled on John and the girl, his stride hitching just enough to register surprise. He took in the armour, the dust, the unconscious weight in John's arms and the rest of the stadium spreading out behind them with no pattern left to exploit, and he did what people like him did when the scene was bigger than the briefing: he swore under his breath and went to work.

"Status?" he asked, voice already in the detached register of procedure. John shifted the girl enough to let him get at her face and neck but did not loosen his hold more than required. The medic jammed a sensor pad under her jaw with hands that shook only slightly, then another against the inside of her wrist, reading from a wrist unit that had seen too much use and not enough maintenance. "Breathing on her own," he said after a second, more to his own checklist than to John. "Irregular. Tachycardic, but not the worst I've seen today. Neuro's a mess." He flicked through menus, eyes tightening. "Post-collapse seizure activity, residual Theta patterning, counteragent markers all over." He glanced at John once, measuring how much word choice mattered here. "We can move her. We can monitor. I can't tell you what she is now." John gave him a brief nod, the closest thing to permission he planned on issuing, and shifted his grip again as a second medic came up with a collapsible stretcher.

They got her onto it with the kind of care reserved for explosives and spinal injuries, strapping her in at shoulders, hips, ankles, lines already snaking from the stretcher frame into portable monitors. John kept one hand on the side rail until they had it settled, fingers hooked under metal, not in protest but because his body didn't seem willing yet to register that someone else's hands were allowed to touch her. When procedure forced him to let go, he flattened his palm briefly against the fabric by her ribs, feeling the small, stuttering rise and fall through the straps, then straightened. Legs obeyed, but the motion had more calculation in it than he liked. His joints moved in the right sequence because the list of tasks still running in his head had "stand" sitting above "fall over" and he hadn't checked it off yet. The medic watched his face the way he would have watched any casualty on their feet in a hot zone and didn't quite tell him to sit down.

More teams spilled into the bowl, spreading out into the chaos with triage tags and bundles of kit, breaking the mass into smaller problems: this cluster breathing, that cluster not; this group conscious and oriented enough to answer basic questions, that one staring at nothing and humming broken remnants of patterns that no longer went anywhere. Radios crackled with sector calls and casualty counts. The drones rose another few metres and widened their loops, handing detail work to the ground in favour of wide-angle coverage and route mapping. John let his eyes run their own sweep across the stadium one last time, not hunting for threat signatures now but assembling a picture out of habit. Bodies where the first counteragent waves had hit too hard, too fast. Pockets of people helping each other upright. Stretcher chains forming at the main tunnels. No hum under any of it. His skin still expected that wrong vibration to slip back in at the edges, but the concrete under his boots had only its own weight to manage.

They took him out with the first lift because Voss had put his name in a box marked priority before the rotor blades ever spooled. A helicopter had set down on the cracked apron outside the stadium, skids biting into tarmac that still held ghost imprints of tyres from a world that had queued for sports and concerts. The air around it tasted of burnt fuel and disinfectant, the combination too familiar now to register as anything but functional. They slid the girl's stretcher into place along one bulkhead, securing it with clips that snapped home with a series of cheap metallic sounds, then strapped in two other stretchers parallel, leaving just enough room for one more body on the inward-facing bench. John took that spot without discussion, hands finding webbing out of training while his eyes stayed on the line of the girl's jaw. The rotor wash beat at the open door, sending dust and atomised counteragent spiralling away from the bowl as the pilot pulled them up.

The ride back was noise and vibration in the old sense, machine rather than parasite, and his body catalogued it automatically as acceptable. Across from him one of the other survivors stared at nothing, irises dilated, lips moving around a sequence of numbers or syllables that refused to settle into words. The third lay entirely still under a foil blanket, eyes closed, chest rising in the shallow, controlled pattern of someone whose nervous system had decided movement was currently someone else's problem. Every time the aircraft shuddered through a pocket of rough air, the girl's stretcher jolted a fraction of an inch, and John's hand came off the bench to steady it before he could think about it. He hadn't been given any guarantee that the thing lying under those straps was something that could be stabilised, but until someone told him otherwise, he treated her like any other fragile piece of mission-critical equipment: you kept it intact, you kept it powered, you kept it where the people who understood the internals could get at it.

The fallback site showed itself first as geometry rather than safety: clean lines of concrete and earthworks cut into a range that had been chosen for distance and angles, not views. The pad they came down on had been poured in a hurry and reinforced in fear, its surface already oil-stained despite the facility's short life. The rotors wound down under the hands of a crew chief who moved with the twitchy economy of someone who had slept in fragments for too long. The girl's stretcher came out first, med team already moving as the skids kissed concrete, then the others, then John. The shift from vibrating metal to solid ground made his knees voice an opinion he ignored. Voss was there because there was nowhere else she could justify being while one of her critical unknowns came home. She had her hair tied back in a knot that had long since stopped being about neatness and started being about not getting caught in equipment, powder from gloves and old plaster ground into the cuffs of her sleeves.

She took him in with one pass of her eyes: armour scored, dust patterns, that slight fractional delay when he straightened from the crouch he'd used to clear the helicopter. "You stayed upright," she said. "That'll do." There was no praise in it, no warmth; just a line entered into a mental ledger that had far too many names in other columns. Her gaze ticked to the stretcher for a heartbeat. "Straight to isolation," she told the med team. "Full neuro, full lattice scan, no contact with general wards. If any of you so much as think about touching an exposed rail on the way, I will pull your licence and your fingers." The threat was dry enough to get a flicker of grim humour from one of the nurses. Then the stretcher was gone through the double doors and the rest of the survivors followed, pushed along a corridor already lined with temporary screens and equipment that hadn't found permanent homes before the city went bad.

The war-room did not move to meet him; it stayed where it was, buried under concrete and cables, humming in its own, strictly electrical way. When he stepped through its threshold later, after a perfunctory check that confirmed he wasn't about to fall apart in the hallway, the conversations inside clipped short not out of deference but because people's brains were switching context. Screens along one wall carried live feeds from Sector 0 and beyond, now showing rescue operations instead of synchrony maps. Another bank held graphs: Theta-9 residues, counteragent binding curves, infrastructure status. Singh stood at a transparent board dense with marker lines, Holt sat half-perched on a console edge, fingers stained with whatever he'd been using to scribble earlier. No one clapped. No one said "you did it." They looked at him the way engineers looked at a device that had gone out into the field and come back altered, and then their attention slid to the doorway that led toward the med wing and the thing lying behind glass.

The ride from war-room to med wing was short in metres and long in weight. The corridor smelt of antiseptic and human stress, the kind that seeped out of walls when too many people had paced them in short, anxious circuits. Lee waited just outside the access point, leaning against the wall with his hands in his pockets like someone trying very hard to pretend he wasn't guarding a door. The beard stubble was thicker than John remembered, hair mashed flat on one side where a camp pillow or vehicle seat had had its way with it. His jacket had dust ground into the seams, the kind of ingrained grime that didn't come from a single bad day but a string of ones that had all blurred together. When he saw John, something in his shoulders lowered a fraction, a breath leaving him that had clearly been held on one long manual override from the point Voss had first told him "lost" and then had to amend it to "maybe not."

"Thought I'd have to ID a body," Lee said, pushing off the wall. The words came out matter-of-fact, the only place the line caught being at the very back of his throat. John stopped a pace away, enough room to take him in whole. "Would've been a short job," he said. "Not many options for ugly bald bastards on a slab." It earned half a laugh, short and snapped off, but it was there. Lee stepped in and, for once, did not bother with whatever distance they usually pretended lay between them. He hooked an arm around John's shoulders and pulled him in hard for a second, the kind of brief, bone-checking contact people used to make sure something was solid and not just a projection someone had sent to keep them from breaking. John's ribs informed him that they had had enough for one week; he tolerated it anyway.

"How bad is it?" Lee asked when he pulled back, eyes flicking toward the doors. "Out there, I mean. Camps are full of rumours and the ones that sound true are worse than the ones that don't." John leaned a shoulder against the wall, letting his weight find contact, more for physics than comfort. "Out there?" he said. "Depends which street you're on. Some people woke up, found their kids, started crying. Some didn't wake up. Some woke up and didn't recognise anything." He shrugged slightly. "City's not humming anymore. That's the important part." Lee nodded, jaw tightening. "And in there?" He jerked his chin at the med wing. "She's still breathing," John said. "Machines say she's alive. No one's prepared to put a word after that yet." Lee's mouth twisted, something wry trying to get past exhaustion. "You look like you stopped a freight train with your bones," he said. "And from what they're not quite saying in there, you saved the world doing it. Not cleanly, not gently—but you did." John kept his eyes on the far wall. The weight of it sat where all the other weights sat. No answer improved the position, so he didn't give one.

Inside the isolation bay the light was flat and soft, designed to keep pupils steady and instruments honest. The girl lay under a thin blanket that had more tubes and wires across it than fabric, monitor leads tracing out from scalp, chest, limbs into a bank of equipment at her bedside. The machines spoke in numbers and graphs: EEG traces crawling in uneven tracks, heart rate plotted in slow peaks, blood oxygen a percentage that made the doctors frown but not call for intervention. There was no hum under any of it. If Theta-9 still lived anywhere inside her, it did so as isolated lattice fragments, unable to reach out into anything larger than the few cubic centimetres of tissue they occupied. Holt pointed at one of the EEG overlays with a capped pen, the tip describing a stuttering pattern that refused to settle into either normal human rhythms or the old coherent field. "Residual Theta signature," he said. "No network to sync to. It's like listening to a radio with the station blown up."

Voss stood at the foot of the bed, arms folded, eyes moving between screens and the girl's face. When she spoke, she did it without decoration. "The parasite's cut off," she said. "We've confirmed that much. Whatever's left is trapped. Her brain is either going to clear the lattice over time, or it's going to find a new equilibrium with it in place." She didn't look at John when she added, "We don't get to know which way that goes until she wakes up. And we don't get to push. If we force her into any kind of induced state, we risk giving the residue a pattern to climb." Singh, further back, watched the EEG like an engineer looking at a damaged circuit board. "No evidence of external coherence," he added quietly. "Whatever she is, she's not their reference node anymore. She's just... a person with bad wiring."

Nobody invited John to stay, but nobody asked him to leave either. He took the chair by the bed as if he'd always been headed for it, the legs scraping softly against the floor. He left his hands on his knees where they wouldn't interfere with lines or sensors, spine straight because his muscles didn't trust relaxation yet. From that angle he could see the slow rise and fall of her chest, the way her fingers twitched occasionally against the sheets as residual impulses misfired. The urge to reach out and put a hand over hers sat somewhere between habit and something he didn't plan on naming; he left it where it was. He watched her breathing pattern the same way he had watched the hum in the walls for too long, counting intervals, noting irregularities, cataloguing them for no one but himself. If her face looked younger now that Theta-9 wasn't using it, it wasn't his place to decide which version counted as true.

Behind glass, the med staff rotated through in shifts, checking readouts, adjusting drip rates, murmuring to each other in low, tired voices. Holt came and went, leaving new notes for himself on a tablet he barely glanced at as he wrote. Singh stayed longer, eyes on the EEG, as if waiting for the graph to resolve into an equation he recognised. Voss checked other bays, yelled at a junior for touching a grounded rail without gloves, then came back to stand in the doorway of this one, arms folded again, expression somewhere between calculation and something harder to read. She took in John, the girl, the steady beep of monitors that had replaced the city's old rhythm. "We can rebuild a city," she said eventually, voice low enough that it barely carried past the threshold. "We just need the people left to want it." It wasn't a speech. It was a line entered into another ledger, one she didn't yet know how to balance.

John did not respond. There wasn't anything useful to say to that that wasn't already written in the bodies outside and the quiet inside. He watched the girl breathe, watched the numbers on the monitors continue their uneven climb toward something that might someday qualify as stable, and let his own eyes close for the first time since the field had tried to decide whether he was part of its body or not. He didn't lean back. He didn't slump. He let his weight rest just enough that his muscles stopped sending urgent messages about failure, and listened past the machines to the thin, unpatterned noise of a facility full of people moving on their own timing. Outside, in a city that no longer shared a brain, traffic would not yet be moving, water would not yet be clean, power would fail and fail again. Inside, one girl's chest rose and fell without a hum behind it. It wasn't victory. It was what was left.

END

Acknowledgments and Creative Contributions

The ideas, plotlines, and creative concepts in this book are entirely original to the author. The author extends heartfelt gratitude to OpenAI's ChatGPT for its valuable assistance in brainstorming, structuring, and refining elements such as dialogue, description, and narrative flow throughout the writing process. Its support was instrumental in shaping the final work.

Disclaimer

This is a work of fiction. All names, characters, places, and incidents are either products of the author's imagination or are used fictitiously. Any resemblance to actual persons, living or deceased, or to real events is purely coincidental.

Made in the USA
Coppell, TX
19 January 2026